Where Do We Go From Here?

BOOKS BY NICK ALEXANDER

The Case of the Missing Boyfriend
The French House
The Half-Life of Hannah
Other Halves
The Photographer's Wife
The Other Son
Things We Never Said
The Bottle of Tears
The Road to Zoe
From Something Old
The Imperfection of Us

nick alexander

Where Do We Go From Here?

bookouture

Published by Bookouture in 2025

An imprint of Storyfire Ltd.
Carmelite House
50 Victoria Embankment
London EC4Y 0DZ

www.bookouture.com

The authorised representative in the EEA is Hachette Ireland
8 Castlecourt Centre
Dublin 15 D15 XTP3
Ireland
(email: info@hbgi.ie)

ISBN: 978-1-83618-500-0
eBook ISBN: 978-1-83618-499-7

PROLOGUE

At first, Wendy had scrolled straight past it. She'd been mindlessly scrolling, thinking about work and what to make for dinner, so the image had nearly been lost forever in the endless stream of nonsense that is Facebook.

But eventually, once the picture was out of sight, she'd realised something had registered after all – an imprint persisted in her mind's eye. So, after reading a heavily punctuated rant from a friend, she'd paused, frowned, and scrolled back up.

The image – a *meme* the youngsters call them, don't they? – was of a rustic log cabin on the banks of a misty lake. The photo looked as if it had been taken in Norway or some similarly beautiful, chilly place. The fluorescent yellow text, in a horrible cutesy font, read:

> *You can live here, free, for a year. You have food, water, and wood to burn, but no phones, no shops, no internet & NO OTHER PEOPLE. If you make it, you walk away with $100,000. Do you accept the challenge?*

Who needs payment? That had been her first clear thought, followed closely by, *How is that even a challenge, anyway?*

She'd read the text again and murmured out loud the words, 'NO OTHER PEOPLE.' *Other people are hell*, she'd thought. *That's the whole point!*

Next, she'd read the comments below the image. Her friend Jill had written, *No dosh required. Packing my bag right now.* Other people, people she didn't know, had said similar things. A woman had asked if she could bring her dog, another, a pile of books. Someone even wanted to bring a horse! The cabin, Wendy had thought with a smile, would end up pretty crowded, and that truly *would* be hell.

But then her smile had faded and for a few time-stretched minutes she'd frozen, lost in thought, as she imagined herself in that cabin – imagined how profoundly ecstatic it would feel to be that far away from the chaos and complexity of her everyday life. A strange thing had started to happen: a long-forgotten feeling of desire had begun to rise within her, an emotion so powerful that it would drive everything that came next.

She hadn't truly *wanted* anything for so long, that was the thing. None of the options ever seemed to appeal in any way. This meal or that meal? This restaurant or that one? Here, there? With, without? Who gave a damn about any of it? She feared she had lost the ability to care.

But suddenly here was something she wanted – no, it was more than that – something she needed: a break, alone, away from *all* of it.

And to think she'd almost scrolled straight past!

ONE

ESCAPE

How long ago had it been, then, since she'd had the initial idea? Five months? Six? She counts the months, tapping her fingers against the steering wheel as she does so. Seven and a bit, then. And now, here she is, on the fifteenth of October, peering out at the landscape, scared to step out of the car.

She works at slowing her breathing and sits listening to the click-click-clicking of the cooling engine. *So here I am*, she thinks. She's not sure how she feels about that.

In front of her, through the windscreen, is a stunning view over hilltops – the sky starting to redden – while to her right she can see the building that will be her new home for the next six months. It's not quite the cosy cabin that sparked the whole thing, because, after all, this is France, not Norway, and the cabin is made of beautiful grey stone rather than wood. Plus, instead of looking out over a misty lake, the view is of mountains and, in the distance, about twenty miles away, the Mediterranean Sea. It would have been nicer to be at the actual seaside and she'd tried her best to find somewhere further south, but her finances just wouldn't run to it.

Because that, of course, is the other big difference here: no one's paying her to do this. She's had to fork out almost five thousand pounds to rent this place for six months – such is the chasm between internet fantasy and real life. But despite this, amidst all the other emotions of apprehension and yes, fear, she's feeling proud. She'd realised seven months ago that she needed this escape, and now, unaided by anyone, here she is. She has actually made it happen.

Of course, as a mother, as a nurse, as a wife, she has made plenty of things happen over the years, but they've almost always been done for those around her. This is the first time she can think of when she has chosen, as an adult, to do something for herself without taking anyone else into consideration.

Even before the car door is fully open, she gasps at the influx of cold air.

It's freezing up here – something she hadn't been expecting. After all, this is meant to be the south of France, isn't it?

At Nice airport a mere forty-five minutes ago, the temperature had been a lovely eighteen degrees, and she'd even broken out in a sweat as she dragged her three suitcases to the car hire station in the warm October sunshine.

Of course, it's higher here, and the higher you go the cooler it gets – she knows this. But all the same... She can still see the turquoise Mediterranean in the distance. If she squints, she can just about see the landing strip of Nice airport jutting out into the sea. How can it be so much cooler here?

Because she can't quite believe the sensations her body is giving her and wants to be able to tell best friend Jill something concrete, she leans back into the car and turns on the ignition. According to the dashboard the temperature is seven degrees. Seven! They didn't mention that in the Airbnb advert.

She rounds the car and pops the boot, then unzips her

biggest suitcase to pull out a purple puffer jacket which she wriggles into as she crosses the scrubby lawn to the front gate.

She finds the key box as specified on the gate pillar and the code she's been given works, too. She's often been accused of catastrophising and it's true she'd half expected that the code wouldn't work, or the keys would be missing, or perhaps the house wouldn't exist at all. She had even made a mental note of every hotel she'd driven past, just in case. But here she is, opening the creaky gate, crossing the stepping-stone path to the front door, slipping her key in the lock and – open sesame – stepping inside.

Gosh, she thinks, *stunning! Truly as beautiful as the photos in the advert.* Closely followed by, *Wow. Freezing. Arctic! Even colder in here than outside!*

The cabin consists of a huge, high-ceilinged living room with a kitchen along the rear wall. The south-facing side is all glass, showing off the view of the mountains and the sky, and when she stands on tiptoe she can still see a strip of distant sea. The decor is Scandi style – a big, grey L-shaped sofa, a curvy wooden-framed armchair and on the left a spiral staircase leading to the mezzanine – her new bedroom.

Sunlight is streaming in making it one of the brightest, most beautiful spaces she's ever seen, but though the sunlight feels warm where it hits her skin, the air in the room is icy – cold enough that she can see her breath rising in steam-train puffs as she explores. The bathroom is tiny but beautiful and also shock-ingly cold. *The cheapskates could have put some heating on*, she thinks with a roll of the eyes and a dismissive shake of her head.

She spins on one foot, scanning the walls for radiators, boil-ers, thermostats – basically anything she can switch on that might improve the situation, but other than a trendy cylindrical wood burner in the middle of the room, there are no obvious signs of alternative heating options. She'd known there would be a wood burner – it had been mentioned in the advert – but she'd pictured it as a luxury extra for special cosy nights in, rather than her only source of heat.

The view is so breathtaking she feels drawn towards the window, but halfway across the room a postcard propped on top of the wood burner catches her eye.

You are welcome to Caussols, she reads, once she has flipped it over. *The pan is ready to burning and there is basic nourishment in the frigo. Enjoy your stay and any demands, demand.*

My French might be better than your English, she thinks, even as she acknowledges that this isn't remotely true. She'd promised herself she'd work on her French before coming here, but she simply hasn't got around to it.

She crouches down and peers in through the curved glass window of the stove. A pyramid of kindling constructed around a fire lighter is waiting, ready to go. She opens the door, strikes a match and holds it until a thin blue flame starts to flicker.

As she waits for the fire to get going she walks around the space again and tries to imagine herself living here, then as the realisation takes hold, tries instead to convince herself that she *is* living here now.

She rubs her hands together and blows through pursed lips to marvel at the spectacle of her breath, hanging in the air like tiny, home-made clouds. *Maybe there's underfloor heating*, she thinks hopefully. But as she can't see any kind of switch, maybe not. She'll send the owner a message, but right now she needs to keep moving, so after a quick glance at the bed upstairs (king size, comfortable, clean), she heads back outside.

By the time she has dragged her cases across the crazy paving, the wood burner is starting to take the edge off and she has generated enough body heat beneath her puffer jacket for the place to feel bearable – just.

One by one, she opens her suitcases and hangs her clothes in the wardrobe behind the staircase. That done, as the sun plunges behind a rocky outcrop to the west and the temperature outside drops to glacial (confirmed during her first cigarette break), she checks the contents of the fridge where she finds eggs, cheese and milk (albeit in single-portion quantities). There are packs of pasta and coffee in the cupboard, too, along with a tin of tuna which, because she's semi-veggie, she'll probably never eat. Eggy, cheesy pasta will do fine, she decides, for now. She can tackle the excitement of a French supermarket by daylight.

She picks up her phone to call the owner but hesitates about whether to try to speak French or be rude and go for it in English. On reflection, she chickens out entirely and sends a text message – a message that she knows the app will translate. She informs them that she has arrived and thanks them for the food. She mentions the cold and asks if there is any kind of supplementary heating.

The reply comes back almost immediately. Another, *You are welcome to Caussols*, which makes her smirk, followed by, *Don't worry the wood-pan is excellent*, which she decides really means 'no'. *Cheapskates!* she thinks again. Imagine renting a place for 1,000 euros a month and worrying about the electricity bill. She'll buy a little blow heater at the supermarket. That'll show them...

She considers, momentarily, texting best friend Jill, but when she picks up her phone to do so and sees that she doesn't have a single message she's overcome by a pique of resentment, closely followed by a ripple of melancholy. Because how the hell has she got to a point in her life where no one, not her kids, nor her husband, nor even best friend Jill, has thought to inquire how she's doing, whether she arrived safely, let alone worry about her, on her lonesome, out here in France?

Jill will most likely be tipsy by now. Wendy can picture her perfectly, singing along to *The Voice* before dozing off in front of the telly next to husband Frank. As for her own family, well... It's not for no reason she's here, is it? It's precisely to get away from them – or rather, if she's being honest, to avoid being confronted by the fact of their absence.

But it's not just that either. She isn't only running away. She's here to think about it all, calmly, quietly. She's here to take stock of her life and she has given herself six months to work out what's gone wrong and what it all means.

It's going to be her personal *Into the Wild* adventure, only hopefully without the starving-to-death-in-a-bus bit. So, taking a breath, she decides there's no need to think about any of them tonight. Tonight, she will be proud of her achievement in getting here and if they can't be bothered to ask, then at least she won't have to tire herself replying.

By the time she has cooked and eaten, the cabin is a tiny bit warmer and within half an hour of returning to the sofa to stare at the flickering flames (more appealing this evening than any TV), she's asleep.

At some point during the evening, she wakes up to find herself utterly disoriented until the chill in the air and the eery moonlit plateau beyond the window remind her where she is.

Up in the mezzanine it's a bit warmer – hot air rising and all that – but as she slides under the covers, the sheets are still quite shockingly cold. She rolls herself in the quilt, using it like a sleeping bag, and adds an electric blanket to her mental shopping list.

She wonders briefly why – seeing as hot air does rise – the tops of mountains are so cold, and then, despite the indisputable fact of that cold, she slips back into sleep where she dreams of running through an abandoned airport hunting desperately for a lost boarding pass. At one point she thinks she hears a wolf howl and sits up in bed with a start. But did the noise come from her post-apocalyptic dream airport, or from this lonely mountain in France? She really isn't sure.

* * *

She wakes from a momentarily remembered dream of being suffocated to find she has pulled the quilt over her head and truly is struggling to breathe. The second she peeps her head from beneath the covers, she understands why she has done so, though. The bedroom is icy cold again.

She pulls the quilt back over her head but realises that the fire must have gone out and that the only way to make the temperature bearable is to get up and relight the damned thing. Dragging herself from the warmth of the bed and grimacing, she hops barefoot down the chilly steps of the metal staircase. Downstairs, she grumbles angrily as she hunts for her tracksuit bottoms and a jumper followed by her thickest pair of socks.

Once dressed, she hops over to the wood burner and runs one hand across the metal to confirm that it truly is stone cold. She should have loaded it up before going to bed – obvious, really.

She searches for fresh kindling in every cupboard and, finding only full-sized logs, steels herself and pulls on trainers and her jacket.

Outside, the sun is peeping over the hills to the east and the air feels tingly with cold. There's a magical mountain purity to the air that seems to make her blood run more freely – that's the sensation, anyway. She pauses to look into the distance where a massive bird of prey – perhaps it's even an eagle – is circling. She consciously takes in another icy lungful of air and tries to remember when she last thought to breathe consciously for the pleasure of it. It's not something you do a great deal while living on a main road.

She's overcome, momentarily, by the beauty of it all. The vista is quite astounding – a vast, flat, vibrantly green plain stretching into the distance bordered by a grey rocky outcrop on the left and greener hills to the right. Beyond the plain she can see a thin strip of turquoise sea and above that an impossibly blue cloudless sky.

A shiver rippling through her, rising from deep within, forces her to remember that she's on a mission to find kindling so she stamps her feet and drags her eyes from the view.

Along the right-hand side of the cabin she discovers a lean-to woodpile, but again there are only full-sized logs. At the rear of the cabin she discovers a vented metal door from behind which comes a vague electrical hum, but it's locked with a padlock and she's fairly certain she doesn't have a key.

So no kindling anywhere...

'Ridiculous!' she murmurs as she starts to scramble around gathering twigs. She feels like she's fallen through a wormhole to prehistoric times. 'Absolutely bloody ridiculous!'

As soon as she has an armful of kindling, she returns inside to discover the one advantage of having had to go out – it now feels relatively warm.

With the help of some scrunched-up kitchen roll and the twigs she manages to get the fire going again and this time piles it high. That done, she returns to the safety of her quilt vowing not to re-emerge until the cabin is warm enough to support human life.

She sleeps for almost two hours and when she wakes up she's soaked in sweat – the room suddenly feeling like a sauna! Fearing that the place might be on fire, she jumps from the bed and rushes downstairs. The wood burner is so hot it hurts her eyes to look at it but otherwise all is well. Squinting against the heat, she kneels down and manages to close the air hole along the bottom which seems to calm things down a bit, then crosses to open a window.

Her breakfast is made up of leftovers from the previous night and a strong cup of coffee which she takes outside so she can smoke.

With the sun now fully risen – her phone says it's 9.30

though she's unsure if that's UK or French time – the temperature outside is almost pleasant. She turns a chair towards the light and sits and closes her eyes, letting the red warmth soak into her eyelids. A gentle breeze flutters against her cheek and in the distance, somewhere behind her, a donkey brays. Sunlight, clean air, donkeys... *Not in Kansas anymore*, she thinks. She corrects Kansas mentally to Maidstone and then smiles and murmurs out loud, 'Not in Maidstone anymore.' So, she's already talking to herself. She wonders if she needs to worry about that.

She pulls her phone from her pocket and rattles off another message to the owner.

I need an electric heater, she types. *Do you have one you can lend me or do I have to go and buy one myself?*

She checks her email and Facebook.

She finally has a message from Jill in Messenger: *How did it go? Did you get there? Call me!* Plus another from her sister-in-law, Sue: *When are you going to France? Is it soon?*

The Airbnb app chimes, so she opens it to find a reply from the owner: *Not possible, I am sorry. Too much electricity in the house. But the wood pan is very good and we have supplying wood for you.* She gasps in amused disbelief. They really are quite mad.

She stubs out her cigarette on a rock and turns back towards the house. She needs to shower and get out for supplies otherwise she's going to have to go without lunch.

Food, wine, heater, cigarettes, she thinks, glancing back briefly at the incredible view – now her view. *Food, wine, heater, cigarettes, plus slippers and an electric blanket.*

* * *

Google Maps lists only one nearby supermarket but when she locks up the cabin and drives to the exact point on the map –

the specific spot where Maps announces optimistically that her 'destination is on the left' she finds herself in the middle of a tree-lined road. There's not a single building in sight.

She tries to use her phone to search for an alternative, but it isn't picking up a signal anymore so she just carries on driving until it does.

Half an hour later, she enters a village called Saint-Vallier-de-Thiey. It looks pretty and she'd like to explore. She's tempted by the idea of a quick drink in the little sun-soaked bar overlooking the green, but she resists and sticks to her mission and soon enough she has found the Intermarché car park, and is pushing a caddie through sliding doors.

The shop is bigger than she expected, the size of her local Sainsbury's, but to her wonder-filled eyes everything looks so much better. The bread is crusty and fresh, the vegetables are deformed and fragrant and the cheese section takes up two full aisles. As for the wine department... oh lordy, Jill would die.

An hour later she's the best part of 400 euros down and back out in the car park with her clinking caddie filled to the brim.

It's my first shop, she tells herself. It was bound to be expensive. Plus, she's had to buy one-off items like the blow heater. No electric blanket, though – it would seem they're not everyday items in the south of France.

Once she's found the tabac and stocked up on cigarettes, she drives back up the twisty mountain roads to the house and, no longer stressed about finding a supermarket, she's able to marvel at the views. At some turns she can see far enough to make out two or three different seaside towns bordering the turquoise sea. She'll have a look at an online map when she gets home and work out whether they're worth visiting.

Back at the house she rewards her successful expedition with a generous glass of red and then, between sips, sets about unloading her shopping, moving the cheeses into the fridge, the cans into the cupboard, and piling the baked goods up on the counter. She's probably overdone it with the baked goods, she thinks. She grimaces guiltily. She has bought a lot of wine, too, though wine, unlike baguettes, will keep.

Once the bags have been squashed into a corner, she refills her glass for the second time. This 4 euro pinot noir is shockingly good. She sandwiches a wedge of not-as-ripe-as-she'd-hoped Brie between a third of one of the baguettes and heads back out to her view.

As she bites into her sandwich, the wine is just hitting the sweet spot, and she experiences a moment of pure ecstasy. Red wine, cheese and crusty bread – the view, the smell of pine needles in the air... *Christ!* she thinks, *the French sure know how to do things, don't they? Why on earth do I live in England?* It's amazing really, how we all just stay where we're born. There's a whole planet out there to choose from, after all.

She should probably call Jill and tell her how well she's doing. She's been putting it off, and she's not sure why. She tries consciously to think about that now, scrunching up her brow to help her concentrate.

She's been feeling anxious, she decides – understandably anxious about getting here, living here alone and surviving for the full six months. When she calls Jill she wants to sound triumphant, even though she has no idea why. After all, Jill never does anything particularly challenging.

Now would be a good time to call her, though, wouldn't it? Just look at her in her mountain garden with a glass of wine and a baguette! But still she hesitates. Because what if it all goes wrong and she has to run home with her tail between her legs? Failure after declaring triumph would be a bit pathetic, wouldn't it? Not perhaps to Jill, because why would Jill even care? But to Wendy, it definitely would. And she doesn't want to sound pathetic to herself. You have to be careful about that. You have to take care of your self-image because sometimes the story you tell yourself *about* yourself is the only thing stopping you falling apart completely.

She sips her wine and takes another bite of the sandwich, then returns her attention to her phone. She sighs and clicks her way onto Messenger where she crafts an optimistic yet understated reply to Jill: *I'm here. All good so far. Place is lovely. Shopping done. Wine is so cheap you'd never have to sober up.*

She replaces the bit about sobering up with a simple 'so cheap you wouldn't believe it'. That would have been a bit close to the bone, and depending on her mood Jill could take it either way. She frowns and thinks about the fact that Jill will almost certainly phone her the second she receives the message and adds, *Just off to explore. I'll call you when I get back.*

Am I going to explore? she wonders. She supposes she might as well.

She thinks about the fact that she still hasn't had a message from Harry nor even a text from the kids. Honestly, they're dragged screaming from your womb; you devote your entire life to them and they can't even...

Don't think about it. Don't spoil the moment.

She sighs and slides her phone into her pocket then swigs down the rest of her wine and stands. The half-eaten sandwich is losing its appeal for some reason. And no, she can't be bothered to go exploring yet. She has 180 days to explore, after all. Well, 179 and a half now remaining. It feels like she's done a million things in the last twenty-four hours and she's really bloody tired.

She looks out at the view again and notices that the colours are more bleached, less vibrant in the midday sun.

Harry would go crazy hillwalking here, she thinks. He'd absolutely love it.

She imagines how he'd be cajoling her to go walking right now, this minute.

At the realisation of how dangerous it is to follow this line of reasoning, she raises one eyebrow and swallows, catching herself, freezing out the thought through sheer willpower. *No,* she tells herself. *Harry's not here. Not in person or spirit. And that's the whole bloody point.*

She turns and heads towards the cabin.

TWO

HARRY (PART 1)

We met when I was twenty-three. Harry was almost two years older than me but looked, if anything, a bit younger.

Funnily – and this is the thing that got us talking – we were both in our final months of training, Harry to be a teacher and me to be a nurse.

They'd sent him to one of the worst schools in Maidstone and, that morning, one of the more difficult kids had stabbed his hand with a chisel.

As for me, it was my first day in A&E. I was meant to be shadowing a friendly nurse called Nigel, but his mum had been admitted to Cardiology that morning, so he'd vanished upstairs to attend to her.

Once the doctor had confirmed that nothing important had been damaged by the chisel, I was left alone to disinfect, close and bandage the wound.

'Sorry, I'm still a student,' I informed him, as I started to irrigate the gash in his hand. 'But I think I can probably cope. I am in my final year, so you probably won't die today.'

'I'm in my final year, too,' he said. 'Teacher training. I

thought I could cope as well, but look at me now...' He nodded towards his hand.

'He really got you, didn't he? It's deep.'

'Are you going to have to stitch it?' he asked.

'Oh, don't worry,' I said. 'My sewing's brilliant. I made this entire outfit myself. I just have to decide whether to do you with cross-stitch or zigzag.'

He didn't look reassured by my humour, so I added: 'Not really. We use these sticky clip things now, you'll be fine.'

He was still looking a bit green so I tried humour again. 'Someone needs to be more careful with his DIY.'

'Never did like woodwork,' he said. 'Now we know why. It's dangerous.'

Once I'd pulled the wound closed and stuck a clip on to hold it together, I started to wrap a bandage around it. The patient, now visibly perking up, joked by repeatedly trying to shake my hand. 'Harry,' he said, each time the bandage came round to his palm. 'Harry Rawling. How do you do?'

'Are you always like this?' I asked, jerking his hand back into position.

'I am,' he said, grinning.

'Then I'm not surprised he stabbed you,' I said. 'Hold still!'

'Harsh,' Harry said. 'But fair.'

Once I'd finished, I went off in search of Nigel. I didn't know if I could send young Harry back out into the world or if some paperwork needed to be done. But I couldn't find Nigel anywhere and, not wanting to get him into trouble for spending time with his mum, I didn't dare ask the locum. So instead, I pulled the curtain around us and hoped no one would spot Nigel's absence.

'Cosy!' Harry commented with a sloppy grin. 'Intimate, even.'

'Don't get any ideas,' I admonished.

To pass the time I pulled a bag of M&Ms from my pocket

and offered him one. 'You still look a bit green,' I lied. 'The sugar will do you good.'

'The sugar will do me good,' Harry repeated. 'Now that's not something you hear often in a medical situation.' He peered into the bag. 'Do different colours have different... um ... medicinal qualities? Which one do you think I need most?'

'Nope,' I said. 'They're all the same.'

Harry fished out a blue one and held it up between finger and thumb.

'Oh, except for those...' I said, with mock seriousness. 'Blue ones have contraceptive side effects.'

'Sounds perfect, then,' he said, popping it into his mouth theatrically.

'Not keen?' I asked, leaning over and peeping out through the curtain in case Nigel had returned.

'I'm sorry?'

'Not keen on becoming a dad? Or maybe you already are?'

Was I flirting? Probably. But I don't think even I had realised it, yet.

'Oh, um, no, or rather, *yes.*'

'Make up your mind!'

'I mean, um, no, no kids yet and yes, I rather like them. When they're not stabbing me, I do, at any rate. Hence the... um... vocation. Teacher.'

'Right. Of course.'

'Hopefully one's own children are a little less...' He flopped his bandaged hand from side to side and wrinkled his nose thoughtfully. 'Stabby?'

'If they are stabby then you're probably doing something wrong,' I said, simultaneously tuning in to a conversation I could hear taking place further down the ward. Someone was asking where the hell everyone was today and I was worrying I'd get into trouble.

'I'm single, actually,' Harry said, surprising me. 'So no kids planned right now.'

'OK,' I said doubtfully.

'Oh, I wasn't, you know... hitting on you,' Harry said.

I raised one eyebrow.

'I'm sure people do,' he continued. 'I'm sure you have to put up with that all day every day.' He grinned inanely and wobbled his head from side to side. 'What with that home-made outfit and everything,' he added saucily.

'OK, now you're scaring me,' I told him, glancing down at my horrible uniform and trying to picture how someone might think it was sexy.

'Right,' Harry said. 'Shut up, Harry! Stop being a dick.'

'And they don't hit on us that much, actually,' I added, because I thought he was being a bit harsh on himself. I was rather enjoying the banter, after all. 'My patients are generally too busy dying. I have a very low success rate.'

At that moment, Nigel dragged the curtain back and stood, hand on hip, frowning deeply at Harry. 'Why are you still here?' he asked. Then, turning to me, 'Sorry I was so long, but... it's not looking good. My mother, I mean. And why *is* he still here? I've been gone twenty minutes.'

'Oh, that's my fault,' Harry said chivalrously. 'I've been pretending to feel faint so she'll let me stay. I love it here.'

'Do you now?' Nigel said dryly. 'Well, time to toddle off back to school, I'm afraid.'

'Just didn't want to leave without a phone number,' Harry said. 'You know... in case I relapse?'

Nigel began to look annoyed on my behalf so I sent him a wink and a tiny shake of the head to calm things down. 'It's fine, Nigel,' I said. 'I didn't know if there was something – some paperwork or whatever – I have to do before I send him on his way?'

'Oh,' Nigel said, belatedly picking up on the cheeky vibe

Harry and I had going. 'Well, yes, there is, nurse. You must always give every patient your phone number before they—'

He stopped mid-sentence because our scary locum, who was at that moment striding past, had spun on one foot and doubled back to peer in on our little gathering. 'Nigel! So you are here. So good of you to show up!'

'I...'

'I don't care. Come with me. Ambulances on the way. Car crash. Big one.' He nodded at me then marched off, shouting over his shoulder, 'And bring mini-me with you. Time for her to see some gore. Can't spend the whole day hiding.'

'Don't be long,' Nigel said, trotting off in the locum's wake.

'Gore,' Harry said. 'Sounds fun.'

'It's what we do,' I told him. 'No gore – no job. Anyway, I think you're free to go. Keep it clean. Change the dressing if it gets wet or dirty. You can take the clip off in forty-eight hours. It just pulls off like a plaster. Oh, and go to your GP if there's any sign of infection. But I basically think you'll survive.'

'Can I have it?' he asked. 'Your number? I promise I'm not a psycho.'

'That's what they all say,' I said, as I pulled a sterile wrap from the trolley and scribbled my number on the packaging. 'That's *exactly* what the psychos say.' I glanced around as I handed it to him. 'I'm not supposed to do this... most unprofessional...'

'I won't tell a soul,' Harry said, slipping it into his pocket.

* * *

Does it sound *easy*, that I gave him my number? I expect it probably does. And if I tell you that I was already dating someone – a guy called Martin from my course – it will no doubt sound even worse.

But Martin had never been right for me and that was something I'd always known. Actually, I'm sure Martin knew it, too. It's one of those weird things really where, looking back, I'm not even sure why we bothered. But I'd been fed up with being single for a while, I suppose, and Martin had bought me dinner in a French restaurant and stroked my hair after sex. For a bit, that seemed like enough. After a series of let-downs I'd maybe set my expectations too low, or perhaps it was just that between my nursing degree and part-time job I didn't have enough time to care.

But now here was someone new and shiny to think about and it took mere seconds for me to make the switch. Because Harry, with his curly hair and wonky nose, with his lopsided grin and piercing green eyes, was the photofit of my ideal man. He had a studious geeky cuteness about him that made him seem substantial, combined with a desire to amuse that promised future happiness. He was like a Kentish version of Hugh Grant in a way – all that bumbling charm without the irritating posh accent.

So yes, I gave Harry my number there and then. And even as he was walking away I was wondering how to end it with Martin.

My first ever date with Harry was in Pizza Hut. Some might say (in fact a nurse friend did say at the time) that it wasn't a particularly romantic place to take me for a first date. But Pizza Hut suited me fine.

I'd come off a twelve-hour shift and was starving, plus Martin – who I'd broken up with twenty-four hours after meeting Harry – had, of course, taken me to a posh French restaurant for *our* first date six months prior. So the contrast between Montmartre Gastronomie and Pizza Hut reassured me. It was proof that Harry was not Martin, and when you're young and you change partners that's always the main quality you're looking for: that the new flame is nothing like the previous one.

By the way, Martin – in case you're wondering – didn't seem too upset. 'Oh, OK,' he said when I told him. 'As long as you're sure that's what you want.' Based on his reaction I felt *very* sure and I told him so.

Anyway, Harry made me laugh from the outset. It's not that he was ridiculously funny – I mean, he wasn't a stand-up comedian or anything – but he did have excellent delivery and a way of using his body to emphasise the point that really got me going. So he'd say something averagely amusing but wiggle his eyebrows and wobble a hand from side to side in a way that made me giggle. So there's a tip, any hopeless single men out there: forget the candlelit dinner. Just make the girl laugh!

Afterwards we walked together to the crossroads where our paths diverged. It was raining that special kind of English drizzle that makes an umbrella seem absurd but leaves you soaked through without one.

'So,' Harry said, smiling lopsidedly and shrugging.

'So,' I repeated.

'The question is, um...' Harry continued hesitantly. He pushed away a wet curl that had fallen over one eye.

'My place or yours?' I offered, cheekily completing his phrase.

'Oh!' he said. 'Christ! You nurses... I would never have dared ask that. From a guy that would count as sexual harassment or something. At the very least unbridled misogyny.'

'Oops,' I said. 'Go on, then. Feel free to finish the far more boring thing you were about to ask.'

'I was only going to... um, ask...' He had a confused expression. 'God, I feel like I'm being a bit stupid here... sort of asking for beer when I've just been offered Champagne.'

'Just say what you were going to say,' I told him. 'Really. I'm winding you up.'

'I was going to ask if I could see you again, but it appears that maybe I can.'

'Yep,' I said. 'Anytime you want.'

'Oh,' Harry said. 'Wow. And that includes the option of, um, right now, does it?'

'It does. So, the question then is...' I said, nodding at the crossroads.

'Your place or mine?' Harry said.

'God, that's so misogynistic!' I exclaimed. 'How dare you!'

'Some chicks like that stuff,' Harry said, with a weird snarl that made me laugh.

'Look, my place is fine,' I told him. 'But I do have a nosy flatmate...'

'Me too, only mine's gone home for the entire week, hehe,' he said, still doing a funny voice. 'So we'd be all alone, just you and me, chicky babe.' He winked and clicked his tongue against the roof of his mouth.

'That's settled, then,' I said, taking his arm and pulling him on along the pavement.

'Right,' Harry said. 'So is this a nurse thing? Because I'm used to girls playing much harder to get. I mean, don't get me wrong. I like it.'

'No, not a nurse thing at all,' I said. 'I think it's more of a "I'm really into you" kind of thing.'

'Right,' said Harry. 'Gosh!'

'Don't sound too happy,' I said.

'Oh, I'm happy,' he said, sliding one arm around my waist. 'I actually can't remember feeling happier.'

Now, when Harry has told that story over the years, he always says that it was love at first sight. But though this will sound cynical on my part, that's not something I believe in. No, what happened was more a question of *compatibility* at first sight. Harry just fitted me like a glove.

I found him pleasing to look at – I suppose that was the first thing, the thing that happened back in A&E. I liked the size of him, his big hands and feet. I liked his curly hair and chunky jumper. I liked his old-school brogues.

The conversation felt easy from the outset, too, and I think that was as important as anything else. Harry seemed solid, comforting and amusing, and even during that first meal in Pizza Hut I could imagine us old, still getting on.

The love bit – the hormone rush that makes you unable to think about anything else – did happen, but it happened a few days later. Within a week, tearing myself from him in order to go to work felt like trying to gnaw through my own arm. It's just that didn't happen – and I don't believe ever really happens – at first sight. But I'm sure someone out there will disagree.

Anyway, ours was more love at second pizza and the rest is so classic, so predictable, that I won't bore you with too many details.

I moved into Harry's place – it was bigger, brighter and cheaper than mine – and, after we'd graduated that summer, we enjoyed a few years doing the 'young lovers' thing with some panache, even if I do say so myself. We had lots and lots of sex, went to concerts and dropped occasional ecstasy tabs in night-clubs. We spent wonderful romantic weekends in Paris, Brussels and Rome and had the obligatory massive argument in rainy Berlin. Nowadays I can't even remember what that one was about, but I do remember that it was bad enough that we sat as far apart as possible during the journey home.

Once we'd got over our two-week post-Berlin sulk/separation (because it was never that clearly defined), we felt pretty much invincible and decided to get married and also – virtually without discussion – to stop using contraception.

We bought a wreck of a house with a sixties kitchen, a leaky roof and two extra bedrooms for the kids we assumed we'd have, and spent our weekends and annual leave doing it up. Once the place had been rendered liveable, we shagged until Todd popped out, and once I'd got over that (because, of course, babies do not *pop out*) we did it all again so that Todd would have a sister he could spend his entire life resenting – Fiona.

Life changed so gradually that we didn't really notice it happening. But the sexy trips to exotic cities gradually got swapped for weekends painting walls, and then fraught weekenders in kid-friendly campsites... Life became packed lunches, sports kit and driving kids around. Lots and lots of driving kids around.

We weren't unhappy about any of this, I do want to make that clear. We loved our kids more than anything, and we enjoyed the lives that having children imposed on us. But it was definitely a different kind of happiness and I'm not sure there was ever a moment when we consciously realised where we were heading. That's my main point, I suppose, because if we had known what we were choosing, would we have still done so?

It felt, in a way, like we were following someone else's groove – or rather, everyone else's groove. It did lead, as society promised, to a kind of contentment that was enough to get by on – it wasn't awful in any way. But if one were to compare and contrast (which I was always too terrified to do), it would probably rate poorly against the joyful freedom of youth. Life certainly felt less unpredictable, less exciting, less alive.

People label this 'settling down', 'growing up' and 'being sensible', which makes the process feel inevitable. In the end, you just get on with it, and try not to question things too much, don't you?

But then suddenly, one day, you might wake up, the way we did, and find that you can't hold the thought off any longer. *Is this really what I want?*

* * *

Along with the love-at-first-sight thing, I've known people who claim their relationship has been one long honeymoon, but I never really believe that either, do you? Not unless they're admitting that they argued on their honeymoon, too.

No, I'm sure that every marriage has its ups and downs not to mention a few make-or-break crises.

Because we had such exhausting careers, I suspect we didn't have as much goodwill in reserve as other people. It took less to throw us off our matrimonial stride than maybe it should have. Major life events often left us at each other's throats.

We had a noteworthy bust-up, for example, around the time Harry's father died, simply because that was when Harry ran out of patience with everything – the everything including me. Because nobody wants to be the woman who dumps her partner while he's grieving, we got through that one and lasted until – with the help of some excellent anti-depressants – Harry got his mojo back.

Other life changes that caused havoc were the birth of Fiona (and specifically the sleepless nights she imposed), buying a bigger house, moving houses, Harry changing schools and me writing off Harry's brand-new car. Each of these led to a moment where at least one of us doubted wanting to continue.

Sometimes a mere run of bad luck – a toaster fire, for example, combined with a recalcitrant insurance company at the same time as a roof leak, a missed promotion and a damning report card from one of the kids – could be enough to have us feeling divorcey for a week. But then the leak would get fixed and the kitchen repainted and I'd wonder why I'd ever cared.

But our jobs, thanks to successive austerity governments, got harder and harder to bear.

When Harry arrived home ranting about a lack of textbooks, lack of discipline and lack of staff, I'd counter with my own list of missing drugs and beds and hours in the day. From about 2010 onwards we were too exhausted to even listen properly to each other's complaints. And then Covid happened and it didn't just rock our little boat, it sank it.

Being a nurse, I was one of the first to feel its full force.

Our health system had been struggling for years. Expensive new drugs, an ageing population and million-pound scanning devices could all be paid for from existing budgets, we were told, as could all the money being siphoned to the shareholders of private companies the government increasingly chose to contract out to. So even before Covid we had eighteen-week waiting lists because operating theatres and surgeons were fully booked. But when the pandemic happened, well... Unless you were there to witness it, you really can't imagine how bad it was.

Within days, we'd run out of beds, respirators, anti-virals, face masks and gowns. We were working eighteen-hour shifts with disposable, non-reusable masks we'd laundered at home, held in place with gaffer tape because the elastic had broken.

I remember walking through our front door at 10 p.m. on 31 March and bursting into tears. We were less than ten days into the first lockdown, it was my birthday and my only gift was discovering that the pandemic had already broken me.

Harry held me and made me dinner that night, but within a few weeks no one at home even had the energy needed to empathise with me. They were all too busy fighting battles of their own.

Harry was in a blind panic from mid-April, a state in which he remained for almost two years. He'd been instructed to create a new online curriculum for both Physics (his subject) and Biology (which was not). Within a month he'd been told to run off-campus Chemistry teaching as well because the poor asthmatic Chemistry head was in the wheezy process of dying, very slowly, in my hospital. The pressure from Harry's principal was apparently unbearable – and I mean that quite literally. None of his staff could bear it. Two had breakdowns and three left teaching forever.

Add to this Harry's responsibility for homeschooling Fiona and Todd – because *Yours Truly* was simply never at home – and you can probably see why he was as close as one can get to a breakdown without ending up in a psych ward.

By then, it didn't matter if I complained, cried or shouted about my lot – all Harry had to offer was a selection of platitudes combined with his newly developed wide-eyed stare. Occasionally he'd still get up and hug me, and that was probably the thing that worked best. But once my colleagues started getting ill with Covid no one wanted to hug me much either, in fact they avoided being in the same room.

And who could really blame them? I mean, it's all very well isolating from other people, avoiding groups, sticking to your bubble, washing your shopping and all that malarky... But what to do about Mum when she's breathing the same air as a hundred Covid patients every day?

THREE

WAITING FOR WISDOM

She wakes up feeling ill and her first thought is that she might have caught a cold. She did sleep right through (something that's rare enough to merit celebration) so, microbes aside, she should be feeling tickety-boo. Perhaps she slept for too long? That can sometimes leave you feeling like a zombie, can't it?

She pushes one foot out from under the covers and is relieved to discover the cabin is warm. She remembers loading the stove up last night and setting it to its lowest setting, and when she gets downstairs this morning she can see from the glow that it's still burning.

She pulls on extra clothes and crosses to look out at the view, as spectacular this morning as yesterday. The sky is a deep blue again and a flock of birds is crossing the skyline, shifting in and out of formation, no doubt preparing to head to warmer climes. It crosses her mind, in a vague, sleepy way, that she too has migrated for winter.

She stretches and turns to face the room, and as she does so a heaped ashtray and a half-empty wine bottle catch her eye. There are two empties on the kitchen counter, too. Of course! She'd called Jill last night on WhatsApp, and they'd spent hours

gossiping and getting drunk. She can't remember much of what
was said, but it had been fun, that's for sure – almost like being
down the pub. She smiles at the memory. She'd needed that.
She'd been feeling lonely.

A specific memory tightens her jaw. She suspects she
invited Jill to come and visit. Not having that much life of her
own, Jill is always on the lookout for any opportunity to tag
along, and with her being so pushy, avoiding inviting her can be
hard. Wendy can't remember specific dates being discussed, so
she'll probably be OK. She looks around at the tiny space. No,
she definitely can't have Jill here. That wasn't the point of this
at all.

She makes coffee and spreads slices of already-stale
baguette with a thick layer of butter and jam then takes it all
outside to a little table placed strategically so she can sit in the
sun while enjoying the view. It's warmer this morning, almost
hot. Maybe the icy temperatures of yesterday were a mere blip.

She sips her coffee and bites into her breakfast. Why does
French apricot jam taste so much better?

She wonders what to do with her day. She thinks about all
the wine she consumed last night and decides she'll be healthy
and go for a walk. That's definitely what Harry would suggest.

If only he were here... *Don't let your mind go there, Wendy!*

Is a walk enough of an activity for a whole day? It seems a
little bit lazy. Maybe a big walk, then – something ambitious
and sporty.

Alternatively she could drive down and explore the coast.
She could go back to St-Vallier-de-whatever-it's-called and have
a drink in that bar on the green. But that's not how she'd imagined her time here, was it? She'd imagined herself sitting cross-
legged staring at a mountain until a bolt of enlightenment
zapped her. Which she knows is more than silly. With the
exception of those three yoga lessons she did with her sister-in-
law Sue all those years ago (that time she put her knee out) she's

never even tried to sit cross-legged for any amount of time, let alone meditate.

Perhaps walking *is* a kind of meditation, especially if you're doing it on your own. She'll give it a try, anyway. She used to have quite good ideas while walking Whitey, Fiona's childhood dog.

If all else fails, she could buy a notebook and write things down. She doesn't know what she'd write, but maybe if she tries the ideas will come? She briefly imagines herself writing a novel. The idea – at least the sitting around holding a pen while sipping tea bit – is appealing, but again rather daft. She hasn't written anything longer than a shopping list since school.

What if I go home none the wiser? she wonders, and a sense of dismay pops up from nowhere. What if this all amounts to nothing?

Yes, what if she spends six months and a chunk of her inheritance only to go home without a clue as to how to fix her life? Wouldn't that be a kick in the teeth?

She showers and pulls on shorts, a T-shirt and trainers, then drives down the track, through the tiny hamlet (there's a single shop here – a bakery – but she's not yet seen it open), and then on along the winding road to a place she spotted yesterday on her way back from the supermarket – a gravelly parking area at the roadside next to a vivid green meadow. Yesterday there had been four cars parked up and she'd seen a woman pulling on walking boots.

Today, she finds herself alone, but that's OK because the track heading off from the car park leaves no doubt. She locks the car, pockets the keys, and starts off along the trail.

This is a bit mad, she thinks, as the trail starts to rise, winding its way past a series of waist-high grey boulders. *Harry would be amused!*

She's always been the reluctant one when it comes to exercise, though if she's honest, she's not sure why. Perhaps it's simply that you have to have these roles in every couple: a keen walker and a reluctant complainer. She's always enjoyed a good walk but rarely admitted it. But yes, those were their roles – Harry the sporty keen one and Wendy the smoking whinger who Harry had to urge ever onwards. She's not sure when she chose to be that person – adolescence perhaps – and she's surprised, momentarily, that she has never questioned it until now.

The track winds back on itself behind a particularly large group of boulders, and as she turns the corner she discovers a bushy waist-high plant – some sort of weed by the looks of it. The tiny flowers are populated by thousands of frenetic butterflies.

'Wow,' she says, crouching down and pulling her phone from her pocket to take a photo. She notices, in the process, that she has no new messages this morning and yearns momentarily for a bygone era when a camera was only a camera and not a device that linked you to the entirety of your life, or in her case, lack of one.

She snaps a couple of photos and a short video of the excitable butterflies and, resisting the temptation to post it straight onto Instagram, stands and continues along the track.

By the time she reaches the top of the hill she's sweaty and out of breath but the view from the top – of brackeny *Wuthering Heights* hills punctuated with spiky protrusions of volcanic rocks – is good enough to make it all feel worthwhile.

In the distance, far away, she sees a huge white sphere perched on stilts. She decides it must be a telescope or a radar for Nice airport down below. It's really quite beautiful, like a modern art sculpture or, in the midst of this strange landscape, an alien spaceship, just landed. There's a scrappy Roman path winding across the hillside so she chooses it as today's destination.

It takes her over an hour to reach the sphere. It's far bigger, and therefore further, than she had imagined, and by the time she gets there her legs are turning to jelly. She actually feels quite faint.

She should have brought some water, she thinks, plonking herself down on a rock. She's dehydrated from the walk, but also from last night's drinking spree. She can almost smell the alcohol leaching out through the pores of her skin.

She should have brought a snack, too. Her trembly legs are almost certainly caused by low blood sugar; still, she'll be fine if she sits for a moment and lets her body catch up with itself.

The view from beneath the sphere is amazing – in fact, it's so unlike anything she sees in her daily life that it's hard to believe it's not a painted backdrop: a crazy, hazy 180-degree panorama of land, sea and sky stretching to infinity in every direction.

She stands and spins on one foot to take it all in – the bank of wispy cloud out to sea, the blur of a distant ferry, the crinkly outline of the coast... She feels proud and tells herself so, out loud. 'Wow!' she says. 'You made it!'

It crosses her mind that this would be a great spot (and moment) for a revelation. *Come to me, wisdom*, she thinks. *Come to me now!* But the truth is that her mind is entirely blank – emptier than it's been in years. A gentle breeze brings the scent of bracken to her attention. She sighs and stares out at all that space, trying to spot the line where the sea meets the sky. It's impossible, though, today. They're exactly the same shade of blue.

Space. She thinks about the depth of it, or at least tries to. *Infinity.* But they're impossible concepts really, aren't they? The thought makes her feel small and lonely. But it also makes her wonder if her problems are really that important in the scheme of things.

As she takes a panoramic photo on her phone, there's a sudden gust of wind. She shivers and her stomach rumbles audibly. My God, she's hungry!

She turns and, with a final glance over her shoulder at the view, starts her way back down.

* * *

By the time she gets home she's so thirsty, her mouth so dry, that she's barely able to swallow.

She gulps down three glasses of water and sets about making cheese on toast with half of one of her prematurely stale baguettes. Rock hard within twenty-four hours – who knew?

After lunch she rewards herself with a jumbo glass of Chardonnay and hurls herself onto the sunlit sofa. She's feeling righteous after her walk – she deserves this.

When she wakes from her afternoon snooze, the sun is already low, illuminating the cabin with a beautiful orange glow.

Intending to post her butterfly photos to Instagram, she reaches for her phone and is relieved to see that she has messages: one from Jill asking if she can come and stay on the fifth of November and others from Fiona and Harry asking her if she's OK. Neither of them have exactly gone to town, but at least they've remembered she exists.

Sorry Jill, she types. *That's way too soon. I've barely got settled in*

Her typing is interrupted by another text from Jill: *I booked it. It was so cheap I decided it doesn't matter. Didn't want to miss out on a good deal...*

'No!' she says out loud. 'That woman!' She gives a dismayed

shake of the head, then sends her reply anyway. Let Jill deal with it, she thinks.

Her phone rings immediately.

'Hello, Jill. I think our messages crossed over. I hope that ticket's reimbursable.' She always feels terrible when she has to say 'no' to people, but it really is too soon. Plus she's been promising herself for ages that she'll stand up more to Jill's pushiness. Now seems as good a time as any.

'Really?' Jill says. 'You're going to make me bin these flights?'

'It's too soon, honey,' Wendy says, weaving a little laughter into her voice in the hope that it will underline how unreasonable Jill's idea is. 'It's way too early. I've only just got here.'

'Aw, Wendy!' Jill whines. 'I mean, they were only a hundred and thirty quid, but all the same.'

'I'm sure you can get the money back, can't you? Or at least some of it.' Even before Jill replies she realises she has probably made a strategic error by asking.

'No, it's not refundable. That's why they were so cheap. But hey, what's £130 between friends. Assuming we are still friends? Seeing as you don't want to see me anymore.'

'I'm just saying come later,' Wendy says. So she has made another error by verbally accepting the idea of Jill coming. This is how Jill works, she thinks. This is how she corners you.

'Damn. A hundred and thirty quid down the drain. Oh well.'

Wendy licks her lips as she prepares to tell Jill she shouldn't have bought the flights – that she should have waited for her to say it was OK, but Jill gets there first.

'I shouldn't have confirmed them,' she says. 'I know, it's my own silly fault.'

'Well...'

'But all the later flights were so expensive, hon. I can't come at all otherwise. And I miss you. I assumed – stupidly – that you miss me, too. You said you did last night.'

Wendy doesn't remember saying this, but then she doesn't remember much of the conversation. Anything's possible.

'Of course I miss you. I'm missing everyone. It's just—'

'Then let me come! Come on! It'll be fun. It's only three nights.'

'It's really tiny here,' Wendy protests.

'Well, I wouldn't know. You still haven't sent me those photos you promised.'

'It's a studio. A one-room studio.'

'Then we'll go somewhere else. I'll have a hunt online and find somewhere nice.'

'I don't want to go somewhere else, Jill. I've only just got here.'

'Then it'll be fine,' Jill says. 'Don't worry. It has a bed, right? And a sofa?'

'Yes, but...'

'The sofa will do me fine, don't worry. It'll be such fun. We'll have a hoot exploring the local nightlife. All those French men!'

'May I remind you that you're married?'

'So are you.'

'Yes,' Wendy says. 'Yes... I am. And there is no local nightlife.'

'Oh, there will be once I get there,' Jill says. 'Oh, talking of husbands, gotta go. Bern's standing in the doorway waving his keys at me. Talk later.'

'OK,' Wendy says.

'And see you on the fifth!'

The line goes dead and Wendy chucks her phone onto the sofa. 'A bulldozer,' she mutters. 'She's an absolute bloody bulldozer.'

. . .

She takes a glass of wine and a bowl of nuts outside and lights a cigarette. The first puff tastes superb – a reality that's impossible to explain to a non-smoker, or even, in fact, to herself. There's nothing to like about smoking, even she can admit that. But sometimes that first drag of a cigarette can really seem quite magical.

She blows the smoke through pursed lips and watches the sun as it slips behind the hills, turning the sky a deep, purply red.

She thinks about Jill and feels annoyed at herself for not being more assertive. Back in her nursing school days she'd had an American friend called Carrie who'd been a living lesson in assertiveness. Carrie could smile at people and say, without a hint of anger or annoyance, 'No, I'm sorry, I don't think I want to do that,' and people would shrug, give in, and smile back. Even the doctors struggled to boss Carrie around.

Wendy has tried over the years to be more like Carrie but she suspects that once you're born British, it's a bit of a lost cause. We're brought up to feel bad about saying no, in fact we're brought up to feel bad about most things. Maybe it's not even our upbringing that does it, maybe it's genetics – a biological desire to please.

She pops a nut into her mouth and notes the sudden chill in the air. It's amazing the way the temperature drops here the second the sun's out of sight.

She hasn't replied to Fiona or Harry yet. Is she trying to punish them for not getting in touch earlier? Probably. But she admits to herself that it's a lost cause. You can't really punish someone's lack of interest in you. Specifically, you can't starve people into missing you. She picks up her phone and types a message to Fiona.

Hello darling. Yes, I'm fine. It's gorgeous here. I'm watching the sunset and sipping some lovely cheap Chardonnay. She starts to ask how things are back home, but then backspaces – she's been bitten by that one before. *Love Mum xxx*, she adds, clicking send before she has to change her mind about the number of kisses, too.

She then takes a snap from where she's sitting and sends that to her daughter.

Pretty! Fiona replies instantly. *But go easy on the Chardonnay.*

How did my kids get to be so puritanical? Wendy wonders.

Jill, whose bank clerk son, Michael, is also surprisingly restrained for a youngster, claims it's a generational thing. Jill says alternate generations are boring, but her son's kids will drive him crazy by becoming rebels. And Jill may well be right about that. Wendy doubts that it has even crossed Fiona or Todd's minds to pop an E and dance till sunrise. Oh, the summer nights she and Harry used to spend dancing. Truly some of the highlights of her life.

And Harry? She sighs. What to say to Harry?

I still love you/I still miss you/I still hate you?

I don't understand what went wrong. We used to be so good together?

Hi Harry, I'm fine, she types. *But thanks a lot for asking. xx*

FOUR

HARRY (PART 2)

When I moved out, it was meant to be temporary. That's what we told ourselves anyway.

Fiona, Todd and Harry were locked down in their Covid-free house while I had to leave every day to work in just about the highest-risk environment in the country. Colleagues were coming down with the illness all the time, and patients were dying every day. It was unfair to put the kids at risk, Harry said, and it was impossible to disagree. Plus, if I'm being totally honest, I'd been finding the atmosphere at home exhausting anyway.

It was obviously nowhere near as 'exhausting' as being at work but in a way, that's my point. By the time I got home I *needed* things to be relaxed. All I wanted to do was slump in front of the TV with a glass of wine. I didn't want to be hassled about drinking too much or smoking too much or what risks I may or may not have taken whilst at work. I didn't want to be asked to wear a bloody face mask in my lounge either, because I'd had one on all day, and I didn't want to listen to my family's whingy – comparatively insubstantial – lockdown woes at all.

So when Jill suggested that I use her empty Airbnb place

for a break, 'until it all blows over', I jumped at the opportunity.
And I enjoyed it there, for a while.

The studio, which was tiny but pretty, was situated at the
bottom of her garden. I could drink and smoke and watch crap
TV without complaint. I slept better, I found, without Harry's
snoring, and didn't miss his complaints about my hours, Fiona's
laziness or Todd's smelly trainers either.

Sometimes Jill and I met in the garden (at a distance) for a
ciggy and a glass of wine and on sunny days when I could fit
him in, Harry and I would walk around the park. But he was
stressed, too, so our conversations became increasingly brittle.
We felt more like strangers every time we met and I remember
having a vague premonition that rather than saving our
marriage we might be breaking it.

We were a month into lockdown before either of the kids
deigned to meet me. It was Fiona who agreed first, so we met at
her favourite place – Vinters Park.

As we walked, we chatted about the pandemic and whether
it was the Chinese who had manufactured the virus, a theory
Fiona insisted was 'gaining traction'. And then I asked her the
dreaded question: I asked how things were at home.

'Oh, good, actually,' she said. 'Everything's quite shockingly
chilled.'

It was such an unexpected thing for her to say that I could
only assume the missing words were 'since you moved out'. I
was so shocked I stopped walking.

After a few paces, Fiona paused too and turned back.
'Mum?' she said.

'I'm not sure what that's supposed to mean,' I told her.

'God, I knew you'd be like this,' she said, instantly leaping
into combat mode.

'Like what?'

'You're always... Oh, you know what you're like.'

'No, I don't know,' I said. 'Tell me.'

'You're waiting all the time to jump on something. It's like you're on the lookout for something to be upset about.'

'I am not! Where's this coming from? I really have no idea what you're talking about,' I told her.

'Look I don't mean anything... you know... bad... by it.'

'Oh, well, that's a relief!' I said sarcastically.

'But even you'd admit your... um... energy... has been a bit off lately.'

'My energy? If you mean that I've been tired...'

'No, I mean your – you know – *spiritual* energy.'

'My spiritual energy?'

'Yes. Or your emotional energy, if you prefer.'

'Well, I'm sorry if I've been a bit too yin for you,' I said, forcing a laugh. 'Or maybe I've been too yang?'

'Ha,' Fiona said. 'Funny.' Then, 'Come on. Let's keep walking. It'll be dark soon.'

We walked in silence for a bit and then she said, 'And now I suppose you're sulking. You see, this is why no one dares say anything to you. Everyone's too scared.'

'I am not sulking!' I was starting to feel quite angry, actually. Or tearful. I sensed it could go either way. 'I don't know what you're trying to say.'

'You don't? Really?'

'No. I've been very stressed, if that's what you mean. My job is incredibly stressful.'

'Everyone's stressed, Mum,' Fiona said dismissively. 'There's a worldwide pandemic on. But we're not all—'

'I'll tell you what we're not all doing,' I interrupted. 'We're not all spending our days watching patients die of that worldwide pandemic, are we?'

'No,' Fiona said. 'No I s'pose not.'

'It's hard, sweetie. My job is really hard right now. Do you understand that?'

'Yeah,' she said. 'Cos you're always telling us how hard it is.'

'And I know it's hard for you, too,' I added, attempting to calm things down. 'Really, I do. But I do think you could try to get where I'm coming from. I think you're being a bit unfair. And a bit hurtful.'

'Of course you do,' Fiona said sourly. 'That's kind of my point.' Then, 'Sorry, Mum, but I need to get home. See you soon.'

'Sweetie!' I called after her. 'Fiona! Come back and talk to...' But she'd already turned off down another path to our left and, blowing a kiss over her shoulder, she strode away.

I was so stunned that I sat on a bench until the cold made me start to shiver.

* * *

Harry phoned me two hours later. I'd barely managed to get warm.

'How are you?' he asked.

'Me? I'm fine,' I replied flatly. The truth was that I was bloody upset and had even had a little cry because my daughter hated me, I'd been banished from my own home and had to return to my impossibly exhausting job the next day... All that, plus the state of the world in general.

Having downed two medium glasses of South African Chardonnay, I was also a tad tipsy which seemed just as well considering the circumstances.

'Fiona came home in a right state,' Harry said. 'I was wondering what you said to her.'

'What *I* said to *her*?'

'OK, what you both said, then. What you said to each other. She's locked herself in her room.'

'Lucky you,' I said. 'I'd make the most of that if I were you.'

'So come on,' Harry said. 'What happened?'

'She basically said things are better at home without me,' I told him, aware, as I said it, that I was paraphrasing to my advantage.

'Did she?' Harry asked. 'Did she really? Because I can't imagine our Fiona saying that.'

'Well, she did,' I told him. 'More or less. She said things are shockingly chilled since I left.'

'Well, I'm sure that's not what she meant,' Harry said. 'I'm sure she was trying to reassure you.'

'Reassure me?' I exclaimed. 'About the fact that you're all so much better off without me? That's incredibly reassuring, Haz. That's exactly what I needed to hear.'

'No,' Harry said. 'And please don't go off on one. Not when I'm trying to help.'

'I am not going off on one. Don't you start too!'

'Look, I'm sure she was just trying to reassure you that we're all OK. Despite everything that's happening. Despite you having to stay at Jill's... Despite the horrific news cycle we're all constantly subjected to, we're OK. And we all miss you like crazy. It's hard.'

'Do you?' I asked. 'Is it hard? Because she categorically did not say that. In fact she said very much the opposite.'

'Yes, of course we miss you,' Harry said. 'The bed's too cold without you.' It was a lyric from a song we'd both liked many years before – a typical Harry attempt at mid-argument seduction, a strategy he used often to calm things down.

'Cute,' I said, signalling that I wasn't buying it. 'Funny guy.'

'It actually is,' Harry said. 'It's bloody freezing.'

'The electric blanket's in the cupboard,' I told him. 'You're just too lazy to put it on.'

'That's probably true. I'll look into it.'

'Anyway, that's not what she said, Harry. So please don't have a go at me. She didn't say you all miss me at all. What she said was that I'm always looking for fights and that things are super chilled now I'm not there to upset everyone.'

'Yes,' Harry said. 'Well...'

I pulled a face at my mobile and waited for him to continue. I could sense he was going to dig himself deeper, quite possibly considerably deeper.

'That's kind of why I'm calling, actually,' he said. 'Because things *have* been fairly chilled. Which, when the world's falling apart, is no mean feat.'

'Congratulations,' I said sourly. 'You win the Single Father of the Year award.'

'And I was wondering...' Harry continued, wisely ignoring my jibe, 'if you could cool it a bit. Just try not to wind them up when you see them. They've got a lot to deal with, too.'

'God, it must be so awful for them,' I said. 'All that extra time they have to spend on the PlayStation.'

'And she's right,' Harry said, ploughing on. 'Everything has been really chilled. Until tonight.'

'Which is my fault, obvs.'

'Well, you saw Fiona and you argued with her, and she came home and shouted at me, and then had an argument with Todd, and now she's upset and locked in her room. Which is the first time in ages that anyone in this house has raised their voice.'

'When you say "in ages" you mean since I moved out.'

'If you must put it that way,' Harry said, 'then, yes.'

A wave of anger rose within me that was so massive it choked my ability to speak. I couldn't even begin to think of words which might express what I wanted to say. Beads of sweat prickled my brow.

'You bring a lot of stress home with you from work and you tend to start dr—'

I ended the call. My finger, as it hit the end call button, was shaking.

Harry phoned me back immediately. 'I think we got cut off,' he said.

After a moment of silence, he added, 'Unless... Did you just...? You didn't hang up on me, did you? Because that would be very childish if it were the case. In fact that would be exactly the sort of th—'

'Oh do fuck off, Harry,' I said, cutting him off before he went full-blown teacher on me. 'Do go and fucking fuck right off.' And then I ended the call again, feeling proud that this time I'd found exactly the right words to express myself.

* * *

Because no one was up for apologising, things could only get worse after that, so that's what happened next. Harry and I avoided contact for almost three weeks (which wasn't exactly difficult, considering the times we were living in) and Todd joined Fiona's war of nerves by never having time to meet me either. Seeing as his courses were online and all his exams had been cancelled, lack of time seemed unlikely.

By the time that first seemingly interminable lockdown ended things had eased all round. The work situation, though still frenetic, was better and, by comparison with the madness of April, almost relaxed. Sure, we'd lost a lot of staff to illness and burnout and one overweight male nurse had died, and yes, we still had a massive backlog of other patients to see and of course there were still Covid patients coming through the doors, some of whom also continued to die... OK, I'm remembering things more clearly as I tell this... So, no, it wasn't relaxed at all. But there were now moments in each day when I didn't need to run and entire weeks when I didn't cry once.

Family matters had calmed down, too.

Fiona was excitedly preparing for a return to school (or so we all believed), while Todd was engaged in a twenty-four/seven *Call of Duty* killing spree while he waited for the calculated grades which it had been announced were to replace his exams.

When our valiant PM announced that the two-metre rule was to be dropped and that schools, if they wished, could re-open, Harry and I agreed it was time I moved back home. I'd pack my things up on the Friday after work, we decided, and for Saturday lunch we'd be a family again.

I didn't quite finish packing on the Friday night because, after my week at work, I felt shattered. As I went to sleep that night, early, it crossed my mind that I was feeling more exhausted than usual and I wondered if I was stressed at the idea of going home.

When I woke the next morning to find the bed sheets soaked in sweat I knew immediately what was going on. There was a poetic absurdity to it that almost made me want to laugh. Almost.

I wasn't surprised that I'd finally caught the damned thing, only that I'd escaped it for so long.

It was horrible, truly horrible – worse by far than the worst flu I'd ever had. I sneezed and wheezed and coughed so constantly that I ended up lacking sleep. I soaked the bed with sweat to the point where – when finally, three weeks later, I was better – I had to buy Jill a new mattress for her studio. But – and let's be thankful for big mercies, here – it wasn't as bad as it might have been. After all, I didn't get long Covid. And as you guess from the fact I'm telling you this, I didn't die either.

People were as lovely as people who are terrified of catching something can be.

A senior doctor from work brought me some Tamiflu (which at the time was being used off-label on a trial basis) so I took that religiously even though I was never convinced it helped.

Jill kept me supplied with soup, pots of which she would leave outside my door before knocking and backing away.

And Harry and the kids came round to shout encouraging

things through the window before blowing kisses as they too backed off.

It was the end of August when I finally moved home.

We had an uptick in fresh cases coming into Maidstone at the time, a fact I shared openly with the family. But after some discussion, we decided I'd been 'vaccinated' by my illness, and I was probably now one of the lucky few who no longer had anything to fear. We still knew so little.

* * *

Things were never quite the same after that, but because the whole Covid drama continued to unfold in its unpredictable way – because there were repeat lockdowns and local variations which affected us all constantly in different ways – I assumed this was par for the course. As Fiona had said: everyone was stressed. We were in the middle of a worldwide pandemic.

Back home, we glided around each other in passive-aggressive semi-silence. When words were spoken they were often terse, occasionally lapsing into downright rudeness.

During periods when I or colleagues at work tested positive (because by then we were too short staffed to stay home sick) I'd go back to Jill's for two weeks, and these were breaks I began to enjoy. When I returned home there was little sense of relief – no real pleasure at being reunited. Harry and the kids were still avoiding me which, considering the risks, seemed sad but hardly unfair.

* * *

In the end, whilst all of our family members survived, the

family itself did not. This didn't become clear until near the end of the whole Covid nightmare.

It was a week before Christmas 2021 – the final Christmas ever to be completely ruined by the pandemic. As an aside, I sometimes wonder, if we'd managed to get through Christmas, would everything have been OK? Because it really was Christmas that blew us out of the water.

The government – if you could call the bunch of chancers running the country a 'government' – had authorised small Christmas gatherings while simultaneously slapping local restrictions on the south-east. This basically meant that even though lockdown was now over, we were right back in – you guessed it – lockdown.

My Christmas leave got cancelled. Yet another of our EU nurses – Gabriela – had vanished overnight back to Madrid. There had been a drip, drip of these desertions ever since the Brexit vote so eloquently informed them all that they were not wanted, but the pressure of Covid made things that much worse. My boss had quite literally begged me to come in over Christmas despite the fact I was overdue for leave.

'Oh, by the way, the Christmas bonanza is confirmed,' I told Harry one morning while I prepared coffee. 'They need me from Christmas Eve through Boxing Day – day shifts only. Legally I can refuse, but things are pretty desperate. You don't mind terribly if I go in, do you?'

'Oh,' Harry said. 'About that. I've been meaning to have a word.'

'A word,' I said lightly. 'OK. Which word?'

'Can you stop and, um, look at me?' Harry asked. I was busy struggling to open a fresh pack of coffee without tipping it all over the place.

'Oh,' I said. I put the package down on the counter and after a brief private frown at the wall, I turned to face him with a forced smile. The quiver in his voice had worried me. 'Go on?'

'This is...' Harry said. He coughed. 'This isn't, um, going to be easy, so please... Let's stay calm, if we can. And quiet.' He glanced behind him at the hallway, presumably thinking about Fiona, who was sleeping upstairs. 'Todd, um, says he probably won't come home for Christmas.'

'Oh,' I said. 'Really? Why's that? What's he doing instead?'

'Not if you're here, that is.'

'Beg pardon?' I said.

'Todd. He says—'

'No, I... I heard you,' I explained. 'But—'

'And Fiona's not that keen either.'

'She's not *keen*?'

'No. Not now we're in tier 4 and everything.'

'But she lives here. Where would she go?'

Harry shrugged. 'I... um...' he stumbled.

'We're all fully vaccinated, anyway,' I said. 'So I don't see...'

'But it's not just that,' Harry said.

'It isn't just what?'

'This hasn't... um... really been... Well... working, has it?' he stammered. 'It hasn't been working for any of us, really. Not for a while, if we're being honest.'

'I...' I shook my head. 'What hasn't been working?'

'Well, you... you know... being at home. Us all being cooped up together.'

'Are you...?' I asked, frowning and cocking my head. 'You're not...? Are you asking me to move out, Haz?'

'Not definitively,' he said. 'Not forever or anything. Just for a bit. I thought maybe if Jill's place is still—'

'But I'll hardly be here anyway. I've just told you. I'm working every day.'

'Well, exactly,' Harry said, signalling with one hand to keep the noise down. 'That's why we thought it probably isn't worth the risk.'

'But it's Christmas,' I said, tears welling up. 'And what do you mean, it hasn't really been working?' His words had only just hit me.

'Well, we feel—'

'Can you stop with the whole "we" thing?' I interrupted. 'It's really weaselly trying to hide behind the kids that way. Just own whatever you have to say, Harry.'

'OK. Then *I* think we need a break,' he said. 'I need some time to myself. And I think you might want to think about seeing someone if there's any chance of making this work.'

I blinked at him. I was flabbergasted.

'You've been stressed for... well, for ages, actually,' he continued.

'Me?' I exclaimed, doing my best to not explode. 'Have you any idea what you've been like?'

'I probably have as well,' he admitted. 'But we've been – *I've* been – walking on eggshells since the pandemic started. So I think you maybe need to see someone to find a better way to deal with all your stress.'

'A better way of dealing with my stress?' I repeated.

'Yes. Better than the way you do it now. And you know what I'm talking about, so don't pretend you don't.'

'Only I don't,' I said.

'Yes, you do,' Harry said. 'You come home and sit in front of the TV with your vat of wine and hope no one speaks to you. And that's not how a family is supposed to work.'

'Oh, so I'm not allowed to watch TV now? I'm not allowed a glass of wine at the end of the day?'

'I'm just saying that it's maybe not as helpful as you think.'

'You sit with your headphones on listening to your bloody podcasts,' I pointed out. 'What's the difference? Plus you drink as much as I do.'

'Well, I actually don't,' Harry said.

'You bloody well do.'

'I don't. But look, that's hardly the point. The point is that I don't get snarky if anyone speaks to me.'

'Snarky?' I repeated. 'Oh, I'm snarky, now, am I?'

'Yes. A bit. And it's not helpful. None of us need the extra stress of that right now. None of us have the space to cope with your stress as well as our own.'

I gasped. 'I...' I said. But I couldn't think what to say.

I thought about my job and wished for a moment that I could take my family to work with me, for one day, so they had some conception of what I was dealing with.

'I don't understand...' I said, sinking into one of the kitchen chairs. 'It all seems so out of the blue. Where's this coming from, Haz?'

'It's been a long time coming, actually,' he said. 'I've been trying to say something for ages. But Christmas and tier 4 have kind of forced my hand.'

I shook my head at the madness of it. 'You really are asking me to move out, then? For Christmas?'

'Look...' Harry said.

'Just say it. If that's it, then at least admit it.'

'The thing is, even I don't want to be around you when you're like this,' Harry said. 'God knows how the kids feel. I actually feel a bit sick about coming home.'

'Then why don't *you* move out?' I asked, my tears morphing to anger. 'This is my *home*.'

'I would,' Harry said. 'I've thought about it. I have. But the kids agree with me. And this is their home, too.'

'God, have you been discussing me behind my back?' I asked. 'Have you been planning this whole little intervention, turning them against me? Is that why they're both so uptight all the time?' I swallowed with difficulty and then repeated, 'This is my home, Harry. This is my family. And it's Christmas. It's bloody Christmas.'

'Yes,' Harry said. 'Yes, I know. But I thought – I mean,

you've done it before loads of times – so I thought if you
could – I mean, if Jill's place is free – and seeing as you're
working all the time anyway – and seeing as there's so
much Covid around right now – well, we... I just thought
you might be able to ask her if it's OK. So the kids can
come home for Christmas stress-free. And then we can
take things from there in the new year. Maybe see
someone together. Or separately. Work out where we're
going.'

'I didn't realise any of us were going anywhere,' I said.

Fiona came downstairs at that moment and, being sleepy,
failed to pick up on the icy atmosphere in the room. She
slouched her way across to the counter, hair falling forwards so
that I couldn't even see her face, then pulled a box of cornflakes
from the cupboard and one of the bowls from the shelf.

I turned my chair so that I could address her.

'Wendy,' Harry said quietly, pleadingly. 'Don't...'

'No,' I said. 'You're the one who keeps saying "we". Let's see
what my darling daughter has to say about it all.'

Fiona turned to face me, the pack of cornflakes still in one
hand. 'What's happening?' she asked, speaking through her
hair. 'Are we arguing already? I mean, it's not even eight
o'clock.'

'Your father says you want me out over Christmas,' I said. 'Is
that true?'

'I thought you were working anyway,' she said, pushing hair
behind her ear.

'Not at nights, I'm not.'

'But if we're not gonna to see you, it hardly seems worth the
risk,' Fiona said, glancing at Harry for support. I saw from the
corner of my eye that he winked at her encouragingly.

'The risk...' I repeated. 'We're all vaccinated. Todd's had it;
I've had it twice. At some point we are going to have to live
with it.'

'Shelley's mum gave it to the whole family even though they was vaccinated,' Fiona said.

'Were,' Harry corrected, I thought rather pedantically considering the context. 'Even though they *were* vaccinated. *They* being plural.'

'Whatever,' Fiona said.

'And please don't say "whatever",' Harry said. 'I've told you about that before. It's chavvy.'

'Anyway, it was like a cold,' I said, interrupting Harry's grammar lesson. 'You told me that yourself. The whole family had a bad cold. Big deal.'

'But it's not just the Covid,' Fiona said. 'It's this.' She waved her hand vaguely in the space between us.

'This?'

'The arguments. Like right now, at 7.45 on a Friday.'

'Well, of course we're having a bloody argument,' I said, raising my voice yet trying my hardest not to shout. 'I'm being told, by my daughter and my husband, to fuck off somewhere else for Christmas.'

'Oh, is that OK?' Fiona asked, addressing Harry. 'Are we allowed to say "fuck" these days, as long as we avoid "whatever"?' She looked at me and gave me a strangely aggressive nod of the chin. 'Eh?'

I lost it – I'll admit it. But talk about provocation! I jumped from my seat and lurched towards her fully intending to slap her face, only Harry grabbed my wrist before I made contact, hurting me as he deflected my swipe.

'No,' he said. 'Not that. Not today.'

'No, let her!' Fiona snarled. 'Go on, Mum. Hit me! That'll definitely make Christmas more festive.'

'Oh... bugger you all,' I said, spinning on one foot – already leaving the room. 'Really. Just go to hell, the lot of you!'

I locked myself in the bathroom where I sat on the toilet and cried. I felt certain that Harry would knock on the door at any moment, either because he was worried about me or he wanted to talk, or at the very least, because he or Fiona needed the bathroom. Between sobs I tried to prepare the best possible comeback for when he did so.

But Harry did not knock on the door, and by the time I'd showered and fixed my face, the house was empty.

Numb with shock, I hesitated all morning about what to do before finally packing two bags and phoning Jill. In the end, I couldn't face the stress of having the whole argument again when Harry got home. I also incorrectly assumed that faced with my absence, he'd feel regret.

I spent Christmas Eve with Jill and Bern watching Christmas specials on TV, and went into work with a gin-and-tonic hangover. The horror of Christmas night itself, I solved by sleeping on a gurney in the nurses' quarters, helping out when things got out of hand. I think everyone assumed I was still on shift.

Because Jill was so used to having me stay she assumed that Covid was once again the cause, and I chose not to correct that assumption.

New Year's Eve came and went without even a smidgin of news from the family. Bern fell asleep just after ten and Jill and I sneaked out to the local pub. But I can't say I enjoyed it. I just went through the motions for Jill's sake.

On the second of January, Todd posted a photo of Christmas dinner on Instagram. In it, he, Harry and Fiona, plus a girl I'd never seen before (new girlfriend, perhaps?) were grinning broadly, cutting into the cake I'd made a month before.

They all looked so happy, it broke my heart. Like poking a sore tooth, I kept going back and staring at that photo and it made me cry almost every time.

Eventually, on about the fiftieth peek, I couldn't resist commenting, *What could be more important than family at Christmas?* And yes, I know it was snide, but in my defence, I had been down the pub with Jill...

By the next morning, Todd had deleted the photo which at least saved me from ever having to look at it again.

* * *

On the fifth of January, Jill came knocking to ask what was 'really going on?'.

She'd received a booking request for February, she said, and wanted to know if she could accept. So I told her the truth and bless her, I think she cried more than I did.

Jill's point of view was that they were a bunch of ungrateful pigs who wouldn't know a woman sacrificing her family life to keep them safe even if she walked up and slapped them in the face. Which, by the way, was exactly what they deserved. I found it hard to disagree.

FIVE

FIRST CONTACT

The next morning, Wendy wakes up to discover a day that is as cold as it is grey.

The thermometer stuck to the outside of the bathroom window tells her the temperature in the garden is seven degrees. It's a bit of a shock really – she had stupidly imagined it would be sunny every day.

Actually, that's not strictly true. Logically, she'd known there would be grey days, it's simply that she failed to ever imagine what she would do with herself.

She switches on some lights, re-stokes the wood burner and makes a pot of coffee. She points her new blow heater at her feet until the fire begins to roar.

I need a plan for dull days, she thinks.

She could visit one of those coastal towns, but in the end wouldn't that be a better thing to do in the sunshine? It would be more fun to do it with Jill, too, if she's really coming. Wendy can't remember exactly how they left things but she suspects that, knowing Jill, she'll be here soon enough whatever was officially decided.

She takes her mug of coffee to the window and peers

outside, searching for a break in the cloud cover but it's wall-to-wall grey.

She returns to the sofa and checks the weather app on her phone. Cloudy all day with a 60 per cent possibility of rain in the afternoon. Yuck.

She has never been good at dealing with winter, with the cold, or even with rainy days in summer, for that matter. Which is silly really, because she knows logically that without rain we'd all be dead. She suspects she suffers from that SAD thing everyone's always on about. Grey days inevitably make her feel lethargic and, when she'd been living alone at Jill's, she'd sometimes struggled to even get out of bed. Which of course is why a six-month sabbatical in the south of France was so much more attractive than the original idea of a cabin in Norway.

Come on, she tells herself, fighting a rising sense of melancholy. *You can do this. You're British!*

She showers in the chilly bathroom and dresses warmly then steps outdoors. Just as she does so, a little yellow van pulls up next to her hire car. A woman with a military-grade haircut – young, not much older than Fiona – jumps out and strides towards her.

'*Bonjour !*' she says enthusiastically. '*J'ai du courrier pour vous – enfin, pour Madame Blanchard.*'

'*Bonjour,*' Wendy replies, smiling as she crosses the garden to meet her. She has no idea what the girl said but she did hear the word 'Blanchard' which she knows is the name of the woman she's renting from.

She takes the three letters from the post lady's outstretched hand and checks the envelopes. They aren't for her; how could they be? All the same, she feels a stab of disappointment. There are few things she likes more in life than getting letters.

'*Vous êtes la nouvelle locataire ?*' the girl asks.

Wendy has no idea what that means either. '*Désolée,*' she

says, with an exaggerated shrug designed to communicate cluelessness.

'You're English?' the girl asks. 'Or American? Or...'

'Yes, English,' Wendy replies.

'Is OK,' the girl says. 'I speak it. My good subject in the BAC. The only! How long you stay here?'

'Six months,' Wendy says.

'Six month!' the girl says. 'Is long. Maybe I practise my English with you.'

'Yes,' Wendy says, sounding vague because, in her mind, she's busy trying to concoct a phrase in French. '*Oui !*'

'Cool,' the girl says. 'You give these to Madame Blanchard? Or I put in the box of letters?'

'No, I'll give them to her. No problem.'

'Good. So *ciao* until next time!' And then she turns and strides back to her van, jumps in, reverses jerkily out then, spitting gravel, accelerates off down the track.

'*Bonjour ?*' Wendy admonishes herself out loud. '*Désolée ?!*'

She shakes her head at this miserable failure to seize the moment. After all, that was the first time she's had any real contact with a French person, and a keen friendly French person at that. All she managed was *bonjour*, *désolée* and *oui*. Three words. Not even an *au revoir*.

She glances back down at the letters in her hand and returns indoors to get warm.

* * *

She sends the owner a message to inform her she has mail at the cabin. It'll be interesting to meet her, Wendy thinks. She glances around at the mess and immediately starts to tidy up, just in case. She has no idea where the owner lives. She could be a hundred yards down the road. She might knock on the door at any moment.

Ten minutes later, as she's guiltily hiding the new room heater in one of the cupboards, her phone pings with a reply: a friend, Erik, will collect the mail at some point.

OK, thanks, she types back, then, *P.S. Do you know when the bakery is open? It seems to be permanently closed.*

Probably annual holiday, Madame Blanchard replies. *I expect there is a word in the window.*

Grey day project, Wendy thinks instantly. She'll walk to the bakery and find out, and hopefully be home before the rain.

She pulls on her puffer jacket against the cold and locks the cabin behind her. The temperature is still in single digits, yet by the time she has reached the tarmac road, she's sweating like a pig. So she takes the jacket off and ties it around her waist, then, because this leaves her feeling too cold, walks as fast as she can.

It takes twenty minutes to reach the bakery and twenty-five more to get back home, but the trip is entirely fruitless. There is no indication whatsoever if the bakery ever intends to re-open. She should probably have asked the post lady, who would almost certainly have known.

The rain begins while she's eating lunch – stale baguette dipped in ready-made soup. The droplets are tiny at first, almost mist, but they slowly morph into a downpour.

After lunch she moves to the sofa and watches the raindrops slithering down the windowpane. The rain makes her think of home and when she checks the weather forecast for Maidstone she sees that, ironically, it's sunny there. She wonders what the kids are doing. She wonders if they hate her.

Her phone rings with an incoming call.

'Hello,' Jill says, the second Wendy answers. 'What you up to?'

'Just watching the rain and—'

'Rain?'

'Yes. Lots of.'

'God, it's lovely 'ere.'

'And I was wondering if my kids really hate me,' Wendy says, 'if you must know.'

'Oh, of course they don't,' Jill replies without hesitation.

'I wish I had your confidence.'

'No news at all, then?'

'Three texts,' she replies. 'One from each.'

'Harry as well, then?'

'Yep. Short and sweet. Well, short at any rate. It wasn't particularly sweet.'

'You two will have to talk at some point,' Jill says. 'You do realise that?'

'Yes, of course.'

'I know I keep saying it, but it's true.'

'Sure. But I need to work out what I want, first. What my end game is. And that's why I'm here, isn't it? To think about it all.'

'Is it better, then?' Jill asks. 'For thinking? I mean. Are you having better thoughts than in my studio?'

'I'm not sure yet, if I'm honest,' Wendy says. 'But I think the distance helps a bit. Not having them all playing happy families down the road definitely feels less... I don't know. Less suffocating, maybe?'

'Perspective increases with distance,' Jill says.

'I'm sorry?'

'Oh, it's just something Dad used to say. He used to go for long drives when he needed to think about anything important. And that's what he used to say to my mum when he got back. Perspective increases with distance. Anyway...'

'Anyway...'

'So, can I come? Because I still need to buy a train ticket to the airport. The flight's already booked – as you know – silly me! And I honestly do think we'd have fun. But if you really don't want me there then I'm obviously not gonna force—'

'No,' Wendy says. 'It's fine. Come!' Even as she's saying it, she's not quite sure why. It's the result of a sort of 'oh sod it' instinct. Something about bowing to the inevitability of Jill's visit. And perhaps it's better to get it over with so she'll have a proper long block of time to think about her life once Jill has gone.

'Brilliant,' Jill says. 'I'll book the train, then. It'll probably cost more than the flight! When I get there, do I get a taxi, or...?'

Wendy laughs. 'I'm in the middle of nowhere,' she says. 'I hope you're not going to be disappointed.'

'Not if you're there, I won't,' Jill says sweetly.

'And, yes, I'll pick you up from the airport. What time do you get in?'

'Just after three,' Jill says. 'Three in the afternoon.'

'Well, that's easy. A very respectable hour.'

'Yeah... you're not gonna like the flight back so much,' Jill says. 'It's six in the morning. So I probably need to be there at four or something.'

'Ouch!' Wendy says.

'I know. I'm sorry.'

'It's fine. We'll just have to be sensible the night before.'

Jill laughs. 'Like that's gonna happen!'

* * *

The next morning, she wakes up early, well before the sun has risen above the hills.

She lies in bed, slowly coming to, and as she does so she realises she's feeling down. She has no idea why – it's perhaps simply the way some days are. Maybe it depends on what she's been dreaming – where, in her mind, she has spent the night. She tries for a moment to remember, but draws a blank.

She lingers in bed for half an hour, at first trying to tune in to the voice inside her head to find out why she's feeling so blue, and then once she's identified the culprit, trying to tune it back out.

Because what the voice is saying, this morning, is that this whole adventure is doomed, that it's nothing more, nothing less, than a waste of time, money and energy.

Maybe I should pack up and go home. Maybe I should just kill myself! That would show them, wouldn't it?

Eek! she thinks. *Where did that one come from?*

If thoughts like that are going to bubble up maybe it's a good job Jill's coming after all.

Still troubled, she pulls on a dressing gown and descends the stairs, then adds wood to the burner and opens the slats. This is starting to feel like a morning ritual – starting to feel like the normal way one starts a day. The sensation of following a routine is reassuring.

She makes a pot of coffee and sits staring out at the colourless landscape waiting for the sunrise to light everything up.

She sips her coffee and thinks about her conflicting thoughts. Stay. Go home. She refuses to reconsider the other one.

She imagines returning home to reclaim her family. Because she really could do that, couldn't she? She could pack her bags right now, drive to the airport and buy an overpriced ticket to fly today. She imagines Harry finding her on the sofa. She imagines the look of surprise on his face. That would be a thing to see!

But what if she arrives to find a mystery woman has replaced her?

A mystery woman. There! That horrific thought is out in the open.

It's not the first time she has imagined Harry might be having an affair, but it *is* the first time she has really let her mind go there since she got to France – since she left Harry alone, for months on end, to get up to whatever the hell he wants.

So might she really get home to find another woman in their

bed? And if she did, would Wendy even have the gumption to tell her to leave?

Perhaps moving out is where she went wrong. Because though her reasons were good ones – because she really was protecting her family by doing so – she can't help but feel that it was that specific gesture that, ironically, made them think she didn't care.

If a new woman really is there, then Wendy's moving out would definitely be the act that created a vacancy.

She regrets inviting Jill. Because of course, with Jill coming, she can't go home, can she? No, she thinks. That's rubbish. Jill wouldn't mind at all. She'd probably be overjoyed for her.

Is going home really what I want?

She pictures the scene again. She'd let herself in while everyone was out and have dinner ready when they all got home. 'Enough is enough,' she'd tell Harry. 'This has all gone on for too long. I'm back.'

The idea feels exciting. She has butterflies in her chest just thinking about it. And it's got to be more constructive than sitting here, on her own, on a freezing mountain in France, hasn't it? Because what did she ever expect to achieve by being here?

The backlit peak she's been staring at starts to blaze as the sun moves above it. A ray of sunlight hits her left cheek.

She moves her head lower so that she can feel the rays warming her eyelids, then sits back and watches as the strip of sunlight begins to stretch downwards with surprising speed, along her arm and leg, and then onward across the floor until the whole apartment is bathed in orange light.

She pulls her new slippers on and steps outside to sniff the pine-scented air.

The frost on the grass is already melting and steam is rising from the ground creating horizontal strips of brilliance where the sunlight cuts through the trees.

My God, it's so beautiful. It's like a little treasure, purpose designed to send her a message, a message she really needs this morning: that being alive to see this is a gift.

Of course she's not going home! This is why she's here – to reconnect with life.

She blows through pursed lips at her own madness.

You're all over the place today, she tells herself. *But that's OK, too.*

* * *

She eats muesli and throws the leftover bread out for the birds.

She locks the cabin and starts the car. She has decided to return to the supermarket for a longer-life form of bread.

But as she passes by the bakery she sees that it's open, so she swings around the roundabout and returns, pulling up in the little car park.

The shop, overnight, has been transformed. Where yesterday it looked almost derelict, today it's sparkling. The windows have been cleaned and are bordered with coloured flashing lights. The wooden interior glows orange, like a lump of luminous amber.

As she pushes the door, an old-fashioned bell announces her arrival. A woman appears from another room, backing into view, her arms laden with baguettes. The smell of freshly baked bread is intoxicating.

'Bonjour !' the woman says brightly, speaking over one shoulder as she loads the bread into a rack.

'Bonjour,' Wendy replies, taking a deep breath and promising herself she'll do better than she did with the post lady.

'Deux secondes !' the woman says, as she continues to organise the bread.

Wendy scans her surroundings. There are four or five kinds

of fresh bread, pizzas and quiches, and shelves stacked with honey and jam. There's even a tiny vegetable section in the far corner.

'*Voilà !*' the woman says, turning to face her. '*Je suis à vous.*'

Wendy's not quite sure what that means, but the hands on the hips and the inquisitive smile are easy enough to interpret.

'*Une baguette, s'il vous plait ?*' Wendy says, trying to sound like the woman in her French language app, trying not to think about how bad her accent must sound.

'*Tradition, aux céréales, ou normale ?*' the woman asks.

Wendy grimaces. Whatever she's been asked definitely didn't feature in the bakery lesson. In the app, the woman asks for, '*Une baguette, s'il vous plait ?*' and the baker replies with the price.

The baker smiles at her and repeats her question more slowly, this time pointing to each kind of baguette. '*Tradition ... céréales ... ou normale ?*'

'Oh,' Wendy says. '*Um, normale, s'il vous plait ? Non, tradition !*'

'*Et avec ça ?*' the woman asks, placing the bread on the counter. 'Anything else?'

'Oh, um, *une croissant et une pain au chocolat.*'

'*Un,*' the woman corrects her. '*Un croissant et un pain au chocolat.*'

'*Oui,*' Wendy says, missing the point. '*C'est ça. S'il vous plait ?*'

As she steps back outside, she's feeling pleased with herself. It's only the smallest of victories, but it's a victory all the same.

As she climbs back into her car, the postal van pulls up beside her and the post lady jumps out with a handful of letters. '*Bonjour !*' she says brightly. 'How you are today?'

'*Très bon !*' Wendy replies, emboldened by her success in the bakery.

'*Très bien,*' the young woman corrects. Then, faced with Wendy's silence, '*Moi, ça va aussi.*'

Wendy frowns as she tries to decode individual words.

'It means, I'm OK too,' the girl says, as Wendy manages to work it out.

'*C'est bon,*' Wendy says. '*Um, non... c'est bien ?*'

The girl laughs. 'We need to make work on your French,' she says.

'Yes,' Wendy says. '*Oui.* I agree.'

'Have a good day. I must...' And then she waves the letters at Wendy and skips off in the direction of the bakery.

Back home – so, she's starting to think of the cabin as home! – she eats the bread with the remainder of yesterday's soup. The baguettes from the supermarket weren't bad, especially when compared with the baguette-shaped pappy mush they sell back home. But this bread is on a whole different level. There's a complex yeasty sourness to it that is so delicious she has to force herself to stop otherwise she could easily munch her way through the lot.

Lunch over and the dishes washed, for want of a more worthwhile project, she returns to the car park at the foot of the hiking trail from where she starts to make her way back up to the sphere.

Her legs are stiff and achy from the last time but it is this stiffness – and the lack of fitness the stiffness implies – that motivates her. Perhaps she'll do this walk every day. Imagine how fit she'd be then!

As she reaches the final rise to the radar, she crosses paths with a couple coming down. They say, '*Bonjour,*' but without making eye contact, and she can tell that they've been arguing. There's something in the atmosphere around them – she can almost see the purple haze. Their little terrier, Samson, would rather walk with her, too, and who could blame him for that? He has to be sharply and repeatedly called to heel before, looking sad, he waddles off down the track.

The view from the top is obviously the same as yesterday, but in a way it's completely remade by this different day. The atmosphere is more transparent than yesterday, making the blues of the sky and sea that much deeper.

She starts to take another photo, but then imagines how cool it would be if she could take identical photos from the exact same spot every day. She could get them all printed up on a big poster, the panoramic strips shifting tint from top to bottom as the seasons progress. So she checks the previous image and then chooses a landmark so she can stand on a specific rock every time.

It's a pointless project in a way, and she can imagine how Jill or the kids would cynically roll their eyes if she told them. Only Harry would get it. In fact, Harry would be positively enthusiastic about her venture. He'd probably buy her an expensive camera and a tripod, just so she could do it properly.

Oh, Harry... We used to see eye-to-eye on so many things.

Anyway, enough of them, because it pleases her, this little project, and she's not going to be put off by the fact that the right people wouldn't like it, nor that the wrong person (Harry) would approve. She's going to do it every day.

By the time she gets back to the car she's cold – in fact, she's positively chilled to the bone. She needs a different kind of coat, something breathable but warm – something midway between the draughty duffle coat she has chosen today and her boil-in-the-bag puffer jacket. Perhaps she'll buy one when she's out with Jill.

As she drives, she thinks about the reality of Jill's impending visit, and she's at a loss as to how it will go.

She can imagine Jill hating the remote cabin and

complaining twenty-four/seven as easily as she can picture her falling in love with it and refusing to leave.

As she locks the car door, her phone buzzes in her pocket and once she's indoors in the warm, she pulls off the duffle coat and perches on the back of the sofa to read it.

Harry: Can you give me a call this evening? I want to hear how it's going. If I'm honest, I'm a bit worried about you. Haz xx

Two kisses, she thinks. *That's a turn-up for the books.*

Perhaps this is going to turn out to be a good strategy after all. Perhaps it's not absence but distance that makes a heart grow fonder.

'A good strategy,' she murmurs, echoing the thought out loud. Is that what she's doing here? Is she strategising to get him back?

She shakes her head and sighs as she rises to make tea. Because once she knows the answer to that one, she'll know the answer to everything.

SIX

HARRY (PART 3)

I moved home on 20 January. I used Jill's need to accept bookings as my excuse, even though (information I chose not to share) she'd offered to delist the place so that I could stay on.

A part of that decision was my sense of injustice at having been asked to leave, and part of it was a desire to put things right. But on top of this, Bern had told me a cautionary tale about a friend of his who'd moved out of the family home and lost everything in the divorce that followed. Possession, Bern said, was nine-tenths of the law. Though I didn't know if this was true, it worried me enough to make me act.

Back home the atmosphere was ghastly. Fiona had reverted to full-on adolescent sulking, and Harry seemed to have decided that the best way to deal with me was to avoid me. He'd come home late from work, by which time I was dozing, and leave extra early in the morning before I was in any state to talk. On weekends, if I had a day off, he'd vanish without explanation.

Harry started sleeping in Todd's room, too – now free because Todd was at university. He made this change the first time I complained about his snoring, and we never discussed it again.

My job remained hellish and my shifts changed so often that – if I'm being honest – it wasn't that difficult to avoid thinking about it all.

But occasionally there were moments when I found myself with enough mental space to reflect on our marital car crash and it was hard not to conclude we needed to talk.

On three separate occasions – because Fiona was sleeping elsewhere and I was off – I decided that I would sit Harry down and force a conversation but he came home way past midnight every time. It was as if being in the house with me alone terrified him.

In early February, my best nurse-mate Cathy announced she was resigning and going to work in a shop. I was flabbergasted. We'd worked together for over nine years.

'It's the job,' she told me, over lunch. 'It's wrecking my mental health. I've been feeling on the edge of actual madness ever since Covid started. And it's either the job or my family. It's simply not possible to do both.'

'God!' I told her. 'I'm stunned. I don't even know what to say.'

'Why the surprise?' she asked. 'You know what it's like as well as I do. It's like being in an abusive relationship every single day. It *is* being in an abusive relationship, with the doctors and the managers and the idiots running the country. By the time I get home, I'm a bloody nightmare for Joe to deal with. Christ knows how you manage to stay so calm. I hope Harry realises what a gem he's got.'

I thought about her claim that working for the NHS was like being in an abusive relationship all the time after that. And the more I thought about it the truer it felt.

We hadn't received a proper pay rise in decades and due to lack of staff our shift patterns chopped and changed constantly. Half the time I'd wake up and not even know where I was, let alone if I was supposed to be at work.

So yes, I began to notice that everything Cathy had said was true for me, too. You could have a family or work as a nurse, but you almost certainly couldn't do both.

* * *

'Harry,' I said one morning. 'We need to talk.'

'I'm sorry,' he said, 'I'm in a rush. Can it wait?'

'Not really,' I replied. 'I've been trying to talk to you for weeks.'

'Oh,' he said. 'Um, OK. Hang on.' He continued to riffle through a pile of paperwork searching for whatever it was he was looking for.

'Haz!' I said sharply. 'I've resigned!'

'Oh yeah?' he murmured, continuing his search for a split second until my declaration reached his brain. Only once the words registered did he pause and straighten, his expression slipping to a frown. 'What?'

'I quit my job,' I said. 'I couldn't take the pressure anymore.'

I'd pictured this moment a few times and tried to guess his reaction. My best bet was that he'd be glad. After all he'd complained repeatedly that I was bringing too much stress home from work. Perhaps leaving the job would fix us, I thought. Perhaps that was all we needed.

Harry glanced at his phone and then, visibly deciding that it wasn't so important after all, slipped it back into his jacket pocket. 'Christ,' he said, after a moment. 'Everyone's resigning right now. It's almost a national trend.'

'What do you mean, everyone's resigning?' I asked, feeling peeved that he'd turned my groundbreaking announcement into a mere symptom of a national trend.

'Oh, sorry. Um, yeah, two work colleagues, last week. And the secretary the week before.' Then, 'What are you going to do?'

'For money, you mean? Or with my time?'

'Either,' Harry said. 'Both.'

'Um, take a break, mainly,' I told him.

'And for money? Because you know how tight things are. What with the mortgage rate and the bills going up and everything. They've upped the gas bill to two hundred a month, by the way.'

'I still have that money,' I said. 'I'll just have to use some of that.'

'Your inheritance?'

I nodded.

'But...'

'Yes?'

'No, nothing,' Harry said, swallowing and licking his lips.

'No, really. Go on.'

'Well, it's just... I mean, it's obviously your money for you to do whatever you want.'

'Obviously.'

'But you always said you wanted to do something – you know – *special* with it.'

This was true. Though I'd used almost half of it to bail us out of various tight spots in the years since my mother had died, I'd wanted to keep some back to use on something memorable. It seemed a bit disrespectful to fritter it away on bills.

'Well, yes,' I told Harry. 'And maybe this is it. Maybe this is the special thing I've decided to do with it.'

I was chewing over the idea of adding, 'Is using it to save our marriage really such a waste?' but because I wasn't sure if that was even my intention, I hesitated.

Harry spoke before I could decide anyway. 'So you're going to use it to just... I mean... I don't mean to be, you know, critical or what-have-you. But I don't really get it. You're leaving your job without *any* idea what you want to do?'

'Yes. That is kind of the idea of a break.'

'OK, but you're gonna do what? Just sit around at home doing nothing? Because I'm not sure how healthy that's going to be.'

In an instant I went from wanting to save my marriage to wanting to stab him with one of our excellent Japanese knives. I opened my mouth but nothing came out, and after a few seconds with his eyebrows raised in expectation, Harry gave up waiting and glanced at the kitchen clock.

I could sense my anger was about to burst forth, and because an argument wasn't at all what I'd intended, I managed to say, through gritted teeth, 'Go to work. We can talk about this tonight.'

He didn't need telling twice.

* * *

By the time Harry got home that evening – early, for once, so that we could talk – I'd at least worked out how to sound coherent about it.

'I'm going to rent somewhere and go away,' I told him. 'I'm going to take a six-month sabbatical to de-stress. I've been working like a dog for decades, and it's the only thing I can think of that I can do to stop myself going completely mad. And it's not a waste of money at all. I'm saving my mental health.'

'Right,' Harry said. 'Yeah, sorry. I didn't mean to sound so... this morning... I was surprised. And in a rush.'

'I thought it might be something you'd want to do, too, and that we could talk about doing it together. But if not, I'll do it on my own.'

'Right,' Harry said. 'OK. Gosh.'

'Do you think it might do us good?' I asked. 'Do you think we maybe need to see some new horizons? Together?'

'Yeah,' Harry said, looking shifty. 'Maybe.'

'Maybe,' I repeated.

'Look it's just...' he said. 'To be honest, I think maybe what we need is more of a break.'

'Well, that is what—'

'From each other,' he added.

'Oh... But that's all we've had, these last few years. Lots and lots of breaks from each other.'

'Yeah,' Harry said. 'I know.'

That was the first time the thought crossed my mind. Almost instantly I found myself wondering how I could possibly have missed it. The late nights, the weekend disappearing acts. His lack of enthusiasm for anything to do with me. His shifty avoidance of eye contact, like right now.

'You've met someone else,' I said. 'D'you want a divorce? Is that it?'

'No, no, I haven't,' Harry said, still avoiding eye contact. 'And I don't know. About the... you know... divorce. Do you?'

'I don't know anymore either,' I told him, and though I'd never named the idea in my head before, as I said it, it became true. I honestly didn't know.

'So maybe a proper break...' Harry said. 'That's what I'm thinking. If you went off and did your thing for six months, then maybe by the end, we'd know where we're at.'

'Fine!' I said. 'I'll do it alone.'

'Do you re...' Harry started, but then his voice petered out.

'Yes?'

'Actually, never mind. I've forgotten what I was going to say.'

I didn't believe him about that. I was sure that he knew exactly what he'd been about to say but had changed his mind. But I was annoyed enough not to want to know.

'Have you decided where you'll go?' he asked instead.

'Norway,' I told him convincingly, the destination plucked out of nowhere – plucked from a silly meme I'd seen on the internet. But Norway seemed as good as anywhere. The important thing was to sound certain.

'Norway?' Harry said. 'Wow!'

'Yes, I'm going to rent a cabin on a lake and spend six months clearing my head of all this nonsense.'

'Wow,' Harry said again. 'Norway! I wasn't expecting that.' And for the first time in many years, he looked as if he admired me.

In the end, I didn't choose Norway at all. But by then I don't think Harry was that interested in my destination. By then he just wanted me gone.

SEVEN

JILL

Somehow, she's aware of Jill's presence before she sees her. The airport is surprisingly busy for November, and she has been momentarily distracted from the stream of people spewing from the arrivals gate by a particularly attractive man in bottom-hugging combat trousers.

She watches him petting his bulldog for a moment and wonders who he's waiting for. You see so many lives in airports, she thinks. So many different ways to live.

She briefly imagines a pretty woman arriving who will kiss this sexy man – an image that morphs rapidly into kissing his unusually plump lips herself. Harry's lips are thin and rather British and his kisses always leave her feeling a bit cheated, but this guy... well, he must be an Olympic-level kisser. Just as she thinks this, the man raises the dog so that it can lick his face – so that it can kiss him. Yuck!

She remembers Harry letting Whitey lick his face when they'd first brought him home for Fiona. She'd told him there and then that he needed to choose – told him he could kiss the dog or he could kiss her, but that he couldn't do both, and they'd laughed about that as though it was a joke, even though they'd both understood that she was being entirely serious.

He'd done his best to avoid doing it in front of her after that, but she'd caught him in the act once or twice. 'You know he licks his arse with that tongue,' she reminded him every time.

'Yes, but their tongues are antiseptic,' Harry always retorted. From such repetitious dialogues are marriages made.

It's at that moment, as she's watching the no-longer-sexy dog-kisser, that she becomes aware of Jill's presence, moving towards her from the right. She's almost completely beyond Wendy's field of vision but there's something familiar about her aura – or perhaps it's the clip-cloppy, wobbly kneed way Jill walks. What-ever it is, without having seen her, Wendy turns, and there she is, her friend, grinning, dragging a little green suitcase behind her.

'Darling!' Jill trills, for some reason putting on a silly posh voice. 'How absolutely spiffing to see you!'

'Hello, you!' Wendy says, opening her arms to accept Jill's theatrical embrace.

'How jet-set is all of this, eh?' Jill asks, gesturing at their surroundings. 'Quite the change after Luton, I can tell you. English airports are always so scummy, aren't they? All chipped Formica and worn lino. Why is that, do you think?'

'This way,' Wendy says, guiding Jill by one elbow towards the exit. 'Unless you're hungry or thirsty or need to pee?'

'No, I had an easy-sandwich and a gin and tonic from the easy-bar so I'm fine,' she says. 'Absolutely disgusting. The sand-wich, that is. Not the G&T, obviously.'

'Obviously,' Wendy repeats – a little repetitive joke of theirs. Old friendships are much like marriages in that way.

They cross the arrivals hall and step outside, walking over tramlines towards the various car parks.

'Drizzle!' Jill remarks. 'Did you order that for me? To make me feel at home?'

'Of course. I know how you like it.'

'You shouldn't have. Really.'

'The forecast is terrible, actually,' Wendy tells her. 'Sorry about that.'

'You should have gone further south,' Jill says. 'Alicante or Tenerife or Rwanda or something.'

'I nearly went to bloody Norway,' Wendy says. 'So consider yourself lucky.'

Once they have found the Renault, negotiated the ticket barriers and a couple of manic roundabouts, Wendy asks how the flight was.

'Fine. On time!' Jill says. 'It was even a bit early, which is a miracle these days.'

'That is a miracle.'

'But the sandwich – lord, it was epically awful. Why do they do that? I mean, it's a sandwich... It's hardly complicated. Two bits of bread and some cheese. But no. Plastic simulated cheese between two slices of rubbery bread. It was virtually inedible. My teeth kept bouncing off.'

'Yuck,' Wendy says vaguely, distracted by the heavy traffic.

'Ooh, ooh!' Jill says, visibly remembering something exciting. She pulls a bottle of Bombay Sapphire from her handbag. 'A little something from the easy-kiosk.'

'You!' Wendy laughs. 'And guess what? I bought a bottle, too. Though mine's the other one. You know, the one everyone used to buy before they started bombarding us with a thousand different brands of gin. They all taste the same to me anyway.'

'Oh, Gordon's, then?'

'Got it.'

'That's true, actually,' Jill says, unscrewing the top of the gin bottle. 'Gordon's was all we had in the olden days, but we somehow survived, didn't we?'

'Stop that!' Wendy tells her, glancing over concernedly. 'You'll get me pulled over!'

'I'm only sniffing it, dear,' Jill says, proceeding to do just that, 'Umm!' she says. 'Better than Chanel No 5.' She then tips the bottle and takes a swig all the same. 'God, I love gin,' she says as she screws the lid back on. 'Did I ever tell you that?'

'Not as such, but I somehow knew,' Wendy laughs, fumbling for the windscreen wipers.

'*Somehow*. You're quite the psychic, really, aren't you?'

'Now, shush a minute,' Wendy tells her. 'There are wa-a-ay too many roundabouts along here.'

'I wonder why they drive on the wrong side,' Jill says. 'I mean, I wonder who made that decision and when. "I don't like this side anymore. I think I'd prefer it over there." Must have been mayhem.'

'I believe...' Wendy says hesitantly as she indicates, changes lanes and then exits the roundabout, then checks her mirror and GPS, 'that... um... that we're the ones who swapped sides. On our horses, way back when. So we could stab people going the other way more efficiently with our swords. Without, you know, all that impractical having to reach across.'

'Nice,' Jill says. 'A friendly nation, the English. Welcoming.'

'We are!'

* * *

Once they leave the autoroute and start to drive through the various villages along the way, Jill begins to ooh and aah. She also reads almost every sign they pass in an exaggerated French accent. '*Travaux !*' she says. '*Rappel ! Boulangerie !*'

As they snake through the centre of Roquefort-les-Pins she comments, 'And there *are* bars here, you liar! I've seen three just along this stretch. *And* there are men in them.'

'But we're nowhere near home. Not by a long stretch. You'll see.'

Once they've passed through Châteauneuf-de-Grasse the

road starts to rise into the mountains, twisting and turning. Below them, fluffy low clouds swirl in the ravines. Jill clings onto the panic handle until her knuckles start to turn white.

'You OK?' Wendy asks, glancing briefly across. She's used to these roads now, and she's only just remembering that Jill isn't.

'Sure. I just get a little carsick on roads like this. Vertigo, too. But carry on, I'll be fine. I just need to remember to look at the road. Must not take my eyes off the road!'

Wendy slows down a little, and they drive in silence for a few minutes with only the noise of the engine and the rhythmic swish-swashing of the windscreen wipers.

'Do you want some mus—' Wendy starts, but Jill has started speaking at the same time.

'So how have you been?' she asks.

'Oh,' Wendy says. 'Um, fine, I suppose.'

'You've been pretty quiet lately,' Jill says. 'You OK?'

Wendy struggles momentarily to formulate an answer. Since she invited Jill two weeks ago – or rather since Jill invited *herself* – it's true, they have barely spoken. This is partly because Wendy has had little to say that she considered newsworthy, but it's also because she's been saving the nuggets of chatter she does have for Jill's arrival. She's been feeling uncharacteristically nervous about having nothing to talk about. Her life these past weeks has been so peaceful, so repetitive – so *empty*, some would say. After all, there are only so many times you can tell someone you ate breakfast, walked up a hill and drank a few glasses of wine.

Wendy swallows and licks her lips. 'You know, I have no idea. I'm sorry but that's the truth. I'm kind of all over the place, so it's hard to say. I actually might be going a bit bonkers.'

'Oh?' Jill says, briefly dragging her eyes from the road to glance concernedly at her friend. She knows she'd go loopy in a day if she had to live alone on a mountain top.

'I can be... like... ecstatically happy, you know, totally in love with life, and all this clean air and the trees and what-have-you. It's very beautiful up there. You'll see, well... if it stops raining, you will. And then a minute later – not even a minute, actually, more like ten seconds later – I feel utterly, utterly depressed, as though everything's so hopeless – the world, the climate, my life, my marriage – that I might as well kill myself and get it over with.'

'Right,' Jill says. 'Wow.'

'Yes, wow indeed.'

'But you wouldn't actually...'

'No! Of course not!' Wendy says, even as she wonders if that's true.

'But then— Ooh, careful!'

'Seen it,' Wendy tells her as she swerves around the rock on the road. 'Don't worry. You get quite a few of those. It's like a video game dodging them all.'

'But you are happier than back home?'

Wendy shakes her head and sighs. 'I'm still not sure about that either. It's different, I suppose? More intense, if that makes any sense. The ups are more up and the downs are more down. I kind of feel like I had everything buttoned up before. I smoothed things out all the time, well... because I had to. But now it's just me... it's as if I've got licence to be more... I don't know...'

'Emotional?'

'Maybe,' Wendy laughs. 'I was thinking more along the lines of *hysterical*, actually. Anyway, I'm glad you're here. I'm glad you came. I could do with someone to talk to, I think.'

'Yes,' Jill says. 'It sounds like it.'

* * *

They get drunk. Well, of course they do.

While Wendy makes her famed mushroom carbonara, Jill pours bowls of snacks and mixes gin and tonics.

By the time the spaghetti is on the boil, they're halfway through their second glass, because when the first drink tastes that good, how could anyone ever resist another?

'You won't get it to work,' Wendy tells Jill, who is trying to connect her phone to the Bluetooth speaker. 'I tried for almost an hour the other day. It just beeps like that and nothing happens.'

'Yeah, I think you might be right,' Jill concedes. 'I think it's officially buggered.' But no sooner has she said this than 'Fast-love' starts booming from the little speaker.

'Excellent,' Jill says, clapping her hands and starting to swing her hips. 'Wow, it's louder than I thought for such a little thing. You see, that's why you've been feeling depressed. Not enough George Michael, hon.'

'I'm not feeling depressed,' Wendy calls back, having to speak loudly because of the music. But as she says it she wonders if her friend might not be right. Because two gin and tonics and George Michael sure feels like a recipe for happiness right now. In fact, the only thing missing is... 'Cigarette break?' she asks. 'We've got time, while the spaghetti cooks.'

'Perfect,' Jill says, already grooving towards the front door.

They step outside and close the door on George Michael. The night is cold and damp after the rain and, other than a window which vibrates occasionally in time with the bass line of the music, utterly silent.

'Christ, it's freezing,' Jill says.

'I know, it's a shocker, isn't it?' Wendy agrees as she lights up two cigarettes and hands one to Jill. 'We've had frost a few times – like a proper hard, everything-white frost. I wasn't expecting that at all in the south of France, but it does make everything pretty.'

'Yes, I'm sure,' Jill says.

'So what do you think?' Wendy asks. Jill, most uncharacter-istically, hasn't passed comment since they arrived.

Jill studies the view and then turns to Wendy wide-eyed. 'I...' she says. She takes a drag on her cigarette and pulls a face. 'I think I might be speechless.'

'That bad, huh?'

Jill shrugs and grins. 'I'd go batshit crazy up here, hon. I mean, it's lovely. I can see that the nature and everything is... appealing and what-have-you. But I'm at a loss, really, as to why you're here. I think it's all a bit nuts, to be honest.'

'I know,' Wendy agrees. 'Sometimes I don't get it either. And I'm the one who chose the place.'

'Aren't you... I don't know... scared?' Jill asks, looking around. 'I think I would be.'

'Scared?'

'Yes. Out here in the middle of nowhere. I'd be terrified up here on my own!'

'Of what, though? Lions, tigers? There aren't that many of those in France. Though I suppose there may be the odd wolf.'

'I was thinking more in terms of slipping and breaking a hip and not being able to get to a hospital, actually. Or French rapists, tapping on your windows in the night.'

Wendy laughs. 'You know I haven't seen a single man since I arrived. The post is delivered by a woman. The baker is a woman. Even the owner of this place is a woman. Actually, that reminds me. A guy was supposed to come and pick the letters up – the owner's friend – but he never came. I was quite looking forward to it, actually. I was hoping he might be sexy. The rapist aspect didn't cross my mind.'

'Too cold,' Jill says, an audible quiver to her voice. She stubs her cigarette out on a rock. 'I'm going back indoors.'

'Me, too. It's freezing.'

Back indoors, George has moved on to 'Freedom! '90'.

Jill moves to stand in front of the stove and, when she knows the words, sings along, while Wendy returns to the kitchen area. It's then Wendy notices that the letters she'd left on the counter are gone. 'God, he's been in,' she says. 'Someone's been in here without me knowing.'

'What do you mean, someone's been in?!' Jill asks.

'The post,' Wendy explains. 'There were three letters here for the owner. The friend must have been in while I was out one day. I'm not sure how I feel about that.'

'Perhaps he came while you were sleeping.'

'Well, if he did, I can't say I noticed,' Wendy laughs. 'But I am a very heavy sleeper.'

When she wakes up the next morning, everything seems off-kilter.

She has a headache and a foot is digging into her thigh – those are the first things she notices. She has to raise herself onto one elbow and look to confirm that the foot belongs to Jill. Jill is in her bed. She can't remember how that happened.

She lies back down and stares at the ceiling, listening to Jill's breathing which is on the quiet side of a snore.

Something else is strange, too, and it takes her a moment to work out what.

The light in the cabin is peculiar, she realises. It's both brighter than usual but also whiter – like when an incandescent bulb gets swapped out for an LED one. It must be a bright, grey day out there, she decides.

The cabin is deathly quiet, too. Of course, it's always fairly quiet, but this morning the wood burner isn't clicking or crackling, which would explain why the place is so cold. The refrigerator is unusually silent, too. This is the first time it has shut up since she moved in.

She sits up and glances again over at Jill, who murmurs but

does not wake. She swings her feet to the floor and, still struggling to focus properly, stands.

Halfway down the staircase she understands that it has snowed overnight – hence the strange piercing light filling the room.

She crosses to the window. Outside, a thin layer of whiteness has covered everything. It's pretty like a postcard but the brightness of the landscape hurts her eyes. 'Wow!' she murmurs, out loud.

'Snow?'

She turns to see Jill, up on the mezzanine, peering out from the foot of the bed. 'Crazy, huh?' she replies. She crosses to the kitchen, located beneath the mezzanine, and fills and plugs in the kettle but when she switches it on, nothing happens. She tries a light switch but that's the same. 'There's no electricity,' she calls out.

'I know! Don't you remember?' her friend replies through a yawn. 'That's why I came in with you. I was freezing.'

Wendy frowns and looks around the room, trying to understand how the one might lead to the other. 'Oh, the blow heater, you mean?' she says, when her eyes settle on it. 'Did we use that?'

'I plugged it in because I was cold,' Jill calls out. 'But then it stopped in the middle of the night. That's why I climbed in with you. To avoid freezing to death.'

Wendy rolls her eyes and does not say, *All you needed to do was throw a bloody log on the fire.*

She crouches down and relights the fire, pulling kindling from the package she bought at the supermarket. 'It must have blown a fuse or something,' she mutters, thinking back to the owner's comment about heating using too much electricity for the house. Perhaps this is exactly what she meant.

She hunts amongst the detritus of last night's meal for her

phone and finds it plugged in to a no-longer functioning wall socket. Thankfully It's fully charged

She sends a message to the owner. *No electricity this morning. Where is fuse box please? Urgent.* And then for want of a better option, she returns upstairs to bed while she waits for the place to warm up. She elbows Jill to move over, perhaps a little more vigorously than she needs to. But she isn't particularly keen on sharing her bed, no matter how cold it is downstairs. Plus she's fairly sure that Jill's decision to plug in the heater instead of throwing a log on the fire is the reason she can't now have a cup of tea. And boy, does she need a cup of tea.

But Jill doesn't seem to notice her subtle violence. She merely snuffles and rolls away.

* * *

The owner replies an hour later that 'a man is coming quickly'.

'Let's hope he doesn't come too quickly,' Jill jokes. 'I hate it when they do that.'

By the time he arrives they have cleared up the mess, washed up (miraculously, there's still hot water) and eaten an omelette, cooked (read: burned) on the stove top.

The man, Enzo, who's too young to really to be called a 'man', has acne, a shaved head, and an unkempt straggly beard.

He fiddles in the electrical cupboard at the rear of the cabin for a while, plugging his laptop into a panel adorned with flashing lights, before returning to give them the good news. 'It's all OK,' he says, in perfect, accent-free English. If anything he sounds American.

Wendy tries one of the light switches and when nothing happens she pulls a face. 'Or maybe *not* OK,' she deadpans.

The young man laughs. 'It will be OK,' he says. 'Soon.'

'OK...' Wendy says, doubtfully. 'When?'

'When the battery fills up.'

'The battery?'

'Yes, you must wait for the battery to fill. It's empty. You have emptied it. Completely.'

Wendy glances at Jill in case she has understood something Wendy herself is missing, but Jill is simultaneously pouting, shrugging and shaking her head.

Enzo glances between them, then breaks into a broad grin. 'You know it's solar, here, right?'

'Solar...' Wendy repeats. 'Oh, like solar panels, you mean?'

'Yes. *Exactly* like solar panels,' he says in a mocking tone. 'It's off grid here. There's no... you know...? I don't know the word.'

'No mains?' Jill offers. 'No grid, I suppose you could say.'

'Yes. Exactly! No grid. Off grid,' Enzo says. 'Just panels on the...' He points to the ceiling. 'And batteries. I think maybe you used a lot of electricity last night?' He looks around the room as if searching for proof of the crime, but the blow heater has been hidden in a cupboard.

'No,' Jill says, reflexively, habitually denying everything. 'We didn't do anything except cook dinner, did we, Wendy?'

The man raises one eyebrow disbelievingly, then flips open his laptop and frowns at the screen. 'Thirteen point three kilowatts in one night. From twenty hours yesterday to four this morning. That's a lot.'

Wendy rolls her head and sighs. 'Yes, it's true,' she says. 'We didn't know. I'm sorry.'

'But how?' Enzo asks, scanning the room again. 'How do you use thirteen point three kilowatts in one night?'

'Um, an electric heater, that's all,' Wendy tells him, wincing. 'We didn't know, so I bought one. From Intermarché. We won't use it ag—'

'An electric heater!' Enzo interrupts her, as if this is the worst off-grid crime he's ever come across. 'You can't do this. Never!'

'Yes, I get that now,' Wendy says. She's beginning to feel like a child being scolded by the headmaster and is beginning to resent being made to feel that way.

'No, never! Never!' Enzo says, wiggling his finger at her to emphasise the point.

'OK, OK! I got it!' Wendy says, raising her voice despite herself.

'And no...' he makes a weird gesture near his ear, 'for the 'air.'

'For the air?' Wendy repeats.

'Yes. No drying the 'air.'

'Oh, oh. I know,' Jill says, sounding like she's found the answer to a game-show question. 'Hairdryer!'

'Yes. No 'airdryer. Not today. Not tomorrow. Maybe after, if it's sunny, maybe five minutes, it can be OK. But you must let the battery fill before this, otherwise it will happen again. The sun will maybe come this afternoon, so this is good.'

'And if it doesn't come back on?'

'It will, when the battery hits 17 per cent.'

'But what do I do if it doesn't?'

He pats the top of his laptop. 'It will. In one hour. Maybe two. I check. It's already 11 per cent. At seventeen it's all OK. I promise.'

Once he has left, Wendy slumps onto the sofa. 'Wow,' she says. 'Solar panels. Who knew?'

'And they didn't warn you about this? I'd be asking for a refund.'

'No, they didn't, really,' Wendy says. She grimaces and sucks through her teeth. 'If I'm being honest the place is listed as an off-grid eco-cabin. I mean, that's the actual title. So they weren't exactly hiding the fact. I just didn't think enough about what that meant. So it's partly my fault, I think. A tiny bit my fault, at any rate.'

Jill fiddles with one of the light switches and twists her

mouth sideways. 'Maybe a good time to go out?' she offers after some thought. 'While we wait for the stupid battery to charge?'

'Yeah, that's kind of what I was thinking.'

'So a drink in a nice bar somewhere, to cheer ourselves up, and then a posh dinner somewhere with a sea view.'

'A meal out sounds good but I'm a tad concerned about the electricity,' Wendy says. 'I mean, suppose we get back – it'll be night-time by then – so what if it still doesn't work?'

'We can leave the fire going, can't we? So the place won't be freezing cold. And if we've eaten then it won't matter that we can't cook. And if we've had enough to drink then we won't care much about any of it.'

'This is very true,' Wendy concedes. 'But if I can find one, I might buy myself a torch.'

'Considering the circumstances,' Jill says, 'that sounds like an excellent investment.'

* * *

By the time they leave, the snow, thankfully, has vanished. Wendy heads south, in the general direction of the coast, without having really decided where they're going.

The first village they pass is the pretty hilltop village of Gourdon, which she's been intending to explore, so they perform a brief comedy lap around the car park before rejoining the main road and heading on down the mountain. It's all too grey and cold up here today to be any fun at all.

For the simple reason that nearly all the road signs seem to point that way, they end up back in Nice, and miraculously, when they step out of the underground car park, the sun has reappeared.

'That's got to be a good omen if ever there was one,' Jill declares.

Drawn by the lure of the horizon, they walk the length of a long, narrow park to the seafront.

'Is it chemicals, do you think?' Jill asks, when they finally reach the railings overlooking the pebble beach.

'Is what – oh, you mean the colour?' The sea, it has to be said, is an uncannily bright shade of blue.

'Yeah. That can't be natural, can it? It looks almost nuclear.'

'I read somewhere that it's silt,' Wendy explains. 'The rivers wash it down from the Alps, I think – it's a kind of chalk or something. And it's all the little particles reflecting the sky that make the sea look that crazy colour.

They walk along the sun-soaked Promenade des Anglais until they come to the point where, below Castle Hill, it swings around the headland into shadow, towards the port.

They turn back towards the town centre and after a few hundred yards Jill asks, 'What about one of these?' She's gesturing at a row of seafront bars.

'A drink?' Wendy asks, glancing at her watch. 'Already? It's not even three o'clock, dear.'

'God, you can have coffee if you want,' Jill says. 'I just thought it might be nice to have a sit up there.' She points to a seafront balcony on the first floor of one of the bars. 'The view's got to be fabby from up there plus it's in the sunshine and there's space.'

'You're right,' Wendy says. 'Let's do it.'

The bar is called Wakka, and the downstairs area looks much like the interior of an English pub. The staff seem to speak only English, which Wendy is a little disappointed about. She'd been hoping for a more authentic French experience.

But the view, from the narrow balcony – 180 degrees of blue – is spectacular, and even though the cloud cover is hovering only a few hundred yards behind them, the sunshine is so warm that, once they've been served their drinks – fluorescent orange glasses of Aperol spritz – they have to remove first their coats, and then their jumpers.

'Amazing!' Jill says, sipping her drink and turning her face towards the sun and sea.

'Yes. This was an excellent idea,' Wendy concedes, lighting up a cigarette.

'My ideas always are,' Jill mugs, nodding discreetly at a young man who has sat down at the far end of the balcony, behind Wendy.

'You're incorrigible,' Wendy says once she has managed to steal a glance.

'It's called being alive,' Jill says, with a smirk, still tilting her head so that she can peer past her friend. 'It's *called* having a pulse.'

When one spritz tastes this good, who could possibly resist a second? So by the time they leave Wakka an hour later, they're both feeling vaguely tipsy.

'Did you *see* that guy?' Jill asks, as they step back out onto the street. 'Imagine living somewhere where the men all look like that.'

'The young one, behind me?' Wendy asks, perplexed. 'Are you really still on about him?'

'Yes. The Italian one. He was speaking Italian; I heard him. But more importantly, did you see the chest hair on him?'

'I did not,' Wendy says, pulling a face. She's not keen on chest hair anyway. One of Harry's great advantages is his downy barely visible body hair. It almost makes up for the lack of lips.

'God, you know, I love Bern and everything,' Jill laughs. 'I do. But if a guy like that tried it on... I'd lose myself in that chest and never leave.'

'For God's sake, he was about eighteen!' Wendy laughs, feigning shock. She knows her friend is only joking.

'He was old enough to have chest hair,' Jill says. 'And that's old enough for me. Plus, cougars are very much in fashion, I'll have you know. Fifty is the new thirty.'

They walk through an arch leading inland. 'I can't drive home, you know,' Wendy says. 'Not for hours. Not after those spritz things. I'm feeling quite light-headed.'

'Who said anything about going home?' Jill replies. 'We're eating here, aren't we? We don't even know if we *can* cook once we get home.'

On exiting the archway they find themselves in the vast pedestrian zone that is the Cours Saleya. It's walled by open-air bars and restaurants sprawling across the pavement beneath multi-coloured façades in faded oranges and yellows and reds.

'Wow!' Wendy says. 'This is beautiful.'

'Gorgeous!' Jill agrees.

They walk the length of the pedestrian zone, people-watching, before meandering off into smaller streets.

'I always wanted to live in Brighton,' Jill says. 'On a sunny day it can feel a bit like this. But that's the other problem, of course. The bloody weather. They keep trying to scare us all with their global warming, but the sad truth is most of the people in Britain are just praying it will happen within their lifetimes so they can go to the bloody beach.'

They buy croissants at a little bakery, with the intention of saving them until the morning, but Jill can't resist sampling hers and once she does so and has encouraged Wendy to do the same, all is lost. They are fresh and warm and buttery, and within a hundred yards, they're gone.

'I need to wee,' Jill says eventually, nodding at a bar/tabac on the corner. 'Shall we sit here and have a coffee so I can use the loos?'

'Sure,' Wendy says. 'I need to get more ciggies anyway... the rate you're going through them.'

'I've smoked, like, five since I got here!' Jill protests, feigning outrage, starting to weave her way through the tables.

'Five?' Wendy pulls a face and takes a seat.

'OK, ten, then.'

'Ten?'

'OK, a thousand, then. Whatever. Christ, I'll buy some, OK? I'll buy you a jumbo multipack. Calm down, dear.'

A waistcoated waiter appears behind them. *'Bonjour.'*

'Two Aperol spritzes, please,' Jill says, not even attempting to order in French.

'But...' Wendy protests.

'Shhh, you! Two spritzes, please!'

The waiter spins on one foot and leaves.

'You said coffee!' Wendy protests half-heartedly.

'Oh, do bloody relax a little, won't you, darling?' Jill says. 'You're going to end up bringing me down if you carry on being a killjoy.'

Once the sun dips behind the rooftops, they start to feel chilly and decide to move indoors. Shockingly, despite an EU law that made indoor smoking illegal decades ago, smoking is exactly what everyone is doing. 'God,' Jill says, waving her hand in the smoky atmosphere. 'It's like being back in the bloody eighties.'

No sooner are they seated than a man crosses the room to speak to them.

'Hello, ladies!' he says in a thick, slightly drunk French accent. 'You are English?'

'We are!' Jill says, smiling and fluttering her lashes, causing Wendy to roll her eyes in dismay.

'I love the English,' he says, already pulling up a chair to join them. 'I am Théo.' He holds out his hand so they shake and introduce themselves. 'So you are here on holiday?' he asks.

'We are!' Jill tells him. 'It's beautiful here.'

'I like too,' Théo says. 'It's... how you say... good to look at. *Jolie.'*

'Pretty?' Jill offers.

'Yes. This. More pretty than Lille where I am coming from. But Lille is maybe more easy for the talking.'

'Really?' Jill says, as if that's the most interesting fact she's ever heard. 'I didn't know that.'

'Yes, people in the south are not so easy. You talk to me because the English same. The English are easy like the people of Lille, I think.'

'Oh, we're very easy, aren't we?' Jill giggles.

Wendy smiles despite herself. She'd been in the process of thinking up exit strategies – calculating ways of getting away from Théo. For her, it's an automatic reflex. But now they've been labelled friendly representatives of their country, it's become more difficult to do so politely.

'You are from London?' Théo asks, glancing between them.

'No, but not far. The south-east. Maybe an hour away. A one-hour drive from London.'

'My best friend live in London. I visit him two time. I like. Maybe you know him...'

So they stay, and Jill and Théo natter easily, randomly, about anything and nothing, frequently talking at cross purposes because of the language barrier. And once the third spritz kicks in Wendy finds herself joining the party.

Théo explains that he's an ex-teacher become estate-agent 'because the money is more big' and touchingly reveals that his wife is currently in hospital undergoing chemo.

When he returns to the bar to refill his glass, Wendy suggests they slip away while he's distracted.

'Oh,' Jill says, checking the time on her phone. 'Really? It's still early, babe. The restaurants serve late here, don't they? I think it's like Spain.'

'We can go somewhere else first, if you want,' Wendy says.

'In the meantime, I mean. I just think it might be a good idea to lose you-know-who. He's a bit insistent, don't you think?'

'Oh, don't be like that,' Jill says. 'I think he's cute.'

'You're drunk,' Wendy says. 'He's not cute at all. He looks like a frog in a suit.'

'... bit racist...' Jill mocks.

'Oh I didn't mean... *that...*' Wendy says. 'But you get my point. If his eyes were any further apart he'd be a fish.'

Jill laughs so suddenly, so unexpectedly that her drink goes up her nose. 'That's true, actually,' she whispers, once she's pulled a tissue from her bag. 'I'm struggling to look at both eyes at once. But I'm enjoying having a chat with an actual Frenchie, aren't you? He's sweet. Anyway, he's married. His poor wife, though. I wonder how bad it is. I didn't dare ask.'

'He's drunk,' Wendy says, glancing over at the bar. 'And so are we. And wife or no wife, he's definitely chatting you up.'

'You're only jealous because I've still got it,' Jill laughs.

At that moment, Théo returns carrying a tray of drinks – a pint glass of beer and two fresh glasses of spritz.

'Oh, no, really...' Wendy says. 'I couldn't possibly.'

'Théo, honey, that's sweet, but we can't,' Jill agrees. 'We have to go soon.' But her tone of voice and body language are expressing the exact opposite.

'You do not refuse my drink, please,' Théo says, sounding serious, as he slides the tray on the table. 'This is how we do it in Lille. We buy our friend a drink. Do not be like the Niçois!'

In the end, even Wendy relaxes into the moment, though after four spritzes in three hours, this isn't something for which she can claim any credit – the alcohol is fully to blame. But an hour later, when they stumble from the bar, they are easily as drunk as Théo, and he's unarguably their new best friend.

. . .

After a random stumble through Nice, and without anyone visibly deciding, they end up in a strange old-fashioned ballroom where Théo's best friend Cyril just 'happens' to be waiting to make up a foursome.

'What was it you were saying about the eighties?' Wendy giggles, as they check their coats into the cloakroom.

'More like 1955,' Jill says, looking around wide eyed. The ballroom, with its glitter balls, gold-painted chairs and white tablecloths wouldn't look out of place on a cruise ship.

They choose a table at the edge of the dance floor and watch the elderly yet spritely crowd jiving to a French version of 'Rock Around the Clock' performed by an equally old-school five-piece band.

'Isn't this amazing?' Wendy murmurs in Jill's ear. 'Who even knew that places like this still exist?'

'That's what I love about being on holiday,' Jill says. 'Mad things happen out of nowhere.'

A bottle of blanc de blanc that Théo has apparently ordered arrives, and once they've clinked glasses and taken sips, Cyril stands, bows, and offers Wendy his hand.

'Oh, no...' Wendy splutters through laughter. 'I can't dance rock-and-roll at all.'

'If she can do it, you can do it,' Jill says, pointing at a woman in her late seventies, being twirled around the dance floor by a bejewelled man channelling Liberace.

'No, I mean I don't know how,' Wendy says. 'I've never danced with a partner in my life. Not so much as a tango.'

'Is OK,' Cyril says, taking her hand by force and yanking her to her feet. 'All you do is follow me.'

* * *

'That was the most fun I've had in years,' Jill slurs, as the two women stumble along the wet pavement back towards town. It is almost midnight and, this being a rainy Thursday in November, the streets are all but deserted. 'But Christ my feet hurt.'

'Mine too,' Wendy agrees. 'How old do you think he was, by the way? I kept wondering.'

'Mine?' Jill asks. 'Or yours?'

'Cyril. He must have been in his seventies, right?'

'Mid-sixties, I'd say. Just ravaged by drink and cigarettes, which should be a warning to us all. But it's hard to tell. Théo said he's sixty-four, which came as a bit of a shock. I thought he was more my age.'

'And did he really not try anything on?' Wendy asks, tripping up the kerb and grabbing Jill's hand to steady herself.

'He did not,' Jill says. 'Not so much as a grope. They really were perfect gentlemen.'

'You sound disappointed.'

'Nah,' Jill says. 'Not really.'

Wendy laughs. 'I know you. You're feeling snubbed.'

Jill snorts. 'By the end I was starting to find him quite attractive.'

'Beer goggles,' Wendy says, 'or rather, spritz goggles,' and Jill finds this so hilarious that she momentarily has to stop walking so that she can double over and laugh.

'Spritz goggles,' she repeats, when she can speak again. 'That's exactly what it was.'

It seems to take forever to reach the car park, but eventually Jill stops walking and points. 'That's the one, right?' she says. 'That's where we parked the car. I remember because of those funky lamps.'

'Yess!' Wendy agrees. 'Now all we have to do is find the car.'

'And you're sure you're OK to drive?' Jill asks, as the lift descends.

Wendy, who has eaten a plate of chips at some point during the evening, and who quite valiantly refrained from drinking anything else from that point on, suspects she's over the limit. In fact she's sure she must be over the limit. All the same, she *feels* reasonably straight. 'I'm not sure,' she says, analysing her own gait as they leave the lift. 'I think I'm OK...' She tries, successfully, to walk along a painted line on the floor of the car park.

'Perfect,' Jill says. 'See? Now my turn.' Jill's mere attempt at walking in a straight line is enough to make her crumple to the floor in a fit of giggles.

'Good job you're not driving,' Wendy says, as she holds out a hand to haul her friend back to her feet.

'I don't think they bref-le-lies people in France anyway,' Jill says, enunciating with difficulty. 'You know what continentals are like. Drink driving is almost compulsory.'

'Bref-le-lies?' Wendy repeats mockingly.

'Oh, you know what I mean,' Jill says.

'Luckily, I do.'

It takes ten minutes of traipsing up and down various ramps for them to locate the Renault, and by the time they're seated, the icy chill of the car park and the stress of worrying about finding the car have left Wendy feeling perfectly sober.

Yes, she struggles a little more than usual opening Google Maps on her phone, but that's only because her eyes are tired. And maybe she does forget that the gearstick is on her right, not once, not twice, but three times. But overall she's fine. She's quite sure she's totally fine.

'More bloody rain,' Wendy mutters, blinking repeatedly in an attempt at getting her tired eyes to focus on the shiny road-surface of the Promenade des Anglais. 'And why did they have to make these lanes so bloody narrow?'

Jill, who a second ago had been drifting into sleep, forces her eyes open and peers out, but the drunken blur of her vision plus the droplets sliding across the glass just combine to make her feel woozy. 'Windscreen wipers, maybe?' she offers.

'Good idea,' Wendy says, then, 'I was about to do that, actually. But do you see what I mean? Do you see how narrow they are?'

'Umh,' Jill agrees, already closing her eyes again. 'They are *very* narrow, honey.'

Luckily there is little traffic at this time of night and Wendy feels proud when she realises that she has managed to negotiate the full length of the seafront without incident, narrow lanes and all.

When she reaches the autoroute, however, she discovers that the lanes still feel unusually narrow. And it's only now – because she finds herself correcting her steering over and over again simply in order to remain within those silly white lines – that she realises that it's not tiredness causing her problems at all. It's the alcohol. She's drunker than she'd let herself realise.

'Jill, I'm...' she starts, glancing over at her friend, but seeing that Jill's head has fallen to one side and that her mouth is wide open, she shrugs and smiles to herself. 'Looks like you're on your own here,' she murmurs.

A signpost comes into view for the next exit and she wonders if it wouldn't be wiser to get off the motorway. There does seem to be something particularly criminal about drink-driving along a motorway, but what would they do then? It's – she glances at the dashboard – six degrees outside, and raining. If they tried to sleep in the car they'd wake up frozen, and finding a hotel at – another glance – almost 1 a.m. would prove challenging, if not impossible, and would probably involve more driving than simply going home. Plus the GPS says the next exit is 'her' one anyway.

So no. The road is almost straight and she has four empty lanes to choose from. If she concentrates and keeps her speed down – if she constantly reminds herself that she's had a few and that her reflexes are going to be slow – they'll be fine.

She can't believe that she's let herself do this. It's criminal, is what it is. But that's kind of the problem with alcohol, isn't it? It makes you unable to do most things properly. And that includes making you unable to realise you *can't* do them.

The GPS is telling her to leave at the next exit, and initially she feels relieved about this. But once she's negotiated the toll gate, a complicated underpass and two roundabouts, she finds herself feeling even more stressed than before. Because these small roads with their signposts and traffic lights are infinitely more challenging than the long straight lines of the autoroute.

Anyway, thank goodness for the GPS, eh? Because God knows how people managed in the old days. Actually, she remembers perfectly how they managed in the old days. You had the map open on your lap, or folded small and wedged in the middle of the steering wheel, and you just did your best not to run anyone over while you were trying to work out the route.

Coming out of a roundabout, her rear right wheel briefly mounts the pavement, making the car jerk noisily.

'Whoa!' Jill says, waking, sitting bolt upright and grappling for the panic handle.

'Kerb,' Wendy says. 'Sorry 'bout that.'

'God, I though' you'driben over someone,' Jill says. She sounds more drunk now than when they left Nice.

'No,' Wendy reassures her. 'Everything's fine. Just go back to sleep.'

'I wasn't *sleeping*,' Jill says, sounding offended at the suggestion.

'Right,' Wendy says. 'Fine. Well, go back to whatever you were doing.'

Once Jill has drifted off again, Wendy opens her side window in the hope that the fresh air will make her feel more alert – which it does. She drives past a police car, blue light flickering, and holds her breath until they've vanished from the rearview mirror. But the French cops were far too busy harassing two Arab lads on mopeds to even think about glancing her way. *Thank God for white privilege*, she thinks.

And then suddenly, without her having really noticed, she's leaving the final proper town on their route and heading up into the hills.

The roads here are dark, wet and winding, but at least there's no other cars on the road and hopefully zero chance of coming across more police. She takes a deep breath of cold air and forces her shoulders to relax. 'You're fine,' she tells herself. 'You can do this.'

She thinks how they'll laugh about this in the morning – imagines telling sleepy Jill how drunk she was – and, for the first time since leaving Nice, she smiles.

'Whoa!' Jill says, once again jerking to attention from her slumber. 'What was that?'

'Just another stone in the road,' Wendy tells her.

They're almost at the Gourdon roundabout now, passing by the car park they did a lap of this morning. So, in a way, they're nearly home which is just as well because Wendy has had enough. She's feeling far more tired than drunk now – in fact, she thinks she has sobered right up. But she wants to be home safely in bed. This journey feels like one of those nightmares where every bend is followed by another and another, and then another.

The rain, which stopped a few miles back, has now returned, the droplets slapping strangely against the windscreen. She focuses, briefly, on the peculiar splatter pattern they're making rather than on the road beyond the windscreen and almost misses the bend. *Concentrate, Wendy*, she tells herself, once she's jerked the steering wheel to save the day.

After a couple more bends an alert appears on the dashboard with a 'bong' sound, but she doesn't immediately recognise what it means, essentially because she's too busy staring at the road to give the dashboard her full attention. It wasn't a particularly worrying 'bong' anyway, more like the noise a lift makes when it reaches the desired floor. Perhaps she needs to buy petrol.

After a couple more bends and rises up the side of the mountain, the raindrops change form again, and it's exactly at that moment she understands what the warning meant – what the weird orange symbol represents.

'Shit, Jill, wake up. It's snowing!'

'Oh my God!' Jill exclaims, leaning forward and wiping the windscreen with her arm. 'Oh I love it! How absolutely beautiful!'

Wendy rolls her eyes at this. *Beautiful!* she thinks, as if snow were something to be admired rather than something she's going to have to drive through.

'... not settling, though,' Jill comments, sounding disappointed.

'No, for the moment it's fine.'

But 'fine' doesn't last for long because as they rise, leaving Gourdon behind them, the road surface turns from black to grey, then to light grey, and then to a scintillating white purity that puts the willies right up them both.

'It's going to take forever to get home at this rate,' Wendy says as she slows to forty, then thirty, then twenty kilometres an hour.

'Don't worry,' Jill says. 'It's fine. It's not like we have a train to catch.'

Which gets Wendy thinking about Jill's flight from Nice airport in less than forty-eight hours. Because what if it *really* snows? How will Jill get home then?

Another bend, another rise, and now they're driving

through a bloody snow globe. Despite all the danger and stress of the situation, it's incredibly beautiful. The pine trees at the side of the road look like images on a Christmas card.

'It is just so—' Jill starts to say, but suddenly Wendy is slamming on the brakes and the car is shuddering, sliding briefly out of control before, thankfully, slithering to a halt.

'Look!' Wendy says, once they've stopped. She points out of her passenger window to where the deer she almost hit has paused, sniffing the cold night air.

'Oh!' Jill says, her voice almost tearful with awe. 'God, I've never seen a Bambi before. And in the snow!'

'She's not going *anywhere*,' Wendy says. 'I think she wants to say hello.'

The deer sniffs the air again, snorts, and then turns and bolts off into the trees.

'Abso-bloody-lutely amazing,' Jill says.

'That was,' Wendy agrees. 'Scared the shit out of me, though. She ran right in front of the car. One second earlier and she'd have been dead meat. One second earlier and we'd *all* have been meat.'

After a couple of nerve-wracking failures, Wendy manages to re-start the engine. And now they're off again, moving even more slowly than before.

'That's, like, proper inches of snow, isn't it?' Jill says as they round a bend into ever more perfect whiteness. 'We are going to make it, aren't we?'

That is, after all, the real question, isn't it? Wendy has been trying to picture the road ahead, trying to recall the various twists and turns. Because if there's one more proper hill they need to climb then they might not make it. She's never really driven in snow before. You don't get a lot of it in Kent and when you do you tend to leave the car at home. She's having trouble predicting how the car will react.

The steering wheel is getting less and less precise the

thicker the snowfall becomes. The car is starting to feel more like a boat, where you steer and then wait a bit for something to happen.

'Should we turn back?' Jill asks, unnerved by the fact that Wendy hasn't answered.

But Wendy has been picturing that option, too. She's been imagining driving back *down* those hills and trying to brake for all the hairpin bends, in snow, in order to avoid sliding over the edge and dying. 'No, I think that might be worse,' she says, glancing at Jill. 'We're nearly home anyway.'

When she looks back at the road, though, she sees a bend she has failed to anticipate. It's not a *crazy* bend by any means, and the downhill slope they're on is only a gentle one, and they're travelling at less than twenty kilometres an hour, but all the same, when she tries to brake nothing happens, and when she tries to steer that doesn't seem to work either, so they continue to slither gently, undramatically forward, as if in slow motion, in an almost perfect straight line on a road where they really do need to be curving to the left.

She turns the steering wheel one way and then the other until she can't even tell which way the wheels are pointing anymore. She tries braking, accelerating, anything, but nothing makes the slightest bit of difference. They slide inexorably onwards.

'Wendy?' Jill cries, reaching for the wheel herself. 'Wendy! Do something!'

The car is now slewing sideways, and nothing either of them do makes the slightest bit of difference. 'Wendy!' Jill screams. But they're both realising there's nothing to be done except wait and see where the car comes to a stop.

In a ditch at the side of the road. This is where they have landed.

With the exception of the wipers, which continue to swipe fresh snowflakes from the windscreen every couple of seconds, all is silent.

'Christ!' Jill eventually says when, after a few swishes of the blades, she finds herself able to speak. 'Jesus! Are you OK?'

'Yes, I'm fine,' Wendy says, though as she says it her hands start to tremble. She folds them beneath her armpits and forces herself to breathe. 'Boy, that was...' She's momentarily lost for words.

They sit like this for a moment, trying to take it all in.

'That has to have been the slowest, quietest car accident in history,' Wendy finally says.

'Like slow motion,' Jill says.

'Like in a dream.'

'Do you think we can get the car back on the road?'

'I'm not sure,' Wendy says. The ditch they're in is only about a foot deep, but will the car want to leave it? Will the tyres now decide to grip the snow?

She releases her seatbelt and tries to open her door but it's impossible to push it further than an inch because of the height of the embankment to her left.

'Shit,' she says, turning to Jill. 'Try yours.'

But – and they both gasp in relief at this – Jill's door does open, so they tumble inelegantly from the car and stand in the cold light of the headlights from where they attempt to appraise the situation.

Things aren't looking good, it has to be said. The ridge of the road is higher than the bumper of the car and the snow is falling more heavily now than before: huge, fluffy, in any other circumstances beautiful flakes drifting past the headlights.

'It's not going to work, is it?' Jill says, with a shiver. 'It's too high.'

'No, I don't think so. Unless... maybe in reverse? It's a bit lower there,' Wendy says, pointing.

So Wendy climbs back over the gearstick to the driver's seat. She starts the engine and engages reverse. But the second she releases the clutch it becomes apparent that the car isn't going anywhere. The wheels merely spin and slide more deeply into mud that's lurking beneath the snow.

'Stop. Stop!' Jill shouts. 'You're just making it worse.' She rounds the car and climbs back in beside Wendy. 'Bloody freezing out there,' she says, fiddling with the heater controls.

'Quite literally,' Wendy agrees.

'So what now? Do we call a breakdown truck? I suppose they have French AA or something, don't they?'

'There's a number on the paperwork in the glovebox,' Wendy says. 'But d'you think they'll come out in this?' A wave of despair washes over her and to avoid crying she buries her face in her hands and makes an angry 'agghhhh!' sound.

Jill pats her shoulder. 'Oh, honey,' she says.

'If we phone for breakdown I'm worried we'll get the police,' Wendy says, her voice trembling.

'And?'

'The drink,' Wendy says. 'I can't afford to lose my licence. What would I do if I couldn't drive up here? Or back home. Life would be impossible.'

'I'm sure you're fine by now, aren't you?' Jill says. Even she's feeling sober after all the drama.

'I don't know. I really don't. But am I willing to take the risk?'

'And why would the AA call the police anyway?'

'Because it's a hire car? Because I've wrecked it? Because that's maybe what they do when you have an accident in France? How would I know?'

'You can barely call this an accident,' Jill says. 'You just slid off the road, really, didn't you? And the car's probably fine. It's not like we hit anything.'

'Maybe,' Wendy says. 'Maybe not. That was quite a drop. We're lucky it didn't roll over.'

'God,' Jill says. 'Don't!'

'Anyway, no, I'm not calling the hire company until the morning.'

'Fair enough, but then what?' Jill asks. 'Because we can't just stay here. We'll freeze to death. Actually, would we? Would we free—'

'It's maybe not that far,' Wendy interrupts.

'You want to walk it?' Jill says. 'In this?'

'I think it's less than a mile. Or maybe *about* a mile. But honestly not much more.'

'But look at it,' Jill says, nodding.

When Wendy raises her eyes to the windscreen she sees that the view is almost completely obscured by snow. 'I know. But shall we try? If it's awful, we can always come back and phone that number.'

'Crazy,' Jill says. 'You are absolutely batshit crazy.'

'I know,' Wendy says. 'But you love it. Come on. Grab your coat.'

'If I'd known, I would have worn flats,' Jill says, as they slip-slide their way along the road.

'If I'd known, I would have worn skis,' Wendy replies, mimicking Jill's intonation.

The terror of the accident is now behind them and a hysterical adrenalin buzz is taking over, that almost makes this seem fun. Both women are already picturing how this will be a story they'll be able to tell forever.

The moon is peeping through a gap in the clouds lighting up the stunning whiteness of it all, and now they're walking it doesn't even feel that cold.

'I'm sorry I made you drink,' Jill says, giving Wendy's hand, which she's holding for stability, a squeeze.

'It's fine,' Wendy says. 'We're both alive. That's the main thing.'

'For now,' Jill says. 'Until the wolves get us. But I am feeling guilty here. None of this would have happened if I hadn't kept plying you with drinks.'

'Oh, I think it probably would have,' Wendy says.

Jill assumes that Wendy means she's not that drunk – that her drinking had nothing to do with the accident. But what Wendy is feeling is more mystical. It's as though the accident was somehow pre-determined – their strange slide into the ditch caused by the push of an unseen hand. She has no idea why she feels this way, particularly because it's not the kind of mumbo-jumbo she generally favours, but she thinks it all the same. That's just how it felt in the moment: as if they were being pushed – like the accident needed to happen.

They walk for half an hour, making slow but steady progress. Both women fall over twice, once together, Jill dragging Wendy down with her in a heap of giggles, and once each on their own, more abruptly. The road surface is turning into an ice rink but they discover that by walking along the edge their heels cut through to the mud and gravel beneath, enabling them to stay upright – just about.

Eventually they reach the little parking area from where Wendy hiked up to the radar. Which means they're still more than a mile from home. She decides not to tell Jill this.

She thinks, as they pass the parking area – now a flat expanse of virgin snow – how she'd promised herself she'd hike up there every day. Jill's arrival put paid to that particular good intention. But how beautiful it must be up there in the snow! She wonders how difficult it would be to get up there without snow boots or whatever.

'Car!' Jill says suddenly, so Wendy glances back down the

road to see a pair of yellow headlights sweeping the plain behind them.

'Oh, thank God,' Wendy says, pulling her friend to a stop.

'You're not... Are we really going to flag down a serial killer?' Jill asks, only half joking.

Wendy laughs. 'Stop it,' she says. 'You're giving me the heebie-jeebies.'

The car, advancing slowly, is almost upon them, so Wendy starts to wave.

'If we end up chopped into steaks,' Jill says, 'then don't say I didn't warn you.'

The car rolls to a gentle halt beside them and the steamy window winds down.

'Oh, is you!' a familiar voice says, and Wendy thinks once again, *Destiny!* 'You scare me in the night like this!'

'Our car,' Wendy says, pointing back down the road. 'We had an accident in the snow.'

'It's OK,' the post lady says. 'I take you. Get in!'

Once they're seated, Wendy in the passenger seat, Jill on the bench seat in the rear, the car slowly pulls away.

'I'm so glad it's you!' Wendy says. 'What are the chances?'

'Me too!' Jill says, with meaning, then, 'And who *is* this, Wens?'

'My post lady,' Wendy explains. 'I'm sorry. I don't even know your name.'

'I'm sorry?' she says, then, 'Oh, my name. Manon. My name is Manon.'

'Like *Manon des Sources*?' Wendy asks.

'Yes,' Manon says, sounding bored by the choice of reference. 'Just like *Manon des Sources*.'

'That's a lovely name,' Wendy says. 'And I'm Wendy. And this is my friend Jill.'

Manon raises one hand and wiggles her fingers back at Jill. 'I see a car back in the snow. Is yours?'

'Yes, we were going slowly, but we slid right off the road.'

'Is very bad tonight. You need snow wheels. This is obligatory here in winter. New Europe law. Everyone must have.' Manon's English isn't quite as good as usual tonight and Wendy wonders if she's been drinking or is just tired.

'Right,' Wendy says. 'I didn't know.'

'I have,' she says, 'the good wheels. And this one...' Here she caresses the steering wheel. 'She is old, and small, and heating not so good, but in snow she is *perfection*. She is four four, you see. I drive through anything.'

'Four four?' Wendy repeats.

'She means four-wheel drive, I think,' Jill offers.

'Yes, this,' Manon says. 'So she is perfect to live here.'

'Because it snows a lot here?' Wendy asks.

'Oh, every year,' she says. 'Though more December, *janvier*. Is early this year.'

And now, they're home, slamming the doors to the rusty Fiat Panda and waving goodbye.

'Well, that was a stroke of luck,' Wendy says as the taillights fade into the distance.

'She's sweet,' Jill comments. 'She reminds me of one of Michael's friends when he was at school.'

'She is sweet,' Wendy agrees. She's actually feeling a fairly unreasonable surge of love for this young woman who, against all odds, has appeared to save them from their nightmare.

They crunch through the snow to the door and let themselves in. The cabin is way too cold for comfort – the wood burner long since extinguished – but at least the lights are working again. 'Electricity!' Jill exclaims. 'I'm assuming we can't use the heater?'

'Absolutely not,' Wendy replies, already crouching to relight the fire.

'Can I come in with you?' Jill asks as she kicks off her muddy shoes. 'Please? Pretty please? Pretty, pretty, pre—'

'Yes,' Wendy interrupts. 'Please do. I'm frozen through to the bone here. But you have to warm my side up first. That's the deal.'

'I'm not sure I can warm anything up,' Jill says, already clambering up the spiral staircase. 'My feet have turned to ice.'

* * *

The next morning, they awaken to a still-cool, shockingly bright cabin. It's like opening your eyes to find yourself in the chiller cabinet.

Jill is first downstairs so Wendy calls out to put a log on the fire. When she eventually gets downstairs she finds her friend staring out of the big window at the blinding landscape beyond.

'Have you seen?' she asks, when Wendy joins her. 'It's amazing. I don't think I've ever seen a sky that blue.'

'Wow, that's a lot of snow,' Wendy says. 'That's not going to make getting the car back any easier.'

'But it'll melt, won't it?' Jill says. 'Surely the sun will melt it. Because, don't forget, I have to get to the airport tomorrow.'

'I've really no idea,' Wendy says tersely, a bit irritated that Jill's main concern seems to be for herself. She glances up at the overhanging gutter. 'Drips. That's got to be a good sign,' she says, softening her tone.

They spend a lazy morning drinking coffee and chattering about nothing in particular. Both women have hangovers and between getting the car out of the ditch and getting Jill to the airport Wendy feels overwhelmed. She doesn't know where to start.

It's one of those rare occasions where she'd like someone – her father, her husband, a friend – to step in and tell her what to do, or even better, take control and deal with it. She tells herself off for the un-feminist nature of the thought but acknowledges the truth of it all the same. Where are the bloody men when you need them?

By lunchtime the snow has compacted to half its previous height and become shiny, but there's no real sign of it melting.

They eat soup from a carton with long-life bread, and as they're washing up (in cold water – yet another problem to be solved) Jill says, 'You know, I do think we need a plan.'

In the end, after some discussion, Wendy trudges off through the snow to pick up the paperwork she has stupidly left in the glove compartment, while Jill is tasked with googling local taxi companies to find out how much a taxi to the airport will cost, and if it's even doable.

The road, thanks to passing traffic, is walkable even if she does have to step into the snowdrift every time a car passes by. She puts her thumb out for a lift from the first three cars, but surprisingly they don't stop. She'd expected snow to bring out more solidarity in people, but she resigns herself to walking. It's gorgeous out here and lord knows she needs the exercise.

The car, when she finally reaches it, is almost invisible beneath the snow.

She scrapes at the snow and yanks the passenger door open, then phones the breakdown number. They speak English, thankfully, and tell her they'll be there at 4 p.m. Then, on their advice, as she walks home with the sun on her back, she attempts to phone the car hire company. She's transferred so many times that on reaching the cabin she's still listening to their awful music.

To her surprise, she finds Jill packing so she puts the phone on speaker and, to a background of looped plinky-plonky piano, Jill explains: 'I've booked a hotel at the airport. The taxis won't come up this far that early – not with the snow and everything. He actually asked me if there was snow and I said yes. Perhaps I should have lied, but...'

'So you're leaving today and staying near the airport?' Wendy asks.

'Yeah. It looks horrible, and I'm sure I'll get bed bugs or the pox or something, but at least I won't miss my flight.'

'God, what a bummer!' Wendy says, feeling sorry for herself, being left to deal with all the mayhem alone. She wonders if Jill really does have to leave today or whether she just prefers to escape, even peering into her eyes in case the truth of the matter is visible.

'You don't mind, do you?' Jill asks, looking genuinely embarrassed.

'No, not at all,' Wendy lies. 'It's really the only way, isn't it? I'm glad you worked out a solution for yourself.'

'Oh, by the way,' Jill says. 'More bad news, I'm afraid.'

'Yeah? What now?'

'The electric's gone off again.'

* * *

Jill's taxi arrives at three thirty, which at least means it can drop Wendy at the car as it passes by, en route for Nice.

'Good luck!' Jill calls, wiggling her fingers through the window of the Tesla as it pulls silently away. 'I'll call and see how it's all going!'

'That's generous of you,' Wendy mumbles through a forced smile, once she's out of earshot. 'Don't put yourself out.'

She watches the car vanish around the bend and tries to work out why she's feeling so forlorn. Actually, it's worse than forlorn. She's really feeling quite angry. Because none of this would have happened had Jill not come to visit. And now Jill has left, leaving her stranded, in snow, without a car.

It makes her think of the parties she and Harry used to host when they were younger, parties that filled the house with guests who would spend the whole night drinking and smoking and slopping stickiness all over the kitchen floor, even occasionally vomiting in inappropriate places. They'd sleep on chairs, sofas and inflatable mattresses and then in the morning – by which time virtually the entire house needed to be renovated – they'd all be in a hurry to leave, due to baby-sitters or train tickets or work. She can't remember any of them ever hanging around long enough to pick up a mop.

She's getting cold and is feeling a bit silly standing at the roadside, so she sits in the car, but that feels even colder. She tries starting the engine, but when she turns the key nothing happens, so she returns to the roadside and watches the occupants of sporadic passing cars staring at her as they pass by. She'll be the talk of the village by nightfall, she reckons. That mad English woman out in the snow.

Four o'clock comes and goes with no sign of the tow truck.

The sun dips behind a hillock so she starts to pace up and down the road to keep warm, but she's shivering all the same. The road starts to freeze over again. It's getting more slippery by the minute.

What am I even doing here? she wonders. Because, lord knows, there are a lot of bad decisions between their lovely warm home in Maidstone and right here, right now, aren't there? She could cry at the stupidity of it all.

But then, oh joy! A throb and a rumble as a bright red breakdown truck rounds the corner, belching diesel fumes into the pristine mountain air.

It drives past her, just far enough to have her waving her arms and running and shouting and then feeling silly because obviously it was always going to pull up in the siding just along the way.

The cabin door opens jerkily, and then an overweight mechanic clambers down. Without any kind of acknowledgement, he strolls towards her, still rolling and then lighting his cigarette. The sun is almost gone now. The sky behind the truck is shifting to red.

'*Alors !*' he says, on reaching her. He nods at the car-shaped snow sculpture in the ditch and asks, '*C'est celle-là ?*'

'*Oui,*' Wendy says, doing her best to make sure no irony enters her voice. Because which other car could it be? '*Oui, c'est ça.*'

He wrinkles his nose, pouts and shakes his head. 'Nah,' he says. '*... peux pas.*'

Wendy feels her life force slipping away. 'I'm sorry?'

'*... peux pas !*' he says, with a lazy shrug. This is followed by his rambling incomprehensible mansplaining of all the reasons he can't. If he removed the cigarette from his mouth it might make his diction a little bit clearer, but when she gestures for him to do so he misunderstands, generously, *unhygienically*, offering her a drag on his roll-up.

'Do you speak any English at all?' Wendy asks, once she's refused his kind offer. '*Parlez Anglais ?*'

He laughs at this and says, quite simply, rather dismissively, '*Non.*'

'But *vraiment ? Vous pas pouvez ?*' Wendy asks, dredging the depths of her French and wincing at the subconscious knowledge that her grammar is all wrong.

She'd meant to ask if he really can't move the car, but he seems to think she's asked if he really can't speak English, and this makes him laugh again but in a sour mocking way. '*Non, je peux vraiment pas,*' he says, followed by something about being a *mécano*, not a *professeur*.

'*Mais la voiture !*' Wendy says, miming winching it from the ditch.

He makes a tutting noise and wiggles a finger at her before producing another long cigarettey phrase from which Wendy manages to extract only two words: damage and insurance.

He's such a sad little archetype, this man, that she feels she knows him, feels she has *always* known him. The lazy, unfit garage mechanic who starts every day determined to do the minimum with as little joy as possible. In a way, she hated him before she ever met him.

Anyway, it's over. The man – her supposed knight in shining armour – has already turned, is already slouching his way back to his lorry, flicking his cigarette butt into the snow-covered bushes. There's one last moment of hope when he looks out of his window back at her, and Wendy thinks he's going to reverse and hitch his pulley thing to the car, after all. Instead, he simply beckons to her.

'*Allez !*' he says. '*Je vous dépose,*' a phrase she correctly interprets as, *Come on, I'll drop you off.*

So she walks to the passenger side of the truck and, feeling guilty for having hated him, climbs in.

* * *

She's up at silly o'clock the next morning. This is partly because she had a couple of glasses of wine last night (enough to bugger up her sleep pattern but not enough to knock her out for the count) and partly because she was cold and had to get up to add logs to the fire. But mainly it's because she's stressed out by her not inconsiderable list of problems: no car, intermittent electricity, hateful snow everywhere and, worst of all, zero remaining minutes on her mobile because she wasted them all trying to call the dreadful car hire people. These problems, which have been churning around in her mind on their evil merry-go-round, even wormed their way into her dreams.

Add to this unpleasant mish-mash, a sprinkling of Jill at the airport going home and a dash of Harry, still at home in their bed with whatever-her-name-is, and it's become impossible to avoid the most agonising question of all: should she give in and pack her bags this minute?

So yes, it's not even six thirty, and she's been up for an hour, stoking the fire, and staring at the flames while she waits for the electricity (and hence the wifi) to return so that she can buy more bloody minutes for her phone and give the owner and the hire company what for. And maybe, just maybe, buy a plane ticket home for tomorrow, or even (why not?) today.

She eventually manages to boil water on the stove for tea, and after half an hour of picking up and then discarding her useless connection-free phone, she digs her Kindle out. After a couple of glassy-eyed false starts she begins to read, but after a few pages the damned thing tells her that it too has a low battery, and a few pages after that, it shuts down.

She resists the urge to hurl it across the room and, stuffing it down the side of the sofa, allows herself a few tears.

Two astonishingly stretched hours later, the sun finally comes over the mountain, and an hour after this the electricity returns, shortly followed by the wifi, so she immediately buys two hours of overseas minutes from Tesco and connects to Airbnb to send an angry message to the owner.

I send someone, Madame Blanchard replies immediately. *You are at the cabin this morning?*

Yes, she replies. *I'm here. I'm waiting.*

She tries to shower but the water temperature is at the low end of 'lukewarm', so instead she washes with a flannel from a saucepan of water heated on the stove. 'Welcome to the Stone Age,' she mutters. 'Only £900 a month.'

* * *

Just after eleven a car pulls up – an ancient orange Lada four-wheel drive, crunching its way through the snow.

The driver, an elegantly dressed retiree whose clothes must

cost more than his car, climbs down and crosses to the gate where she's waiting.

'Hello,' he says, holding out a hand. 'I'm Erik. Florence – Madame Blanchard – she tells me you are having some problems.'

'I am!' Wendy says, shaking his hand. 'Wendy.'

'Well, I am here to help, Wendy. Let's have a look and see what we can do,' he says, following her through the gate.

Wendy feels tearful again, but this time it's in relief that the man speaks such perfect English.

'Thank you,' she says. 'The electricity keeps going off, and there's no hot water either. And I also crashed my car, so everything's basically bloody awful.'

'Gosh, that does sound bloody awful,' he says. 'We'll have to see if we can sort at least some of that out.'

'Your English...' she comments, as they step indoors. 'It's excellent.' His accent is so vague as to be unidentifiable.

'Well, I'm from Sweden,' he explains, smiling as he removes his coat. 'Unlike the English, we have to be good at languages. Because no one else on the planet ever even *tries* to learn Swedish.'

* * *

It turns out that Erik can't do much about Wendy's electrical problems nor indeed her lack of hot water. The only thing he can do is explain, which he does, in painful detail.

The short version – the version Erik does not choose, the version that someone with the ability to summarise would give – is that there are two panels on the roof heating the hot water when the sun is out and nine others charging the battery – also when the sun is out. And when (she should be so lucky) the battery is full, the excess electricity heats the hot water further still.

Wendy's problems stem from multiple facts, namely a) no one has ever rented the cabin all winter before so no one knew it wouldn't work out, and b) she and Jill not only emptied the battery with the stupid blow heater, but also drained all the hot water (Jill did spend an extremely long time in the shower) and c) there is still snow on the roof obscuring the solar panels she's depending on to recharge everything.

'I really do think that if you can be careful for two, maybe three days – you know, not use too much hot water, not use too much electricity – then the battery will fill again, and everything will be fine,' Erik says.

'I do understand,' Wendy says, 'but it's not really good enough, is it? I paid 900 euros a month to stay here, and that was supposed to include electricity. No one ever mentioned quotas.'

'You are right,' Erik says. 'It is not good enough. This is why Florence will refund 20 per cent of your... um... you know... the money you have paid.'

'My rent.'

'Yes, that's it. Your rent.'

'Oh,' Wendy says. She'd prepped herself to slowly go ballistic, had been mentally listing all the reasons this situation was making her life intolerable, and steeling herself to progressively raise her voice. Erik's offer has knocked the wind out of her sails.

'Sorry, but are we talking about 20 per cent of the *entire* fee?' Wendy asks, hunting for the catch. 'For the whole six months?'

'Yes, it comes to thirty-six days, I believe. She will refund that to you today, if you agree.'

'Oh,' Wendy says, mentally totting up how much that will represent. It's about a thousand pounds.

'This is OK for you?'

'Well, I suppose,' Wendy concedes. 'As long as the electricity does start working again. Because I can't really live here without it.'

'Of course. But we think it will. This is what the engineer – you had a man come to check the system, yes? – well, this is what he says. Two or three days, being careful.'

'OK,' Wendy says. 'Well, I can try. But if it doesn't sort itself out I will have to leave early.'

'Of course. Now your car...' Erik says. 'You say you are having an accident?'

'Yes. Well, more just slid off the road, really. On the snow. It's in a ditch down the way.'

'So how can I help you with that?'

Wendy sighs deeply and recounts her attempts at calling the hire company: how they always pass her to the breakdown division who then transfer her back to the insurance division, who then attempt to transfer her to an English-speaking insurance assessor, at which point nothing further happens. 'Then I'm on hold for like half an hour until the line goes dead.'

'How French!' Erik says with a wry smile. 'Maybe I can call them for you? *With* you, I mean.' An offer which produces a fresh welling up of tears.

'Yes!' Wendy says. 'Yes, please!'

The phone call is as torturous as Erik is methodical and patient. But the news when it finally arrives – that nothing can happen until an insurance assessor has seen the car, and that this can't happen until a new different kind of breakdown truck has taken the car to a Renault garage, and that this can't happen either until the snow encasing the car has melted – is not good.

'Can they at least lend me another car?' Wendy asks.

Erik translates this request and argues valiantly in Wendy's favour, but at the end when he hangs up the phone, he's shaking his head and looking glum. 'Until the car is assessed, I'm afraid there will be no other car.'

'Ugh!' Wendy exclaims. 'I somehow knew that was going to happen.'

'If you want to rent another car, maybe from another company, I can take you.'

'I need to think about that a bit first,' Wendy tells him. 'It costs an absolute fortune. I mean, that one cost me a fortune, but if you're doing it day by day it's much worse. And I wouldn't know for how long, would I? So I can't even sign a long-term contract... So I don't know.'

'Yes,' Erik says. 'Of course. Well, if you need me to take you, send Florence a message.' And then suddenly he's standing, pulling on his coat and rather hurriedly leaving. There's a distinct whiff of 'enough of your problems' suddenly floating in the air.

Once he's gone Wendy goes around the cabin unplugging appliances with the exception of the refrigerator and her Kindle charger. And then she pours herself a glass of wine and hurls herself on the sofa in despair.

After a few sips, she reaches for her phone.

She has a text message from Jill telling her she's back in Maidstone and another from Harry asking if she's up for a 'chat'.

'No,' she mutters putting the phone back down again. 'No, I'm not up for a bloody chat, Harry.'

EIGHT

ISOLATION

She eats pasta with cheese and opens a bottle of superbly fruity Fitou. Outside, the weather is shockingly cold but sunny, if a little hazy. The snow still isn't melting, though. It's just becoming ever more compact and slippery as it slowly morphs to ice.

Indoors, with the fire stoked, she is warm and also a little hazy under the combined effects of tiredness, warmth and wine.

She tries to read but her mind is refusing to focus so that every time she reaches the bottom of the screen she realises that she hasn't taken in a single word and has to go back to the top again. Eventually she puts the device aside and turns around on the sofa so that she's facing out towards the view.

She's relieved that Jill has left, she decides. She can be quiet and thoughtful and reflect on her life now, which after all was the whole point of coming here. But she's lonely, too. She misses Jill's upbeat company. And she's a bit disappointed that Jill hasn't called. *Out of sight is out of mind*, she thinks. Then, *she's probably just sick to death of me.*

She's stranded here now, as well. No car! She hadn't expected that particular plot twist. It's going to become a real problem soon. Her supplies will probably last for a few days, but after that she'll absolutely have to get to a shop.

She thinks about going for a walk, but the compacted snow, when she tests it, is like a skating rink and after a minute of Laurel and Hardy slip and slither she abandons the idea. It's almost impossible to stand up, let alone walk, and a broken leg would be an almost biblical final straw. So no. She's going to be stuck inside until it melts. But she can do this. She knows she can. After all, during Covid she spent months alone in Jill's little studio.

So why did she want to come here? Wasn't the deprivation of the past few years enough for her? Perhaps she really is losing her mind.

Her phone pings with a text message from Fiona.

R U OK? Dad says you're not answering texts.

She will phone her daughter shortly. It will be good to hear her voice. But first she needs to decide not only how she is, but also how she's going to spin it. How does she want to appear?

So number one first: how is she? She consciously scans her body.

She's exhausted, actually, which seems silly, but there you are. And a bit lonely. And stressed. Her chest is tight – breathing feels like a challenge – which probably means she's very stressed.

Plus – and this is most likely the main one – she's feeling bored, which is even sillier. If she's exhausted because the last few days with Jill have been full on, and she's stressed because she has so much shit to deal with, then a rest, doing nothing, is precisely what the doctor would order.

When did she lose the ability to do nothing and relax? she wonders. When did doing nothing come to automatically equal boredom? It's an interesting thought, really, and one that says quite a lot about her life.

But she is at least now asking herself these philosophical

questions, so perhaps this whole 'retreat' thing is working after all.

Yes, she decides. Philosophical. Fiona will love that.

'Mum!' Fiona says, the second she answers. 'We've been worried.'

Wendy thinks (but does not say), ~~Two text messages in ten days doesn't make you look particularly worried.~~

'But why, sweetheart?' she says, instead. 'Everything's fine.'

'Oh, thank God,' Fiona says. 'Dad was worried, too, because apparently you haven't been answering him either.'

Either, Wendy thinks. A weasely word slipped in to imply that they've all been trying to contact her, which they haven't. She lets it go.

'So how is it?' Fiona continues. 'Are you having fun? Tell me everything. I have, like, a whole ten minutes before my next class.'

~~A whole ten minutes? Gosh, thank you!~~

'Oh, it's really quite the adventure, sweetie. It snowed! And not just a bit, either. It covered all the solar panels on the roof – the snow, that is – so the electricity has been on the blink as well. I feel like I'm living in the Middle Ages.'

'I'm not sure they had solar panels in the Middle Ages, Mum.'

'No. But you know what I mean.'

'I didn't know the place was solar. That's cool.'

'Yes, off grid, I think is the term. And Jill came to stay for a few days, so that was fun. We went dancing down in Nice.'

'Dancing?' Fiona says. 'You?'

'I can dance! You've seen me dance.'

'I've seen you dance really badly, if that's what you mean.'

'Now you're being mean to your old mum.'

'I am. Your dancing's fine. So is Jill still there?'

'No. She's gone. She left yesterday. She only came for a few days.'

'I didn't realise you were accepting visitors. I might pop over and see you myself. You can show me your moves on the dance floor.'

~~But we both know you won't.~~ 'Oh do, sweetie. That would be lovely.'

'So now you're on your own?'

'I am.'

'And you don't mind it?'

'No, I'm feeling quite philosophical about it all. It's good, having time to – you know – reappraise things.'

'Gosh,' Fiona says.

'Don't sound so surprised! That is why I came here, after all. You know that.'

'Yeah, but it's not really you, is it?'

'What isn't?'

'Well, relaxing. Being zen. Thinking about things.'

Wendy snorts at her daughter's hopefully unintentional insult.

'Sorry, I didn't mean...'

'It's fine. And I am, thinking about things. So perhaps it's a whole new me.'

'OK. If you say so, Mum. I mean, great! That sounds good.'

'It *is* doing me good, darling. So don't be... you know... dismissive. Anyway, enough of me, how are you? How's everything back home?'

'Oh fine,' Fiona says. 'Just boring day-to-day stuff, really. The shops are going full-on Christmas already, which is absolutely ridiculous. It gets earlier every year...'

Once the conversation has ended precisely ten minutes after it began, Wendy sits and thinks about Fiona's eclectic selection of news, namely that: Poundland has closed again, Todd's girlfriend has a genuine Ferragamo handbag and the latest opinion polls say that no one is ever going to vote Conservative ever again. Ever.

Fiona, having never forgiven the Conservatives for taking away her dream of living in every country in Europe, seemed particularly thrilled about that one.

Wendy runs the whole conversation through her mind again, analysing it for tone, phrasing and hesitation in case she missed some clue, even a hint of a clue as to the one bit of news she'd really like to know, namely has Harry moved his new bit of fluff into the house? But there was nothing to even begin to interpret.

Perhaps she'll ask him outright. He'd probably answer honestly. But is she ready to hear it?

She scrolls through her old text messages and sees that she hasn't replied to her sister-in-law Sue who'd enquired a while back when she was going to France.

Why hasn't she replied? Well, because she's angry. Sue, of course, should know. Sue should be interested enough to have not forgotten.

She remembers before she introduced them, when Sue was still her best friend and her brother Neil was her other best friend. Who could have imagined that by putting them together they would merely cancel each other out? Best friend + best friend = sweet FA. By meddling, albeit with the best of intentions, she has managed to swap two wonderful relationships for none.

She will reply, though, to stop things getting worse. Because worse is always a possibility.

In the old days, she would have phoned Sue and told her everything – in fact, she would have hauled Sue over the coals for forgetting such an important date and they would have laughed about it together. But in the old days she wouldn't have had to do any of those things. Sue would have known exactly when she was in France because back then Sue actually gave a damn.

She doesn't want to feel too bitter, though. Feeling bitter towards her ex-best friend, now sister-in-law, hurts physically. There's a sensation somewhere in the region of her heart that feels (she marvels at the perfection of the English language as she realises this) bitter. Bitterness feels bitter. How brilliant is that?

It's amazing that people can change like that, though, isn't it? Amazing that they can change each other so quickly and so profoundly.

She shoots off a text which she hopes is neither friendly nor unfriendly, merely informative.

Sorry, just got this. I am in France! Been here about three weeks. All is well. Hope you're both OK. Wendy x

She wonders if she should have put more kisses, and then shrugs and lifts her gaze to the window. It's dark outside now (when did that happen?) so she lowers the blinds and turns inwards to face the fire.

She wonders if she and Harry changed each other, too, and even before she has finished asking herself the question she knows the answer.

She's way more uptight than she ever was pre-Harry, and Harry for his part is far less fun. He'd been funny when she met him. He'd been really funny, actually.

She wonders where that went and if it's her fault. She's aware of consciously refusing to find him funny these last few years, even though she's not sure why she started to do that. To punish him for something, probably. At the beginning that was it, anyway. Later it was more of a habit. But yes, for years, Harry has been playing to the worst, least amusable audience in town. And that would do it, wouldn't it? That would make anyone give up on their failing comedy act. Then again, perhaps it's just the inevitable result of spending so many years together, as a couple.

Uptight, irritable woman with dull un-funny husband. Lord, she's known so many couples the description would apply to that it's virtually a definition of middle age. She thinks back to her parents, who were very much that way. She thinks back to her parents' friends and pictures the wives' pinched expressions and nods to herself. Maybe the stale nature of her relationship with Harry is nothing more, nothing less than inevitable.

More from boredom than actual desire, she refills her glass. She adds a fresh log to the fire, and watches as it smokes and splutters before bursting into flames.

She thinks again of Sue and remembers that first fated holiday as a foursome – the Greek one where she'd thrown Sue and her brother together in the first place. My, that had been a great trip, hadn't it? The beaches, the bars, those incredible sunsets – it had all been brochure-style perfection. She remembers Neil attempting to teach Sue to windsurf and almost laughs out loud at the memory of her endlessly falling off.

And then she's holding her breath and feeling stressed again, because a different memory has popped up. After all, the beginning of the end had been present even during that first holiday.

The specific memory is: sitting with Harry in a posh restaurant and explaining to the waiter that the other two seats were going to remain empty after all.

Harry: I expect they're shagging or something. Don't let it get to you.

Wendy: But it's rude. Don't you think it's rude, not turning up like this?

H: A bit, maybe. But, you know...

W: And anyway, they can't be at it twenty-four/seven.

They do have to come up for air sometimes. And food. Think of all the calories they'll be burning.

H: I thought it was what you wanted. I thought that was why you invited them.

W: Just because I *thought* it was what I wanted doesn't necessarily mean it's what I wanted.

H: It doesn't?

W: No. And even if I did want it, that doesn't mean it was a good idea.

H: Right. Gosh. I don't think I'll ever understand women.

W: No. You're right. Your best bet is not to try.

Yes, every single relationship – every single combination you could make out of the members of that foursome – was already shifting to a new, far-less-pleasant version, and it was all entirely her fault because matching Sue with Neil was what she'd thought she wanted.

Now, five years later, here we are, she thinks, still staring at her sister-in-law's text. *Just about as far apart as friends, or couples, or family for that matter, can be.*

* * *

She is woken by heavy rain drumming on the roof of the cabin. She glances at her watch; it's 3.30 a.m. – about the worst possible time for her to have woken up.

Jill, for some – no doubt mythological – reason, calls it 'the witching hour', and certainly for her (and for Jill, for that matter) between 3 and 4 a.m. is the specific time slot in which she knows she won't get back to sleep. She has no idea why this is the case, but it is so. It's been that way for decades.

She wonders if the electricity is still on and tries to listen for the buzz of the refrigerator, but the drumming of the rain is too loud so she fumbles for the switch of the bedside lamp. It works, thank God! She didn't know she could feel so grateful for something as basic as electricity.

She switches the lamp back off and tosses and turns for half an hour before giving in to the inevitable and getting up.

At the moment she switches on the downstairs light she spots a pair of animal eyes looking in through the gap beneath one of the blinds, but in the fraction of a second her eyesight takes to focus they've vanished.

She fully opens the blind and peers out into the night. The rain is falling in sheets and it's pitch black.

Poor animal, she thinks, imagining it out there, soaked through, peering in, dreaming of a spot on the sofa next to the fire. Had it been a cat? A dog? A fox? It's impossible to know.

She adds a log to the fire and pulls a blanket around her shoulders.

The drumming of the rain intensifies abruptly, sending a ripple of excitement through her body that feels like some primitive reaction to the terrifying power of the elements.

She picks up her phone and scans the messages and the call list. The last two entries are both 'missed' calls from Harry.

She's going to have to pick up at some point, and if she's honest, she does want to hear his voice. But how to go about it – how specifically to talk about her situation without sounding like a damsel in distress? And how to talk about anything without discussing the elephant in the room? The elephant in Harry's bed.

Perhaps he isn't phoning for her news at all. Perhaps he has news of his own: that he wants a divorce so that he can marry his elephant woman.

She sighs and puts the phone down, and only as she does this does she consciously realise something she has seen outside.

She jumps up and returns to the window, and yes, she's right: no more snow! The rain has washed it all away.

Thank God for that! she thinks, marvelling again at how basic her joys and triumphs are becoming. 'Electricity, good!' she grunts. 'Big snow, gone! Also good!'

Now they'll have no choice but to sort out the bloody car.

* * *

It continues to rain for two days solid. Other than to bring in a few fresh logs, she doesn't step outside. Without a car, without a sou'wester, how could she?

So she finishes the novel (not bad, but a lazy ending) and starts a new one she struggles to get into. She concocts weird meals from the diminishing contents of her cupboards, and phones and hassles the car hire company to no avail. They're waiting, as far as she can understand, on news from Renault, and Renault are waiting for the tow truck to bring them the car, and the tow truck people appear to be waiting for the rain to stop. *Imagine if the British waited for the rain to stop*, she thinks. *We'd never get anything done at all.*

On the third morning after Jill's departure she wakes to drizzle, and the forecast promises that even this will give way to sunshine by mid-afternoon.

Deciding to kill two birds with one stone – bird one: pushing through the boredom of this final wet morning, and bird two: getting the damned call out of the way – not to mention her difficult-to-admit-but-nevertheless-true bird three: the desire to talk to her husband, she braces herself and initiates the call. *Hello, Harry, Hallo, Haz*, or plain *Hello*? How chummy does she want to be?

Wendy: Hello, Harry.

<That sounded colder than she'd intended. The use of his

name for some reason sounded like reproach. Oh well... Too late to change that now.>

Harry: Ahh! Finally! I was beginning to think you were ghosting me.

W: Ha! Not really my generation's thing, ghosting. You've been spending too much time with the kids.

H: Yeah. Well, that was meant to be a joke...

W: Yes, I got that. My sense of humour's not entirely gone yet.

<She's trying to be friendly, honest she is, but it's coming out all wrong. Wow, this is tense!>

H: Anyway, jokes aside, I have been a bit worried. We all have.

W: Well, still here. As you can see. Or rather, hear.

H: We can FaceTime if you prefer.

W: No, this is fine. Otherwise I'd have to put on an evening gown and tiara, wouldn't I?

H: Oh, are you starkers, then?

W: I am! Absolutely starkers.

H: Good. I like it. So, how's it going? How is La Belle France?

W: Oh, you know. Pretty *belle*.

H: Clever.

W: I'm sorry?

H: Pretty. *Belle*. Two languages, one meaning.

W: Oh, yes. I'm afraid that was entirely unintentional.

H: Is the place nice? Was it a good choice?

W: Um, yes, it's lovely. The, er, off-grid thing is more challenging than I anticipated.

H: You mean, you're missing Facebook? I saw you haven't been on much.

W: Oh, no. No, internet's fine actually. But if I use too much electricity, everything goes off. And then I have to wait for the bloody battery to charge up again. It's all solar panels and what-have-you.

H: Wow. You go, eco-warrior!

W: Yes, eco-warrior despite myself. I didn't think enough about what the term *off grid* implied, unfortunately.

H: Still, no lack of sunshine down your way, so I'm sure you're fine.

W: <laughs> You'd be surprised. It snowed for two days. And now it's been raining for three.

H: Really? Funny cos it's been lovely here.

W: Yes, so I've heard.

H: So you're enjoying yourself, anyway. That's great!

<Wendy frowns momentarily at her phone. She retraces the conversation to work out whether she has at any point intimated that she's enjoying herself, but no, she's quite sure she hasn't. It's funny when people tell you so clearly what they want to hear, isn't it? And surprisingly hard to deliver up anything other than what they're asking for.>

H: You *are* enjoying yourself, aren't you?

W: Yes, it's fine. I've been going for walks and reading lots. Jill came down for a few days which was a fun interlude. We went dancing.

H: Well, good for you. Like I say, it's great that you're enjoying yourself.

W: So, how's everything at your end?

H: Oh, you know, same old, same old. I'm feeling fairly jealous of your adventure to be honest. Maidstone or the south of France? Hum. Let me see.

W: ~~Well you could have come. I did invite you and you said no.~~ And the kids?

H: Oh, Todd is enjoying uni. D'you remember how worried he was about it being the same as school?

W: I do.

H: Well, it's not, obviously. So he's happy. He's not telling me much, but I think it's wall-to-wall parties to be honest. Standard first term stuff. And Fiona's good.

W: And you? How are you, Haz?

H: Oh you know... snowed under with assessments. The usual.

<Wendy licks her lips. How to ask the burning question? What combination of words might she be able to get through in their entirety? Best, perhaps, to aim for simplicity.>

W: Are you...?

<Her throat seizes up before she can say, *Seeing anyone?*>

H: Am I ...?

W: Are you OK, Haz? I mean, really OK?

H: Yes. Like I said. We're all fine.

W: And is there anything... you'd... you know... like to discuss with me? Anything you want to tell me?

H: ...

W: Harry?

H: Yes, still here. Um, I mean, well, no, not really. It's a bit early for that, don't you think?

W: Is it?

H: Yes. I mean, you're away for six months, aren't you? And that's fine. That's good. I'm sure we'll see things more clearly by spring.

W: Right. Sure. OK, then.

H: But it's good to hear your voice. Seriously. It is.

W: And it's good to hear yours, too.

H: Oh, there's someone at the door.

W: Yes, I heard the bell. You expecting someone? ~~New girlfriend maybe?~~

H: Nah, probably just a delivery. More fast fashion that Fiona's ordered. She's absolutely addicted. Most of it doesn't even fit so she ends up giving it to her mates. No wonder they love her.

W: Those cheap sites are terrible for the planet, you know. It's all made by slave labour in sweatshops and then shipped halfway around the world.

H: I know and I'm fairly sure she knows it, too. But all her mates are into it. Hopefully it's just a phase.

W: Which bit? The not giving a shit about human rights, or not giving a shit about the planet?

H: Hello, thanks. Um, do I need to sign? No? OK, thanks. Yes, you, too.

H: See! I told you. More rubbish direct from China.

W: Personally I blame the parents.

H: Ha! Yes! Good one. Look, I'll talk to her about it. I'll tell her again. I'll tie her to a chair and make her watch a documentary about Chinese slave labour if you want.

W: I wasn't saying I blame you, Harry. It was just a throwaway line.

H: Sure. It always is. Anyway, gotta go. You know how it is. Papers to mark.

W: I do. And I really was trying to be funny, Haz. Plus I said parents plural. So I was including myself in that.

H: Hey, relax. It's fine. But I really do have to go.

W: OK, well, you have a good one, OK?

H: I expect yours will be wa-a-ay better than mine to be honest. But anyway... talk soon. Love ya, miss ya, merely getting by without ya! *Ciao ciao.* <click>

She stares at the phone in her hands and notes the way it's trembling, then places it on the coffee table. Is she shaking because she still loves him or because she hates him? Is she shaking because the call was too much for her or too little? Is it possible that she's shaking because all of these things are simultaneously true yet entirely contradictory?

She checks her watch. It's only eleven and she could do with a drink. Eleven is a bit early but after all, it's midday in England, isn't it? No, it's the other way around. It's ten in England and ten is definitely too early. But she could have an early lunch, she supposes. That would make it OK, wouldn't it?

She heats up the last of the soup, makes a terrible toasted cheese sandwich with the last of the bread and the waxy rind of the cheese and pours herself a vat of red wine to compensate.

Everything is awful. She's been avoiding acknowledging the fact but there it is. Everything truly is awful.

She finishes her lunch and empties the remainder of the bottle into her glass telling herself it's Dutch courage for today's battle with the car hire company and that as soon as her glass is empty she'll place the call.

When she does, miracle of miracles, she's connected straight to Letitia, whose English is nigh-on perfect.

So she re-tells Letitia her story. She has had to do this every time, but at least she's getting better at it. Her tale is becoming more succinct but also increasingly dramatic.

'Now I'm stuck in the middle of nowhere with no food and no way to get to a supermarket,' she says, summing up. 'So, I really need this to be sorted out today otherwise I'm literally going to starve to death.'

'Yes... hang on... I've just got access to your file. Sorry the system is so slow today. Computers! You are calling yesterday, I see. And the day before?'

'Well, yes. I'm calling every day. I need my car back!'

'I wasn't...' Letitia says. 'I was checking I have the right file. And I'm sure we are doing everything we can to get this car back to you, but after an accident there are procedures which must be followed.'

'Well, maybe you could follow your procedures more quickly.'

'You wouldn't want me to give you back a dangerous car, would you?'

'No. I want you to give me a drivable car. With you being a car hire company, that surely can't be beyond the realms of possibility, can it?'

'I see you were simply crashing the car.'

'It slid off the road. It's called an accident.'

'Yes. An accident while you were driving.'

'And?'

'I'm sorry?'

'I don't see what you're trying to imply?'

'I am not trying to imply anything.'

'It sounds like you're saying it was my fault.'

'Oh! It was not your fault? I did not know this. Did you turn to avoid another car? Or a person? Or an animal? Because that doesn't seem to be mentioned here in the report.'

'No. You know full well there wasn't anyone else involved.'

'Oh, sorry. I misunderstood. English isn't my first language as you can tell. So it was your fault, or it wasn't? I am trying to understand.'

'It was the snow's fault.'

'Ah. Well, perhaps you can be a little more patient, then.'

'Patient?'

'Yes. You rented a car. And then unfortunately, you crash this car. So perhaps you can be more patient with the people who have to sort out your mess.'

From this point the call spirals out of control, and Wendy finds herself powerless to avoid its slow slide towards the apocalypse.

She tries to keep things calm and polite – she really does – but she simply isn't able to do so. Instead she hears her mouth saying words – rude words that she truly had no intention of saying. She feels like that girl in *The Exorcist* watching in surprise as green bile spews from her mouth. Her 'Dutch courage' is no doubt partly responsible.

Eventually, once Letitia has had her fill and ended the call, Wendy drops her phone onto the sofa to avoid hurling it across the room. So she does have some self-control after all. She pounds a cushion instead, while releasing a wild, animal scream of frustration.

Next, she goes to the cupboard for more wine only to discover that she's out. She gasps at this fresh misery. How can that even be possible? She'd bought twelve bottles before Jill arrived. Twelve! She could get seriously angry with Jill if she decided to let her thoughts run that way. And she will, she reckons, at some point, let them run exactly that way. Just not right now.

Instead of wine, she lights a cigarette. Yes, she's smoking indoors! *Bugger them!* she thinks. *Bugger them all.*

Her phone rings with a call from an unknown number, so she pulls a face and, her heart only just slowing from her argument with Letitia, she answers, but this time it's Letitia's boss on the line. He proceeds to scold her for being rude to his staff, which sends her blood pressure through the roof, but goes on to inform her – luckily before she starts spouting bile again – that the car will be towed in the morning.

* * *

The good weather holds, so the next day Wendy pulls on still-damp trainers and her duffle coat before heading out for a walk. She can hear Harry's voice telling her what a good idea this is and how proud she'll feel once she's done it.

First, she walks the two miles down the road to the car, or rather where the car used to be, because (oh joy!) at 10 a.m. it's already gone.

Relieved, she returns halfway home before taking the hiking trail back up to the radar. The view from beneath it this morning is stunning; the air after the rain is as clear and crisp as she has ever known.

Once she has taken the obligatory photo – blue, blue everywhere – she heads back, and then continues on past home until she reaches the bakery where she buys bread, cheese and wine, plus eggs and potatoes to make a tortilla.

When she goes to the counter to pay, the woman says something long, complex and utterly incomprehensible to her in French.

'*Je suis désolée,*' she manages to reply. '*Plus lent, s'il vous plait ?*'

'Very good!' the woman says. 'That was almost perfect! But you must say *lentement* – more slowly. *Plus lent* means "more slow".'

'*Merci. Je... veux... apprendre ?*' Wendy says hesitantly.

'Also perfect. Is good you want to learn. So what I say before is, if you need other thing, you must say, because I have many thing out back...' She points as she says this to the rear door. 'I know you have no car, so...'

'Oh! You know about that?' Wendy laughs.

'In a small town like this, everyone knows everything,' the woman says, smiling gently. 'It was Thursday night, yes? In the snow?'

'Yes. You really do know everything.'

'Were you ...?' the woman asks, making a strange gesture by raising her circled fingers to her nose.

'I'm sorry... Was I ...?' Wendy repeats, mimicking the gesture.

'This means "alcohol",' the woman says, making the gesture again. 'Too much alcohol.'

'Oh, no!' Wendy says, and she can feel she's blushing. 'No, I never drink and drive.'

'You English are so good,' the baker says. 'Round here, on the weekend, they are terrible.'

'But anyway,' Wendy says, deciding to forcefully change the subject before she has to think too hard about the fact that she's lying, '... no car. Which is why I can't buy more today.' She turns her shoulder towards the woman so she can see her tiny rucksack. 'I can't *carry* more.'

'Ahh, but Manon, she can deliver you.'

'Manon, the post lady?'

'Yes. She do this for all the old people. The persons who have car no more. So if you want to buy more, is OK. Manon will bring to you tomorrow.'

'Oh!' Wendy says. 'OK... Um, that would be brilliant. At least until I get my car back.'

'So please!' the baker says, gesturing at the interior of her shop. 'Help yourself.'

Wendy circles the bakery once again, adding tins of tomatoes and jars of sauce and packs of pasta from the mini grocery area plus (just to make the delivery worthwhile) another four bottles of wine.

She pays the surprisingly expensive bill with her credit card and heads home with only the bread, cheese and a bottle of wine.

What a perfect day, she thinks, as she walks. Perhaps she will get those French lessons after all!

* * *

Her delivery arrives the following morning, just after eleven. She's been feeling bored waiting, and is about to pour a glass of wine, thinking once again about the fact that eleven really is a bit too early, when she hears the van drive up.

Despite telling herself she's being silly and that she has the right to do exactly what she wants whenever she wants, she hides the open bottle in a cupboard and heads outside to meet Manon.

'Bonjour !' she announces as she takes the box from the girl's outstretched arms, then, 'Oh, gosh, wow! That's heavy!'

'It is very 'eavy,' Manon says with meaning. 'Is the wine. You buy more wine than food, I think!'

'I know!' Wendy says, forcing a laugh. 'It looks bad, huh?'

She hadn't thought about this aspect of getting her food delivered — the fact that the baker, the post lady and, by extrapolation, the entire village will know all about her shopping choices.

'As long as it is not for this day, is OK,' Manon jokes. *If only she knew*, Wendy thinks forcing another smile.

Declining the offer of a drink but promising to return after work for some 'English conversation', Manon skips off to continue her postal round.

As she drives away, Wendy returns indoors with the shopping, feeling surprisingly excited about the prospect of Manon's return that evening. As she puts everything away she asks herself why and decides that it's probably normal considering how lonely she's been feeling these last few days. But she also recognises that there's something about Manon that reminds her of Fiona – something universal about this new generation of young women, a bit like seeing Fiona in an alternate universe – Fiona without all the baggage of home. *Oh, Fiona!* she thinks. No matter what's going on in your relationship with your kids there's still always so much love.

Instead of pouring wine she finds herself making tea, and once she's gulped this down she pulls on trainers for a walk before lunch. Manon's comment about the wine, which was totally something Fiona might have said, has left her feeling guilty. Actually, it's not so much guilt, she decides as she walks, more a momentary desire to make better choices.

By the time she has reached the car park and started the climb to her alien spaceship she's feeling thoroughly pleased with herself. The day is really quite breathtaking and it feels wonderful to be back out in the fresh air.

And she's not the only one making the most of the sunshine this morning. She crosses paths with four people walking their dogs and a group of retirement-age female hikers. Everyone smiles and says *'bonjour'*, as enthused as she is with the returning joy of sunshine.

* * *

Manon arrives at half past four, just as the sun is dropping behind the hill.

Though lighting fires and switching on lights signals 'aperitif time' to Wendy, and despite the reputation the French have for being constant wine-guzzlers, Manon opts for coffee.

'Well, as long as you don't mind me...' Wendy says, pouring herself a glass. She doesn't wait for Manon to reply. A little social lubricant for her first lesson is non-negotiable.

'So we speak French today, or English?' Manon asks, sipping her coffee.

'Um both, hopefully. Though I think the English is going to be easier.'

'OK, so English first, then French,' Manon says.

Despite her excellent English, it turns out that Manon is shy about her accent, so it is Wendy who does all the talking, answering Manon's short probing questions: why did she come here? Why France? Does she have family in England? Why did she not bring them with her?

And Wendy, perhaps because she likes her, or perhaps because of the wine, but most likely because she doesn't really know her at all, finds herself telling Manon everything. And the telling feels good, like a great therapeutic unburdening.

She explains about moving out during Covid, and living at Jill's, and about falling out with her children and how she feels they have sided with their father. She even tells Manon about her suspicion that Harry is having an affair and it is Manon's reaction to this which is perhaps the most surprising.

'All men have affair,' she declares, sounding ultra sure of herself. 'Many women, too, but definitely most men. If they don't have affair, they leave.'

'Really?' Wendy asks.

'Really. My father has many. At least four. Ones we know...'

'And you think most French men are like this?'

'Everyone is like this,' Manon says with the certainty of youth.

Wendy sips her wine as she ponders the subject for a moment. She's wondering whether French people have more affairs than the English, or if they're simply more honest about it.

'You know, I don't really think that's true,' Wendy says once she has gathered her thoughts. 'Not in England, anyway. Not all men are bastards. They really aren't.'

Manon laughs at this. 'I don't say they are bastard,' she says. 'I say they have affair. It is you who thinks this makes them bastard.'

'Bastards,' Wendy says, because Manon keeps asking her to correct her. 'It's a plural, so it takes an "S" at the end. But I don't agree. I really don't.'

Manon shrugs. 'It is, I think, how you say... the nature.'

'Human nature?' Wendy offers.

'Yes, this.'

The French session, predictably, does not go so well.

Wendy barely manages to ask Manon intelligible questions and understands nothing of the girl's answers. Once or twice Manon repeats what she has said slowly enough that Wendy is able to make out the odd word here or there – just enough to understand that the girl is indeed answering her question – but even then, the bulk of whatever she's saying remains lost in a stream of random-sounding vowels.

'Do not worry,' Manon tells her as she's leaving. 'It will get better.'

'God,' Wendy says. 'I hope so!'

Only once she's alone does the implication of Manon's reassurance hit Wendy. 'It will get better' means they'll be doing this again, a thought which lifts her spirits to the point she finds herself almost buzzing.

For the first time in a week, she heads to Facebook.

Just had my first ever French lesson in France, she posts. *The teacher says I can only get better. Not sure how to take that, haha* :-)

And then she refills her glass, takes a sip, and thinks about the fact that she came here to get away from other people, to be alone and to reflect. Yet what's truly making her happy is human connection. It's a conundrum that for the moment she can't resolve.

NINE

A NICE LITTLE LIFE

Wendy has a new routine, or rather two alternating routines.

Every morning, she rises, has breakfast in the glorious sunshine, and then hikes up to the radar where she snaps her daily photo.

Afterwards, she walks back home before, on Tuesdays, Thursdays and Saturdays, continuing as far as the bakery where she buys food for the next two days. She's careful to make sure she orders enough to justify a delivery but not so much that she ever has to skip one. After all, it's the delivery of these orders on Mondays, Wednesdays and Fridays that guarantee her French lessons.

The walking is making her feel fitter – she can sense it as she marches up the hill each day – and the French conversation sessions are definitely improving her language skills. She can negotiate most aspects of her bakery visit now without ever resorting to English.

It's a little life – she's aware that there's nothing ground-breaking here – but it's a nice life, too. It feels good, it feels healthy, and learning something new is fun. Mentally, she's in the best place she's known since she came here. In fact, she feels so happy with her new routine that on some days she forgets entirely to hassle the car hire company. As they have now assured her that the period during which she is car-less will be refunded, the whole situation feels like something of a win.

She really does like young Manon. There's something about the fact that they have to talk to each other every other day which has led to the strange situation where she feels like Manon is one of the people she knows best on the planet.

She knows that Manon's father is also a postman, for example, and that he makes a wicked cheese soufflé and has a new girlfriend called Louise, who is way too young for him. She knows that Manon's brother is a drug addict who favours 'speedballs' which are a potent mix of cocaine and heroin, and that Manon worries every time the phone rings with an unknown number that it's a hospital phoning to tell her he's dead. She knows that Manon's mother died years ago (though the cause seems to be a taboo subject) and that Manon loved her deeply and misses her so much that occasionally she finds herself crying about it even now. Music-wise, Manon (surprisingly) favours retro Britpop seemingly because that's what her mother liked to listen to, and she has revealed she has a girlfriend called Celine, who lives in Draguignan and who Manon is trying to encourage to brush her teeth more often!

By December Wendy reckons Manon knows her quite well, too, because Wendy has told her how it felt being pregnant, what it was like giving birth, and how she sometimes has hot flushes she fears are the beginning of the menopause.

It strikes Wendy, one evening after Manon has left, that in some ways they know each other better than she and Harry do these days. The thought is absurd, because, of course, she and Haz know each other in ways that she and Manon simply never could.

But it's also true that she really does know things about Manon that she has never known about Harry, things she doesn't even know about her kids. She and Manon, for example, have spoken at length about their first sexual experiences, and these are conversations that she doesn't think anyone really has with their husband, let alone their own children.

Could the answer to her relationship problems with Harry be nothing more, nothing less, than proper in-depth conversation? Certainly, as far as she can see, most of the couples she knows would benefit far more from an hour a day talking to each other than the three hours of Netflix they're getting by on.

* * *

On 4 December, Manon arrives far later than usual – just before 7 p.m. As it's been dark for almost two hours, she finds Wendy firmly ensconced in aperitif time.

'*Vous arrivez plus tard, aujourd'hui,*' Wendy tells her, feeling proud of her perfectly constructed phrase even though she has had the last hour to think about it.

'I know!' Manon says. 'I start work very late this morning. My brother. Big problems. Again!' She proceeds to explain how her father phoned her first thing to tell her he's thinking of paying for a private detox clinic for her brother. The clinic being incredibly expensive, and her brother having already gone through three previous detox sessions only to start using almost the second he got out each time, the discussion had gone on for some time.

'I start very late. So, I end very late,' Manon explains.

'And what did you decide?' Wendy asks. 'About your brother?'

Manon shrugs. 'Oh, Papa will pay. He always pay,' she says. 'Because if he don't pay...'

'If he doesn't pay,' Wendy corrects.

'Yeah, if he doesn't pay, and Bruno is...' she makes a brutal slashing gesture across her throat here, 'then... whose fault can it be? The *culpabilité*... the guilt? For Papa will be terrible.'

'I'm sorry,' Wendy tells her, genuinely touched by the girl's emotion every time she talks about her brother. 'That must be very difficult for you all.'

'It is,' Manon says. 'But it is a family problem, so we are used to this.'

'But I'm glad you feel you can share it with me.'

Manon laughs. 'I share *everything* with you. So you, now. What do you want to talk about, in French?'

'Oh, gosh, I honestly have no idea today. Nothing happens in my life except seeing you and going to the bakery.'

'In French,' Manon insists.

'*Vraiment, je ne sais pas,*' Wendy says.

'*Vous parlez de quoi d'habitude, en Angleterre ?*'

'What do the English talk about?'

'*Oui. Si vous voulez...*'

'The weather mainly,' Wendy says. '*Le météo.*'

'*La météo !*' Manon corrects. 'The weather is a girl. This is probably why she is so unpredictable! *Est-ce que vous avez vu qu'il va neiger en fin de semaine ?*'

'*Neiger ?*' Wendy repeats. 'It's going to snow?'

'*Oui. Beaucoup.*'

'Oh my God!' Wendy says, her eyes widening. 'When?'

'*En français !*'

Wendy laughs. '*Oh, mon Dieu !*' she says, laughing at how much funnier it sounds in French. '*Quand ?*'

'You see,' Manon says. 'You can when you try.'

Slowly, clumsily, they manage to have Wendy's first ever in-depth conversation about the weather in French, during which she learns that heavy snow is forecast for the end of the week along with freezing temperatures. Apparently, French forecasters don't predict the actual depth of the snowfall, but there will be a lot, Manon insists. Three or four days of snowfall, at the very least.

Wendy should get plenty of food and wood in, Manon tells her. And she should probably see if she can get her car back before the bad weather hits. It all sounds a bit worrying, especially considering the chaos the last snowfall caused, yet she feels far more excited than scared. Isn't this why one rents a remote mountain cabin, after all?

As Manon is leaving, she calls for Wendy to join her behind the house and points to a pile of bottle-filled crates. 'Do you want me to take these, before the snow?' she asks.

'Oh, to the bottle bank?' Wendy asks. 'Yes, please! That would be great. It's so far from here that without a car, I just haven't been able to do it.'

But as they load the crates one by one into Manon's little Panda, Wendy starts to feel embarrassed and then – when they have to fold the rear seats down – mortified by the sheer volume of empties. Though some of these are jars that once contained jam or coffee or pasta sauce, the vast majority are indisputably empty wine bottles.

'I'm so sorry,' she says repeatedly as they load the car. 'Do you want me to come with you to put them in the bottle bank?'

'No,' Manon says, with a sigh. 'It's fine.' But Wendy sees a cloud crossing Manon's features, and for the first time since Wendy has known her, she doesn't look fine at all.

'I am used to this,' Manon tells her as they load the final crate into the car and slam the hatch. 'I do it for my brother all the time. And before that I do it for my mother. Like I say, is a family problem.'

Todd: Hello? Mum?
    Wendy: Hello, my lovely boy.

T: Eek, you sounded a bit Welsh there. Is everything all right?

W: Um, yes, sweetheart. Of course it is. Why wouldn't it be?

T: Oh, OK. Just... you know... For some reason I thought it was Dad.

W: You thought I was Dad? Doesn't my number—

T: No, I thought you were phoning because something had happened *to* Dad. You don't tend to phone out of the blue.

W: Sometimes I do. I may not have done so for a while, I suppose, but...

T: Fine. Whatever. Anyway, I'm glad. I was worried there for a moment. So how are things in France? I take it you're still there?

W: Yes. And it's lovely, thanks. We're getting ready for heavy snowfall, actually. So that's exciting.

T: Snow, huh? Will you be able to ski?

W: Ha! You know I can't ski, honey.

T: True. Shame, though. Anyway, it's wet and miserable here. So you're not missing much.

W: Your father said it's been lovely.

T: Oh, you two *are* talking, are you? Good. And, yeah, it was lovely until Sunday. But now it's chucking it down so we're holed up bingeing on *The Boys*. Have you seen it? It's excellent. Violent, but excellent.

W: No, I can't say I have. And when you say we... *we're* holed up...?

T: Oh, just me, my flatmate Matti, and Amanda, of course.

W: Amanda... Is she your girlfriend?

T: Yep.

W: Is this the same one as in the um... ~~Christmas~~ photo? The one where you were all eating cake?

T: Yes, Mum, it's the *same one*.

W: I didn't mean anything, Todd. I've never met her, that's all.

T: Well, you will one day. And you'll like her. She's gorgeous.

W: Good, well, I look forward to it.

T: Are you ...? Um... <coughs> Are you, um, coming back for any, you know, visits? Or are you staying out there until May or whenever?

W: April. I'm out here till April.

T: Right. Yeah, I knew that. Course I did.

<She tries not to think about the question they both know Todd almost asked, namely: are you coming home for Christmas? If she starts thinking about that one, she won't be able to think about anything else.>

T: So are you phoning for a particular reason, or...?

W: No, not really. I was just talking to a friend about—

T: You have a friend?

W: I... Um... Yes.

T: Sorry. I mean, in France. You have a friend in France?

W: I do. She's the post lady. And she was telling me about her brother, and it made me think of you and Fifi. I miss you. I miss you both.

T: Did you phone my evil sister as well, then? I haven't heard from her in ages.

W: No, only you. I spoke with Fiona a few days ago, though. She seems fine.

T: <Snort>

W: Sorry, why is that funny? Did I miss something?

T: Oh, just, you know... Fiona being *fine*.

W: Why do you say that? Isn't she fine?

T: Oh, she's probably fine as far as she's concerned. She always is. It's just to everyone else she's a bloody nightmare.

W: Ahhh! Sibling rivalry.

T: Nah, just observing a family trait, I think.

W: What family trait would that be, then?

T: Being a nightmare, maybe?

W: Haha. Very funny, Todd. So, what have you been up to? Tell me.

By the time she hangs up, she has learned that Matti drove them all to Margate at the weekend, where they had fish and chips and played the slot machines. Margate has quite a 'cool vibe' according to Todd, something she pretended to be flabbergasted about even though she's heard this repeatedly over the last few years. Kids love being reassured that their parents are out of touch, and it's hard not to play up to that.

Other than the Margate escapade, Todd's news had been rather sparse, so sparse in fact that she'd launched into a brief, ill-advised monologue about the honest conversations she'd been having with her French teacher and how nice it would be if they could communicate more openly as a family.

Todd had laughed at this idea. 'Yeah, well, you're not the postie's mum, are you? Otherwise she wouldn't tell you anything at all.'

Wendy steps outside and lights a cigarette. The evening is unusually warm and it's difficult to imagine that snow is on its way.

She blows the smoke into the breeze and retraces fragments of the conversation in her mind. Todd's 'joke' about their nightmare family trait – had that been a dig at her, or merely self-mockery? She suspects it was the former, but she's glad she managed to resist reacting. And Fiona... Does Todd really resent her? Or is that, too, just habit?

And finally, Christmas. God, there it is! Amazingly she has managed to completely avoid thinking about Christmas until now, and for a moment there she still believed she could blank out Todd's almost-mention of it as well. But no, here it is, thundering towards her like a big red steamroller.

Is she strong enough to survive Christmas here alone? Or will it derail her fragile, newly found sense of wellbeing?

An image flashes through her mind's eye, a terrible scene in which she's here, alone, drunk and weeping in front of some dreadful Christmas movie.

Still, she tells herself, attempting to battle the image into submission. She's done it before, hasn't she? But that defence quickly crumbles because the truth is that no, she hasn't. Even last Christmas Eve she'd been with Jill and Bern. And on Christmas Day proper, even with Jill and Bern next door, the idea of being home alone had been so horrific she'd preferred to stay on at work.

At that moment, at the precise instant she feels her resolve might crumble entirely, something catches her eye – a movement on the far side of the cabin. A rat? A rabbit? No, a cat!

She crouches down and makes kissing noises by sucking through her teeth, but instead of being drawn to her as she'd hoped, the cat is surprised by the noise – shocked by her presence. In a single leap it bounds out of sight behind the cabin.

She remembers the face she saw peering in a few days ago and scans the horizon as she wonders how far away the nearest houses are.

A stray! she decides, feeling a little burst of empathy and wonder and, yes, *need* for this cold little animal.

She creeps to the far side of the cabin and peers around the corner but the cat is nowhere to be seen.

'Silly cat,' she murmurs. 'You could have got yourself some tuna there.'

But perhaps it will come back. She decides to put food out just in case.

* * *

The next morning there's not a cloud in the sky and definitely no sign of snow. She wonders if the forecasters have got it wrong.

Before heading out for her walk she phones the rental company, who instruct her to check her emails where she discovers (happily) that they've refunded her half of the cost of her rental, and (less happily) that they've cancelled the remainder of her contract. When she phones them to ask why, they explain in perfectly understandable franglais that as far as they're concerned she's become uninsurable. The only smidgin of good news is that she can 'probably' still rent from someone else.

By the time she hangs up, she's shaking with frustration, but she decides she'll deal with the fallout after her walk, once she's calmed down. She stomps out of the cabin, along the road, and up the hill virtually without noticing her surroundings. It's only when she gets to the top that she reconnects to her environment, to the beauty of right here, right now...

The air is crisp and bracing. Occasional gusts of wind make her cheeks smart, but when the wind drops, the sun is strong enough to prickle her skin. As she raises her phone to take the photo she spots a distant bank of cloud to the west. She wonders if they're snow clouds.

After her walk, the baker greets her with more talk of snow. Perhaps obsessing about the weather isn't a purely British thing after all.

'You must buy more,' the woman tells her, a profiteering glint in the eye. 'Sometimes, when it snows a lot, we 'ave to close. Sometimes even Manon cannot deliver. You do not want to be 'ungry.'

So she fills three boxes instead of the usual one. In go bottles of wine and long-life bread; olives, cheese and butter. In go carrots and leeks and potatoes; biscuits and peanuts and chocolate. And then, because there's still a little space left in box three, another four bottles of wine and two tins of cat food.

'You 'ave a cat?' the baker asks, as she rings up the purchases.

'No. Just a stray I want to feed,' she says, wondering if the cat found the tuna. After the business with the car hire company this morning, she forgot to check.

'A stay...?' the woman repeats uncomprehendingly.

'Stray,' she says, with an 'R'. 'A lost cat. A wild cat. *Sauvage.*'

'Ahh,' the baker says. 'You must take care. If you feed them they are forever. This is 'ow we get our cat! But we do love 'er.'

* * *

Back home, the bowl she put out is empty, though whether it was the cat or birds or some other wild animal that ate the tuna, she can't possibly know. But she moves the bowl so that it's within view and refills it just in case.

Though the temperature is too low for her to be able to sit comfortably outside, the winter sunshine warms the cabin nicely, so she lounges indoors in the sun alternating between reading and doom-scrolling the news on her phone.

She also fires off a few long overdue texts, to Jill, Sue and Harry.

She's feeling uncharacteristically forgive-and-forgetty this afternoon, no doubt something to do with the warmth of the winter sunshine. She considers phoning Harry at one point, but ultimately decides on a more measured, reflective approach. She'll write him an old-fashioned letter instead.

But despite her excellent mood, once she's armed herself with pen and paper, she stalls after the opening line. She still doesn't know what she wants from Harry. How could she possibly know what to say?

At sunset, as the light is fading, she spots the cat creeping up to the bowl, moving in slow motion as though he believes this makes him invisible. She can see this time that he's a long-haired variety gone wild. His fur is dirty and matted.

She resists the urge to rush outside to befriend (and brush) him and instead moves towards the window using the same slow-motion strategy as the cat. After sixty seconds of eye contact he seems to accept the deal, namely that in exchange for the food this strange woman is going to watch him eat.

'You see, we'll be friends eventually,' Wendy says, once the cat starts to dig in. She's surprised when the cat pauses and stares at her, *glares* at her, in fact. He can clearly hear through the double glazing. 'OK, OK, I'll be quiet,' she whispers, and she could swear the cat gives her a nod of approval before gulping down the rest of his meal.

Sue: Good morning, France. *Ici Londres !*

Wendy: Hello, you.

S: I've been meaning to call you for ages.

W: ~~So what happened?~~ Me, too.

S: Anyway, thanks for texting me.

W: No worries. I wanted an update from the old country.

S: How's it going down there? That's what I want to know. You've been in France, what? A month?

W: Yeah. A bit more actually. And it's nice. Remote. Very wild. Tiny village. Typical French cliché, really.

S: Sounds heavenly.

W: Yeah... Mostly it is.

S: Where are you again?

W: ~~I can't believe you don't remember this! Do you not listen, or are you feigning disinterest to drive me insane?~~ Um, down south. An hour north of Nice. In the mountains.

S: That's it! I knew it was somewhere around there. So how are you spending your days?

W: Oh, you know... reading, walking, learning French...,

S: God, I'm so jealous.

W: It's a bit lonely sometimes. But mostly I'm loving it.

S: And Harry?

W: What about him?

S: Is he...? He's not with you, is he?

W: You *know* he isn't, Sue. He's at home. With the kids.

S: But Todd's at university now, isn't he?

W: Yeah, so with kids plural during holidays. And just Fiona during term time.

S: Are things between you still... difficult?

W: Um. Well, yeah, they are a bit. But I think the break is doing us good.

S: Still working through it all, then?

W: Something like that. ~~Please stop talking about Harry.~~ And you two?

S: Oh, we're great. Perfect. Brilliant. And all thanks to you, of course!

W: ~~Introducing you to each other is my one great regret.~~ Ha!

S: No, seriously. I often think I should thank you more for introducing us. It changed everything really. D'you remember how miserable I was single?

W: ~~And how happy I was?~~ Well, you're welcome. So what's new otherwise?

S: Oh, work's terrible. Not that that's new at all.

W: More cutbacks?

S: Endless cutbacks. Child protection is so underfunded that I doubt we're protecting anyone at all.

W: Fifi's convinced they'll get massacred at the next election.

S: Well, everyone in social services is hoping they will. Um, Neil's fine, in case you were wondering but didn't dare ask.

W: ...Well, good. I'm glad.

S: Can I...?

W: Yes?

S: I... um... I mean, I know this is difficult and everything...

W: ~~Oh God, no! Please don't go there, Sue.~~ What is, honey?

S: But Neil won't talk about it either...

W: Ha, the list of things my brother won't talk about...

S: So I'm going to come right out and ask you, I think.

W: ~~Please don't.~~ OK...

S: Did you two fall out about something specific?

W: Oh.

S: I mean, you must have. I know you must have. But I really don't know what it was.

W: ~~Perhaps leaving Mum's end of life care to me and phoning twice between the moment she was diagnosed and when she died might have something to do with it.~~ No, me neither really. I mean, sometimes you drift apart, don't you? Busy with our lives and everything.

S: Really?

W: Yeah. Yes, I think so.

S: So it wasn't anything to do with me? Because I sometimes feel like it was.

W: ~~Well, my brother stopped phoning me, visiting me and in general giving a shit about me when he met you. And you didn't seem to care too much about our mother dying either.~~ No, honestly, Sue. We're good.

S: He was going through a lot when your mum died, you know. I'm sure he'll tell you all about it one day.

W: ~~Was he?! I can't wait for that conversation. I can finally tell him about Mum's final months and exactly what the two of us were going through.~~ Yeah. I'm sure. We all have so much going on, don't we?

S: But we're definitely OK, you and me?

W: I'm phoning you, aren't I?

S: Well, I'm actually phoning you. <laughs>

W: OK, well, texting you or whatever.

S: Yes.

W: Oh, gosh, I've got to go, Sue. My French teacher's coming up the path. She's early.

S: French lessons! Get you! Well, I'm glad we had this chat. Call me soon, OK? Don't leave it so long next time.

W: Yes, I will. Got to go.

S: I miss you.

W: *Moi aussi ! Au revoir !*

* * *

Her French teacher is *not* coming up the path – not at 11 a.m. That, obviously, was a lie. *Why* did she lie? Well, because all the lies she was having to tell to stay in the conversation were making her uncomfortable.

Her relationship with Sue has become so difficult to navigate that every time she does speak to her she remembers why she so rarely does so. Without honesty, it's become completely hollowed out. But if she were to tell Sue the truth about how she feels she knows she'd never speak to her again. Sometimes she wonders if this wouldn't actually be better.

* * *

Manon arrives at 5 p.m. on the dot, carrying the first of Wendy's boxes of groceries.

'You get them please,' she tells Wendy, her tone unusually abrupt. 'They are too heavy.'

So Wendy, after discreetly pulling a face, makes trips to the car for the remaining two boxes while Manon leans against the kitchen counter sipping water.

'Are you OK?' Wendy asks, once the groceries are stacked against the wall.

'*Oui*,' Manon says unconvincingly. '*Ça va...*'

'You look tired,' Wendy says. 'Bad day?'

'Not tired, worry,' Manon says. 'Too many worry.'

'Too many worries,' Wendy corrects. 'With an "S". Your brother?'

Manon nods.

'Do you want to t—?'

'My father goes to pick him up this morning,' Manon interrupts. 'To take him to... I forget this word.'

'The clinic? Rehab?'

Manon nods. 'Rehab is easy. Like Amy Winehouse. I can remember it that way. And he is completely... Again... I don't know this word. He had taken a lot of drugs.'

'High?' Wendy offers with a wince.

'Yes, but more. In French we say he was *complètement perché*...'

'High as a kite, maybe?'

'Maybe,' Manon says with a sigh. 'Though this sounds funny. High as a kite, but not funny.'

'Off his face, then,' Wendy suggests.

'OK, then. He was off his face. On the one day Papa will take him to the clinic. *C'est un manque de respect total.*'

'It's totally disrespectful.'

'So he phone me from the car and Bruno is singing and laughing in stupid way. And my father he sounds so... I don't know. Without hope. I hate Bruno. This morning, I really hate him.'

Wendy places the coffee cup in front of Manon and settles in an armchair with her glass of wine.

'That's hard,' she says. 'It's really hard.'

Manon is glancing at her phone. 'Maybe I don't stay today,' she says. 'I don't think I can think about words.'

'OK,' Wendy says with a resigned shrug. 'But if you feel you need to talk about your brother, that's OK too.'

'No, I don't want this,' Manon says. She chews her bottom lip for a moment, visibly weighing something up. 'Perhaps I tell you about my mother.'

'Sure,' Wendy says, jumping up for a bowl of peanuts she's forgotten on the kitchen counter and giving her glass a quick top-up in the process. 'Anything you want to talk about is fine,' she says, returning to the armchair and settling back in.

'So my mother,' Manon says. 'It's a hard story.'

'I can imagine,' Wendy says. 'And only tell me if you want to.'

'I do,' Manon says. 'I do want to tell you, but I think maybe you will not like this story so much.'

'It's OK,' Wendy says again. 'If you want to tell me, please...'

'She starts drinking, my mother, when she is fifteen. Fourteen, maybe.' Here Manon nods towards Wendy's glass to make clear that she isn't talking about Coca-Cola.

'OK,' Wendy says. 'That's early.'

Manon shrugs. 'Earlier, probably. As a kid they sometimes have wine with water. Many French families do this in the old times with dinner... But she begins to drink really when she is fifteen. She has friends who are like this, too.'

'Party animals.'

'Yes. Party animals. So, at first she drinks like everyone, like her friends. Fifteen, sixteen, seventeen. This is OK.'

'Because *everyone* parties at that age,' Wendy says, nodding, starting to reach for her glass and then arresting the movement before it gets started and pushing her hair behind her ear instead.

'She meets my father in – how you say – a discotheque?'

'A nightclub, probably. Discotheque sounds quite old-fashioned.'

'And they are both drunk. This is the start of their romance. Drunk in discotheque.'

'I think quite a few relationships start like that,' Wendy says with a forced laugh.

'They go out together. They have big fun. For years, it is like this. Big fun. Good fun. And then she gets... how you say? With baby. My brother. So, she must stop drinking. But she does not.'

'It can be hard to suddenly stop when you're used to drinking. I know.'

'So she drink, and my brother when he comes, is not normal. Not really bad, like some, but he is a small baby. A bit slow to walk, to speak... They say this is because of the alcohol.'

'Oh, I'm sorry, that's awful.'

'And now she is pregnant again with me. So, she must stop. And she knows she must stop. The doctors tell her. Papa tells her.'

'Yes. After what happened with your brother...'

'They argue. With Papa. Because she don't stop. They argue a lot. And at the end she stops the last three month. This is probably why I am OK.'

'Thank God,' Wendy says.

'But when I am born, she starts again.'

'Well, motherhood is hard. Sometimes you need a drink.'

'My mother does *not* need a drink. Believe me. They argue. And my father leave her. Because my mother is drinking – always drinking.'

'But was she drinking reasonably? Or—'

'No. She is not. She is drinking like you, one, two bottle every day. She starts at midday dinner, and then eleven, and then ten. And then she is drinking with breakfast, before breakfast, three bottle every day, sometimes four. Then whisky, vodka, anything.'

'Oh, I don't drink that much,' Wendy says with a fake laugh. She can feel herself blushing. 'I couldn't do two whole bottles of wine! I'd be on the floor!'

'You do,' Manon says flatly. 'I bring these boxes. I take the bottles to the... the *recyclage* ?'

'Yes, but my friend Jill—'

'And I see you. Every time I come. One glass, two glass, three glass... First you are funny, like my mother. And then you are... how you say? Noisy.'

'Noisy?'

'You speak noisy. Because you drink.'

'Really, um... this is making me a little—' Wendy can sense beads of sweat forming on her brow. She chews the inside of her mouth and tries to remain calm.

'I see this with my mother. This you must understand. Then she crash the car, because she drinks too much wine. We are in the car, me, my brother, but we're OK. Then she crashes new car and loses her *permis*. So she makes us to go to the shop. We are too young, but she tells the shop man it's OK. And we do this every day. We bring new bottles, and we take away old. Because if we say "no" she will go crazy.'

'I'm really sorry, Manon. That sounds horrific.'

'And then one day, she is dead, you know? I am nine.'

'Oh, you poor things,' Wendy says, tears welling up in response to the tremble in Manon's voice. 'I'm so, so sorry. That's a terrible thing to have to live through.'

'And I am sorry, too, my friend. I cannot do this for you. You are too much like Maman. And I cannot do this same thing twice. Your delivery make me feel sick.' Manon touches her chest, shakes her head and stands before, after a tiny, strange, Japanese-style nod, she turns and walks out the door leaving Wendy wide-eyed, trying to work out what just happened.

She feels numb. She sits staring at the front door, observing Manon's absence as she tries to think some kind of coherent thought. But there are so many different ideas vying for attention that for a while it's all a blur.

There's a dose of resentful 'how dare she', and a dash of 'damn! I've lost my only French friend'. There's a hefty layer of 'poor Manon' dampening her resentment, and a touch of reasonable 'it's not her fault' because she's dealing with the trauma of losing her mother. There's shame of course, too, because for the first time in her life she has been accused of being an alcoholic. There's even a sense of confusion about why that might be, because, yes, Manon may have just delivered three boxes containing ten bottles of wine and enough food for a week, and yes, there perhaps were an embarrassing number of empties to be recycled a few days ago, but though Manon may have seen her sipping a glass or two during their sessions, certainly she has never seen her drunk.

Repeatedly Wendy reaches for her glass but interrupts the gesture every time and returns her hand to her lap until, once she has catalogued all these different thoughts and decided – her most reassuring thought – that Manon is clearly projecting her traumatic past on the situation, she consciously reaches for it, takes a sip and phones Jill.

Jill: Honey! I was just talking about you, with Bern. It's been ages!

Wendy: Yes, we haven't spoken since you left, have we? ~~You forgot about me the second you walked out the door!~~

J: So how have you been? Did you get all that nonsense with the car sorted out?

W: Sort of. Actually no, not really. But Jill, the reason I'm phoning: do you think I'm an alcoholic?

J: I'm sorry?

W: The post lady. She's been giving me French lessons and she just accused me of being an alcoholic!

J: Alcoholic? You? <laughs> What a cheek! Though Bern pulls my leg about that all the time. He says we both are.

W: But are we? Do you think we really might be?

J: Honey, if we're alcoholics then half the population of Britain are. Everyone I know has a glass of wine at the end of the day, and I do mean everyone. I don't think modern life is possible otherwise. Everything's just too awful.

W: You really think that?

J: Of course. Listen, you hold down a job, don't you? Well, you did. For years. You've organised this whole sabbatical thing brilliantly, and paid for it. You're not exactly sleeping under a bridge, honey, are you?

W: No, I suppose not.

J: I think you're bloody reasonable, to be honest. Compared with me you are, anyway. <laughs> Why on earth did... you said it was the post lady? <shouting> The post lady's told her she's an alcoholic! Just telling Bern... Believe it or not he's in the process of fixing two G&Ts!

W: Do you remember the girl who picked us up when we broke down? Well, it was her.

J: Right. And how did the subject even come up? Because you weren't that drunk when we—

W: Her mother died of it, apparently. She was telling me about her and it sort of morphed into a discussion about me.

J: She died of alcoholism?

W: Yes, I think so. She and her brother found her dead when they got home from school.

J: God, that's awful. But there you go. It's her problem, not yours.

W: You mean she's projecting?

J: Exactly. That's the word I was looking for. Projecting. I bet she's tee-total, too, isn't she?

W: Yes, I think she probably is. I've certainly never seen her drink.

J; Well, there you go.

W: And I do think I could stop if I wanted to, don't you?

J: Of course we could, but why would we want to, honey?

W: Well, quite. God, I'd get so bored. That would be the main thing. The sheer boredom of existence.

J: Exactly. Everything's better with a G&T. You know it's true. Anyway, enough of this misery. Tell me what's been happening.

So Wendy tells her about the car, and how she's been unable to rent another one because prices are sky high until after the holidays. And she tells her how she has managed to book one from 4 January until she leaves in April, and therefore only has to manage without until then.

'But how?' Jill asks. 'You're in the middle of bloody nowhere. How are you going to manage? What about shopping and stuff?'

Wendy explains about the bakery and how they've been delivering her orders. She does not mention (because she can't bear to think about it) that the person doing the deliveries is the very same person she seems to have fallen out with.

'Well, if you need me to send you food parcels, just say.'

'No... Actually... God, you know what?' Wendy says. 'Some Christmas stuff would be wonderful. You know, some mince pies and a bit of Christmas cake. Marks and Sparks will do. I'll pay you back. And some marmalade. Oh, and a jar of Marmite. I'm gonna be here and it's gonna be miserable, but a mince pie or two would definitely help.'

'Consider it done,' Jill says. 'And if you think of anything else, just text me a list. I hate the idea of you up there on your own over Christmas. Why don't you come back here?'

'Really, I'll be fine.'

'I'm not convinced.'

'I will. It's just a day like any other day.'

'It's actually a whole load of days. Christmas Eve, Christmas Day, Boxing Day...'

'Stop. It's OK. I'll be fine.'

'Well, think about it at least?'

'OK,' Wendy says. 'I promise, I will.'

'Oh and – in your box – maybe a little foie gras for the festive season?' Jill adds mockingly.

'Don't you dare,' Wendy tells her. 'Ugh.'

* * *

The snow arrives the following morning.

Wendy has been thinking so obsessively about Manon's accusations that she had entirely forgotten about the snow. But here it is, drifting from a grey sky in beautiful, delicate flakes.

She wraps up warmly and steps outside, raising her open mouth to the sky and revelling in the sensation as the snowflakes hit her tongue.

Gentle snowfall continues, but for most of the day the flakes melt the second they hit the ground. It's only when she steps outside for her final cigarette of the evening that she sees it's starting to settle. The bowl she'd put out for the cat is empty but dusted with snow. Damn! She'd hoped to catch it eating.

She watches a film on her laptop featuring not one, not two, but three AA meetings and notices for the first time how ubiquitous they're becoming in modern TV. She studies the ravaged faces of the people in the scenes and thinks, *No, that's not me, thank God.*

She dozes off before the end of the film and wakes just enough to stoke the fire and climb the stairs to bed, where she dreams of a cat in boots drinking whisky from a bowl and dancing an Irish jig. When, at the end of the dream, she wakes again, the image lingering in her mind's eye is so comic that she laughs out loud. Someone should make it into a cartoon, she thinks. She must try to remember the dream in the morning. But as she slips back into sleep, she knows she most probably won't.

* * *

On going to bed last night, she'd expected to wake up to a winter wonderland, but she can tell the second she opens her eyes this has not come to pass. Rather than being lit by that strange icy brightness, the cabin is almost dark and the sound of the world outside is unmuffled. She lies, listening to birdsong for a while, trying to pluck up the courage to leave her warm bed and when eventually she makes it downstairs, she sees there's been only the lightest dusting of snow.

She stokes the fire and, while she eats breakfast, wonders what to do with her day. A walk, then a read, and then some Netflix, maybe? She can't help but feel that's rather a waste of a day, but then who is here to judge? Who's to say that time has to be 'spent' usefully, anyway? Sometimes, managing to just about feel OK is 'enough'.

When she steps out of the shower and opens the bathroom window to let the steam out, she gasps. Outside, the snow is falling thick and fast – as heavily as she has ever seen. The flakes are like massive cartoon-style fractals, and they are so dense that it's impossible to see further than a few feet.

She dresses quickly and steps into the swirling whiteness of it all. The air is icy and fragrant with that unique metallic smell of snow, and under her feet – where more than an inch has already settled – the snow squeaks beneath the soles of her boots.

'God, I love snow!' she says out loud. 'I love it!'

She nips back indoors for her phone and records a slow-mo

video of drifting flakes. She'll get a hundred likes with this video – more probably. Everybody loves snow.

She's in the process of uploading this to Instagram when a message pops up from Madame Blanchard. *There is much snow forecast*, the message says. *Please be* économique *with the* électricité a*nd let me know in case of problem.*

God! she thinks. *Of course! The solar panels.* She crunches her way to the rear of the house and sees that they're already buried.

She returns indoors to ensure that everything is unplugged and then sets off, crunching her way towards the bakery. The snow beneath her feet feels squeaky and delicious. Surprisingly it isn't slippery at all.

She peers up at the white-dusted pine trees overhead and notes, beneath her feet, the tracks left by a single passing car. Just before the village she spots paw marks, too – a reminder that she needs to buy cat food.

The houses in the village look beautiful today, and she finds herself marvelling more generally at the beauty of the world and, unusually for her, feeling lucky to be alive to witness it all. She thinks that this must be why we all love snow so much – because it makes everything seem new, and that newness, that difference, makes reality become visible again. The world doesn't change at all, but this unexpected shift to whiteness makes it all stand out for our tired, bored eyes.

Trudging on, she finds herself thinking about her twenty-five-year marriage and an unusually profound thought strikes her: That if they could only come up with some kind of marital snowfall, she and Harry might be able to see each other properly again, too.

The bread racks in the bakery are almost empty by the time she gets there, and the cold cabinet, usually laden with quiches and cakes, is in the process of being cleaned.

'Hello!' the baker says, looking up at her through glass. 'It's good you come today. Tomorrow we are on holidays.'

'Holidays?' Wendy says. 'In December? For how long? *Pour combien de temps?*'

'Until this is gone,' the woman says, straightening, dropping the sponge into a bucket, then massaging her back while simultaneously nodding at the weather outside. 'As you see, everyone stays home. No customers, no bread!'

Just in case, and despite yesterday's delivery, Wendy buys as much as she can carry, choosing fresh bread, instant noodles, cat food, crispbreads and cheese. She very nearly grabs a couple of extra bottles of wine as well to replace the two she drank yesterday, but then she remembers denying ever being able to drink two bottles and feels too ashamed to get more. She wonders if Manon has already been in. She wonders if the baker already *knows*.

By the time she steps back out, the snow is four inches deep and she can no longer see where the tarmac ends and the verge begins, so, in the absence of traffic, she carves a line down the middle of the road.

As she reaches the turning towards her cabin she spots a distant car approaching, creeping around the bend. By the time it passes she has her back to the main road, but she glances behind her to see Manon at the wheel, leaning forward, feigning concentration as she drives laboriously towards the bakery – a near miss which leaves her feeling nauseous.

TEN

INTO THE WILD

Day One

So, I've decided to keep a journal. As I'm finally getting that *Into the Wild* adventure I was hoping for, I thought I should write it all down. That way, when I'm eaten by wolves, Sean Penn can make the movie.

First (because writing anything original is hard) some facts and figures:

Inches of snow: 5.
Food remaining: Masses.
Electricity: Yes!
Bottles of wine remaining: 7.

Actually, I'm not so sure about the facts and figures. They're a bit Bridget Jonesey.

But I don't know what else to write about. It seemed like keeping a journal would be a Good Thing To Do but other than the fact that things are pretty grim, there's not much to tell. Sorry, diary.

* * *

Day Two

Inches of Snow: 12!
Food remaining: Loads.
Electricity: Yes!
Bottles of wine remaining: 5.

So, *kerazeee* amounts of the white stuff. And it's still snowing.

Last night I demolished a delicious bottle of Beaujolais from the bakery and watched Netflix all evening. Which initially helped (the wine, that is). It made the Guy Ritchie film I chose seem almost like fun. But after the fourth glass, the wine no longer helped because not only did I lose track of the plot, I fell asleep.

Missing the end of the film wasn't that much of a big deal but what was sad is that I missed the cat. I'd put food out for him/her/it and turned everything in the room around so that I could watch Netflix and the bowl simultaneously. But the cat, being a cat, waited until I fell asleep and then swept in to gobble up the food. When I woke up it was past midnight and the dish was empty. Better luck today, hopefully.

Other than that, there's absolutely nothing happening.

Oh, I nearly called Harry last night. I wonder, does that count as news?

I was eating my pasta and watching Sky News when I was suddenly overcome with a burst of love for him. It was so weird because it's been ages since I've felt like that. I suppose it's bound to happen, though. Twenty-five years, the father of my babies, feeling lonely, dying slowly in the middle of an Alpine snow drift, etc. Things are going to get emotional, I suppose.

But I do miss him. I will tell you and you alone this, Dear

Journal. And sometimes it does strike me as utter madness that this is where we have got to.

* * *

Day Three

Inches of snow: 'I'm getting a bit scared' levels of snow. Maybe 2 feet?
Food remaining: Lots.
Electricity: Yes (A miracle!).
Bottles of wine remaining: 3.
Cat sightings: 2.
Primary emotion: Cabin fever.

I think I might be going a bit doolally. And I don't think I'll get eaten by wolves after all. I suspect they'll find me and say, 'Ooh, look, she gnawed her own arm off through sheer boredom.'

I've watched every decent thing I can find on Netflix and am reduced to dubbed Spanish drama. And dubbing really does ruin everything, doesn't it? On my TV at home I know how to switch it to Spanish with subtitles, which even though it's kind of tiring due to all the reading, I prefer. But I can't find any way to do that on my laptop. Maybe I'll ask Todd. He'd know.

Other than Spanish Netflix, I've read three novels in four days, but I think I've already forgotten novels one and two. I'm reduced to pacing around the cabin like a lion in a cage (which makes me think about how that must feel when it's for life. Poor lions! I hate zoos).

Anyway, I can't stand it anymore. I'm heading out. Wish me luck!

· · ·

Well, I didn't get far, Dear Journal. The snow was above the tops of my boots and it sneaked in, crumbled down, and froze my shins. By the time I reached the main road, I'd had enough, so I turned back and promptly fell on my arse.

When I got home, Mittens (I've decided to call it Mittens, a great gender-neutral name if ever there was one) was there, peeping in through my window. I could almost hear it thinking, *Where's my food, human?*

Of course it ran off the second it saw me (actually, more *bounced* off because of the snow), but I stomped some of the snow flat and put more food out so hopefully Mittens will be back.

Right now I'm drying my feet in front of the fire, which is bringing back a whole stock of memories of the kids when they were little. The first time Todd saw snow he was five. I remember asking him what he thought of it while we were thawing his feet by the fire, and he said, 'It's wery wery cold but wery wery lubbly, Mummy.' My God, they were cute. What happened?

OMG, Mittens is back! I wonder if he will ever deign to come inside?

* * *

Day Four

Inches of snow: Compacted down to about 18.
Food remaining: Plenty.
Electricity: Intermittent.
Bottles of wine remaining: 1.
Cat sightings: 3.

Despite falling over, I've been for another walk. I feel so claustrophobic stuck in this tiny place, it didn't even seem like a choice.

I tried to do some sort of yoga-ish exercises first in the hope that would help, but the truth is I couldn't even remember how they go. My last yoga lesson was at least ten years ago, and I only went about three times then.

So, my walk: the snow's really deep, but has also melted a bit and then refrozen overnight which has given it a strange crispy topping. It's like walking through a massive crème brûlée. The result is that you have to do a ridiculous John Cleese goose step and then try to smash your heel back down through the crunchy topping. It must look very, very peculiar. Thank God no one was there to see me.

Again, I didn't get far, but even my short ten-minute military march felt better than staying indoors. I do wonder whether it's possible to actually die from being stuck in a tiny space. Again, a sad thought for all the animals in zoos.

Once I got back I put more food out for Mittens, and then left the door ajar and after only about twenty minutes, he (it's definitely a 'he') appeared. He stuck his head through the door and gave me a long hard stare before gobbling down his food. Definitely making progress there. I think we'll be friends soon.

And now, Dear Journal, we need to talk about something serious. Because I've realised that I've been lying to you. Lying to my own journal. How silly is that?

So the truth is that on Day One I didn't have seven bottles of wine remaining, I had seven and three quarters. And today I don't really have one full bottle left, but merely a half. Which means that I truly have been drinking more than two bottles a day. That's probably too much, isn't it? And it obviously leaves me feeling a bit icky about that weird conversation with Manon.

In my defence, I was wildly bored last night because not only did the electricity go off, taking the internet with it, but my Kindle ran out of juice again, and with no electricity I couldn't recharge it. With nothing left to do but drink, smoke and watch the flames, I authorised myself that extra half bottle which pushed me over the edge into a positively tipsy state I would have to admit I rather enjoyed.

I'm going to have to be good tonight, though, as I only have half a bottle left. Only half a bar of chocolate, too. Things are getting desperate. Dear Sean Penn, if you're reading this then send a search team! And please include a St Bernard (with whisky).

* * *

Day Five

Inches of ~~snow~~ ice: 6.
Food remaining: Random leftovers.
Electricity: Mostly off.
Bottles of wine remaining: ZERO!
Cat sightings: o.

What a thoroughly miserable day. It's stopped snowing but it's grey, grey, grey. In fact, it's like nighttime, which, as the electricity is now off, makes indoors as miserable as outside. There's also a hateful, icy wind out there.

Still, look on the bright side. The forecast for tomorrow is sunshine. Just imagine if I'd chosen Norway! It would have been night-time nearly all the time. I hadn't even thought about that...

So yeah, the electricity is mostly off now. It came on for an hour, just long enough to charge my phone and laptop and then went off again. Lucky I don't have a freezer, I suppose. I sent a message to the owner using one of my precious Tesco mobile megabytes, and she replied that everybody's electricity is off. Apparently the snow has pulled down the wires or something.

She didn't offer any solutions to my problems, though. I think the fact that I'm in the same boat as everyone else made her feel she doesn't need to bother. I'm praying that tomorrow's sunshine is strong enough to reach through the snow to my solar panels!

But the truth is that I don't care as much as I should. I think I'm coming down with the flu and I'm also feeling quite depressed. I'm eating weird combinations of food (instant noodles with cheese this lunchtime, for example) and mainly just dozing in front of the fire. I hate it here. I hate my life. And I'm pretty sure I hate me.

Update: Still no sighting of Mittens today. I wonder where he is, poor thing. And I'm definitely coming down with the flu. I'm shaky, and I feel sick. The only tiny bit of good news on this horrid day is that I found an inch of gin which I'm swigging right now with orange juice. It definitely seems to be helping.

* * *

Day Six

Inches of ice: 4.
Food remaining: Not much.
Electricity: Gone.
Alcohol: None.
Cat sightings: 0.

The sun has returned, but I don't care because I'm dying. I barely slept at all last night and when I eventually did it was for an hour or something and then I woke up soaked in sweat with a splitting headache.

I ventured outside briefly to empty the ashes from the wood

stove (it left a horrible stain in the pristine snow) and it's like an ice rink. It's absolutely bloody lethal and there's no way whatsoever I could make it to the main road, let alone the bakery.

Luckily I still have rice, two eggs and a tin of mushrooms, so I'm going to attempt egg-fried rice.

I'm so over this all now. I've been thinking I need to phone Harry, because I really, really want to go home as soon as I can get out of this damned place.

* * *

Day Seven

Inches of Ice: 1.
Food remaining: Scraps.
Electricity: Yes, it's back!
Alcohol: Zero.
Cat sightings: 5!

God, I'm so ill. I woke up feeling sick and sweaty again, and very, very anxious. My heart was racing so fast that for a while I worried I was having a heart attack.

I wish I'd kept a bit of that gin back for emergencies because it was the only thing that made me feel better. Today I'm dosing on paracetamol, but it's not doing anything at all.

I wasn't going to write this down – because it somehow makes it even more real to do so – but whatever: I saw my mother this morning. I woke up and she was sitting on the end of the bed. Not transparent or ghostly or anything – totally solid and there. I could even feel her weight through the covers.

She wasn't doing anything, just sitting there quietly in that placid way she had with her hands crossed on her lap.

I think I cried out, then felt surprised that it wasn't enough to wake me up. I mean, I was obviously dreaming but it didn't feel like a dream after that

Mum smiled at me and said, 'Calm down, silly. I'm just checking in on you, but you'll be fine.' And then she added, 'Then again, I'm dead, so what do I know?' Typical Mum humour there.

I got the shakes then, and kept closing my eyes, sort of blinking really hard, but every time I opened them, she was still there.

I went through a whole range of emotions in less than a minute. At first I was shocked, and then I was scared, and then kind of happy for a bit – I came over all emotional, and had a cry. And then I got scared because I decided that I really was going mad and hid my head under the quilt instead. Eventually I must have fallen asleep (or more likely, I was asleep the whole time) and when I woke up, she was gone. And now I feel sad and a bit angry with myself for not making the most of the moment. There are so many things I should have asked her. Now, every time I look around the room I'm excited but terrified in case she's back.

The snow has almost melted, so I'm going to be brave and try to walk to the bakery. I need bread and cheese and butter, at least. And I could really do with a drink.

But, honestly, I feel so ill. I think I must have got Covid all over again. Not sure if I'm going to make it.

Update: I suddenly remembered Erik's kind offer so I phoned him. He answered, but he's in Stockholm for Christmas. Damn! He said to ask Madame Blanchard for help, so I've sent her a message but for once she's not answering. Perhaps her internet is down. Hell, I tell you, is right here, right now.

I made it halfway to the bakery but it was so slippery, and I was so wobbly on my feet, that I was about to give up and come home when Manon pulled up in her yellow post van. She told me that the bakery isn't opening until tomorrow and then drove me back home. She didn't mention our previous discussion, and I was feeling so rough I didn't broach the subject either. She kindly offered to get me some shopping if I need it but I can manage fine until tomorrow. I've lost my appetite anyway. The only exception is that I would really, really like a bottle of something, but of course that's the one thing I can't ask her to bring.

I've been thinking about the drink thing, and I suppose the truth of the matter is that I don't only want a drink because I'm bored. It goes deeper than that. There's some surgical alcohol in the bathroom cabinet and I even found myself considering that.

OK, look, cards on the table time. I didn't just consider it, I actually tasted it. I thought it might taste like vodka, but it was disgusting – even with tonic. But that can't be normal, can it? Tasting random bathroom products in the hope they taste like vodka?

On the good news side of things, the electricity has returned and Mittens has been back five times today. Five times! On his last visit I managed to get him to eat indoors on the doormat. His fur is all matted and dirty and I'm gagging to get a brush to him. It's probably a bit pathetic, but when he's here I don't feel quite so alone.

ELEVEN

A SURPRISE

Wendy: Hello?

Harry: Hey there, French eco-warrior girl. How goes?

W: I'm fine thanks. Actually, that's not true. I don't know why I even said that. I'm ill. I've caught a cold, but I'm OK. I'll survive. Probably.

H: Oh, poor you! Everyone's coming down with it here, as well. 'Tis the season to be fluey and all that. How ill are you? Do you need me to organise an airlift?

W: Nah, it's just, you know: tired, fever, headache... I'll be fine in a few days, I expect. I've been having weird dreams, too.

H: What kind of weird dreams?

W: Oh, you know... Just dreams. That are weird.

H: Right. So, um, you all ready for Christmas? I'm just about to head out for another load.

W: ...

H: Hello?

W: <laughs sourly> I'm ready for nothing at all, Harry. I'm ill in bed with the flu.

H: Sure. I just mean, are you, like, staying over there this year?

W; Why, are you inviting me this year?

H: No, I...

W: Then what else would I be doing, Haz? Of course I'm bloody staying here.

H: Right. Sorry. Of course.

W: Is there an actual reason you're calling me? I mean, other than to make me feel bad about being on my own for Christmas?

H: Do I need a reason to call my wife?

W: No. But it has to be said, you usually do have one.

H: Actually, there is something I need to talk to you about.

W: You see? I knew there would be.

H: And, as it happens, it's about Christmas.

W: OK...

H: Specifically about Fifi's Christmas present.

W: Christ, Harry... Really?

H: Jesus! What have I done now?

W: Don't you think that's a bit...?

H: A bit what?

W: A bit insensitive? Asking about Christmas presents... When you banished me last Christmas, and when this year you know I'm—

H: Nobody banished you, Wens.

W: Um, well... Except you kind of did.

H: OK. Maybe we did, a bit. But it was only because of Covid.

W: Yeah. Right.

H: Anyway, she's told me what she wants – Fiona has. But I need to run it by you first. So don't, you know, go off on one before you know what I'm going to say.

W: <sighs> Go on then. What does she want this time?

H: She wants a flight. To France. She wants to come visit you. Though frankly, God knows why.

W: God! Really?

H: I know. Crazy, huh? I'm thinking of taking her to a shrink instead because she's clearly losing her mind.

W: Harry...

H: Hey, I'm joking! She wants to spend Christmas with her mummy. You can't be that shocked.

W: For Christmas, though? She wants to come for *Christmas*?

H: Yeah. I think she feels bad about last year. Well, we all do, actually. And she's a bit worried about you, out there on your own. And ... I don't know... I think she thinks it might be nice. To reconnect with her mummy over mince pies or frogs' legs or whatever it is the French eat.

W: Gosh.

H: Plus, if truth be told, she's not Amanda's biggest fan.

W: Amanda being Todd's girlfriend?

H: Yeah. He's bringing her to ... ~~mine ours~~ ... to the house. Fifi thinks she's snobby. Which she probably is, a bit. So... Anyway. Lots of good reasons. Lots of perfectly reasonable reasons. And the flights are doable – I've checked. A bit pricey, but totally doable. But of course, in the end, it's up to you. Because you're the one who will have to entertain her.

W: ...

H: So?

W: ...

H: Hello? Ground control to Wendy. Anyone home?

W: Sorry. I'm a bit stunned, actually.

H: But in a good way?

W: Yes. But gosh... Look... I don't know what to say, Haz. I... ~~I don't have a car. And I feel like shit right now. And I'm living in a studio. And I don't have a tree or decorations. Or cake. And Fiona will hate it here anyway. I have no idea how to organise any of this. Plus Fiona hasn't had a good word to say to me in ages. And what if we argue the whole time?~~

H: Look, if you don't fancy it that's perf—

W: No, of course I fancy it. I'd love that. Yes! Obviously, it's a yes.

...

The phone call over, she lies back and stares at the ceiling and tries to catch her breath. She checks the calendar on her phone. She has eight days to get better, organise a car, get food in and clean the place (and herself) up. She probably needs a haircut. She's starting to look a bit wild. And the car part is going to be expensive, but it's possible, she supposes. It's all just about possible. As long as it doesn't snow again, it is, anyway.

* * *

She drags herself out of bed and takes an unpleasant lukewarm shower before wrapping herself warmly and stepping outside into the sunshine. She's been feeling so ill that she hasn't even noticed the weather until now.

The snow is all but gone this morning and there are only tiny patches remaining in the undergrowth to prove it wasn't also a dream.

The walk to the bakery feels much farther today and by the time she gets there she's soaked in sweat and her legs have gone all rubbery. But the bakery, thank God, is open, so she buys pasta and sauces and instant noodles, fresh bread, chocolate and, to cheer herself up, a couple of bottles of that lovely Beaujolais, plus a croissant to eat en route.

'You don't want more?' the baker asks, as she rings up Wendy's limited purchases. 'No delivery this time?'

Wendy just shakes her head and taps her card against the payment machine.

'You are OK?' the woman asks, one eyebrow arched. 'You look... *je ne sais pas... fatiguée* ?'

'*Oui*,' Wendy says flatly. '*Je suis fatiguée.*' And then she hikes her heavy backpack onto one shoulder and turns towards the door. She's in no mood for small talk this morning. Not in any language.

She has to rest repeatedly along the way, and by the time she gets home she's so exhausted that she considers it a result to have made it home at all. But the sun is streaming into the warm cabin and after a Pot Noodle, a hefty serving of wine and an unplanned three-hour snooze on the sofa she wakes up feeling a bit better, though not really well enough to deal with what happens next: a tap, tap, tap on the window. A familiar face peering in.

'Hello!' Manon says brightly, the second Wendy opens the door. 'It's OK? We take our lesson?'

'I... I didn't think you were coming,' Wendy says, blocking the doorway with her body, effectively keeping Manon on the doorstep.

'Of course I come,' Manon replies. 'It was just so much snow.' She gestures around her at where the snow was only yesterday. 'I don't even deliver post for three days because the road is closed. But if you don't want...'

'I'm ill, actually,' Wendy tells her, faking a cough and wiping non-existent sweat from her brow.

'OK,' Manon says. 'Maybe *mercredi*, then? Wednesday?'

Wendy shrugs. 'Maybe.' She's feeling angry towards Manon, though having just woken up from her snooze, she's struggling to remember quite why.

'If you feel better,' Manon says and Wendy sees her glance at the bottle on the coffee table, and remembers. Then with a wave, Manon turns and walks away. '*À mercredi !*' she casts over her shoulder.

* * *

She tries not to think too much about Manon, but it's hard. Specifically, every time she takes a sip of wine, her accusations come to mind. But as a sip of wine seems to be the only thing which momentarily clears the flu from her head she doesn't feel like she has much choice.

She is efficient, though, despite her illness and these occasional sips of wine. Between alternating waves of fever, nausea and general tipsiness, she manages to text Harry for Fiona's flight details and book a ridiculously expensive car from Hertz for the three days Fiona will be here over Christmas, plus a taxi to get to the airport to pick the car up in the first place.

With all this sorted, she gives herself permission to finish the last of the bottle before crawling back upstairs to her bed.

She's woken just after ten in the evening by her telephone, and through bleary vision she manages to see that it's Fiona calling.

Fiona: I'm so excited. Thank you! Dad's just told me!

Wendy: Well, I'm excited, too. I only hope you don't hate it here. It's very, very rural you know.

F: How could I, Mum? It's France! For Christmas!

They discuss places Fiona might want to visit during her trip (Nice, Antibes and a perfume museum in Grasse) and items Wendy might like from home (mince pies, Christmas cake and crackers). The conversation is unusual in that none of Fiona's usual reproach leaks out. She genuinely does just sound excited.

The next morning, Wendy feels well enough to throw herself back into her routine. She hikes back up to the spaceship to take her photo, and then trudges back down and onward to the bakery where she picks up a few slightly more thoughtfully chosen supplies.

It's a gorgeous sunny day and she ends up tying her jacket

around her waist. It's almost impossible to believe that only three days ago she was snowed in.

Back home, she feeds Mittens (he's almost stroke-able now) empties the wood stove and neatly stacks a batch of logs beside it. She cleans the cabin from top to bottom and, noting that the water is now hot, even hand-washes a batch of laundry and hangs it out to dry.

Finally, feeling the particular joy one feels when an illness finally fades, she settles down to make a Christmas shopping list. Her daughter is coming for Christmas! Perhaps she still loves her old mum after all.

* * *

The weather continues to improve and by the time the twenty-third comes around it's almost like an English summer day. This is a massive relief for Wendy. After all, she'd far rather her daughter see her enjoying the Mediterranean sunshine than have her witness the misery of snow, cold and blackouts.

The Hertz office being rammed with Christmas travellers, picking up the car takes longer than planned, so despite her best efforts, she's almost an hour late getting to arrivals.

'I'm sorry, I'm sorry, I'm sorry!' she exclaims as she trots across the hall to where her daughter is seated, looking bored and a bit annoyed.

'It's fine, Mum,' Fiona says, but then, unable to resist, she adds, 'It's nice to know you're so keen to see me.'

'Oh please don't be like that,' Wendy says. 'The whole car thing has been a nightmare – I'll tell you about it all later. But my lateness has nothing whatsoever to do with keenness or lack of. I'm thrilled to bits you're here.'

Fiona scrunches up her nose and smiles. 'I know,' she says, finally deigning to stand. 'I'm only pulling your leg.'

After a hug they trundle Fiona's suitcase to the short-stay car park where Wendy has parked the rented Clio.

'Not an electric, then?' Fiona asks as she heaves her case into the back. 'I thought you were all eco-everything nowadays.'

'Huh!' Wendy snorts. 'There was a Tesla option, actually, but it was twice the price of this one. Plus, I think I'd be a bit lost, to be honest. I wouldn't know where to begin.'

'Neil's got one,' Fiona says. 'Todd keeps going on about how cool it is. He thinks Dad should get one.'

'I'm not sure anything from that Musk guy can be considered "cool",' Wendy says, a comment she knows will please Fiona.

'That's exactly what I keep saying.'

Wendy drives them to the nearby port of St-Laurent-du-Var where they choose a pizzeria overlooking the bay.

'It's amazing!' Fiona says, taking her seat and looking out to sea. 'I can totally see why you chose here.'

'This is nothing like where I live,' Wendy says. 'You'll see.'

The waiter arrives so Wendy orders two pizzas, a Coke for Fiona and a small pitcher of red wine for herself.

'Wine, Mum?' Fiona comments. 'Really?'

'Yes, it's fine,' Wendy replies. 'It's 250 mls; it's tiny.'

'I'd rather you didn't, though. You are about to drive and everything.'

'God, I'll just have a glass, then,' Wendy tells the waiter, shaking her head. *'Juste un verre.'*

'Mum, I really...' Fiona starts. But the waiter shoots Wendy a knowing 'kids today, huh?' smile, and vanishes before the discussion can go any further. His complicity with her mother makes her feel outnumbered.

'Anyway, as I was saying...' Wendy says, signalling that the subject is now closed. 'It's very rugged and remote where I live. It's not coastal, at all.'

Fiona sighs in frustration then gives in. 'But it's nice?' she asks. 'You like it?'

'It's... interesting,' Wendy tells her. 'You'll see.'

The drinks arrive, closely followed by the pizzas and they are thin and crispy and delicious.

'So how are things with you?' Wendy asks, taking a tiny sip of her wine. 'You look well.'

In truth, Fiona has put on weight since Wendy last saw her but she knows (as only a mother can) that the subject is taboo.

'Thanks. Yeah, I'm fine.'

Wendy wants to ask her if she has a boyfriend, but that subject is off limits, too. 'And school?' she asks, instead.

'Oh, that's all fine. Pretty much caught up with everything now. Though I have to say I'm a bit jealous of Todd. He escaped his finals completely.'

'He did, didn't he? The lucky bugger. Though I read somewhere that employers can be a bit snooty about A level results from that year.'

'Yes, I read that, too. Not that it seems to have bothered Manchester uni.'

'No, apparently not.'

They eat for a moment in silence, then Fiona says, 'Look, I know this is a bit of a—'

'Ooh, look,' Wendy says, pointing. On the horizon an enormous cruise ship is sliding into view. 'That's massive! It's like a bloody hotel on a boat – look, Fiona!'

'Yes,' Fiona says, turning her head. 'But—'

'And look at all the smoke pouring out!' Wendy says.

'God, yeah,' Fiona says. 'That's gross.'

* * *

It's eleven the next morning and it's Christmas Eve. Mother and daughter are enjoying a late breakfast in the warm sunshine.

Wendy had all but forgotten her daughter's famed capacity for sleep.

The afternoon following Fiona's arrival had been taken up with food shopping and the evening with general catching up. This had mostly consisted of Fiona telling her mother random stories about her friends, during which Wendy had done her best to feign interest.

She sometimes worries a little about her daughter, because she seems that bit more innocent than Wendy remembers being at her age. The stories Fiona tells her mother about her friends' exploits seem designed to shock and amuse, but they're generally so tame that instead Wendy worries Fiona has grown up to be too timid, too cautious – that she's not having enough fun. She's seventeen, for God's sake! Where are the motorbike trips, the wild nights out, the noisy demos against the government, or for that matter the all-night raves in muddy fields?

It's an unusual thing to be concerned about as a mother, because you can hardly tell your daughter to take *more* risks, but Wendy wonders if she can't find a subtle way to suggest Fiona has more fun.

'These croissants are lovely,' Fiona says, delicately ripping off a corner and popping it into her mouth with her long violet fingernails.

'I know,' Wendy replies. 'I think most of the food tastes better here. Everything back home seems so industrial by comparison.'

'That's because it is,' Fiona says. 'I saw a thing the other day about all the veg they throw away just because it's too ugly or whatever. The amount of food we waste is criminal.'

Wendy pours herself another cup of coffee and waves the pot at her daughter, who nods by way of reply.

The conversation seems clunky this morning. Apparently Fiona has run out of stories about her whacky friends, and though there are many things Wendy would like to ask, most of them seem out of bounds. She's left feeling a bit shell-shocked at how brittle their relationship has become.

'So how are things back—' Wendy starts, but she's interrupted and probably saved by Fiona's phone, which chooses that precise moment to start vibrating.

'Sorry,' Fiona says, dragging the phone towards her and standing. 'Gotta take this.'

Wendy watches her daughter walk towards the cabin and hears her say, 'Hi,' but nothing further, because she vanishes around the corner where she's out of sight and earshot.

She sighs and wonders what's going on. Because as Fiona dragged the phone across the table, she'd glimpsed Todd's name through the gaps between her fingers. Perhaps that's normal, it being Christmas Eve and everything.

Wendy crosses to the cabin where she locks herself in the tiny bathroom. She's right: through the air vent she can hear the conversation – well, Fiona's half of it at any rate.

'No. Not yet,' she's saying.

...

'Because.'

...

'Well, because I've only just got here!'

...

'Look, I'll try. I told you I would. And if there's a right time then I'll do it.'

...

'No, Todd, I'm not going to promise anything.'

...

'I know.'

...

'Yes, I know.'

...

'Look, I know, all right? Jesus!'

...

'If it's that important then talk to her yourself.'

...

'Exactly.'

...

'Well, then!'

...

'And don't hassle me. It'll just make her suspicious if you keep phoning me up.'

...

'I know. I'm just saying. Yeah, you, too. Oh, and don't forget to wish her a merry Crimbo.'

...

'No, not today, you twat! Tomorrow! Honestly, sometimes you scare me, Todd.'

...

Wendy flushes the toilet and washes her hands before returning to find Fiona seated sipping coffee.

'Who was that, then?' she asks, as casually as she can.

'Oh, just a friend. Someone from school,' Fiona says.

'Really?'

'Yeah.'

'I thought I saw Todd's name flash up.'

Fiona laughs convincingly. 'Um, more than one Todd on the planet, Mum.'

'You know multiple Todds?'

'I do. Well, two... Todd at school is actually quite nice, though. So I guess some of them are OK. You didn't think my stinky brother was calling me, did you?'

'No,' Wendy says. 'I s'pose not.' Wendy has found out something new today, something she didn't know. Her daughter has learned how to lie. And she's really rather good at it.

* * *

They drive to nearby Gourdon and wander through pretty village streets peering in souvenir shops full of glassware. They stop briefly for pancakes in a creperie and then continue to the far end of the village where the cliff the village is built on drops to coastal plains below.

'Wow,' Fiona says. 'There's a view.'

'Yes. And look, that's the airport,' Wendy says, pointing out to sea where the reclaimed land of the runways juts out.

'Nah,' Fiona says. 'Don't be daft. Nice airport was way further than that.'

Wendy shakes her head in surprise. 'It's not a guess, sweetheart,' she says. 'I'm telling you that's where I picked you up from yesterday. That's the runway, right there.'

'OK,' Fiona says. 'If you say so, Mum.' Annoyingly, Wendy can tell from that 'Mum' tagged on at the end that her daughter doesn't believe her. But she decides it's of little importance.

'And that bit?' Fiona asks.

'What bit?' Wendy asks.

'That green blob sticking out to sea.'

'Oh, that's part of Antibes, I think. But I haven't been yet. It's supposed to be pretty. And there's a great walk around the coast apparently. We can go tomorrow, if you like.'

'But tomorrow is Christmas Day,' Fiona says.

'So...?'

'So... OK! Sure! Why not?'

'We can take a picnic,' Wendy says. 'A Christmas picnic. Could be nice. Especially if the weather's like this.'

* * *

As Wendy drives back to the cabin, she thinks about Fiona's conversation with Todd. She wonders what her daughter is meant to ask and runs through potential subjects as she drives. It's probably to do with the state of her marriage, she concludes – they probably want to know what's going on. She would, if she were them. She'd like to know, herself, come to think of it. She continues to drive in silence as she tries to decide how she'll reply but they are home before she has worked out a strategy, and as she parks the car she realises not a word has been spoken since Gourdon.

'You OK, Fifi?' she asks.

'Um?' Fiona says, turning from the window. 'Oh, me? Yeah, I'm fine.'

'Good. Well, let's get indoors and put the kettle on. I'm gasping.'

'Sure,' Fiona says. 'Actually, there's something I want to ask you, OK? And I don't want you to get upset.'

'OK,' Wendy says, pulling the keys from the ignition and pausing.

'Inside,' Fiona says. 'Let's make that cuppa first.'

Wendy boils the kettle and drops teabags into mugs. But at the last minute, kettle in hand, she changes her mind and pours herself a glass of wine instead. She's not sure what her daughter is about to ask, but she doubts that the conversation will be fun.

'Really, Mum?' Fiona says as Wendy puts the drinks on the coffee table. 'It's not even five o'clock.'

She has been expecting this. She's getting used to Fiona monitoring her wine consumption and is prepared. 'It may not be five o'clock yet, but it is Christmas Eve,' Wendy says lightly. 'Normal rules do not apply.'

'Mum!' Fiona says.

'Lordy, do take a chill pill,' Wendy says. 'It's a glass of bloody wine, not a syringe filled with heroin.'

Fiona makes a gasping noise and shakes her head.

'What?' Wendy asks sharply. 'Seriously? *What?*'

'I wanted to talk to you, that's all.'

'And? How does me having a sip of wine stop you talking to me?'

'Because that's—' Fiona says.

They're interrupted by a tap, tap on the window and both turn to see Manon's face peering in.

'Hello, Wendy!' Manon says, when she opens the door. 'I come on Wednesday but no one is 'ome.' She glances over at Fiona and nods a hello.

'Sorry,' Wendy says. 'My daughter's here, so... Fiona, this is Manon, our post lady. And my French teacher, too.'

'Hi, Manon,' Fiona says, with a wave and a tight smile that's the antithesis of 'invitational'.

'So, no lesson today?' Manon asks.

'Sorry,' Wendy says. 'Maybe after Christmas?'

'Ah, yes! I almost forget!' Manon says, before jogging off, presumably to her car.

'What did she forget?' Fiona asks.

Wendy shrugs. 'Search me,' she says, and then Manon is back, a cardboard box in her arms.

'You have mail!' she says brightly. 'It's good time, yes? I mean, with Christmas tomorrow.'

'Oh, gosh!' Wendy says, taking the box from her arms and studying the label. 'It's my Christmas supplies from Jill. I'd forgotten all about that.'

'There is forty-four euro to pay,' Manon says, pulling a slip of paper from her pocket. 'I'm sorry. It's you know... new. Since Brexit.'

'Customs, then?' Wendy asks.

'Yes. Customs.'

'Forty-four euros!' Fiona mutters. 'Another Brexit benefit, then.'

'It's fine,' Wendy tells Manon, plopping the box on the sofa and heading to the kitchen for her purse. 'Really.'

Once Manon has wished them a '*Joyeux Noël*' and headed off, they open the box to find mince pies, a Marks and Spencer mini Christmas cake, a lump of Cheddar, a bottle of port and a Christmas card which Wendy props up on the bookshelf.

'That's ruined half my surprise, then,' Fiona says, hands on hips.

'What has?'

'I've got mince pies and cake in my suitcase. You know that stuff won't even have cost forty-four euros in the first place, right?'

'I know,' Wendy says. 'Still, it's sweet of her.'

They warm mince pies in the microwave and then both burn their mouths biting through the pastry. 'Better leave those for a bit,' Wendy says, pulling a face.

'Indeed!' Fiona says. 'That's molten lava in there.'

'So you wanted to ask me something,' Wendy reminds her, raising her glass, now refilled with Jill's port, and clinking it against Fiona's mug.

'I did,' she says. 'But now we've gone all Christmassy so I'd feel like a bit of a killjoy.'

'It's fine,' Wendy says. 'Really. Go on.'

'She seems nice,' Fiona says, buying some thinking time. 'The post lady.'

'She is. She's really nice,' Wendy says. 'A bit, you know... puritanical for my tastes. But nice.'

'Puritanical?' Fiona repeats, looking surprised.

'Yeah, you know... doesn't drink, doesn't smoke. I'm sure she has her reasons, but all the same. It seems strange at that age. Plus, she's gay, you know? She has a girlfriend.'

'Which makes her more puritanical or less?'

'Er, neither really. I was just saying.'

'OK, you were just saying, but why?'

Wendy frowns, and takes a gulp of port. 'No reason,' she says. 'I was just making conversation.'

'Would you have told me she was straight, do you think?'

'I might! Jesus, Fiona! I can never say anything right, can I? I was merely imparting a bit of information. I suppose I was thinking that the not drinking, not smoking thing was even more unusual because she's gay. But I guess that's my own silly prejudice in assuming the gays are more fun. Now, can we move on?'

'Because drinking and smoking are *fun*?'

'Well, most of the Western world certainly seems to think so.'

'OK, fine. Whatever, Mum.'

'So is that what you wanted to talk to me about?' Wendy asks. 'Are you gay, sweetheart? Is that it?' She'd intended it as a tease, but once the question is out there she finds herself holding her breath.

'No, Mother!' Fiona says icily. 'That was not what I wanted to talk to you about. Forget it. I can see there's no point even going there today.'

'Going where?' Wendy asks, genuinely confused.

'No... forget it. Here's another one for you instead. Are you and Dad getting a divorce?'

'Oh!' Wendy says, feigning surprise. 'Gosh!' She's not sure quite why she's feigning surprise. After all, it's the exact question she'd been expecting. Perhaps she thinks that revealing she'd been expecting it might affect the believability of whatever she says.

'I mean, you've hardly lived together for years, really. Not properly. Not permanently, anyway. You must have thought about it, haven't you?'

'Um, no, honey, I haven't. Not really. Not in those terms.'

'Hum. I'm not sure I believe you, Mum.'

'Has your father said something about it? Is that why...?'

Fiona shakes her head.

'I...' Wendy shrugs, twice. She sips her port. 'I don't know what to say, sweetie. I know that's not... I mean, things have obviously been... difficult. But you know that.'

'Yeah,' Fiona says, with meaning.

'But I'm not sure we necessarily... I mean, most couples go through rough patches, you know. At some point they do, anyway.'

'So this is just a rough patch?' Fiona asks. 'And you haven't thought about splitting up once. That's your honest answer?'

'Yes. No. No, I really haven't. Not in any concrete way. Because we still... Well, I do, anyway. I still love him.'

'You do?'

'Yes.'

'Then why are you here, Mum? Why is he there?'

'I don't know the answer to that one.'

'Right,' Fiona says. 'Great.' She sips her tea and sighs deeply, then puts the mug down and raises her fingers to her temples.

'What?' Wendy asks. 'Tell me.'

'I just don't believe you. Not after all this...' She gestures at the room as if it sums up the state of their marriage, which in a way, Wendy supposes, it does. 'I mean,' Fiona continues, 'I get that you might not want to tell me about it. And that's fine. But—'

'Honey,' Wendy says. 'That's not what's happening here. These things... they aren't easily explainable; they aren't black and white like that. The truth is... I don't know. What *is* the truth? I suppose the truth is that I don't know what's going on in my own head, let alone what's happening in your father's.'

'You know there's a thing for that,' Fiona says. 'They invented this thing for working out what's going on in someone else's head. It's called—'

'Conversation, yes, I know. And we will. We're going to. We've even talked about having that big conversation. But we need time to... to... I don't know... To sort our own heads out first, I suppose. That's what I'm trying to do by being here.'

'So this isn't a trial separation?' Fiona asks.

'No, it's not. Not really. It's just space, really. Space and time, to think.'

Fiona looks away, out through the darkened window. 'The cat's outside,' she says, and Wendy turns and sees Mittens peeping in. 'Shall I let him in?'

'You can try,' Wendy says. 'But he's pretty skitty.'

Fiona crosses and opens the door, but as soon as she does so the cat runs away.

'You could fix it if you wanted to,' she says when she returns. 'This isn't my... It's not fair, really. I mean, it's not my role. Or it shouldn't be, anyway. I'm, you know, the child. Not the marriage counsellor or whatever. But you could fix it if you wanted to. You just need to be a bit less...'

'Less...?'

Fiona shrugs.

'Less what, Fiona?'

'I don't know. Just *less*.'

Wendy smiles at this. 'Right,' she says. 'Good to know. I might try that.'

'You can smile, Mum, but it's true.'

'You know there are two people in this equation. It takes two to tango, and all that.'

'Meaning?'

'Meaning that your father may not want to make it work. I mean, I know you think he's the bees' knees and everything, and that's good, that's fine, that's how it should be. But he may prefer... something... different... But you probably know more about that than I do.'

'I'm not sure what that's supposed to mean,' Fiona says.

'Well,' Wendy says, downing the remainder of her glass of port in search of courage. 'It means—'

But Fiona interrupts her. 'Actually. Can we change the subject? This is all starting to make me feel a bit queasy '

'Sure,' Wendy says. 'Me, too.'

'Cat's back,' Fiona says coldly, tipping her head toward the window.

'Already!' Wendy says, jumping up, feeling thankful to the cat for the distraction. 'I'll put some cat food in a bowl and you can try to give it to him.'

* * *

It's Christmas morning. Wendy wakes up early and takes pleasure in lying still, listening to her daughter's gentle breathing. Fiona had complained about both the hardness *and* the softness of the sofa after her first night, claiming that the mattress magically managed to combine both faults in a single bed. So, this time, they've shared the upstairs double and Wendy hasn't slept so well in years. Memories have come flooding back of how the kids used to crawl in with them when they were little and scared or ill, or indeed simply fancied a cuddle.

She'd quite like to roll over and cuddle her daughter now, but that, she knows, would seem weird... It's such a shame that happens, though, she thinks. As she dozes in and out of sleep she wonders if it's that way in all cultures or just ours, before sliding from the bed to creep downstairs where, as quietly as she can, she stokes the fire.

It's eight thirty and the sun is still hiding behind the mountains lighting the landscape in a strange almost monochrome tint, but she can tell it's going to be a lovely day.

She puts a bowl of food out for Mittens – it's not even particularly cold this morning – and makes herself a mug of tea which she nurses as the fire starts to flicker, and then roar.

She thinks of Christmases past, remembers the obscene piles of gifts they used to wrap for the kids, gifts for which

Father Christmas got all the credit. Again she wonders how they went from that warm united family to here and now, and feels sad. But then realising that she's spoiling the moment, spoiling now by comparing it with the past, she forces herself to simply be grateful. Because this – Christmas alone with her daughter in France – is as unexpected as it's delightful. She thinks how awful it would have been on her own and feels tearful with gratitude.

At ten, as the sun starts to creep across the floor of the cabin, Fiona wakes up and begs for tea, so Wendy makes a cup and takes it up to her. She sits on the edge of the bed and pushes her daughter's hair from her face. 'Merry Christmas, sleepy,' she says.

'Umh,' Fiona says, rolling away. 'Merry Crimbo to you too.'

* * *

By the time Fiona comes downstairs the cabin is bathed in sunlight and the sky is deepest blue. 'Wow,' she says. 'Is every day sunny here?'

'No, I told you, I got snowed in. It was dreadful. You're one very lucky lass.'

'Hard to believe, looking at that sky.'

'It is hard to believe,' Wendy says. 'I know.'

They eat breakfast in the garden – eggs florentine, Fiona's favourite – and then exchange gifts in front of the fire. There's a pair of sneakily purchased supermarket earrings and a cheque in Fiona's name, plus a selection of brightly wrapped Christmas staples from home.

'Mince pies!' Wendy says, feigning surprise as she opens them. 'Christmas cake!'

'More mince pies,' Fiona says dryly. 'More Christmas cake!'

But there's also a tin of posh tea, a Union Jack tea towel and some fake vegetarian foie gras which they decide tastes halfway between Marmite and mushroom soup. Having never tasted (nor wanted to taste) foie gras, neither of them have any idea how realistic the fake product is, but it's certainly yummy on toast.

And then, showered and with a picnic lunch packed, they lock up the cabin and climb into the car.

'This is great, actually, isn't it?' Fiona says, as Wendy pulls out onto the main road.

'What's that?' Wendy asks.

'That it's just you and me,' she says. 'We haven't done anything together for years. Not the two of us.'

'No, you're right,' Wendy says. 'And I feel quite bad about that. I should have made sure we did more.'

'Don't feel bad,' Fiona says. 'It's like you were saying before. It takes two to tango, after all.'

'Well, I'm really happy you came,' Wendy says genuinely. 'It's the best Christmas gift you could have given me.'

As they drive towards the coast, they chat pleasantly, sporadically, about Christmases past before moving on to random memories of their various family holidays. The friction of yesterday seems forgotten.

The restaurants on La Plage de la Garoupe are all closed for Christmas Day with only a few vehicles peppering the car park.

'It's weird, really,' Fiona says. 'You'd think Christmas Day would be full-on rush hour.'

'My French teacher says Christmas Eve is the main one. They're probably all sleeping off hangovers.'

Once parked, Wendy pops the hatch and hauls her backpack onto her shoulders, and then they walk down to the beach where Wendy has to re-check the instructions on her phone.

'So it's over there, I reckon,' she says, pointing. 'I think we can just follow that couple with the dog.'

They decide to pick their way across the beach rather than walk behind all the restaurants. The sand is littered with driftwood and they pause to examine some of the prettier sea-worn branches.

'Amanda would take this all home,' Fiona says. 'She'd make stupid mobiles out of it.'

'Mobiles?'

'Yeah... Actually, they're not stupid at all. I'm being mean.'

'What, you mean *hanging* mobiles?'

'Yeah, she strings it all together with fishing line so it hangs nicely and sticks on bits of beach glass and what-have-you, and then flogs them all on Etsy.'

'So she's arty, then?'

'She certainly thinks she is.'

'You don't sound keen.'

Fiona shrugs. 'Oh, she's OK. She's just a bit... you know...'

'Can't say I do,' Wendy says, with a laugh, 'having never met her.'

'She's a bit up herself, is all,' Fiona says. 'She thinks she's like some modern art genius, but she just sells driftwood on Etsy.'

'Ah,' Wendy says. 'Yes, I think I see.'

'But Todd thinks she's amazing, so, hey, what do I know?'

'It's serious, then?' Wendy asks, climbing up onto the walkway and holding one hand out for her daughter.

'Yeah...' Fiona says, frowning.

'And?' Wendy prompts. She's convinced that Fiona's about to say something important.

Instead, visibly changing her mind, Fiona merely adds, 'Oh, you know what he's like, Mum. It's serious or it isn't at all.'

They walk for a while along a narrow path until it reaches a wide promontory where the red volcanic rocks tumble into the sea.

To their left they can see two or three different coastal

towns, and behind those the snow-capped Alps rising to meet fluffy clouds. The sea is deep indigo today – and is tipped with delicate whitecaps whipped up by the breeze.

'This is gorgeous,' Fiona says. 'And look, there's even a bench for lunch.'

Wendy snorts. 'I kind of imagined we might walk a little, first?'

'Oh, OK,' Fiona says. 'Sure. That's fine with me.'

To the west, the path narrows, passing through a rusted steel gate and then weaving along in the shadow of a high, red-brick wall built to protect someone's private property from passing plebs.

'Who d'you think lives there?' Fiona asks, peering through a locked gate.

'Bill Gates, maybe?' Wendy suggests. 'Elon Musk? Sting?'

'Must be worth a fortune,' Fiona says. 'God, imagine living here!'

They've reached the southernmost point where the path turns west cutting through red rocks, winding in and out to follow the coast, and up and down endless flights of steps as it hugs the profile of the land. Sometimes the sea is tens of metres away, and others it splashes over the path so that they have to study the waves and then run, shrieking, to the other side. It's beautiful and fun.

'So how come you chose that particular place?' Fiona asks after narrowly avoiding a wave. 'I mean, it's lovely and every-thing, but it did kind of surprise me. It's not really you.'

'No? What sort of place would be me?'

'Dunno, really,' Fiona says. 'Maybe a little cottage in Corn-wall with roses round the door.'

'I quite like the idea of that, too,' Wendy says. *It's funny how your kids see you*, she thinks. *You never really know.*

'So?'

'Oh, well, it just sort of happened, really. The way these things do. I was looking at places in Norway on the net and—'

'Yeah, Dad told me about that. But Norway's freezing this time of year, right?'

'I think it would have been dark most of the time, too. So, not one of my better ideas. But this one sort of popped up. And it looked nice. So here I am.'

They catch up with the couple with the dog. The woman, who is limping, has had to sit down for a rest.

Once they have petted the dog, exchanged *'Bonjours'* and moved on, Fiona says, 'That dog reminded me of Whitey.'

'That's exactly what I was thinking.'

'I still miss him, you know.'

'Well, he was a lovely dog.'

'Best dog ever, you mean. You know, Todd wants a dog?'

'Todd your schoolfriend?' Wendy teases. 'Or our Todd?'

'Huh?' Fiona asks, then, almost seamlessly, 'Oh, no, Todd at school's scared of dogs. He got bitten by an Alsatian when he was little. He's got a massive scar right here.' She hops and taps her left calf.

She's good, Wendy thinks. Excellent attention to detail, but she doesn't overdo it. *She'll go far*.

Fiona has reached a fork in the path, so she pauses and looks back. 'Left,' she asks, 'or right?'

'Try left,' Wendy says, but after less than a minute, it becomes clear that they've chosen a dead end.

'Back?' Fiona asks, pausing again. 'Unless you want to picnic down there?'

Wendy squeezes in beside her and lets her eyes trace the path down to the sea. There's a small flat area at the bottom, mere feet from the water's edge. 'That's perfect,' she says. 'Well spotted!'

They unpack the picnic: baguette, smoked salmon, a tub of

olives and another of hummus, plus crisps, cashew nuts and Coke.

'It's not very festive, I'm afraid,' Wendy says, once the food is all laid out.

'Nah!' Fiona says, prising the top off the olives. 'Best Christmas ever, this! Better than bloody turkey, anyway.'

The sip their drinks and dip into the crisps, and stare quietly out at all that blue. Far away on the horizon a gigantic container ship is sliding past, cutting a glittering line between sea and sky.

'Did you ever think about living abroad, like, properly?' Fiona asks. 'You and Dad, I mean?'

'No, not really,' Wendy says. 'I mean, we loved our holidays. Spain and Greece. Especially Greece. But it was never really an option. Not with kids and jobs and a mortgage... you know how it is.'

'Amanda's parents have got a house with a pool in Tuscany.'

'Of course they have,' Wendy says.

'See, you're getting the picture already.'

'You used to go on about living in Europe,' Wendy says. 'You wanted to spend one year in each country. Do you remember that project you did in Geography?'

'I do,' Fiona says. 'I've still got that somewhere. Brexit put paid to that one.'

'You can still travel, though.'

'Yeah, yeah... I know. But it's not really the same, is it? A holiday's not like being able to work and live in all those different places. I kind of wanted to know what it felt like to be French. To *be* Italian.'

'I think you just fancied an Italian boyfriend, didn't you?' Wendy asks.

Fiona raises one eyebrow and shakes her head in dismay at the turn the conversation has taken.

'But you're right,' Wendy says, moving on. 'It's not the same. Maybe it will all change again, though. If you wait long enough.'

'Sadly,' Fiona says, 'I doubt it.'

* * *

After their picnic and the walk back to the car, Wendy drives them to the centre of Antibes where she parks so they can walk around. Fiona had been hoping for a cup of coffee and a cake, while Wendy was imagining beer, but everywhere seems to be closed.

'The French take their bank holidays seriously, I guess,' Fiona comments as they pass yet another shuttered brasserie.

'Yes, it sure looks that way.'

'Lovely, though,' Fiona adds. 'It's a very pretty town. It kind of makes me wish I was staying for longer.'

'Well, you can always come again,' Wendy says.

'Careful,' Fiona says. 'I might hold you to that.'

After a few random turns through the streets of the old town, they unexpectedly find themselves back at the car. 'Shall we go home for a cuppa?' Fiona asks. 'We have Christmas cake.'

'Lots of Christmas cake,' Wendy says. 'And yes. Let's do that. My feet are killing me.'

'Careful. You sound like Uncle Neil there,' Fiona comments, as she climbs into the car. 'He's always complaining about his feet.'

'Well, Neil's feet are flat as pancakes,' Wendy explains, 'so that's not really his fault. You know, he wanted to join the army when he was eighteen, but he couldn't because of his feet?'

'God knows why anyone would want to join the army,' Fiona comments, lip curled.

'Well, his best friend joined up. I think that was the main reason. That and, you know... patriotism. But anyway, he was saved by his feet. Too flat for all that marching.'

Guided by the Google Maps lady, they drive through the quiet streets of Antibes, and it's not until they're on the open road that Fiona resumes the conversation.

'Why don't you see them anymore?'

The break in the conversation has been long enough that it takes Wendy a second to join the dots. 'Oh, Neil and Sue, you mean?'

'Yeah. Your, um, brother – remember him?'

'Actually, I spoke to Sue a couple of days ago,' Wendy says, wondering whether she can use this true fact to avoid the rest of the discussion. 'But you're right,' she says, relenting. 'I don't see them much these days.'

'Because?'

'Ooh, that's a bit of a long story.'

'We have time,' Fiona says. 'Go for it.'

'And not a story I'm entirely sure I want to go into with you.'

'OK,' Fiona says, with a sigh.

'But sometimes people change. Let's leave it at that.'

'...'

'They used to be more fun, I suppose. But perhaps we all used to be more fun. I'm sure they say the same about me.'

'Not to me they don't,' Fiona says.

'Well, good, because that would be entirely inappropriate,' Wendy says with a laugh.

'So they changed. That's it?'

'Yeah, they got serious all of a sudden. Stopped drinking. Stopped having parties. Stopped coming to *our* parties. It happens to a lot of people when they get older. I'm not entirely sure why, but it does.'

'Hum,' Fiona says markedly.

'Hum?'

'I don't even know why you think that. I don't think they've changed at all. And they definitely haven't stopped drinking.'

'They haven't?'

'No.'

'And you know this, how?'

'Look, I probably shouldn't tell you this, but they came down last weekend.'

'OK.'

'Yeah, see. I shouldn't have told you.'

'Not, it's fine. It's just... a bit strange. I mean, he's my brother, after all. Sue was, for many years, my best friend. My *only* real friend.'

'Well, he's our uncle too. And Sue's our aunt. So it's not that strange.'

'No, I suppose not. And they stayed the night, you say?'

'They did. And it was lovely.'

'Good,' Wendy says, but even she can hear that her voice is sounding brittle. 'And you're sure they're drinking again?'

'I don't think they ever stopped.'

'Oh, they did. I can assure you of that. And they got very, very judge-y about me not following suit.'

'Judge-y?'

'Yes.'

'And that's why you stopped seeing them?'

'Partly.'

'Hum.'

'Oh, please do stop with the "hums", Fifi. You're starting to sound like Sue. If you have something to say, then say it.'

'Well, it doesn't sound like a brilliant reason to me.'

'A brilliant reason for...?' Wendy asks, momentarily distracted by a roundabout.

'For not seeing your only brother. And your supposed best friend.'

'OK,' Wendy says.

'I mean, if I stopped talking to Todd because he was a bit

judge-y – which by the way, he totally is – then I don't think you'd be thrilled, would you?'

'No, I don't suppose I would. But there was other stuff. Of course there was.'

'Like when Gran was ill?'

'Oh, you know about that, do you?'

'Dad mentioned it vaguely.'

'He did, huh? What did he say?'

'Just that they weren't brilliant when Gran was ill.'

Wendy laughs sourly at this. 'Bit of an understatement,' she says.

'So that was it? That was the big one?'

'Yeah, more or less. I'm not sure about there being a "big one". It was more of a drip, drip, drip really. Sometimes you just realise that a relationship isn't... I don't know. That it's becoming too much like hard work. There's a sort of accounting you do in your head at some point: energy put in versus benefits received. And ours was in deficit.'

'It still doesn't sound like a reason for ex-communicating your only brother.'

'Well, there were other things. Like I say, it was a drip, drip kind of situation.'

'Tell me.'

'No, I don't think that's... I've already said too much. Like you say, they're still your aunty and uncle.'

'OK. Fine!'

'Now, I think we just have to go up here,' Wendy murmurs, 'and we're on the road to Gourdon.'

'So, how come they never had kids?'

'Lord, are we back to Neil and Sue again?' Wendy asks, exasperation leaking out.

'I only wondered. If you don't want—'

'I just don't think they wanted any,' Wendy says, a little

more sharply than she'd intended. 'I think kids would have made too much mess.'

'Sue is ultra tidy,' Fiona agrees.

'And Neil is even worse. But seriously? I think they enjoy their lovely lifestyle. Their trips abroad and their gardener and the cleaner and... I don't know... You know what they're like. It's all about the new kitchen and the new sunroom and—'

'The new Tesla...' Fiona offers.

'Exactly. I think they like their lifestyle too much to go messing it up by having kids. Kids cost a lot of money.'

'It sounds kind of selfish when you put it like that,' Fiona says.

'No comment. Those were your words, sweetie, not mine.'

They drive on in silence for a while.

Wendy is concentrating on the road, looking out for fallen rocks, while Fiona enjoys the views. 'It is amazing here,' she says, at one point, swivelling to glance at Wendy before looking back out at the vista.

'I know. I'm glad you like it too.'

They continue to rise into the hills. The interior of the car feels warm and full of love, more love than Wendy has felt around her for some time. It's unexpected. She reaches across and gives Fiona's knee a squeeze. 'This is nice,' she says.

'It is,' her daughter agrees.

They pass by the village of Gourdon, and as Wendy turns and starts up the final hill towards Caussols, Fiona says again, 'You know, you really could fix things with Dad if you wanted to.'

Wendy struggles for a moment to reply, opening her mouth repeatedly and then closing it again without a word.

'Yes,' she finally manages. 'You said.'

'I was thinking about Sue and Neil, that's all. You've kind of been falling out with everyone lately. And I really do think it's all fixable.'

'Oh,' Wendy says, devastated that the gentle atmosphere has evaporated so quickly. 'Well, thanks for your opinion!'

'But, you know I'm right, right?'

'And you know that what's going on with your father is a little more complicated than that.' She switches on the radio in the hope of curtailing the discussion, but Fiona isn't going to be intimidated by a mere French love song.

'Is that it, then?' she asks, speaking loudly to be heard over the radio. 'No comment? End of?'

'Honey...' Wendy protests, with a sigh. 'It's just... things aren't that simple. *Life* isn't that simple.'

Fiona reaches out to turn the radio down low. 'Why not?' she asks.

'Honey... it's... Look, it's kind of like you said the other day. This isn't your role. To play marriage counsellor or whatever. You're our daughter.'

'Well, someone has to bang your heads together,' Fiona says.

'That's as may be. But that person isn't you.'

'Then see someone,' Fiona says. 'See an actual marriage counsellor.'

'Well, your father would have to want to do that as well.'

'He would. I'm sure he would.'

'I think we both know he wouldn't.'

'You keep saying I know things when I don't know them at all.'

'OK. Well, he'd have to... Look, I really don't think we should be talking about this. It isn't appropriate.'

'And there was me thinking we were finally having an honest conversation for once,' Fiona says. 'Fine. Whatever. Let's just talk about the weather.'

'Sweetie,' Wendy protests. 'Please don't do this.'

'Really. It's fine,' Fiona says, turning to look out of the window. 'Forget it. We can go back to not talking about anything important the way we always do in this family. Cos that's been working so well for us all, hasn't it?'

Wendy sighs deeply. She licks her lips as she forms then abandons various phrases in her head.

'OK,' she finally says, 'You want an honest conversation?'

'I *dream* of an honest conversation,' Fiona says.

'OK, what the hell? Why don't you start by stopping all this pretence that you don't know what's going on back home. And then I can stop pretending I don't know, too. That would be a great start if you want honesty.'

'What's going on at home...' Fiona repeats flatly.

'I'm assuming you've met her, have you? So stop pretending you're all innocent and have no idea why we are where we are with all of this.'

Fiona does not reply to this and when Wendy glances across she sees her daughter red faced, wide eyed and chewing her lip... She looks like she might burst into tears.

'I'm sorry,' Wendy says, as she turns off the main road onto their track. 'But as you can see, honesty's not the easy option after all, is it?'

Wendy parks the car and they sit silently for a moment listening to the metallic clicking of the cooling engine, both wondering if the other is about to speak and trying to guess what it is they'll say. But eventually, realising that Fiona isn't going to speak, Wendy opens her door and says, 'Right, let's get that kettle on!'

As they round the corner of the cabin they find Mittens sitting on the wall and for the first time ever he doesn't run away.

'Someone wants his dinner,' Wendy says. Fiona does not reply.

Indoors, Fiona heads for the bathroom, so Wendy busies herself making tea and forking cat food into a bowl.

'Here,' she says, when her daughter returns. 'You give it to him. I think he likes you better.'

Without a word, Fiona takes the bowl and places it outside for the cat. On returning, she scoops the teabag from her cup and drops it in the sink, adds milk and heads to the base of the stairs. 'I think I'm gonna have a lie-down,' she says.

'Have you got the hump with me?' Wendy asks, and Fiona pauses and looks back just long enough to say, 'No, Mum. No, not at all. I'm just tired.'

Wendy sits sipping her tea, listening to Fiona fidgeting on the bed up in the mezzanine, and watching Mittens wolf down his food.

She's feeling stressed and is gagging for a glass of wine. She even glances behind her to look at the open bottle sitting on the kitchen counter. But she fears she couldn't cope with another round of reproach from her daughter and so she continues to sit and sip her tea until she's sure that Fiona has settled, whereupon she heads for the bathroom, silently swiping the bottle of Bordeaux from the counter as she passes by.

This is utterly ridiculous, she thinks as she sits on the toilet lid swigging at the wine. *Still, she'll be gone tomorrow*. She feels guilty at the sense of relief this thought provides. *Maybe I am a loner*, she thinks. *Maybe I truly can't put up with anyone anymore.*

Back in the lounge, she sits on the sofa and watches as the cat cutely washes his face with his paws and then saunters off, as the light fades slowly to grey. She analyses the sounds from the mezzanine. Fiona, she thinks, must be on her phone.

It's 7 p.m. and pitch dark outside by the time Fiona finally comes back downstairs. 'God, I totally fell asleep,' she says.

'That Christmas afternoon snooze is virtually a family tradition,' Wendy says, unsure if she believes her.

They eat ready-made pumpkin soup from a glass jar and dip carrot sticks and toasted baguette into a Camembert that

Wendy has melted on the wood burner. It's very much Christmas dinner-lite but it's delicious all the same.

'We are OK, aren't we?' Wendy finally asks, as she cuts into the second mini Christmas cake.

'Sure,' Fiona says. 'Of course.'

'There's nothing we need to talk about? Nothing urgent?'

'Tomorrow,' Fiona says. 'I think I need a break from all that.'

'Yes, me too,' Wendy agrees. 'It's all got a bit intense, hasn't it? But you do realise you're leaving tomorrow?'

'Yeah,' Fiona says. 'But not till three, I don't think?'

'The flight's at five past three,' Wendy says. 'I checked. But we'll need to leave here about twelve.'

'Sure,' Fiona says. 'No problem. Oh, by the way: everyone at home says happy Christmas.'

'And happy Christmas right back at them,' Wendy says. Then, 'You would tell me if you were upset with me, wouldn't you? I couldn't bear you being upset with me on Christmas Day.'

'I'm not,' Fiona says. 'Not at all.'

'OK,' Wendy replies. 'Well, good.'

'Maybe we can watch a Christmas movie or something?' Fiona suggests. 'You've got Netflix on your laptop, right?'

'I have,' Wendy says, wondering what her daughter intends to say tomorrow and starting to feel worried all over again. 'Let's do that.'

But then the movie is up and running, her daughter has leant in against her so that Wendy can slip one arm across the back of her shoulders, and she has a glass of wine in the other hand about which Fiona hasn't said a word. It feels like Christmas after all, and she only notices that she's been holding her breath when she realises she can breathe again.

TWELVE

AN ULTIMATUM

It is Boxing Day and after a leisurely breakfast and some frantic packing, they've driven to Nice airport.

Wendy has dropped the car back at Hertz and is now trotting back to Terminal 2 to join her daughter. She'd been expecting The Conversation to happen during the drive down but the chatter has remained pleasant and of no consequence, so it's probably yet to come. She can't quite decide whether she hopes that it will happen or not. Fiona, at any rate, seems relaxed. So whatever it is, perhaps it's not so bad.

She finds her daughter standing beneath the departure board. Her flight, it would appear, is on time.

'Departures is all the way down there,' Wendy tells her, pointing.

'Yeah, I saw,' Fiona says. 'Might as well head over that way. Everything OK with the car?'

'Yep,' Wendy says. 'I just parked it and dropped the keys in a box.'

They walk past shops and bars and then across a vast glass-roofed concourse before reaching a row of turnstiles where people are scanning their boarding passes.

'Looks like this is where we have to part ways,' Fiona says, hiking her backpack a little higher, then apparently changing her mind and dropping it instead between her feet.

'It does,' Wendy says, thinking that this definitely means that the conversation isn't happening. Should she provoke it? Should she ask her daughter what it is she wanted to say? Or should she let sleeping dogs lie?

'I'm actually a bit early,' Fiona says, glancing at her phone. 'Maybe we can grab a coffee over there?' She nods towards a brasserie set bang in the middle of the space.

'Coffee sounds great,' Wendy says. 'You should probably eat something too.'

'I'll get something on the plane if I'm hungry,' Fiona says. 'Though I might grab a last proper croissant while we're here.'

They buy croissants and cappuccinos and perch on bar stools where they can watch the stream of travellers pass by.

'I kind of like airports, actually,' Fiona says.

'I know what you mean. So do I. Well, except for all that security nonsense. That always makes me feel guilty, like I'm hiding something.'

'Me too!' Fiona says, pulling a face. 'What's that all about?'

'These croissants are stale,' Wendy says. 'I think they must have been made before the Christmas break.'

'Yeah,' Fiona agrees. 'They saw us coming.' Then, 'People are better looking in airports, aren't they?'

Wendy glances around. 'Maybe,' she says. 'Perhaps they're happy because they're going on holiday?'

'Or suntanned because they just got back.'

There's a pause in the conversation during which a man – red faced, sweaty, overweight – sits down next to Wendy with a pint.

'Though there are exceptions, obviously,' Fiona says pointedly.

Wendy follows her gaze and rolls her eyes. 'You're mean!' she murmurs.

She glances at the man's pint, sees the condensation rolling down the side, and wishes she'd ordered beer instead. And then she sees Fiona looking at it with a raised eyebrow and is glad she didn't after all.

'So,' Fiona says, pushing her half-eaten croissant away.

'So!' Wendy says, mimicking her daughter and doing the same. *Now*, she thinks. *Now is when it happens. Whatever she says, keep calm.*

But, 'I think I'd better get going,' is all Fiona says.

'Oh, OK,' Wendy says, hiding her surprise, and offering a sad smile. 'Let's get you posted back to Blighty, eh?'

They stand and return to the turnstiles. 'Passport? Boarding pass? Purse?' Wendy prompts. 'Nothing else is that important as long as you have those.'

'Yep. Got it all,' Fiona says, patting her pockets.

Mother and daughter hug. The time for any major discussion has run out, and that is probably just as well. It's nice to end the visit on a relaxed note.

She decides she'll reward herself with a little glass of wine the second Fiona's out of sight, and then she'll get her taxi back home. Her nerves are completely frazzled.

'Thanks, Mum,' her daughter says. 'It's been lovely.'

'No, thank you for saving my Christmas!'

'You'll be OK, won't you? I mean, with New Year and everything coming up?'

'Of course I will,' Wendy says. 'And you enjoy yours. Try to get up to some mischief! Make up for your boring Christmas with little old me by going out dancing or something!'

'OK, Mum, I will.'

She squeezes her mother's forearms and breaks away, turning towards the turnstiles, but then pauses and looks back.

'Oh, Mum?' she says, and Wendy – who'd been about to walk away has to interrupt her own movement to turn back.

'Yes?'

'There's a couple of things I promised I'd say before I leave and I haven't managed to get around to it.'

'Oh, OK. Don't worry. We can always talk on the ph—'

'Todd's getting married.'

Wendy frowns at her daughter. The words are so unexpected that they don't really compute. 'I'm sorry?' she eventually replies.

'Todd. Your son,' Fiona says pedantically. 'He's getting married.'

'Todd.'

'Yes. In June.'

'Wha... wh... why?'

'Um, dunno. Because he wants to, I expect.'

'But...' Wendy says.

'But?'

'But that's absurd.'

'Yeah, 'tis a bit,' Fiona says. 'But you know Todd.'

'But that's crazy,' Wendy says. 'That's utter madness.'

'I wouldn't necessarily go that far.'

'I mean...' Wendy can't work out which aspect of this moment is the most ridiculous. Is it the fact that her twenty-one-year-old student son is getting married to a girl he met a few months ago – a girl she hasn't even met – or the fact that she's finding this out here, at the turnstile of an airport, from her daughter? 'Why are you telling me this now?' she asks, starting to feel angry that she's being informed in circumstances which won't even let her think clearly. It crosses her mind that perhaps this is Fiona's intention.

'Because Todd asked me to,' Fiona says. 'Sorry, I know it's not ideal.'

'Ideal? No, it isn't. Why the hell didn't he tell me himself?'

'Probably because he's a wimp. Dunno. Look, I really do need to—'

'And why now? Why so soon? They only met a few months ago. Is she pregnant or something? Because even then—'

'They met over a year ago, Mum. And no, her dad's got Parkinson's, actually. And she wants to do it while he can still walk her down the aisle.'

'Oh. Right. Gosh!'

'So maybe more sad than mad after all.'

'It's going to be in June, you say?'

'Yes. It's almost the longest day. The nineteenth or something.'

'Well, I'll be back mid April, so...'

'There's more, actually,' Fiona says.

'More?'

'Yeah... Todd wants you at the wedding—'

'Well, of course I'll be at the wedding!' Wendy says, interrupting.

'OK, but he doesn't want a scene.'

'A scene? Why would there...? Oh, you mean with your father? Of course there won't be a scene.'

'So yeah, he wants you at the wedding—'

'Yes, yes!' Wendy says impatiently. 'I'll be there. I'll phone him and discuss it all.'

'But he wants you to be sober.'

'I'm sorry?'

'He only wants you there if you're sober, Mum. If you're not drinking at all. That's what he said.'

'I... He... *What?*'

'He – Todd...'

'No, I heard you, Fiona. But why are you – why is he saying this? Is she... is it... I don't know, is she teetotal? Is it a religious thing?'

Fiona laughs at this. 'No. Quite the opposite, really.'

'The opposite?'

'Yeah, that's why he's worried. The reception's in a pub and there's going to be a free bar. And you know what you're like when there's a free bar.'

'But I don't understand... And no, I don't know *what I'm like*. I don't even know what that's supposed to mean.'

'OK, well, have a think about it, Mum, and you'll work it out. And if you still can't work it out then talk to Todd because frankly I feel I've gone above and beyond the call of duty here. Plus I really do have to go now, OK? Or I'm going to miss my flight.'

'Sweetie!' Wendy protests. 'You can't just drop this on me and waltz off!'

But Fiona is pecking her on the cheek and spinning on one heel, now laying her boarding pass on the scanner and pushing through the turnstile. Then, with only the briefest of glances back and a flutter of fingertips over her shoulder, she is gone.

* * *

The taxi home is ridiculously expensive but Wendy doesn't notice. On arrival at the cabin, she puts her credit card into the man's reader and types her PIN code without even checking the amount. She might have authorised a 1,000-euro payment rather than the 190 euros the cab actually cost.

Mittens is waiting by the front door for food, and this, too – the washing and filling of the bowl – Wendy does in a trance.

She can't believe what's just been said to her, nor the lackadaisical way the message was delivered. What a spineless so-and-so Todd is! Imagine asking your younger sister to tell your mother you're getting married! And that 'You know what you're like'. The phrase keeps running through her mind. She can imagine Todd and Fiona discussing it. Perhaps even Harry was there as well. *You know what Mum's like. No way we can trust her with a free bar.*

As if she's ever made a scene. As if any of them have ever seen her drunk! Seriously, how dare they! What is wrong with everyone?

She glances through the window and sees Mittens looking in, clearly hoping for a second helping. But Wendy's not in the mood, and when she stares right back he seems to get the message. She watches him blink, avert his gaze, then finally saunter off.

She sighs deeply. She inspects the knuckles of her left hand and rubs them with her other thumb. *Madness!* she thinks. *The whole thing is utter madness.*

She stares into the distance waiting for some kind of useful thought to crystallise. But when a thought finally anchors itself in her mind, it's not particularly useful. *Fuck them!* is the only thing that comes to mind. *Really!*

She stands and crosses to the kitchen where, after a hunt for the missing corkscrew, she opens a fresh bottle of Chardonnay. *Yes!* she thinks. *Fuck them all.*

* * *

Wendy: I suppose you're in on all of this?

Harry: Wendy? Hello?

W: Hi. Well, are you? In on all of this?

H: Oh, sorry, I thought that was a pocket dial or something. I seem to have missed the beginning of the conver—

W: Just answer the bloody question, Haz.

H: ...

W: Harry!

H: And a merry Christmas to you, too, sweetheart. You're drunk, aren't you?

W: No, Harry, I'm stone-cold sober. <takes a sip of wine>

H: You don't sound stone-cold sober. You're slurring.

W: I am not. And do shut up and answer the question.

H: Which was... sorry... what? Am I in on something?

W: On Todd getting married. And his mum not being trusted with a free bar.

H: Oh, that.

W: Yes! That!

H: So you know about that now, do you?

W: Clearly.

H: Did he call you, then? I didn't know he—

W: No, he did not! I had to find out from his sister at the bloody airport, Haz! He didn't even have the balls to tell me himself. Nor did you, for that matter. Like father, like son and all that.

H: Oh.

W: Oh? Is that all you've got to say?

H: Well, I can't say I blame him. I mean, can you hear yourself?

W: Harry, this is not OK.

H: Which bit?

W: Well, any of it. I mean, Jesus, Harry!

H: Look, I can't really talk to you when you're like this, Wen.

W: You can't be OK with this. Tell me you're not OK with this.

H: The wedding, you mean, or...?

W: Yes, the wedding! He's twenty-one. He's a child.

H: Actually, twenty-one makes him what people like to call an adult.

W: He's twenty-one! Do you remember what it was like being twenty-one?

H: I do, actually. And it was a damned sight more fun than being nearly fifty. But, listen, Todd's an adult and—

W: So you're all agreed, then? That's it? Christ, I'm speechless!

H: You don't *sound* particularly speechless. Speechless might be an improvement.

W: Don't get cute with me, Harry. This isn't funny.

H: Hey, who's laughing? Can you hear me laughing? Well, can you?

W: Now you're being—

H: Listen. There are circumstances, Wendy, and—

W: Circumstances?

H: Yes. For one, they're very much in love.

W: Love? Huh! Love won't get them far. It didn't do much for us, did it?

H: I'm going to do my best to ignore that one, because you're clearly drunk. But listen: Amanda's dad—

W: Yes, I know all about her bloody dad. I couldn't give a shit about her dad.

H: Wow. That's one of the worst things you've ever said, Wen. And there have been some pretty bad ones... But that? Right there?

W: Oh, don't get on your teacher high horse with me. I'm immune to that, Harry. Have been for years.

H:. You know, you're horrible when you're like this? And you are drunk. I can hear it in your voice. So I'm going to hang up now.

W: Don't you dare, Harry! Don't you dare hang up on me.

H: Call me back when you're sober, Wendy, if you ever are these days. Call me back when you're sober enough to apologise.

The line goes dead.

She tries to refill her glass, but the bottle on the table is empty.

'Yes, yes, yes, I'm drunk,' she says out loud. 'So hang me!'

She crosses to the kitchen and pulls a fresh bottle of wine – red, this time – from the cupboard. She's shocked to discover that it has a screw top, the first time she has seen this in France.

'Well, that certainly makes things a bit easier,' she says to no one in particular.

* * *

It's Boxing Day evening and, with her daughter gone, Wendy's feeling miserable and lonely. So she drinks until she loses consciousness and then carries on the moment she wakes up the next morning, drinking like she has never drunk before.

She drinks white wine and red wine and then rosé. Occasionally, when the hunger pangs get too much, she eats crisps or lumps of bread with cheese.

Sometimes she tries to watch something on Netflix, but half the time she can't concentrate on the plot and the other half she falls asleep. So mostly, she just drinks and dozes and stares at the changing light beyond the window. She runs snippets of conversations around her head, revelling in the righteous fury they provoke. *Can't be trusted. You know what you're like. You're horrible when you're like this.*

How dare he call her horrible! How dare they plot to keep her from her own son's wedding!

And when all that fury gets overwhelming – which regularly it does – she drinks more. She drinks until the fury stops and she can slip into not thinking anything at all.

She does not shower, change her clothes, or brush her teeth. At some point – she forgets exactly when – Manon drops by for a French lesson, so she hides out of sight in the bathroom. Mittens visits, too, and despite being too drunk to see straight she manages to give him food.

On the twenty-eighth, she wakes up with the worst hangover she has ever had. The pain of her headache is excruciating, like a pile-driver ramming into her temple just behind her right eye.

She drags herself downstairs. She's wobbly on her feet this morning and misses the last step, stumbling into the coffee table and bruising her shin.

She searches the bathroom for paracetamol but she can't seem to find it anywhere, which is unsurprising really because her headache is so bad she can barely see.

She returns to the kitchen and hunts through the debris of yesterday's binge, but she can't find the damned paracetamol there either.

What she does find is a half-finished bottle of Fitou, and thinking 'hair of the dog' she raises it to her lips and takes a swig. But something unexpected enters her mouth – something solid, something alive. She gags and spits the wine into the sink where she sees a bluebottle, still wriggling, drag its hairy body from the red mess onto a teaspoon.

She heaves and runs to the bathroom where she kneels before the toilet bowl. She thinks she's going to vomit and in fact wants to vomit. Instead, she merely retches repeatedly. There's nothing in her stomach to come out.

Eventually, once the retching is over, she stands and washes her face at the washbasin.

She examines herself in the bathroom mirror. This morning, she looks about ninety.

She washes her face again more thoroughly and applies moisturiser. She brushes her teeth, and then her hair, and then, though she knows this is in the wrong order, she undresses and steps into the shower where she stands beneath the flow until it runs cold.

She dries herself and pulls on clean clothes before returning to the devastation of the kitchen. She tips the remaining Fitou down the sink revealing a second, smaller fly, then returns to the cupboard for a fresh bottle which she uncorks,

She pours herself a hefty glass. She hears Fiona's voice commenting on the hour and glances at her phone. It's not even ten in the morning. She looks at the glass of wine. She looks at the bottle. *If I carry on like this I'll die.* She doesn't know where the thought came from, but it feels like a profound truth mystically revealed to her in that moment.

She gasps and then slowly, as if possessed, as if on autopilot, she pours the glass of wine down the sink and then follows it with the rest of the bottle. Glug, glug, glug.

Hurriedly, fearing she'll lose the willpower to continue if she hesitates even for a second, she opens and empties the three remaining bottles one after the other. Glug, glug, glug, glug, glug.

She opens the refrigerator for food and discovers a final bottle of beer – truly the last drop of alcohol in the cabin. She takes it from the fridge and pops the cap off.

She pauses. She stares at it. She sniffs it. She holds it up to the light and thinks of every other bottle of beer, thinks of the parties, and the dances and the summer barbecues; thinks of the chilled delicious bottles of Mythos in Santorini and the draught halves of Mahou in Spain. Gin and tonics. Manhattans. Shots. Alcohol had been fun, once, hadn't it? She's sure it used to be, sure she isn't kidding herself about that. But it isn't now. And the truth is that it hasn't been for some time.

Telling herself it's a final goodbye kiss, she takes a swig. It's delicious! And then she pours the rest down the sink.

Just before eleven, Manon knocks on Wendy's door again, so she forces a smile and opens it.

Her hangover is still horrendous and she has barely slept, but at least she has tidied the cabin.

'Post?' Wendy asks, because Manon generally calls by after her postal round rather than at the beginning of it.

'No,' Manon says. 'I check that you're OK. I come yesterday but there is no answer.'

'I think I must have been out,' she lies.

'You make me coffee?' Manon asks.

'Um...' Wendy really doesn't feel like company right now.

'Go on. I need coffee,' Manon says. 'And I think that you do, too.'

'Don't you have post to deliver?' Wendy asks.

'No, it's OK,' Manon says, checking her watch. 'No one cares what time the post come as long as it come.'

'As long as it comes,' Wendy corrects, emphasising the 'S'.

'Comezzz,' Manon repeats. 'Same mistake every time!'

Wendy makes two cups of coffee which they drink at the kitchen table. It's too windy to sit outside despite it being a sunny day.

'So where do you go yesterday?' Manon asks. 'You are visiting with your daughter? She is still here?'

'No, she's gone,' Wendy says.

'You still have a car?'

'No.'

'So you go for a walk. This is good. Where?'

Wendy sighs. 'OK, I wasn't out at all. I was here, and I was drunk. I was very drunk and I didn't want to open the door, so sorry.'

'Oh,' Manon says. 'OK.'

'And today I have the worst hangover I have ever had.'

'Ah, so this is why you look...' Manon says, nodding knowingly.

'Yes,' Wendy says. 'This is why I look awful. Moving on, how was your Christmas?'

'Bad,' Manon says. 'My father is with my brother in the... um... the rehab? He drives down there for Christmas Day. And my girlfriend, she's with her family in Draguignan. So, I am alone. But it's OK.'

'And is he OK? Your brother? Is the rehab going well?'

Manon shrugs, but then shrugs again differently and rolls her eyes. 'Officially, is all OK. It's just...'

'You're not convinced,' Wendy offers. 'After all the times before.'

'Yes, I am not convinced,' Manon repeats. 'And you? Your Christmas is good?'

'It was... interesting,' Wendy says. 'In a way, it was good, yes.'

'OK,' Manon says. 'Mysterious.'

'Look,' Wendy says. 'What you said to me... about the drinking... I'm sorry I reacted badly. No one ever said that to me, before. I mean, really, *never*. And then, well, some other people have, since. So I've had to think about it and that's been... challenging. I'm a bit shocked.'

'Your daughter, she says something?'

'Yes. Amongst others. So I was thinking... would you... Could you...? I mean, if it's not too hard for you. Could you tell me some more about your mother? I've never really thought about this much before. Not properly. Not seriously.'

'Sure,' Manon says. 'But what is it you are wanting to hear?'

'I don't know,' Wendy says. 'I'm just trying to understand, really. Because I probably have been drinking too much. That's true, I think. I didn't want to... you know... acknowledge that. But it's probably true. And I'm not sure how much is... well... too much, really. You know?'

'I think when it is not funny,' Manon says. 'If you drink and it's not funny, then it's too much...'

'Yes,' Wendy says. 'Yes, I see. I was thinking the same thing this morning.'

'My mother, for years, it is funny,' Manon says. 'Maybe a bit too much, but not crazy. And then she drinks more. Aperitif. Aperitif early, in the morning.'

'Yes, I've been doing that, too,' Wendy says. 'Pushing *apéro* time forward to eleven.'

'Then drinking on her own. Secret drinking. She is hiding bottles in the bedroom, the bathroom, the car. They fight. Proper fights, like this...' Here Manon mimes boxing. 'And then it is too much so Papa, he leaves.'

'Why didn't he take you with him?'

'Oh, he lives in very small place. And he works late every day. Sometimes weekends we go to the house of Mami. This is grandmama, yes?'

'Just grandma,' Wendy says. 'And even then, your mother didn't stop?'

'She tries, you know, but she never gets help. I'm not sure there is help then for this. But anyway it's hard to stop. You can die, you know?'

'From drinking? Yes, of course you can.'

'Of course. But also from no alcohol.'

'Oh, you mean from withdrawal?'

'Yes. If you drink like my mother, and you stop... Sometimes your body cannot...'

'Yes,' Wendy says. 'Yes, we studied that in college. It's the DTs.'

'So, every time she has to start again because she thinks that she will die. She drinks vodka because she thinks nobody can smell this. But it's not true. You can smell it on the skin. And everyone can see she is drunk. So she loses her job. And then she is home, and this is even more bad. We are dirty. House is dirty.'

Wendy looks around guiltily, and is relieved to remember that she cleaned. So she's not the same as Manon's mother. Not yet.

'I'm so sorry, Manon. That must have been really awful for

you,' she says. 'I can't imagine. And how old did you say you were?'

'Nine. I am nine when we come home and she is dead.'

'That's horrific.'

'Yes. The worse. My brother he finds her and puts a *couverture* over her so I don't see. We call Papa and he comes. Ambulance. Neighbour. Policeman... I don't remember so much. But after this we live with Mamie.'

'God, Manon. And – I know this must be so difficult... but – it was drink? Just drink, I mean?'

'Yes, but also some Lexomil. This is a *médicament* to calm her when she stops drinking but it's not so good with the vodka, so...'

'That must have been so traumatic for you both.'

'*Traumatique* ? *Oui*. For my brother more, I think. Because he finds her. This is why he drinks, maybe. The *trauma*?'

'Trauma. It's the same word.'

'So yes, the trauma of seeing her like that. The trauma, it is given like the bad gift, from the mother to the son. You understand?'

'Yes, from generation to generation.'

'Exactly this. And then, me, too.' Manon sighs deeply and glances out of the window before continuing. 'I start drinking. I don't think I am ever telling you this. When I am maybe fifteen I drink too? Because I feel so... guilty? But I can stop. I see my brother. And I think of Maman. And so, I stop.'

'You felt guilty?' Wendy says. 'How could *you* feel guilty?'

'Because I think... I think...' Manon says. Tears have started to slip down her cheeks. Wendy moves closer so that she can take Manon's hand in hers.

'I just... I know this is not true,' Manon says. 'But I think if we come home more early then she's OK. Just five, maybe ten minutes... I miss her so much.' The emotion suddenly too much for her, she wrenches her hand from Wendy's grasp and dashes into the bathroom.

'It's not your fault, you know?' Wendy says, when eventually Manon returns. 'You know, none of this is your fault.'

'No,' Manon says, still standing, visibly angling to leave. 'I know. I see a... you know a doctor? For the...?' She points at her head to make her meaning clear.

'A shrink?' Wendy suggests. 'A counsellor?'

'Yes, this. So I talk about it. But Bruno, my brother, he does not. He will not talk about this. He cannot talk about it. So...'

'So you think that's why he drinks?'

'Yes,' Manon says. 'Yes, I think this is why. Or maybe it is *génétique*, too.'

'I'm so sorry that happened to you.'

'It's OK,' Manon says, then, 'Well, is not OK. But we live with this. Because we must.'

'Well, thank you for telling me.'

'We are friends...'

'Do you think... just... tell me to stop if this is too much. But do you think there's a reason your mother started drinking in the first place?'

Manon nods sharply. 'Yes. It is her father.'

'Her father?'

'He is not a good person.'

'A drinker, too?'

'Maybe. I don't know. But no, he does worse thing.'

'You mean drugs?'

'Oh, no,' Manon says. 'No, this I do not know. But he is bad to my mother. Very bad. Worse kind of bad. But this I cannot... I'm sorry, look...' Here she holds her hand out so that Wendy can see it trembling. 'This is too much now. I must go.'

'Yes, of course. I'm sorry. I shouldn't have...'

'It's OK,' Manon says. 'And you will be OK?'

'Yes,' Wendy says 'Of course.'

'You will not...?' Here she raises one hand and makes that French 'drunk' gesture around her nose. 'Not too much, I hope?'

'No,' Wendy says. 'No, I promise. There's nothing to drink here anyway.'

'Good,' Manon says. 'This is good.'

* * *

Once Manon has left, Wendy makes coffee and smokes a cigarette, followed by another cigarette, then a third which she lights from the second. She wishes she'd bought more cigarettes while she had the car because if she carries on like this she'll be running out within days. She needs to stop chain-smoking and do something. She's nervous, she realises. She's nervous about facing this day without a drink, which is as absurd as it is true.

She decides to walk up to the radar. It's the only thing she can think of to kill the next few hours and at least it will be better for her lungs than sitting here chain-smoking. She imagines stopping off at the bakery on her way home for a bottle of wine, and has to forcibly change the narrative. No, she has food – she can avoid the bakery for now.

She makes herself a packed lunch, fills a bottle with water, and even though her head is still throbbing, she heads out.

The day is delightful, the sky a gentle baby blue dotted with wispy veil-like clouds. The sunlight hurts her eyes, and she's thankful for her dark sunglasses. The temperature is in the high teens and it feels like a beautiful late spring morning back home.

She asks herself what she means by 'home' these days. Does she mean England, or Maidstone, or that house she bought with Harry, the one they decorated and furnished together? She really isn't sure.

Half an hour later she reaches the base of the walking trail. There are seven cars parked there this morning. It's perfect hiking weather, after all.

Just as she starts the climb, she receives an incoming call from Jill which she ignores, switching her phone to silent. Just as a shop selling wine is the last place she needs to visit, Jill would be the worst person on the planet for her to speak to today.

But even though she knows this, and even though she has refused the call and slipped her phone into her pocket, she hears Jill's voice banging around her head, as well defined and Jill-like as if she'd chosen, instead, to answer.

'Oh, don't be daft,' the voice says, 'you're not an alcoholic!' And, 'If you're an alcoholic, then everyone's an alcoholic!' And, 'God, please don't become one of those people! Please don't become a bore!'

Wendy would certainly be bored if she stopped drinking. And she'd probably be fairly boring, as well. Is that really what she wants?

She catches herself using the conditional tense in her head. She *would* be bored *if* she stopped. *Honestly*, she thinks. *Ten seconds of imaginary conversation with Jill and I'm already beginning to backslide.*

So, no, she will stop drinking – well, as long as she can humanly do so without dying. Seeing her son get married depends on it. And she'll stop for... For how long? Until the wedding? But that's months! Just long enough to prove to herself that she can, then. But how long would that be? A month? A week? Christ, even the idea of a week without a drink sounds like hell.

She crosses paths with two early-bird hikers coming back the other way. They are young (maybe thirties?), blond, fit and beautiful.

When Wendy was their age she'd believed that if you did

enough exercise you could prevent ageing altogether. She really had thought that creaky, cranky old people got that way because they hadn't put in enough effort. But no matter what you do the aches and pains come, and no matter what creams you slap on, the wrinkles and sunspots appear.

She can remember it, though: feeling young, feeling fit, feeling almost permanently optimistic and capable – getting over a full-on party during a single night's sleep and slapping make-up on the next morning thinking, *Yeah, girl, you're looking fine*. If only she'd been aware how temporary it all was, she'd have made the most of the feeling.

She imagines herself at ninety, looking back at this very moment. *Appreciate it*, she tells herself, taking a deep breath and consciously looking around at the view. She's been so lost in her mind since she started walking this morning that she has barely noticed her surroundings.

At the top she finds multiple groups of hikers picnicking noisily – chattering like magpies – so she nods and smiles and continues along the ridge until she finds a quiet hollow in which to eat her sandwich.

She thinks about what Manon said about the way her mother passed her own trauma on to her children and wonders what the nature of the original trauma might have been.

Even though it wasn't said or even really hinted at, there had been a whiff of sexual abuse in the air. She reckons she'd realised, at least subconsciously, that this is what Manon was referring to. No wonder the poor woman turned to drink.

At least she doesn't have any trauma of her own to deal with. After all, her own childhood had been pretty damned perfect. Well, OK, perhaps not perfect, because whose upbringing ever is? But it had been good. It had been good enough. Perhaps her father had been a little slap-happy, and her mother a bit of a hypochondriac, always laid up with one of her mystery illnesses. Which is why no one really listened when she really did get ill – not until it was too late to do anything about it, at any rate. Classic crying wolf scenario.

But the love had been there, too, hadn't it? She'd received oodles and oodles of love. Particularly from her mother. Which is why losing her was so damned hard.

A buzzard swoops past, and as she follows it with her gaze she finds herself looking out to sea. She's so distracted today that she hasn't noticed it until now.

It's lighter than usual today – pale turquoise almost white. The colour makes her want to be on a boat, trailing her fingers through the waves. She'd always wanted to live by the sea. They should have made that happen.

Anyway, if she isn't dealing with trauma, then what's her excuse for drinking so much? she wonders. Could it really be as simple as boredom? And if that were the case, then surely it wouldn't be that hard to wrestle under control something that is little more than a bad habit?

She takes another bite of her sandwich even though she isn't really enjoying it. The bread is stale and so chewy that it's making her jaw ache. She picks the cheese from inside and nibbles that instead.

It was the pandemic, really, she decides. And yes, her home life had been a bit boring around that time. After all, they'd stopped going out to restaurants or even visiting other people's houses. They'd stopped hosting dinner parties and going to the cinema, too. But when she thinks back really hard, she can't remember feeling bored. What she remembers is feeling *stressed* – so stressed that she could barely breathe.

The buzzard flies past again in the other direction and so she chucks the bread from her sandwich into the air hoping it will swoop and grab it like prey, but the bird isn't interested and flies on unperturbed. 'Can't say I blame you,' she mutters.

So no, not bored, but stressed. And unable to find another way to wind down at the end of the day.

The horror of those two years washes over her. The patients dying in corridors, the piled-up bodies in the morgue... No wonder she'd been stressed!

Nearly everyone at work had found some kind of chemical crutch to get through it all. Gina got hooked on stolen Valium, and Melody started smoking weed during coffee breaks, something that was known about by everyone, and tolerated. Wendy had merely drunk a little more than usual of an evening and convinced herself that she was doing fine. *So yeah, the pandemic as a nurse*, she thinks. *That'll do it.*

Before that, pre-2020, everything had been fine, hadn't it? She takes a swig from her water bottle and tries again to remember.

In truth, she hadn't been in the best place when the whole thing had started, either – after all, she'd already fallen out with Sue and Neil by then. And she'd needed them during the pandemic. If she'd had her best friend and her brother to lean on, then maybe things wouldn't have been so bad for her. She'd needed them and they hadn't been there, and that had been yet another reason to resent them.

Sitting here isn't working, she decides. Her anger is starting to feel overwhelming, and the stream of fresh reasons to feel angry seems limitless. She needs to move. Action feels better than thought.

She munches on a few squares of chocolate washed down with a swig from her water bottle and stands. She'll walk farther today. She'll explore what's higher up the ridge. And she'll not think of Sue and Neil again.

But it's been interesting, thinking about it, she decides as she starts to walk. Because she's never thought about that aspect of the pandemic before: how even during the pandemic, and even knowing she was a nurse and on the front line, Sue and Neil still hadn't been in touch – well, other than the occasional text message to check they were all still alive, they hadn't.

She supposes that they must have felt submerged by their own worries. That every single person felt that their own experience was the most unbearable was almost a defining aspect of the pandemic, even when, for people like Sue and Neil, the only thing that really happened was that they ran out of things to watch on Netflix.

Still, it was silly of her to expect more of them. Because if they hadn't stepped up when her mother was dying, they were hardly likely to become brilliant people for anything else.

But, God, the pandemic had made her angry.

Actually, anger is probably an even better word to describe how she was feeling than 'stressed'. She can remember being so angry when she got home of an evening – angry at the government, at her bosses, at the lack of funds and material; angry at bloody Brexit for sending her gorgeous EU colleagues away right when they were most needed; angry at her family, too, for not trying harder to understand what she was going through at work, and yes, angry at Sue and Neil for seemingly not giving a shit. She'd felt angry at the news every evening, angry at the clapping – bloody hell, the clapping! The clapping had made her absolutely furious, and the sight of Boris Johnson clapping the NHS staff on the doorstep of 10 Downing Street had made her feel nauseous. She could have strangled him with her bare hands for that.

It's not like they'd got any help, either. There had been no counselling, no discussion groups, no vouchers for sessions with a shrink... So, yeah. She'd started coming home and getting tipsy. Because being tipsy made her feel less angry or at least, it made her anger seem manageable.

It's so obvious, now she thinks about it, that she wonders if she doesn't have alcohol to thank for the fact she got through the whole thing intact. Well, perhaps not intact, but semi-intact, at least. She didn't throw herself off a bridge, after all.

She pauses and looks around. She has scrambled so far up

the ridge that the globe of the radar is now the size of a ten-pence piece silhouetted against the sky. It's wild and craggy and dramatic up here. It's beautiful! She sniffs the air and then pulls her phone out to take a photo.

She's feeling happier, suddenly – fancy that! Perhaps it's this new narrative doing the trick – this idea that it's the alcohol that enabled her to survive. As a theory, it certainly sounds right. It feels true. And now the pandemic is over she needs to calm down and get her drinking back under control. With the source of her anger now gone, why on earth would that be hard? It's hardly rocket science, is it?

* * *

Somehow, she gets through the afternoon and most of the evening.

Time drags strangely, which in a way seems reasonable. After all, she's sitting in a cabin on a mountain in France, alone. There's quite literally nothing going on.

She reads until her eyes are tired then watches a detective series on her laptop until she gets bored with that as well. But unlike every other day when she has performed these same activities with a drink (or three) she does not fall asleep and so is surprised by how little time they take up. Has she been using drink to fast forward her life?

She phones Jill and has a long chat during which she doesn't say a word about what's been going on, a conversation during which the word 'alcohol' is not mentioned once. But even after that it's still only 6.30 p.m.

She cooks dinner (tomato sauce with pasta and cheese) and eats it in front of Sky News. Mittens appears, and she feeds him not once, not twice, but three times, and though the cat can't believe his luck, it's still only 8 p.m.

After another hour of staring at the fire, she retires upstairs to read but finds she can neither concentrate on the story nor fall asleep. She's feeling nervous and irritable and other than this round robin of trying to sleep, trying to read and doom-scrolling on her phone, she can't think what else she can possibly do to pass the time.

And then, suddenly, it's morning and she realises that at some point she must have dozed off, straight into a world of nightmares.

She lies in the pale morning light and tries to remember the nature of her dreams, but other than a few images that are so vague they're more like sensations than stories, she's unable to grab hold of any specifics. But her mother had been in the mix somewhere, she's sure of that. Her mother, and the hospital, and Harry.

She picks up her phone and sends him a message, a message which remains undelivered because his phone is still switched off.

Ping me when you wake up, she types. *I could do with a bit of a chat.*

It's ten o'clock (nine in England) by the time Harry switches on and replies.

Gimme five, he writes. *I need a coffee and a poo first.*

She makes herself a fresh cup of coffee and stokes the fire with logs – it's cold in the cabin this morning.

Harry: Good morning, beautiful. <His voice is still deep and thick with sleep.>

Wendy: It's a good job this isn't a video call because you wouldn't be saying that at all. I swear I look like I've been dragged through a bush, murdered, buried, and dug up again. Plus I really, really need a proper haircut.

H: Well, seeing as it isn't video, we'll just pretend you're looking gorgeous, right?

W: Certainly works for me. How are things in sunny Maidstone?

H: Everything's fine. Fiona seems to have enjoyed her little trip and is actually smiling from time to time. Todd and Amanda are being astoundingly dull looking at wedding stuff all day and trying to get everyone else interested.

W: You mean dresses and flowers and what-have-you?

H: Yeah. And suits and ties and shoes for Todd. The shoes are very important, apparently. Can you imagine? I can't believe how traditional our children have turned out. Do you think we went wrong somewhere?

W: Sounds like fun to me. I love all that stuff. And Todd will look great in a suit with those square shoulders of his.

H: Yeah. I suppose so. And you? How are you?

W: I'm OK... Look, I'm sorry about the other day. I know I was a bit...

H: ...

W: A bit *antsy*, I suppose you could call it.

H: Not the word that comes to my mind, but OK. You were shocked. Understandably. So did you want to talk about something specific? Or did you just want to hear my gorgeous morning baritone?

W: Specific. Definitely.

H: Oh. OK, then.

W: But your gorgeous morning baritone is definitely a plus, if that helps.

H: Yeah, it does a bit.

W: So I've got two quite full-on questions for you as it happens. Are you on your own there?

H: Um, yeah, I am. But hang on. Just let me... There. Door closed. Lazy youngsters sound asleep in their beds. Go for it.

W: So. Um. Wow, this is hard!

H: ...

W: OK. Are you seeing someone, Harry? Actually, it's OK,

I know you're seeing someone. So I suppose my real question is: is it serious?

H: Oh. OK. Wow!

W: Sorry, but I need to know. I've just... sort of reached a point where I have to know.

H: Sure. It's not a conversation I thought I'd ever have to have on the phone, that's all.

W: No. It's not ideal. But this is where we are.

H: Yeah.

W: Yeah?

H: I mean, yeah, OK. As for the question, the answer is 'no'.

W: No?

H: Yeah. I mean, no, I'm not seeing anyone.

W: Harry...

H: Honest, Wens, I'm not.

W: I really do need you to be honest here, Haz. And I promise not to kick off about it. Well, I promise to try my best.

H: Good. That's good. But the answer is still 'no'.

W: OK, then have you *been* seeing someone? Past tense.

H: That'll be a 'no' to that one, too.

W: I...

H: Really, Wendy. No.

W: I'm finding that hard to believe. Sorry.

H: And yet I can assure you it's totally true.

W: I felt sure you were.

H: Yes. I know. I picked up on that.

W: Back in... I don't know exactly. March, maybe? When you started coming home really late every night.

H: Ah. OK. God, do you really want to do this right now?

W: Yes, I think I do.

H: Right. Fine. OK.

W: So?

H: So... In that case, define seeing someone.

W: You see. I knew it.

H: It's not... I'm not... Look, it's hard to...

W: To admit?

H: No! Stop it! No, it's hard to define really. But if you really want to know...

W: And I think we've established that I do...

H: Then I *was* sort of hanging out with someone, in March.

W: And April. And May.

H: Yeah, if you want.

W: Define hanging out.

H: Um, I was, you know... spending time. With one of the supply teachers. She'd moved down from ... from up north... and she didn't know anyone here.

W: Poor her.

H: Don't be like that. It won't help.

W: Sorry. Carry on. She didn't know anyone there...

H: So I started hanging out with her a bit.

W: You want me to believe that's it?

H: And if I'm being brutally honest, there was maybe a moment when – I mean, you and me, it wasn't really working, I think we can agree on that, right? And so I thought it might go somewhere with... this person.

W: This person?

H: This woman. It was a woman, you'll be pleased to hear.

W: Oh good. Yeah, I'm thrilled.

H: But it didn't. I mean, we were friends, and then we were sort of close friends, and then when... you know... the thing... between us... when it didn't come to pass, then the shine all sort of wore off a bit. I think that happens if you wait too long. And we did wait too long. Because I'm married. So I wasn't in a rush.

W: That's good of you.

H: Wendy...

W: No, I get it. Seriously. I do.

H: And now we're back to being workmates again.

W: Right. OK. I think I see.

H: But we never... ever... you know...

W: Had sex?

H: Yeah. We never had sex. I promise.

W: Define sex.

H: Ha... Funny. Seriously, we didn't.

W: I'm *being* serious. Define sex.

H: Wendy, we didn't do anything. No matter how you choose to define sex, we didn't do it. OK?

W: Kissing?

H: No one defines kissing as sex.

W: So you did, then? You kissed?

H: ...

W: That's a yes, then.

H: Christ, OK, sure, we kissed. We kissed a couple of times. And we nearly, you know, went further. But we didn't. And now it's over.

W: You sound sad about that.

H: No, I'm really fucking happy about that.

W: Because?

H: Because otherwise this conversation would be a whole different kettle of fish. Because – oh, hang on. We've got an early bird here. Just, um, let me move to another room. Morning, Fiona. Yeah... on the phone... No, no, you're fine.

...

...

...

H: OK, I'm back. God knows why she's up before lunchtime. Anyway, where were we?

W: You were kissing another woman. And nearly shagging her.

H: But not shagging her. Let's concentrate on the positives, shall we?

W: OK. Though not doing something's actually a negative.

H: Funny.

W: Yeah. I'm hysterical, me.

H: You OK?

W: Uh huh.

H: Uh huh, meaning?

W: I need to think about it. Can we put a name to this mystery person? It might make things easier.

H: I don't think that would make things easier at all. So no.

W: OK, point taken. Maybe not. Do I know her?

H: No. You definitely don't.

W: Right. OK, then. Oh, one last question on... all that... Is she still around? At your school?

H: Yes, she is. But she's dating... She's, um, in a relationship with someone else from work now.

W: Is he married too?

H: No, as it happens, he isn't. Which is probably why their story has... you know... blossomed.

W: Blossomed?

H: Yeah, you know, worked out or whatever...

W: OK. And how do you feel about all this blossoming?

H: Fine. Relieved.

W: OK.

H: So are we good? Did I pass the test?

W: I'm not sure. We'll be in touch.

H: You'll have your people get in touch with my people?

W: Something like that, Haz, yes.

H: So.

W: So... On to my next question.

H: Please don't tell me there's more?

W: Yes, I'm afraid there is. Though this one's more about me than you.

H: Why? Are *you* seeing someone?

W: No. Most definitely not. No, it's just... Do you think I'm an alcoholic? Be honest. Be totally honest.

H: Oh, OK. Bit left of field and all that, but OK...

W: Because everyone else seems to think I am.

H: Define everyone else.

W: Fiona, Todd, my post lady.

H: Your post lady?

W: Yes. Just answer the question, will you?

H: If I'm being totally honest: I'm not sure.

W: You're not sure?

H: No. I mean... I'm thinking about it now, and it's a bit of a technical question, isn't it? A bit of a medical one, really. And I'm not an expert. I don't know the actual definition.

W: Right. OK. I see.

H: Will that do? As an answer, I mean?

W: I suppose. But it sounds like a cop-out.

H: I do think you drink too much, though. Actually, I don't just think that. I know it. You definitely drink too much.

W: Define too much.

H: Erm, enough to make you... How can I put this politely?

W: I think we're beyond politely, don't you?

H: OK, then. Bombs away: your drinking has made you impossible to live with.

W: ...

H: And now you're pissed off with me. That's the trouble with these total honesty situations. No one really wants honesty no matter how much they say they do.

W: No, I do.

H: Anyway, now you have your answer.

W: That I may or may not be an alcoholic, but that I'm impossible to live with.

H: Yeah.

W: Do you mean that, like, literally?

H: Sorry, which bit?

W: The impossible to live with bit. Or is there still hope?

H: I think maybe if you stopped there might be hope.

W: If I stop being impossible or stop drinking?

H: I think they're linked. I think one leads to the other. In a sort of strange circular fashion.

W: OK. Do you really mean that, Haz? Because...

H: You're not crying, are you?

W: ...

H: Wendy?

W: No, no, I'm fine.

H: You are. Babe...

W: Maybe, a bit.

H: I'm sorry.

W: Don't be. I asked. And you don't think it's just me, then? That I've become impossible to live with, full stop?

H: No, I don't think that. I mean, you have. But that isn't you. It isn't all of you at any rate. I'm not sure I'm making any sense now. But it's the drink. The drink is definitely part of the problem. Quite a big part, I suspect.

W: You think?

H: Look, Wendy. OK... Take right now, yeah? This conversation. You're sober, aren't you?

W: Yeah. It feels awful. This conversation has me gagging for a drink.

H: But that's why this conversation is going the way it is... It's reasonable, isn't it? It's a proper conversation between adults. Do you see?

W: Is it?

H: Yes. It is. And compare it with the one we had on Boxing Day when you were drunk.

W: Look, I've apologised about that. I was upset. You know I was. Because of Todd.

H: You were. But you were also drunk.

W: ...

H: Can you at least admit that?

W: OK. Fine. I'd had a few.

H: And it made the whole conversation unreasonable.

That's my point.

W: You hung up on me. You actually hung up on me.

H: Yep. I did. But not today. Today I'm still here. See the difference?

W: OK. Yes, I see the difference.

H: Drinking makes you angry. That's the thing, Wendy. And being angry makes you drink. You think it helps, but it doesn't.

W: ...

H: You still there?

W: Yes. Still here.

H: You're crying. Honey... God. Please don't cry. I hate it when you cry.

W: It's OK. I'm fine. I'm just... You know... A bit brittle, today. But I'm fine.

H: Good. Because I really want that. I really want you to be fine again.

W: I've been trying to think about it all, you know. I really have. About the drinking, I mean, and us, and everything else. I think I've worked out when it started, at least. I think it was the damned pandemic.

H: OK.

W: I think the pandemic made me so angry. Because of my job. And I didn't know how to deal with all that... anger. You know? So I started drinking just so I could breathe again. Because otherwise I thought I might explode.

H: ...

W: You've gone quiet now. What's that about?

H: Do you really want to know what I think?

W: Yes. You know I do.

H: No, I'm not sure that I do know that. Because I've tried to talk to you about this countless times, Wens. And that conversation has never gone well.

W: You have?

H: Hundreds of times. Well, tens, at any rate.

W: Well, I don't... I mean... OK, if you say so. But that doesn't really... match... my experience, if that makes any sense. But, go on.

H: It didn't start with the pandemic. You're wrong.

W: It didn't?

H: No. It got worse during the pandemic. But Covid wasn't the start.

W: But—

H: It started when your mum died, Wens. I'm sorry, but I'm absolutely certain of that.

W: ...

H: Really. Think about it and you'll see I'm right.

W: ...

H: Wendy? You're not crying again, are you?

W: No, no... I'm trying to remember. Honestly, I am. But... I mean, are you sure? *Was* I drinking when Mum died? Because I don't think—

H: Not the drinking, so much, Wendy. I didn't really mean the drinking. I'm talking about the anger.

W: The anger?

H: Yeah. You changed when your mum died, Wendy. And you've been angry ever since.

She has just put her phone down when Manon bangs on the window making her jump.

'*Bonjour,*' she says quietly. She's raw from her conversation with Harry, and if possible she would have hidden in the bathroom all over again, but she's been caught in broad daylight. 'I don't usually see you at this time,' she says.

'Yes, I am working!' Manon replies. 'You have mail!''

She takes the envelope from Manon's outstretched hand and immediately recognises the weight and shape of the envelope – a Christmas card. The handwriting she knows well enough, too. It's from Harry.

'Thank you,' she says, forcing a smile and waving the envelope like a fan.

'You are OK?' Manon asks.

'Yes, I think so. I didn't sleep well, so I'm tired. Very tired, actually. But I'm fine.'

'You look... I don't know...' Manon says.

'I'm trying not to drink,' Wendy announces. 'Everyone seems to agree I have a drink problem, so I'm trying to find out if they're right.'

Manon nods. 'I think you are very brave.'

'Or very stupid.'

'No,' Manon says, reaching out to touch Wendy's shoulder. 'Never this. I can phone you? To see you are OK?'

Wendy feels suddenly tearful at this young girl's concern for her wellbeing. 'That's very sweet of you. So yes. Please do. And thank you!'

Manon glances at her phone. 'You know, I don't have your number?'

'Oh gosh, yes, that's true.'

'You put in?' Manon says, handing Wendy her phone.

'Yes, of course.'

Once Manon has left, she sits in the sunshine and takes stock of the sensations in her body. She's feeling anxious – which strikes her as fairly normal, all things considered, but also clammy, and a bit slow of thought, as if suffering from the beginnings of a fever. She's also still shell-shocked from her conversation with Harry, but more hopeful about the future, too.

She remembers the flu she had when she was snowed in and ran out of wine. Perhaps that wasn't viral after all. Could it just have been lack of booze? Either way, she got through it, she thinks. So she'll get through it again this time. She'll be fine.

* * *

She is not fine.

She is not fine at all.

But the worse she feels the more convinced she becomes that what everyone has been saying is true: she really is dependent on alcohol. It's madness that she has never allowed herself to realise this before, but now she has, she's determined to push through to the other side.

She barely sleeps that night and when she does manage to doze off, she wakes up feeling panicky a couple of hours later. Even when asleep, she has terrifying nightmares that are so vivid they're more like hallucinations. These are bad enough sometimes to make her doubt that this is humanly achievable without help. But when she imagines returning home as the new, sober Wendy and compares this mental image with the alternative in which she has to admit that she tried and failed, and that her addiction – something she hadn't even accepted as existing – turned out to be more powerful than the sum total of her willpower, she steels herself to push through.

She will simply attack the problem like the medical professional she is. So she takes half a tab of Oxazepam from time to time – enough to calm herself down when her anxiety starts to feel unmanageable. And whenever she feels particularly agitated or restless she checks her heart rate, promising herself that if it ever goes over 110 she'll get help. She's not sure quite what kind of help that would be, but she reckons Manon or Madame Blanchard could get a doctor to her if things get bad. At worst, they could always bring her some wine!

Though she sweats profusely and trembles a little, though she feels utterly, utterly awful, and irritable and angry, her heart rate does not go above ninety-six. When Manon texts her, she lies, texting back that she's 'fine' to avoid having to speak to her. She doesn't have the patience for conversation.

While dozing she dreams of her mother flying like a kite, being dragged high into the sky until the string breaks, and of her father snoozing on a hammock above a precipice, and of a terrifying eight-legged spider-cat who looks a lot like Mittens, catching birds in his enormous web. When awake she fawns on the real four-legged Mittens, who, seeming to understand her need at this time, finally deigns to let himself be stroked in exchange for food – an act of generosity that makes her cry.

Unable to concentrate on the book she has been reading, she instead reads everything she can find about alcohol, addiction and getting sober.

She reads about clinical trials of new drugs to help with withdrawal and scientists who have performed brain scans, and the twelve steps used by Alcoholics Anonymous. She reads dozens of personal horror stories, and success stories, and the best advice currently available from the top American hospitals.

At one point, after a random turn in the network of rabbit holes she's been sucked into, she stumbles upon an article which says that rats left alone in barren cages self-administer alcohol and cocaine, while rats in rich social environments do not. Lack of social connection leads to addiction, the article concludes, and this ties into her own experience in such a profound way that it feels like a lightbulb moment.

After all, didn't her own story with alcohol start with the disappearance of her beloved mother and her rupture with her best friend and brother, only to be topped up with the lashings of isolation supplied by Covid? Her life is quite simply stuffed with severed connections these days and rather than spotting the issue and trying to deal with that in any meaningful way, she has chosen to shut herself away and drink – to shut herself away *through* drink. And when that failed to help, as it surely must, her decision was to come here, to a lonely mountain in France – the land of the 3 euro bottle of wine.

She pulls out her journal and rereads her previous diary

entries, written when she was snowed under, to confirm that she is re-experiencing the same symptoms. And then she writes a couple of fresh entries about the general state of her life and everything she seems to have lost or given up during the last fifteen years. Her father. Her mother. Her best friend. Her brother. Her husband. Her kids. Her workmates...

When you line it all up like that it's a lot. And like a jigsaw puzzle at the beginning of the construction process, she senses that a picture is forming. She starts to believe that if she carries on, it may one day all make sense.

On the evening of the thirtieth, fifty-nine laggardly hours after she stopped drinking (because, yes, she's counting the hours), she manages to watch a film in its entirety and fall asleep without taking a pill. But less than three hours later, she's awake again, soaked in sweat and trembling from the most dreadful nightmare.

In the dream, her mother had been screaming in pain – begging for morphine, and struggling to breathe – and Wendy had been weeping herself, tears rolling down her cheeks as she pleaded with a lazy hospice nurse to summon the night doctor for her mother.

She sits up and switches on the light. She notes the wet pillow, the soaked sheets, and holds out her hand to watch it trembling. Is this the beginning of the DTs? she wonders. Or is she merely trembling in rage at that dream nurse who would not listen?

She gets up and makes her way downstairs; she plugs the kettle in for tea.

She looks outside into the darkness and tries to push the horror of the nightmare from her mind's eye, but it won't go away. The images from that hospital ward feel as real as here and now – more real in fact, than this strange dimly lit cabin.

She goes into the bathroom and sits down to pee. And it's there – in the cold white bathroom with her knickers around her ankles – and then – at 3 a.m. on New Year's Eve – that she realises: the nightmare was no nightmare. It was a memory, an actual memory of a very real moment – perhaps the most real, most horrific moment in her life – a memory she has somehow shut out until now.

The choking, the begging, her mother's pain, the tears, that imbecile nurse insisting that her mum had taken all the morphine that was 'allowed'... every detail of the nightmare is true, every sensation, every feeling something she most definitely lived through, every image intense with uncanny photographic accuracy.

And now she remembers the rest, too. She remembers how ten minutes later another nurse had finally paged the doctor and how ten minutes after that he'd sleepily sauntered in. She remembers how, when she finally managed to push him into her mother's room – because she had quite literally *pushed* him through that door – it had been too late.

He'd removed her hand from his shoulder and shot her a glare in irritation that she'd dared touch him, and then he'd said, in the most supercilious manner possible, 'So, what's all the fuss about then, Mrs Wilks?'

And that's when she'd realised that her mother, the fussing Mrs Wilks, was no longer choking, no longer begging, no longer wheezing, no longer screaming in pain – that her mother was no longer experiencing anything at all. And she hadn't even been there to hold her hand.

She stares at the tiled bathroom wall as the film plays out in her head. She realises that she's been holding her breath and forces herself to breathe, and finally starts to pee.

And then, with a gasp of her own, with a gurgle, with a squeak, she starts to weep here in real life, fresh tears rolling down her cheeks until they drip, one after the other, onto her knees.

God knows how this is possible but she really had forgotten

this scene. Yes, she'd wept for the loss of her mother, for her absence, for the ache in her heart, for the impossible-to-comprehend fact that the most important person in her life was no longer on the planet... But that precise moment – the cinematographic horror of those thirty minutes – well, she truly had locked it away. And now, it is back, playing over and over in a high-speed loop, like a horrific best of, like the recap at the beginning of a television show. And she really doesn't know what to do with it all. No wonder she was angry. No wonder watching all those people gasping for breath during the pandemic felt so personal. And no wonder she started to drink. If she could, if she had some alcohol in the cabin, she would drink herself into oblivion right now.

THIRTEEN

A NEW YEAR

It's not until Wendy gets up again just after ten that she remembers it's New Year's Eve. As every morning since she stopped drinking eighty-two hours ago (she's still counting them), the first thing she does is scan her body.

She has woken up feeling tired and depressed. Is the cause this newly surfaced memory, the New Year's Eve effect, or giving up alcohol? It's probably a unique combination of all three, she concludes. After all, New Year's Eve alone, sober, with all of *that* to ponder... Well. That's quite clearly going to be hell.

She gets up; she stokes the fire. She makes coffee and cradles the warm cup between her hands. It's cold outside this morning – the thermometer says six degrees. But the sky is entirely free of clouds, so it will at least be sunny. She should probably try to take a little pleasure from that.

She feeds Mittens and manages to stroke him a couple of times before he decides that's quite enough of that and wanders off into the bushes. She wonders where he sleeps. She wonders if feeding him is even a good idea, because, after all, what will happen when she leaves? She imagines him peering through the window at the empty cabin and feeling desolate, cold and hungry once she's gone. Maybe befriending him is an act of cruelty.

She slouches around until mid-morning, reading the news on her phone (miserable but at least distracting) and checking Facebook and Instagram, too, which (as they largely feature people's preparations for New Year's Eve) are depressing in their own way.

It's gone eleven by the time she manages to drag herself out the door. She walks to the car park at the base of the hiking trail, lost in thought. She doesn't want to be here, today. She doesn't want to be here at all.

Is she at least fitter than when she arrived? she wonders as she begins the climb. Yes. So at least there's that.

But even fitness will fade when she gets home – once she closes the brackets of this trip. And then will anything remain at all?

Just as she's nearing the radar she hears a noise behind her and turns to see a man and dog catching up fast. He's no spring chicken, but by God, he's fit – he's almost running.

Wendy ups her pace, determined not to be shown up by being overtaken, and as he gets closer behind her she can hear him urging his dog on. 'Come on, Fifi,' he keeps saying. 'You can do it.'

Wendy takes her usual panoramic shot and then turns to face the man, now crouched down, rewarding his dog. 'There you go,' he says. 'Good girl!'

'I'm assuming your dog is English,' she says, offering the man a smile.

'Ha!' he says. 'Yes. I'm actually Scottish, but Fifi's most definitely English.'

'My daughter's name is Fifi,' Wendy tells him. 'Well, Fiona really, but we call her Fifi. She'd be mortified.'

The man smiles warmly. 'My wife called her Fifi,' he says.

'She's French. So it's just *fille-fille*, if that makes any sense. She looked very girly when we got her. She had these long lashes as a puppy, didn't you, Fifi?'

'She still has a very pretty face,' Wendy says, nodding at the dog and then turning to look back out at the view. An orange paraglider is swooping gracefully in the distance.

'We love this walk, don't we?' the man says, petting his dog.

'Me too,' Wendy tells him. 'I try to do it every day.'

'Ah, a local, then?' the man says.

'Not really. More a long-term tourist. I'm staying here for six months. Well, if I stay until the end. I may go home a bit early.'

'Homesick?' the man asks. 'Or obligations?'

'A bit of both, really,' Wendy says.

'And where is home?'

'England,' Wendy says. 'Maidstone. Kent.'

'Ah, well, make the most of this,' the man says, gesturing at the view. 'Because you'll miss it once you're gone.'

'Yes,' Wendy says. 'Yes, I will.'

And with that, the man stands, says, 'Come on, Fifi! Upward and onwards!' And with a wave and a 'You have a good day,' the man and his dog head off, continuing up the ridge.

Wendy sighs and sits down on a boulder. She stares out at the view. Yes, it's true, she will miss this. Perhaps she should stay longer after all.

She takes a deep breath of the cool mountain air and starts her way back down. She's feeling a bit better – that smog of depression is lifting.

Is it the exercise, she wonders, or the mountain air? Or is it the fact that she has been forced to think about how she'll miss all this beauty once she's home?

But no, it's that brief connection with another human being, she decides. Those few pleasant words exchanged with a stranger have somehow lifted her spirits. She thinks about those rats in their cages and thinks that the research is probably right – social connection probably is the answer after all.

On the way back she walks as far as the bakery to find it as busy as she has ever seen it. The queue of people picking up cakes for their New Year celebrations spills right out into the sunshine.

When eventually she gets inside, she fills her basket with food – cheese, a jar of posh pickles and a fancy pasta sauce containing artichokes and truffles. If she's going to spend New Year's Eve alone for the first time in her life, she can at least try to make it special.

At the counter she adds fresh bread, a raspberry charlotte for dessert, and two croissants for the morning.

'Nothing to drink?' the woman asks as she nears the end of Wendy's basket.

'No,' Wendy says. 'New Year's resolution.'

'*Ah, ça, c'est pour demain,*' the woman says – that's for tomorrow. '*Vous êtes seule ce soir ?*' she asks, then in English, 'Tonight, you are alone?'

'Yes,' Wendy says, feeling irritated at the intrusive nature of the question.

'We 'ave this,' the woman says, 'if you want.' She's pointing to a half bottle of Champagne on the counter. 'It's only thirteen euro.'

Wendy looks at the bottle. She imagines it chilled, imagines the pop of the cork at midnight and thinks how much less miserable the moment would be if she let herself cave in. 'Yes, OK,' she says, then, 'No. Sorry. No. Really, no.'

'You're sure?' the woman asks, her hand floating near the bottle. 'New Year is only one time.'

'Oh, go on, then,' Wendy says. 'Just the one.'

It'll be fine, she tells herself as she walks home. *It's the only alcohol in the cabin.*

She can start the New Year with a bang and then get serious about her New Year's resolution. She'll save it until midnight, and it won't even be enough to get her drunk.

* * *

Back home, she makes a sandwich for her late lunch and, doing her best to ignore the Champagne, calling to her from the fridge, she feeds Mittens half a tin of cat food. By way of thanks he sits beside her licking his paws while she eats her sandwich in the sunshine. 'If you come and keep me company at midnight, I'll give you some more,' she tells him, but though he does look up when she speaks, she's not convinced that he has understood the invitation. Perhaps she should lure him indoors and keep him hostage until midnight?

Her phone starts pinging mid-afternoon with concerned messages from all and sundry. Fiona, Harry, Todd, Jill and even Sue text to ask if she's OK, or more pointedly, if she's going to be OK. Though well-intentioned, these end up leaving her even more anxious than before.

She copies and pastes the same reply to everyone. *Yes, I'm fine. I'm having a nice night in with cake and Netflix.* Both Harry and Jill reply that they'll phone her at midnight.

Manon texts her, too, inviting her to spend the evening with them. But though the invitation is generous the sad truth is that she can't imagine a worse way to spend New Year's Eve than trying to make conversation in French with someone she doesn't know. Especially sober. She really *would* rather spend it alone.

* * *

It's a quarter to twelve – which is to say, a quarter to twelve French time – and she's alternating between watching the news on her laptop and staring at the beads of dew forming on her chilled mini bottle of Champagne. She's been thinking about the bottle all day and Christ knows how she has resisted opening it until now. But should she open it at midnight in France or at midnight back home so she has a glass in her hand when Harry calls? She probably should have bought two half bottles, she thinks, so that she could open one for each. She also shouldn't have bought any at all.

She glances at the screen, now showing for the hundredth time the 'best of' firework displays from around the world. She should have bought *ten* bottles and started with Australia this morning, she thinks.

She focuses on the Champagne bottle again and her brain manages to superimpose the horror reel of her mother's death all over again. Now that she has dug these images from the depths they are going round and round in a loop, like some tragic event on a rolling news channel. She winces in pain at the visual and blinks it into oblivion. She waits for it to start over.

This is a terrible idea, she thinks, as the on-screen UK countdown falls to 01h.14m.59s. *I'm not strong enough for this at all!*

You'll get through it, she forces herself to think instead. *You'll be fine.* She finds herself unconvinced.

Christ, there's so much going on in her head this evening, so many voices battling for dominance. Perhaps she's lapsing into clinical schizophrenia. Wouldn't that be a great way to start the year?

There's a tap-tap-tap on the window which is so unexpected she wonders if it is even real. But Manon's familiar face peeping in would seem to confirm that it is.

'Manon?' she says, once she has unlocked and opened the front door.

Manon is wearing what looks like a boy's suit, with a crinkled white linen shirt and a loosely knotted tie. Behind her is an extraordinarily pretty girl in jeans, silver trainers and a (somehow incongruous up on this mountain) sparkly top.

'We decide to come to you,' Manon says, brandishing a full-sized bottle of fizz. 'It's OK?'

'Oh, yes, that's lovely,' Wendy says, her voice wobbling a little with emotion. 'Come in!' She hadn't wanted this at all but now they're here she can't think of anything she wants more.

'This is Celine,' Manon says, dragging her girlfriend into the cabin. 'And this is Wendy.'

'Hello,' Celine says, then in surprisingly formal fashion, 'I am very pleased to meet you.'

'Thank you!' Wendy says, laughing. 'Come in, come in! Please, sit down!'

'Is nearly time,' Manon says, checking her phone, then, 'Sorry, *it is* nearly time.' To her girlfriend she adds, 'Wendy is very hard teacher.'

'Oh, yes, I'm well hard,' Wendy says, and she can tell from their blank expressions that her joke has gone over their heads.

'We bring Champomy,' Manon says, handing the bottle to Wendy. 'It is apple. So no alcohol. It's good, yes?'

Wendy glances guiltily back at the coffee table where her half bottle of Champagne is waiting, prompting Manon to follow her line of sight.

'Oh,' Manon says, frowning slightly. 'You are drinking tonight? I think you said...'

'I just...' Wendy says, pulling a face. 'What can I say? You've saved me from myself.'

'*Est-ce que...*' Celine starts, but Manon raises one finger like a stop sign. '*Un moment,*' she says. 'If you want to drink, Wendy, it's OK. I just—'

'No,' Wendy says. 'No, this is perfect. Because I don't. Really. I don't.'

'*Est-ce que j'ouvre le gâteau ?*' Celine asks, once Manon's finger has been lowered.

'Ah, yes,' Manon says, lifting a box from the carrier bag her girlfriend is holding and handing it to Wendy. 'We bring cake.'

'I hope you like,' Celine says. 'We don't know, so...'

Wendy takes the box and places it on the kitchen counter so she can cut the sellotape and peer inside.

'It is nice here,' Celine comments.

'Thanks, yes,' Wendy replies distractedly, then, 'Oh, croquembouche! I love that.'

'*Croque-en-bouche?*' Manon repeats, sounding surprised, now moving to stand beside her and peer in. 'You call this *croque-en-bouche?*'

Wendy nods. 'Um, yes. Something like that. But surely that's French, isn't it?'

'It is,' Manon says, laughing. 'But they call it like this in your country?'

'Yes, we call it by the French name. Is that funny? Or did I pronounce it—'

'It is French,' Manon confirms. '*Croque-en-bouche* is French for, um, "bite in the mouth". But we do not call it this, so yes, this is funny for me. We call this *une pièce montée*.'

'*Une pièce montée*,' Wendy repeats. 'I'm not sure what that means.'

Manon shrugs. 'It means, er, like a construction.' She turns to Celine and adds, '*Les Anglais appellent ça croque-en-bouche ! T'imagines ?*'

'I heard this before, I think,' Celine says. 'In France, too. But now it is late.'

'Ooh, ooh!' Manon says, checking her phone. 'Wendy, you must be quick. We have one minute fifty seconds. One minute forty-nine. Forty-eigh... seven, six...'

'Gosh, OK,' Wendy says. 'Um... Glasses!'

'Yes, Wendy,' Manon says. 'Glasses, quick! Go!'

* * *

By twelve thirty the girls have already left, but their brief presence has transformed Wendy's New Year's Eve from something so terrifying she wasn't quite sure how she was going to get through it to a beautiful memory she doubts she will ever forget. *What a wonderful, generous girl she is*, Wendy thinks. *I am so lucky to have met her.*

She sips her fizzy apple juice and tries to remember the brand her mother used to give them as children. Appletise, that was the one. They'd felt so grown up sipping it and eating Wotsits.

She thinks of midnight and how the girls had counted down in French – thinks how sweet they had been – sweet and somehow a bit... what's the word? Unpretentious? Childlike? Naïve? Unembarrassed, certainly.

Fiona and Todd would pull faces about having to count down. They would both consider it the height of uncool. Well, unless they were drunk, that is. Perhaps that's why the English have to drink so much: to escape the clutches of being cool.

She pops the final half a croquembouche into her mouth. *My God, fresh choux pastry tastes amazing, doesn't it?* Her mother had been a dab hand at profiteroles, and they'd tasted exactly like this. Maybe she should learn to make them herself when she gets home.

Home!

Just after midnight, Celine had initiated a round robin of who wanted what in the new year.

Manon had said the only thing she wanted was for her brother to stay 'clean', while Celine hoped to pass her driving test. As for Wendy, she'd surprised herself by saying she wanted to go home.

'You mean now?' Manon had asked. 'You wish to go home early?'

'Yes, I think I do,' Wendy had told her, considering it as she spoke. 'I think I need to go home and sort my life out.'

'But this is why you come here,' Manon had pointed out. 'To think. To sort your life?'

'Yes, that's exactly why I came here,' Wendy had agreed. 'But... I don't know... I kind of feel like I have. Or I've started to, anyway. I feel like I've sorted my head out, a bit, at least. And the next step involves everyone else, really.'

'Your husband?'

'My husband, my kids... my brother, my sister-in-law. I think I need to go home and fix it all.' As she spoke, an internal monologue had started trying to trip her up, saying, *You'll go home and everything will be exactly the same as before, and what will you do then?*

Manon had raised her glass then and said, 'I think you can do this. I think you are a strong woman now.' And by Christ, Wendy had loved her for that!

She drags her gaze from the flickering fire to check the screen on her muted laptop. The UK countdown has now reached eleven minutes to midnight. Harry will be calling soon.

She goes to the fridge for her Champagne, but even as she crosses the room she's realising that she can't remember having moved it from the coffee table. One of the girls must have done it.

She opens the fridge door but the bottle isn't there.

She scans the room. There's no sign of it.

Her phone, on the coffee table, lights up with a message, so she returns to check if it's from Harry. Instead there's a message from Manon.

I take your Champagne. Do not look for it. You will not find. Bonne année my friend. P.S. Celine really like you. :-)

'Cheeky!' Wendy mutters, but then realising that this was not an act of theft but support, she shakes her head and tries to laugh instead. But genuine laughter is hard to come by. She has been looking forward to that Champagne all day. She's salivating just thinking about it.

At five minutes to midnight – UK time – her phone rings with a call from Jill, which she ignores letting it go to voicemail. And then at exactly midnight, as the Sky News fireworks burst into the night sky, it rings again with a call from Harry.

Harry: Sorry, I bloody missed it. I called five minutes ago, and it was busy. And then by the time I'd made a cuppa, midnight had come and gone.

Wendy: Hey, it's fine! It's not even a minute past.

H: So who were you on the phone to?

W: Just Jill. I didn't even take the call. I probably have a very drunken voicemail.

H: Because?

W: Well, she'll be drunk, won't she?

H: No, I meant, why didn't you take it?

W: Oh, because I was waiting for you.

H: Eek. Good job I remembered, then.

W: Yes, it really is!

H: I just got in, actually.

W: In? From where?

H: ... had to take Fifi to a party at that Paradise place. She was raging because we were late.

W: Fiona? In a nightclub?

H: I know. But her mate Cindy got free tickets or something, so... Are you worried about her drinking? She says they ask for ID at the bar. Though I'm sure they can get around that. I always did.

W: To be honest, I'm relieved to learn my daughter has a social life.

H: Yeah, me, too, actually. She has a tendency to play safe, doesn't she?

W: She does.

H: Which is all very reassuring and everything...

W: But not *only* reassuring.

H: Quite. So how was midnight in froggy-land?

W: Oh, I'm right in the middle of nowhere, here.

H: So...?

W: So it was very much like being in the middle of nowhere. But a friend called in with cake, which was nice.

H: That is nice. Your post lady friend?

W: Good guess. With her girlfriend and a bottle of Appletise.

H: God, Appletise. Does that still exist?

W: Apparently it does in France, though it's called Chappony or something.

H: Well, I'm glad you had company, Wens. I worry about you, out there on your own.

W: And you? Do you have company?

H: I do as it happens. You.

W: Cute.

H: We try.

W: Haz, this is all very nice and everything. But I need to... Look, do you think I can maybe come home early?

H: ...

W: Don't sound too keen.

H: No, it's not... I just thought we'd keep it light and fluffy tonight, for New Year's Eve.

W: Oh, we can, if you want. Though it's hard not to take that as a 'no'.

H: Even though it isn't. It really isn't. It's just, well, that's quite a big discussion, isn't it?

W: Is it?

H: Well, yeah. I mean, er... Are you sure you want to come back early? Are you sure it's a good idea? Don't you feel you might regret cutting things short later on? And, you know, home to where? And to do what? Which seems like a lot to be talking about at four minutes past midnight.

W· OK, fair enough. I get your point. Even if the answers are quite simple.

H: You think?

W: Yes. I mean: yes, I'm sure. And no I won't regret it. And home to our house, to patch things up with you and the kids and Neil and Sue.

H: Gosh. OK.

W: Don't sound so surprised, Haz. It's hardly the plan from outer space.

H: No... But it sounds... I don't know...

W: It sounds what?

H: Like you've had some kind of epiphany? Have you had an epiphany?

W: Maybe a mini one. A sort of half-a-piphany, if that's possible.

H: If you've had a half-a-piphany then I suppose it must be.

W: Look, I think – sorry you're right, this isn't light and fluffy at all, is it?

H: It's fine, Wens. Go on.

W: Well, you were right. About Mum. When she died, that was it, wasn't it? That's when I veered off the rails. You know it's all come back to me now. How Mum actually died, I mean. It was quite traumatic.

H: I bet.

W: Bloody traumatic, actually. Horrific.

H: Yep, I can totally believe that, Wendy. Even if you never did say a word.

W: You know, I couldn't?

H: You couldn't?

W: No. I couldn't even remember it myself. I think I scrubbed it because it was so awful. To sort of... survive. So that I could carry on functioning. Otherwise I would have imploded or something.

H: That makes sense, I guess. You had so much to organise.

W: Yes, I'll tell you about it at some point. I want to. And I need to tell Neil about it, too. He doesn't even know about when she died so he can't really know why I'm angry, can he? It's unfair of me to expect him to. I can see that now.

H: I think that might be a bit of a fiery conversation. Do you mind if I opt out?

W: Yes, I'm sure. And yes. It'll just be Neil and me for that one. And I'm not going to rush into it, either. I might see someone first to talk it all through.

H: You mean, like a professional?

W: Yes. I should have done that ages ago. Maybe *we* should see someone, too.

H: I think you're right. Maybe we should.

W: Anyway, there you go. That's where I'm at.

H: And it all sounds shockingly reasonable.

W: Good.

H: And the... um... drinking? How are you feeling about that, dare I ask?

W: Well, for the time being, I've stopped.

H: You've stopped?

W: Yeah. I haven't had a drink for ninety-um... three hours.

H: Ninety-three hours? That's precise. And do you think you might want to see someone about that, too?

W: About the drinking? Oh, I don't think so. I think I've got it sorted.

H: ...

W: Why, do you think I need to see someone?

H: Maybe. Probably. Yeah.

W: OK, well... Like I said, Haz, I've stopped. And if that gets hard, or, you know, impossible, then I promise I'll see someone about that, too. But I honestly think I'm through the worst of it now.

H: Great. Well, I'm, um... reassured, I suppose is the word.

W: Good. I'm glad.

H: So... D'you mean... erm, you haven't had a drink tonight? Not even on New Year's Eve?

W: I've had two glasses of Appletise.

H: Wow. Call me impressed.

W: OK, *Impressed*. But seriously, Harry, what do you think – about me coming home early, I mean?

H: Can we talk about it some more tomorrow?

W: Yes. Sure. Of course.

H: And don't take that as a 'no'. I know what you're like and I'm really not saying 'no'. As if I have the power to say 'no' anyway... Because as an adult, with free will and whatever, you're obviously free to do whatever you want.

W: Obviously.

H: But I just want us both to sleep on it. And talk it all through properly tomorrow.

W: Sure. That's fine.

H: I was going to suggest I come out and visit you for half term if you must know. I quite fancied seeing your place before you leave, but—

W: Ooh, I quite like that idea. I've been feeling a bit sad about the fact you might never see the place. That it would always be sort of the one adventure we didn't share. So, yes, let's do it.

H: You're sure?

W: Yes. Definitely. When is half term, anyway?

H: Mid-February. The twelfth or so.

W: That could work. Maybe I'll stay on till then.

H: We can discuss that tomorrow too.

W: Yes. In 2024.

H: It already is 2024. How crazy is that? The years do fly by, don't they?

W: They do. You know, I do love you, Harry. I don't say it enough, but I do.

H: Cool. Because I love you, too.

W: Goodnight.

H: Goodnight.

W: You have to hang up now.

H: Or you do.

W: D'you remember when we used to do that for hours?

H: I do. You were a student nurse sleeping on a gurney.

W: When I was a student, still, that's right. That was a *long* time ago.

H: Decades.

W: Goodnight, Haz.

H: Night night.

FOURTEEN

CONVERSATIONS AT HOME

Fiona

'I can't believe you came home early.'

Wendy turns to see her daughter, still in pyjamas, standing in the doorway to the kitchen.

'Hello, you!' she says, standing and crossing the room to hug her. Her daughter smells of sleep. She smells the same way she has smelt for eighteen years. It's wonderful.

'Stop! Stop it!' Fiona says, laughingly pushing her mother away. 'I can't stand it when you snuffle me like that.'

'Apologies, I'm sure,' Wendy replies, smiling wryly as she returns to her seat at the table. She resumes reading the news while her daughter pours a bowl of cereal. She knows better than to initiate conversation in those first few minutes. And yet once Fiona has made tea and sat down she finds herself saying, 'You know that's not a proper breakfast, right?' Mothering. It's impossible to resist.

'I'm sorry?'

'You do realise that chocolate's not a reasonable breakfast staple.'

Fiona leans back in her chair, almost falling over in the process, and swipes the cereal box from the counter. 'Choco Crispies – breakfast cereal,' she mumbles, running her finger across the words on front of the box.

'Fine, whatever,' Wendy says. She'll have this battle another day.

'Anyway, I didn't buy it, Dad did,' Fiona says. 'So have it out with him.'

'I will.'

'I know you will. And then we can all eat gruel every day and be thrilled that you came home to save us.'

'Gruel would probably be healthier,' Wendy says, trying to turn the almost-spat into banter.

'Anyway, why did you come home early? I mean, look at it,' Fiona says through a mouthful of Choco Crispies. She nods at the kitchen window, beyond which sheet rain is plummeting from a slate-grey sky onto their extremely muddy lawn.

'Well, not for the weather, that's for sure.'

'But seriously. I thought you were staying there till April.'

'Maybe I missed you too much,' Wendy says, then, 'Actually I did. I missed all of you.'

'I can almost believe that,' Fiona says. 'Almost. Are you and Dad tight now, too, then?'

Wendy frowns at her daughter as she thinks about this.

'Are you two getting on?' Fiona rephrases.

'I do know what tight means,' Wendy says. 'I'm not that much of a fuddy-duddy.'

'Enough of one to say "fuddy-duddy", though,' Fiona says, grinning. 'And please don't say *it's complicated*. I hate that.'

'No, even if it is... But I suppose I'd say we're working on it. How's that?'

'OK. That's good news, I guess. Did you two talk last night?'

'No, I got in too late. I was shattered. We both were.'

'Right. Well, in that case I'll stop being nosy.'

'You know, I don't mind you being nosy at all. I'm kind of hoping we can open things up a bit around here. Talk a bit more openly. As a family, I mean.'

Fiona laughs. 'Todd's going to love that.'

'Todd? Why Todd?'

'Well, he never talks about sh— about anything... does he?'

'No, I suppose he doesn't much.'

'And what about...? I thought Dad said he wanted to come to France.'

'Yes, he did suggest it. But it just didn't work out, really. It would have meant I had to stay on till mid-February. And once I'd decided to come home... well, you know how it is.'

'Given the choice between the Côte d'Azur and Maidstone, I'm not sure I do.'

'Oh, you do. It's like, you know, when you've got a long journey and you end up leaving early, because you want to get on with it. Or, when you're on holiday, and you suddenly feel like you've had enough and you want to get back to normal life.'

'Never happened to me, Mum. Never. But OK. I get the point. And what about lovely Mittens? What did you do with him? I hope you haven't left him to starve.'

'Of course not. No, Manon's going to try to catch him and take him to the vet, and then see if she can tame him. And in the meantime she has promised to feed him. She drives past the place three times a day, so... I left some money for food.'

'She's sweet,' Fiona says. 'But I still think you should have brought him home.'

'Well, I would have had to catch him, for one. I never even managed to pick him up.'

'And the cabin? Is it just sitting empty now?'

'I don't know. I assume that she'll re-list it but I don't know. She refunded me in any case – for all the unused weeks. So that was nice of her. I had a new car booked from tomorrow, the fourth – is that tomorrow? So, yes, from tomorrow. Cancelling that before it got started saved me a fortune. So those, you know, financial reasons kind of forced my hand to do things more quickly than I otherwise might have. But I'm good with that.'

'Fair enough.'

'But I may go back there sometime with your dad. I'd like him to see the place. Because otherwise it will always be one thing we never shared. I'm not sure if that makes much sense, but...'

'Sure,' Fiona says. 'That makes perfect sense. Though it does make it sound like you're maybe intending to stay together.'

'Yes. Well, I hope so. We'll see.'

'Thank God!' Fiona says. 'My friend Glen's parents are separating and it's a bloodbath.'

'Is it?' Wendy says, glancing at the kitchen clock. She's about to ask Fiona if she has school today but before she can do so her daughter speaks, pre-empting her.

'I thought I might skive off today,' she says. 'Would that be OK?'

'On your first day back?'

Fiona nods. 'That's why. I won't miss much. And I could pretend I mucked up the dates. That way I can spend the day with you.'

'Oh,' Wendy says, feeling touched. 'Oh, OK, then. Yes. Of course.'

'You don't mind?'

'No. I'd like that a lot. And you know, I am sorry. I know I've been a nightmare.'

Fiona smiles and wrinkles her nose. 'You haven't been a *nightmare*, Mum. Well, maybe a bit of a nightmare. But it's fine. Dad explained a bit.'

'Oh? What did he explain?'

'You know, about Gran and stuff. I know it was a lot. I

hadn't really thought about it much. I'd probably go a bit loopy if you popped your clogs, so...'

'Well, thank you for being so understanding.'

'I probably wasn't at my best back then, either. I was, what, fourteen?'

'It was 2019 so you would have been thirteen. And don't worry, you were fine.'

'Fine for a nightmare teenager, you mean?'

'Yes, fine for a nightmare teenager.'

'So what are we doing today?' Fiona asks.

Wendy looks out at the rain again. 'I thought we might go to the beach. Or maybe have a picnic in the park.'

'Great ideas,' Fiona says.

'Alternatively we could rent a film and eat crisps on the sofa in front of the fire.'

* * *

Harry

'Hey there.'

'Hey! Ooh, kisses in the neck. That's been a while.'

'Well, that's probably because it *has* been a while. What-ya-cookin?'

'Lasagne. My world-famous veggie lasagne.'

'Yum. But you know, you don't have to do that. The freezer's stuffed.'

'I know. But I wanted to.'

'OK. Well, I'm not complaining.'

'Cooking makes the kitchen feel more like home. Well, I'm hoping it will, anyway. It's a bit strange being back.'

Strange is something of an understatement, but how else can she describe this feeling? Everything about being home feels alien, as if the house is perhaps a film set and Wendy an actress pretending to live there. It's awful and anxiety-inducing feeling like an Imposter, and the only real habit calling to her is the one where she breaks out the booze in order to relax. She's hoping she can power through until everything feels normal.

'Strange-good, or strange-bad?' Harry asks.

'Just strange. I can't really explain. I'm trying to just do a normal day and see what happens.'

'Anything I can do to help?'

'Not sure,' Wendy says. 'I'll let you know.'

'OK. So what did you get up to in your normal day?'

'Not much. It's been a lazy one. I'm still shattered.'

'I take it you saw Fifi before she left, though?'

'She actually skived off. With my blessing, that is. She's upstairs.'

'Oh?'

'I know you don't approve. I don't either really. But these are kind of exceptional circumstances. She wanted us to spend a day together, so...'

'So you yielded to emotional blackmail.'

'I did.'

'Well, good for you. And was it nice, your mother-and-daughter day?'

'Yes, it was good. We rented a film and ate crisps.'

'Wow. I think I'm jealous.'

'The film was a Julia Roberts rom-com.'

'OK. Maybe not.'

Harry moves his dripping jacket from the chair-back to a hook above the radiator. 'Can't believe this weather,' he says. 'It's like walking through a car wash.'

'Yes. It's horrid.'

'Must be a bit of a shock for you, too?'

'D'you know, I've hardly noticed it? I'm just glad to be home.'

'Is everything... you know... OK?'

'I'm sorry?'

'You seem a bit... I don't know.'

'... I seem a bit...?'

'I don't know. Have you got the hump with me? Is it because I had to leave early this morning?'

'No, Harry. No everything's fine. I don't even know why you think that.'

'You're, you know, doing the no-eye-contact thing. Like right now. You're staring very intently at your sauce.'

'Well, if you don't pay attention to béchamel it goes lumpy.'

'Oh, OK. And that's all it is?'

'Yes. OK, actually, *no*. Like I said, it feels very strange being back. And if I'm being honest I feel a bit... *shy* around you, too. Is that weird?'

'No. I feel kind of clunky around you. I think it's probably normal. Tea?'

Wendy glances across at her husband, his hand frozen in mid-air before the mug rack, and for the first time since she got home something feels right. *How nice it is to have someone come home and make you tea*, she thinks. *How nice that he'll know exactly how I like it.*

'What?' Harry asks, breaking into an embarrassed grin.

'Nothing,' Wendy says. 'I was thinking how good looking you are. I don't think I've noticed that for a while.'

Harry snorts. 'And you're sure you haven't been drinking?'

Wendy rolls her eyes. 'I'll let that one pass.'

'So? Tea?'

'Yes. Tea!' she says.

Once she has assembled the lasagne and slipped it into the oven, she takes a seat at the kitchen table. Harry is reading something on his phone and above them the distant sound of Fiona's music is making the ceiling thud.

'What's she listening to?' Wendy asks. '... sounds awful.'

'K-pop,' Harry says, reluctantly lowering his phone then pushing it away from him and finally flipping it face down. 'And you're right. It's awful. That's Blackpink, I think. She's obsessed. I would have thought she was too old for it, but hey, what do I know?'

'Right,' Wendy says, clasping her hands together. 'So.'

'So,' Harry repeats, then, after a glance at Wendy's mug of tea, 'Actually, I wanted to ask you something. I don't want you to think I'm on your case or anything, but I do kind of need to ask you about the drink thing.'

'The drink thing?'

'Yeah, are you, er...'

'Am I what? Just ask, Haz. It's fine.'

'So are you, you know, drinking, now? Or not drinking?'

'At this minute, I'm drinking tea.'

'You know what I mean.'

'Sorry. I do. And no, I'm not drinking.'

'OK. Cool. It's just... well... yesterday... I mean, I didn't dare ask. And it's fine, well, maybe not *fine* but normal if you had one, at the airport, or on the plane, or whatever—'

'I didn't.'

'It's just you did sound a tiny bit...'

'Yes?'

'...'

'A tiny bit what, Harry?'

'I don't know,' Harry says, with a shrug. 'A bit slurry, maybe?'

'I was tired, Haz. I was so tired I could barely speak.'

'Really? That's all it was?'

'Yes, that really is all it was. You know I was up at six cleaning the place – which is five here. And then the flight was late, so I spent five hours in Nice airport. And almost another hour sitting on the runway. And then a bus and two trains and a taxi... So by the time I got here at midnight...'

'I'm sorry I couldn't come. But the car—'

'Yes, I know. It's fine. But I was tired. I was very, very tired, that's all.'

'OK. So you didn't drink at all?'

'Harry, I haven't had a single drop of alcohol since Boxing Day.'

'Right. I mean, I want you to feel you can be honest with me, that's all. I'm not asking you this in, you know, a judge-y sort of way. I just want to help. To be here for you.'

'Yes, OK, and I am being honest.'

'Sorry, that's not what I meant. This is coming out all wrong.'

'It's fine. It's all fine, Haz. Please relax a bit. You're stressing me out, too.'

'Right. I will. This is me relaxing. So do we – I mean... Are you going to stay stone-cold sober from now on?'

'I am. For now. I'm going to try to stay stone-cold sober.'

'So should we... you know... get rid of the bottles in the house? Or are you fine about... all that?'

Wendy looks at Harry and then lets her focus relax and stares through him. She's once again picturing the contents of the drinks cabinet behind him – the whisky, the Baileys, the Martini – and salivating at the thought of it all. 'No, I'm fine about it,' she hears herself say. More consciously, she adds, 'Actually, that's not true. Yes, getting rid might be a good idea. If you don't mind. Just for a bit.'

'No, no, that's fine,' Harry says. 'I thought I should do it before you came home, and then I hesitated because I didn't want to offend you.'

'Well, that's sweet. Thanks for being so sensitive about it.'

'I try,' Harry says. He takes a sip of his tea and then puts the mug back down and runs his finger around the rim. 'Is it hard for you? The not drinking thing?'

'A bit.'

'Right.'

'Truth is, Harry, I think about drink a hundred times a day. But I think I nipped it in the bud early enough. Only just, apparently, but all the same. It could have been much worse. I've been reading about withdrawal symptoms and some people have it really bad. And that didn't happen to me, thankfully. I had flu symptoms for a bit and a headache and nightmares. And my sleep was terrible for a few days. But that's about it, really. Some people end up in A&E. I assume those are people who are dosing constantly all day every day. Which I wasn't. Quite.'

'It still doesn't sound like fun. If you're thinking about it all the time...'

'No, it isn't fun. It's miserable. But like I say, it's getting easier.'

'Well, good. That sounds good.'

'But I'm not pretending that I'm out of the woods, Haz. I mean, just you mentioning the Martini in the drinks cabinet—'

'I don't think I specifically mentioned Martini. I'm not even sure we have any.'

'No, but there you go. I'm picturing it, the Martini. And salivating.'

'So maybe I should get to it.'

'Or maybe later? When I'm in the other room?'

'Sure. Whatever you need.'

'I made an appointment to see someone, by the way. It's next Monday.'

'That's quick. You must have connections. A woman at work has been waitin—'

'It's private. I'm going private. Which rankles, obviously, but there you go. I think I need it. And apparently she's very good.'

'Says ?'

'Says?'

'Sorry, I mean, says who? Who says she's good?'

'Oh, Giles gave me her name. You know Giles, the surgeon? He says she's the best he knows around here. She's very cutting edge apparently. Well, in terms of addiction. And trauma. So...'

'Sounds good.'

'We'll see. I only have to commit to one session. Which is good as it's a hundred and twenty quid a pop. But hopefully it'll be worth it. I'm feeling a bit scared, to be honest. I've never seen a shrink.'

'I saw one once. When I was seventeen.'

'Really? You never told me that.'

'No?'

'No. And this was because...?'

'Oh, normal teenage angst, I think. My grades were getting worse when before they'd been quite good. So I had to go see the shrink.'

'And did it help?'

Harry shrugs. 'Not sure. I don't remember much. My grades definitely got better afterwards but to be honest, I think I just worked harder so I could stop going. It clashed with footy, and I remember I wasn't thrilled about that.'

* * *

Kathy

Kathy: Hello. Please, come in. Take a seat. Yes, there's fine.

Wendy: Right. OK. Oh, and hello. Sorry, I'm not trying to be rude. I'm just nervous.

K: Please don't be. I'm not as scary as I look.

W: Well, that's something, at least. Oh, I didn't mean... You don't look scary. My mouth seems to be saying random words today.

K: It's fine. Relax! So my name's Kathy. If it suits you, we can use first names?

W: Yes, that's fine.

K: And you're Wendy. Have I got that right?

W: Yes. Wendy. That's me.

K: Great.

W: Um, thanks for seeing me so quickly.

K: Ah, well, Giles is one of my oldest friends. We were at college together. Plus there was a bit of luck involved. I had a cancellation... So, what brings you here today?

W: Um... Do I just...? Sorry, but is this an introduction? Or is this, you know, the actual thing.

K: Let's say it's a bit of both.

W: I just thought... never mind.

K: You just thought...? Please, finish that sentence.

W: I thought you'd want me to lie down on the couch or something.

K: <laughs> You can if you wish. Would you be more comfortable on the couch?

W: No, I don't think I would.

K: Then let's carry on like this for now, shall we?

W: OK.

K: So.

W: So.

K: ...

W: I don't really know where to start.

K: That's fairly common. Just start anywhere. All roads lead to Rome, as they say.

W: Yes, I'm sure they do. So... OK. Can I ask you a question?

K: Of course. Fire away.

W: How do you define an alcoholic?

K: How do I define an alcoholic?

W: I mean, how does one know if one is an alcoholic. As opposed to a normal heavy drinker.

K: Do you think you might be an alcoholic?

W: Maybe. I'm not sure. That's why I'm asking.

K: OK, well, let's talk a bit about your use of alcohol, then. Does that sound like a good idea?

W: Yes, it probably is.

K: Do you think that you drink too much, perhaps?

W: I think that I *have been* drinking too much. Yes.

K: Do you think you're able to be honest about how much you're drinking? It's not always easy to count these things accurately. Especially when one is drunk.

W: No, I can. I was in denial about it at first. But then I was in this cabin up in the Alps and I had to go get the stuff on foot... Anyway, to cut a long story short, I know exactly how much I was drinking. I was up to about two bottles a day. Sometimes two and a half.

K: These are bottles of...?

W: Wine. White, red... anything, really.

K: Well, two and a half bottles of wine per day is certainly more than the human body can tolerate for any period of time without it leading to health issues.

W: Right.

K: I notice you're using the past tense. You *were* drinking two and a half bottles a day.

W: Yes, I stopped completely on Boxing Day.

K: This Boxing Day, just past?

W: Yes.

K: So that's, what, about two weeks?

W: Yes.

K: And when you say, you stopped... Do you mean you've reduced or—

W: No, I haven't had a drop. Not a single drop since Boxing Day. Well, it was actually the day after, I think, but...

K: So you're entirely sober now.

W: I am.

K: Good. That's helpful. And how about cravings? Have you been craving alcohol since you stopped? Are you craving alcohol right now?

W: Yes, at first it was awful. I was ill with it. I was desperate. I couldn't think of anything else. But now I just feel sort of depressed. Like I'd feel happier if I could have a drink.

K: You're feeling depressed?

W: Yes.

K: How depressed is that?

W: Just, you know, normally depressed, really.

K: You feel sad?

W: Yes, I suppose so.

K: Like everything's a bit pointless?

W: Yes.

K: How about hopeless?

W: No, not really. No, I wouldn't go that far. Everything's just very flat.

K: Are you having trouble getting out of bed, for example?

W: <shrugs> A bit, maybe.

K: How about thoughts of self-harm? Have you had any of those?

W: Oh, no. Nothing like that. I just feel down, really. I did, actually, have some of those sorts of thoughts when I was drinking. Towards the end. I thought about ending it all once or twice. Not that I ever would. But I can't say it didn't cross my mind. Because everything seemed so... bleak. But since I stopped, it's more like disappointment, really.

K: Disappointment?

W: Yes. I think I thought if I stopped I'd feel all fit and, you know, *bouncy* – full of beans. But I just feel a bit deflated, really. Like a punctured tyre or something. Like I've given up something that was fun. So that's a bit of a disappointment.

K: Something 'fun' you say. Was it fun?

W: Sometimes it was. Yes.

K: So why did you stop on Boxing Day?

W: Because... Well, because I realised I *couldn't* stop. I kind of realised I was addicted. And I don't like being out of control. I hate not being in control.

K: I see. So you stopped, cold turkey, on your own?

W: Yes. I took a bit of Valium-type stuff which helped. I looked it up on the web, and a few studies seemed to say that might help.

K: Valium-type stuff?

W: Oxazepam. The doctor prescribed it for me ages ago when I had trouble sleeping.

K: OK. And how much Oxazepam did you take when you stopped drinking?

W: Maybe ten half pills. I can't remember the dosage, but they weren't that strong. And all in the first week. Nothing since.

K: OK. That sounds very reasonable. And very strong willed of you.

W: Yeah. I'm not too bad that way.

K: What way?

W: Oh, I just mean my willpower's never been too bad. You know, if I diet, I diet. If I decide to clean, I clean. I see other people faffing around about going to the gym or whatever and I always think just get on with it, you know?

K: I see. So, to get back to the drinking, for how long were you drinking heavily, do you think?

W: Oh... um... a few years, maybe? It built up gradually, really.

K: Was there a reason you started, do you think? Was there

something specific you were trying to avoid or improve by drinking?

W: Yes, I think I've worked it all out.

K: Go on?

W: Well, my mother died. It was awful. It was very... um... traumatic, I s'pose you'd say. And I kind of forgot, which is weird.

K: I'm sorry, you forgot she had passed, or you forgot how it happened?

W: Oh, no... sorry. No, I mourned her. I was devastated. No, it was more the actual event that I forgot. Do you think that's really possible? Because that's certainly how it seemed. Like I'd wiped it from my mind.

K: You forgot the event of her dying, do you mean?

W: Yes, I was there. And it was awful. But I completely forgot the details. That's how it seemed, anyway.

K: Well, that is perfectly possible. It's a well-studied mechanism called repression. We do it to protect ourselves when memories are too painful to bear.

W: So repression's not a made-up thing?

K: A made-up thing?

W: Yeah, I thought it might be just in films and stuff. You know. A plot device.

K: No, repression is very real. Well studied, and fully documented. And not uncommon.

W: OK, then. Well, I think that's what happened. And I sort of started drinking more around then. Because I felt so angry. Actually, I was already a drinker, even before. But it wasn't every night, you know? I was more of a weekend drinker. But I started feeling so stressed and angry all the time after Mum died. And the alcohol did seem to help.

K: Yes, it feels like it's helping until it isn't helping anymore, right?

W: Exactly.

K: Can you tell me about how your mother died?

W: Oh. OK. Do I have to?

K: No, you don't have to do anything at all.

W: Fine, well, I'd rather not.

K: Perhaps you can tell me why you'd rather not, then?

W: Because it upsets me. I cry. I get angry all over again. And then I can't get the images out of my head. That moment. At the end. In the hospital.

K: So you remember more of it, now, than before?

W: Oh, yes, I remember all of it. It came back to me in a sort of dream. Well, more of a waking nightmare, really. But it all suddenly came back. And I wept and wept and wept.

K: If you don't want to go into detail, can you perhaps give me an overall picture? That might be helpful for my understanding.

W: Oh, OK. Sure. So it was, um, cancer – of course. It's always cancer, isn't it? And she was in pain. A lot of pain. And they were useless – in the hospice, that is. They wouldn't give her enough morphine. I had to fight for it every time. It was like it was on bloody ration or something, which, as a nurse... Anyway... And then, at the end, while I was off hunting for a doctor to see to her – because he wouldn't come, you see, and they wouldn't give her more morphine without his say-so – and then she died. And I wasn't there. I missed it.

K: Please. Take a tissue.

W: Yes, you see? I can't even talk about it without...

K: That's fairly normal, I'd say. Take a breath. That's right. You know, it's good, actually, that you can cry. You need to let that out. So even though you don't want to talk about it, it's probably good if you do. Even when it does make you cry. Because each time you do it will get a little less painful.

W: OK. Well, job done, eh?

K: Were you on your own dealing with all of this?

W: Well, there were nurses and doctors, but as I say, they were all pretty useless.

K: Yes, but what about family? Are you in a relationship?

W: Yes. I'm married.

K: And was your partner present through this? Did your partner support you?

W: No. Not really. I mean, he'd hug me when I got home. And make me dinner, and what-have-you. He was sweet. And supportive.

K: But he wasn't with you at the hospital?

W: No.

K: Why was that, do you think?

W: I don't know. It just didn't seem like his place, really. I mean, she's not – she wasn't – his mother.

K: I see.

W: And Mum wouldn't have wanted him there, anyway. She was quite a private person. And it was a very intimate moment, you know?

K: Yes, dying is perhaps the most intimate moment of all.

W: And my brother was totally absent, too. I really fucking hate him for that. Sorry.

K: Please don't apologise. Whatever language comes to you here is fine. The important thing is to express yourself. So your brother, he didn't support you as you would have wanted?

W: No.

K: Did he support you at all?

W: No. Nada.

K: Why was that, do you think?

W: I don't know. Maybe because he's a...

K: As I said, you can swear if you want to. I won't be shocked.

W: No, I don't think I want to, really. Anyway, you know the word I was thinking of.

K: I think you should say the word so there's no doubt.

W: OK, then. He was a cunt.

K: Do you think there's a reason why he behaved like a cunt?

W: <laughs> That sounds funny, coming from you. It sounds wrong.

K: ...

W: And, no, I don't think there was a reason. He didn't want all that messiness in the middle of his perfect little life.

K: I see. I'm hearing quite a lot of resentment, there.

W: Yeah. Loads. *Bucketloads* of resentment. And his wife, Sue? She used to be my best friend. And she wasn't there for me either.

K: So how did you feel about that? About the fact that Sue wasn't there?

W: Hurt. Angry all over again.

K: ...

W: Hurt more than words can say, really.

K: And angry.

W: Yes, very, very angry. I still feel incredibly angry about it.

K: I see.

W: I mean, who does that? Who lets their best friend, or their sister for that matter, deal with a dying parent, alone?

K: Well, it is probably more common than you'd think, but that doesn't excuse it.

W: Really?

K: Oh, absolutely. Care of elderly or dying parents is one of the biggest reasons siblings fall out.

W: OK. So there are lots of ... you-know-whats out there. Arseholes.

K: ...

W: I don't get it. I just don't understand how anyone can be that selfish.

K: Have you ever asked them how?

W: No! As if...!

K: ...

W: Do you think I should, then? Ask them?

K: I didn't say that.

W: So you don't?

K: I didn't say that either.

W: You actually didn't answer my question.

K: Which question is that?

W: The definition of an alcoholic.

K: Ah. OK. So, to be honest, I'm not sure a definition would be helpful to you right now.

W: You don't?

K: No. Alcohol is a drug. It's a legal drug, but a drug nonetheless. Society, our society – most societies in fact, but not all societies – use it for many reasons. We self-medicate with alcohol. We use it as an anti-anxiety drug, for example or as a social lubricant, because we humans can be so awkward around each other. And sometimes it's used in larger quantities as an anaesthetic for physical or emotional pain. In ancient times they amputated limbs using alcohol as an anaesthetic, so it's a very powerful drug. And like any drug it can be used, or it can be misused.

W: Right. but that still doesn't—

K: I'd say that if your use of it is having negative consequences in your life, or on your relationships, or on your health, or on your wealth, then that's a problem. So I'd say that at this stage – at your stage – asking whether it's a problem in your life is perhaps more important than the definition of the word 'alcoholic'. Do you think your drinking has become a problem?

W: Yes, I think it has. People have told me it has. Family members. Friends. They say it's been affecting my relationships. And I think that's probably true. Actually, it's definitely true.

K: Right. Well, it's good that you've identified that. What I can tell you is that if you've been drinking two bottles a day then it will certainly have started to affect your health, even if you haven't noticed it yet. That level of consumption will end up damaging your liver and your kidneys, for starters. It would have effects that would show up in blood tests, for almost all your vital functions. So health-wise, it's definitely too much, and it's definitely a problem.

W: So it's a good job I stopped.

K: Yes, it's a good job you stopped.

W: ...

K: ...

W: I'm not sure what to say now.

K: That's OK. We can sit and digest for a bit until something comes along.

W: It's a bit expensive to just sit here, really, isn't it? It's like a waste. Two quid a minute.

K: Is that a worry for you? The cost?

W: Not this once. But if it needed to be regular...

K: ...

W: Do you think it will need to be regular?

K: I really couldn't say at this point.

W: What do you think he'd say? My brother? If I asked him. I was wondering about that.

K: Sorry, if you asked him what?

W: Why he left me alone to deal with Mum when she was dying.

K: I don't know. What do you think he'd say?

W: I really have no idea. That's why I was asking what sort of things people say.

K: People often do have their reasons. But they aren't always able to express them. And sometimes those reasons are subconscious, so they don't even know them themselves. But nothing comes from a vacuum. There will always be reasons for everything.

W: When you say, subconscious... Do you mean that people

can be subconsciously selfish? Like, they're selfish but it's not their fault?

K: Well, selfish is a slightly judgemental word, so it's perhaps not helpful. There are no universal standards for defining selfishness, after all.

W: I'd say that not helping your sister with your dying mother would probably fit the bill, though, don't you? As a standard measure of selfishness.

K: <laughs> Maybe so. I just mean that as for the word 'alcoholic' there's no standard definition. And of course you have to consider people's circumstances. Their capacity to help. Their capacity for generosity. There will often be a reason why people become relatively 'selfish' as you say. A past trauma or a childhood experience that limits their ability to be generous, for example. We often become who we are because of things that happen to us.

W: Right. Only we had the same childhood, my brother and me. We grew up together. So I don't think that really gets him off the hook.

K: Yes, but you weren't constantly together. You have had different life experiences.

W: I suppose. I actually think we'd argue if I asked him.

K: That's certainly a possibility. Would that be a bad thing?

W: I'm not sure it would be worse than saying nothing at all.

K: No, saying nothing can be quite painful, too.

W: So you do think I should ask him. Go on. Admit it.

K: I'm really not saying that at all. But I do think it might be a good idea for you to ask yourself why you haven't discussed it with him. And what you might gain or lose if you did. So at least the decision to discuss it, or not discuss it, would be a conscious choice on your part.

W: Yes, I can see that. That makes sense. So do you think I'm having a breakdown? Do you think I need years of therapy?

K; Do you think you're having a breakdown?

W: <laughs>

K: That was a serious question from me to you. And one I'd very much like you to answer.

W: Honestly?

K: Yes, honestly.

W: Quite honestly, no. I think I've got a handle on it all, now. I've worked out why I'm angry. And I've remembered what happened and who was and wasn't there for me. And I think I probably do need to have it out with my brother and his wife. And I think I've probably cracked the drinking thing. So, no. I think I'm doing OK.

K: I agree. I think you're doing OK, too.

W: You do? Really?

K: Really.

W: You're not just saying that?

K: No. If you truly have ceased drinking, as you say you have, on your own, without any help, then that shows quite extraordinary self-awareness and willpower. And if you've managed to push up the repressed trauma of your mother's death from your subconscious – once again, on your own – then that, too, is quite impressive. So I think you're doing incredibly well. And I think you should carry on like that. And, of course, come back to me if you need more support with any of it.

W: Gosh, that is not what I thought you'd say.

K: OK. What did you think I'd say?

W: That I need therapy for a hundred years at a hundred and twenty quid a pop.

K: Ah, well, I guess we therapists aren't all as cynical as you assumed. Are you disappointed?

W: No. I'm a bit scared, I think. Because it all depends on me now, doesn't it?

K: Yes, it all depends on you. But as I say, if you need help with any of it, I'm here for you. If you need help with the drinking, or if the pain of the trauma doesn't lessen, for example, then there are techniques we can use to help that on its way. So yes, it does depend on you. But you aren't alone. I'm here.

W: What happens if I fall off the wagon, do you think?

K: What happens if you start drinking, do you mean?

W: Yes. Do you think I can just have, like, a normal drink?

K: OK. So my best guess, from experience, would be that if you start drinking at all, you'll be drinking heavily within days. Perhaps even within hours. I think you'd snap right back into it like before. There can be miraculous exceptions, but that's generally how these things go.

W: So you don't think I can go back to drinking normally?

K: That depends what you mean by normal.

W: You know. Like normal people.

K: Some people's normal means never drinking at all. And others drink so much they drink themselves to death. There really is no normal. And if you find you need to stop drinking completely then it's important that you don't consider yourself *ab*normal because of that. Because that's very, very common. Alcohol, as I said, is a drug. And for many people it's a very addictive, unmanageable drug.

W: OK. Right. Got it.

K: But if you do fall off the wagon, as you say, then please do come back to me, and we can talk about options.

W: What kind of options? D'you mean like rehab? Because I don't think—

K: No, not necessarily. There are support groups. There are methods that can be useful. Strategies. Books I can recommend. There are even some new drug regimens that can help with the cravings. With the depression, too, if that gets difficult to cope with, you must come back and we can talk about options for that.

W: OK. I'm OK for now, I think, but OK.

K: But as you said yourself, I really do think you've got

this. Not everyone can do it on their own. Different people's bodies – their psyches – work differently. But so far, you've shown quite extraordinary resilience. You're doing extremely well.

W: Gosh. OK.

K: You sound surprised.

W: No, I'm just feeling... I don't know...

K: Pride? You look like you're feeling pride.

W: Yes. Maybe. Flattered, at any rate.

K: Well, good. You really should let yourself feel proud. This capacity you have for knowing yourself is quite rare. So I'd say, make the most of it. <looks at the clock> And that's probably a good point to wind up our first session, don't you think? Unless you have any other questions.

W: No, that's fine. Is this where I have to pay you?

K: Yes, this is where you have to pay me.

W: OK. Worth every penny. Well, every pound.

K: Well, I'm glad that you feel that way.

* * *

Sue and Neil

Sue opens the front door almost the second that Wendy knocks. 'Hello, hello!' she says, sounding a bit too enthusiastic – sounding like she's making an effort. 'Come in. Come in! Neil's, um, tidying the garage. I'll go and get... Oh, here he is!'

Wendy steps onto the doormat. It has an imprint that reads 'I hope you haven't come empty-handed' and she has indeed come empty-handed. She wonders if she should have brought something. She notes the hallway has changed colour again, this time from off-white to pale hospital green. She thinks she preferred it before.

'Hey, sis,' Neil says, stepping forward to hug her quickly

and rigidly. The result is more like being patted down by a secu rity guard.

'Gosh, we were so surprised to hear you were back, weren't we, Neil?'

'Yeah. I thought it was mid April.'

'Come through, come through!' Sue says. Wendy wonders if she's going to say everything twice today.

'So why'd you come home early?' Neil asks.

'Ah, I'm full of surprises, me,' Wendy says, aware that this doesn't really answer the question. She follows Sue through to the dining room, her brother close behind.

'Tea?' Sue asks as Wendy removes her coat. 'I've just boiled the kettle, so...'

'Yes, tea would be good.'

'Did you drive, or...?'

'No, I took the train. Our car's playing up. And to be honest, I think the train's easier. There's so much traffic on the roads these days.'

'As long as you can afford it,' Sue says. 'It's always so expen- sive. I'm shocked every time.'

'It was OK, actually,' Wendy says. 'But I suppose I'm travel- ling off peak.'

'Milk? Sugar? I should probably remember that, so sorry.'

'~~Yes, you probably should remember that.~~ Just milk. Milk is fine.'

'D'you want to...?' Sue asks, turning with the two mugs in her hands. 'Shall we sit in the lounge or...?'

'No, here's good,' Wendy says. There's something about the lounge that might feel too soft for such a hard conversation. They take their seats, equally spaced around the circular kitchen table. Wendy and Sue nurse their mugs of steaming tea.

Wendy reaches out to touch the flowers on the table and is surprised to discover they're plastic. They're exceptionally realistic.

'The weather's been awful,' Sue says, glancing out of the window.

'Yes, it has.'

'So how was France?' her brother asks. 'Did you enjoy it? Or did you hate it, hence the early return?'

'No it was good, thanks. Interesting.'

'And worthwhile?' Sue asks.

'Yes. It was quite life changing, actually.'

'Oh, gosh,' she says. 'Do tell.' She's trying so hard to be enthusiastic that Wendy feels a bit sorry for her. Her efforts to be upbeat seem proportional to how far their friendship has waned.

'It's not that easy to explain,' Wendy says. 'But spending that much time alone was interesting, to say the least.'

'So did you have...?' Sue asks. Then, 'I think Fiona said something about you having a revelation. Or hoping for one? I'm not sure which.'

Wendy laughs. 'Did she? Our Fiona said that?'

'Something like that. Maybe I got it wrong.'

'That's funny. I don't remember saying anything like that. Not to Fiona, at any rate.'

'So no bolts of lightning?' Neil asks, sounding dismissive. He smiles at the end of his sentence to soften his unintentional blow.

Wendy forces a laugh. 'No bolts of lightning. I haven't become a Hare Krishna or anything. It didn't really happen in the way I thought it would. I did expect something... I don't know. Well, I didn't *expect* anything. I was *hoping* for some sort of revelation, I suppose. But it didn't really happen like that. I did have lots of new thoughts, though. But it was more a case of little insights than one big one. I do feel quite different now I'm home, though, so hopefully it wasn't all for nothing. I'm blathering, aren't I? Sorry.'

'No, that's great, isn't it, Neil?'

'Yeah. Totally.'

'Neil! Do try to wake up a bit, honey. I'm sorry, he can be a bit vague sometimes after his snooze, can't you?'

'I'm not being vague at all. I'm just waiting to find out what this is all about. You said you wanted to talk, Wens. And I'm assuming you didn't mean about the weather.'

Wendy blinks at this sudden slip of cordiality, at the glimpse of animosity it reveals.

'Neil!' Sue says, shooting a frown at her husband. 'Sorry, Wendy. Why are you being like this, hon?'

'I'm not being like anything.'

'Well, please just stop it, then.'

'And please don't talk to me like that in front of my sister.'

Wendy raises one hand. 'Please, stop, both of you! It's fine. You're both right. It is nice to see you and chat after so long. But I also do need to get to the point. Because Neil's right. There's no point pretending everything's, you know... And it's true. I didn't come to talk about the weather.'

'Right,' Neil says, crossing his arms. 'Well, good.'

'Though I didn't expect you to be so...'

'So what?' Neil asks.

'So... I don't know... combative?' Wendy offers.

'No?' Neil asks. 'How did you expect me to be?'

'Just... Look. Can we start over?'

'Sure. Go ahead,' Neil says. 'Start over.'

'So first of all. I want to apologise,' Wendy says, launching into the speech she prepared during her train journey. 'I've come to the realisation that I've been drinking too much. And that I've been... a bit difficult, lately, let's say. And I've stopped now – the drinking that is. So I'm sorry if that affected you. Affected us.'

Neil pulls a strange pouty expression combined with a raising of the eyebrows that seems to imply, *And...?*

'Gosh,' Sue says, visibly trying to counterbalance her

husband's lack of enthusiasm. 'Well done you on the drinking. That's great news, isn't it, Neil?'

'Yeah, great. If it lasts.'

'And I actually have a question about that for you, so let's start with that one. Because – unless I got this wrong – you told me way back when that you'd stopped drinking too. I feel sure you said that to me, didn't you?'

Sue glances at Neil, who remains poker-faced.

'But Fiona told me that I'd got that wrong,' Wendy continues. 'So I was wondering what that was about.'

'Well, Neil did stop for a while, didn't you? For what was it? Almost a year?'

'A bit more than a year, actually. For sort of medical reasons.'

'And I did kind of slow down, too,' Sue says. 'The way you do if your partner stops drinking.'

'But you did tell me that, didn't you?' Wendy asks, addressing Sue. 'I'm sure I remember you saying repeatedly that you'd both stopped drinking. I remember because you no longer even had any drink in the house.' She remembers this because she had started smuggling a small bottle in her handbag whenever family gatherings took place at Neil and Sue's. Facing their thin-lipped smiles had felt impossible without a drink just as it feels almost impossible right now.

'No. Yes. I mean... uh...' Sue splutters, turning to her husband. 'Neil?'

'OK. So, we said that for your benefit,' Neil says, stepping in brutally to save his wife. 'If you must know, that's what happened.'

'For my benefit?'

'It's just... the conversations,' Sue explains. 'When you were drinking. They often got a bit... excitable... So we thought it was easier this way.'

'Excitable? You were downright argumentative,' Neil says.

'I'm sorry, but if we're going for the truth here: you were absolutely bloody exhausting.'

'Oh,' Wendy says. She can feel herself blushing. 'OK.'

'You weren't that bad,' Sue says unconvincingly. 'But it's true, we didn't want you drinking when you were here because that seemed to make everything... awkward. So the easiest way seemed to be to stop drinking *with* you.'

'But you used to smuggle in your own and swig it in the bathroom,' Neil says. 'So I'm not sure it helped.'

'Gosh,' Wendy says, blushing even harder. 'OK. I didn't know you knew about that. But OK.' She's imagining all the conversations they must have had about her behind her back and feeling mortified. 'Couldn't you have said something, though? Couldn't you have asked me to slow down, instead of, you know, lying to me?'

Neil laughs sourly. 'Oh, we tried, didn't we, Susie?'

Sue nods quickly, embarrassedly.

'You do remember the bottle of whisky, I take it?' Neil asks. 'At Christmas? A couple of years back?'

Wendy shakes her head. She has no idea what he's talking about.

'When I said you'd had enough and tried to put the drinks away? And you prised the bottle from my hands? You virtually fought me for it, here, in the kitchen.'

'I did?' Wendy asks, looking to Sue for confirmation.

'You swigged it straight from the bottle,' Sue says. 'And Neil got actual bruises on his arm from the scuffle.'

'Well, that was... I bruised more easily back then.'

'But you still had bruises.' She turns back to Wendy. 'He had your fingerprints on his arm for a week.'

'God,' Wendy says. 'I'm sorry. I really don't remember that at all.'

'And that was just one time,' Neil says. 'There are plenty more where that came from.'

'Yes, it happened a few times,' Sue says. 'Not the bruises. But times we tried to get you to slow down.'

'But you wouldn't hear of it,' Neil says. 'You were offended even at the suggestion. So...'

'So we started hiding the stuff before you came,' Sue says. 'It just seemed to be easier that way.'

Wendy starts to cry, silent tears slipping down her cheeks.

'Oh, Wens,' Sue says, standing and moving to crouch beside her so that she can slip one arm around her shoulders.

But Wendy shrugs her off. 'I just...' she says. Then, after accepting the tissue that Sue is proffering, she continues, 'It's mortifying. It's so embarrassing and I don't even remember. It's embarrassing *that* I don't remember, too.'

'Well, it's true,' Neil says. 'We're not making anything up.'

'No, no, I believe you. And I'm sorry.'

'It's OK,' Sue says, returning to her seat. 'Right, Neil?'

'Yeah. Sure. It's fine.'

'And you were going through a difficult time,' Sue says. 'We know that.'

Wendy nods and closes her eyes. She blows her nose and tries not to think about how much of an understatement that is. 'So, about that,' she finally says. 'That's the other thing I need to talk about. That's the main thing, really.'

'What is?' Neil asks.

'My "difficult time",' Wendy says, making the speech marks with her fingers.

Sue glances nervously at Neil and then, after pushing the box of tissues so that it's right in front of Wendy, she takes Neil's hand across the table – a visible sign of solidarity before the onslaught she can sense is coming.

'I've never told you how Mum died,' Wendy says. 'And I've discovered that I need to do that. So...'

'I think we know how Mum died,' Neil says. 'So there's really no need to go there.'

'Yeah, but that's the thing,' Wendy tells him. 'You don't.'

She tells them now. She tells them how she drove her mother to chemo and radiotherapy for months and how she nursed her when she vomited, back home. Through tears, fresh tears, intermittent floods of tears, she tells them of the routine check-ups and the good news, and their shared joy until that one fateful check-up when the results were not good, followed by the devastating follow-up when they announced the cancer had metastasised all over, a fact she had to keep explaining to their mother because it was a concept she seemed unable to hear.

And then finally, she tells them of the day she died, how she hadn't slept for thirty-seven hours because she'd gone straight from a night shift to holding her mother's hand in the hospice. She tells them how their mother had screamed in pain before dying alone, because she'd been stuck down at the main desk begging for morphine.

When she comes to the end of the story the three adults sit in silence. Wendy pulls another tissue from the box and wipes the tear-splattered table and then her eyes, and then, because still no one is speaking, and because the silence in the room is unbearable, she stands and goes to the bathroom to wash her face. She wishes she had a secret bottle of vodka in her handbag and only barely manages to be thankful that she doesn't.

When she returns to the dining room, her brother and sister-in-law are still seated. They don't seem to have moved a muscle. It's as if time has been suspended in her absence.

'I'm sorry,' Neil says, once she has sat back down. 'We didn't know. I suppose we thought we knew, but we didn't.'

'No,' Sue says. 'But how could we? You never said a word.'

Wendy nods thoughtfully at this. She clears her throat before, speaking with difficulty, she says, 'It was so... awful... that I blanked it out myself. So I couldn't have told you even if I'd wanted to.'

'You see?' Sue says, as if this somehow vindicates her. 'We couldn't possibly have known.'

Wendy blinks slowly and turns to look out at the wet garden. Something is happening in her body and it's a moment before she recognises the sensation as rising anger. She'd hoped to avoid that today, but here it comes, bubbling up. She takes a few deep breaths and then turns back and says, in the flattest tone she can manage, 'If you'd been there then you would have known. That's how you could have known. By being there for me.'

'That's true,' Neil says. 'And I'm sorry we weren't there for you.'

Wendy nods at him slowly. 'Oh,' she says. 'OK.'

She looks out at the garden again, and tries once again to calm herself with deep breathing, but this time it doesn't seem to help. When she turns back to face them, she catches a glimpse of something unspoken, something complex going on between them.

'So is that it, then?' she asks after a moment. 'Like, sorry, and we're all OK? Is that how this is supposed to work? After I... After I... Actually, I can't even go there.'

Sue is biting her bottom lip.

'I'm trying here,' Wendy says, fresh tears springing up in spite of herself. 'I really, really am trying. But I'm not sure that "sorry" quite cuts it.'

Sue turns to Neil now and strokes his shoulder. 'I think you need to tell her, honey,' she says. 'I don't think there's any other way.'

'No,' Neil says, squeezing her fingers and then pushing her hand away. 'No, you're right.'

'Tell me what?' Wendy asks, glancing between their faces, trying to read meaning into their troubled expressions.

'Look, there's a reason why we couldn't be there,' Neil says.

'And I know you think I'm an arsehole – and maybe I am that, too – but there was a reason. That's the thing.'

'OK,' Wendy says doubtfully, drying her tears again and blowing her nose. She can feel a fresh bout of anger rising again, already pushing away the sadness. She knows, she just knows that whatever Neil says next is going to make her explode with rage. Because what possible justification could there be for leaving her alone with their dying mother?

'I had it too,' Neil says, blindsiding her. 'That's the thing. I had cancer as well.'

And just like that the balloon of Wendy's anger pops. 'What?' she asks, unbelieving at first. Her mind is trying to tell her that this is some kind of trick.

'I found out I had cancer almost the same time you found out about Mum's,' Neil says. 'Talk about timing!'

'It was just a few weeks before,' Sue says.

'No!' Wendy says. 'Neil... no...'

Neil nods. 'Stage two. Testicular. Horrible.'

'No,' Wendy says again, fresh tears springing up. 'But how can...?'

'It's OK,' Neil says, using the flat of his hand to make a calming gesture. 'I'm fine now. I'm in complete remission.'

'Complete remission,' Sue repeats.

'But for a while back there, things were pretty full-on.'

'For a long time, really.'

'Yeah, we had a bad couple of years.'

'I don't... How can I not know this?' Wendy asks. 'I mean, Christ, Neil. I'm your sister.'

'I know,' Neil says. 'I'm sorry.'

'Why didn't you tell me?'

'We...' Neil glances at his wife and she sighs and nods. 'We were worried about you, really,' he explains. 'We were worried about you even before Mum. What with the drinking and... your general... I don't know... stress levels... And then...'

'We were worried it would send you over the edge,' Sue says. 'I thought you had enough to deal with.'

'And you weren't that easy-going about anything,' Neil says. 'So I didn't want you making a fuss.'

'A fuss?' Wendy splutters.

'Yeah. You know what you can be like. You're hardly the best person to have around in a crisis.'

'I'm not?' Wendy asks. She's shocked about this. She's always considered herself *great* in a crisis.

'No, you're not.'

'OK. Well, I guess I didn't know that,' she says. 'And did anyone else know about this, about the cancer? Did Harry? Did you tell the kids?'

Sue shakes her head.

'Harry only knew—' Neil starts.

'Are we doing that?' Sue says, interrupting him.

'Oh, OK. Sorry, no. Maybe not.'

'What?' Wendy asks. 'Are we doing what?'

'Nothing, really,' Neil says. 'Never mind.'

'But all this was going on when?' Wendy asks, trying to reframe her internal narrative of the last six years.

'Well, they found it in, what – 2018, wasn't it?' Neil asks.

Sue nods. 'It really was a couple of weeks before you told us about your mum.'

'And I was going to tell you. I was, you know, prepping myself to tell you. But then you called about Mum, and I somehow couldn't.'

'There wasn't really any space to tell you,' Sue says. 'If that makes any sense.'

'You were all about Mum, which was normal. And you were really upset about Mum. Which was obviously normal, too. But we did think that you might find out. And we sort of decided to deal with that as and when.'

'Neil was having his first surgery while you were in and out with your mum as an outpatient,' Sue says. 'So we thought we might bump into you then. Or at one of the check-ups. We thought you might find out that way. Or that one of your nurse friends might tell you. But you never did find out, so... so we just... left it, really.'

'We were maybe a bit spineless about it, looking back,' Neil says. 'I still don't know. And if we were, I'm sorry.'

'We honestly didn't know what was best,' Sue says. 'We couldn't decide whether to tell you or not.'

'We talked about it all the time,' Neil says.

'All the time,' Sue confirms.

'Your surgery,' Wendy says, sifting through the conversation, grasping at words that might help her understand. 'You said surgery...'

'Yeah, they had to remove one,' Neil says. 'Replaced it with a plastic fantastic.'

'You can barely tell,' Sue says, resulting in a brief glare from Neil. 'Well, you can't,' she insists.

'God,' Wendy says. 'And you said your first surgery? So there was more?'

'Yeah, lymph nodes,' Neil replies. 'They had to take those out, too. But that was a bit later on.'

'Oh, Neil!' Wendy exclaims. 'You should have told me! I would have been there for you.'

'It's OK,' Neil says, shaking his head. 'You were there for Mum. And I do appreciate that, sis. Because I really couldn't be there, myself.'

Wendy starts to cry again so Neil stands and moves his chair to her side.

'Hey, I'm fine,' he says, caressing her hair. 'And I'm sorry I couldn't be there for Mum. But we really were in the wars for a while back then.'

Wendy sighs and shakes her head. It's too much to take in in one go. She wishes she could go and lie down – wishes she could take a break in her mountain cabin, alone, to digest it all. 'But you're honestly OK now?' she asks, again.

'I am.'

'You're sure?'

'One hundred per cent sure.'

'Thank God,' she says.

'Nah, thank chemo,' Neil, says.

'And are there...? Have you, you know... God, I can't think of the word. Have you got secondary issues? From the chemo and whatever?'

'Side effects, you mean?' Neil asks.

'Yes. Exactly. Have you?'

Neil glances at Sue, silently asking her a question by raising one eyebrow.

Sue nods sadly and chews her bottom lip.

'D'you want to...?' Neil asks. 'Or shall I?'

Sue shakes her head. 'You.'

'So, yeah,' Neil says, turning back to Wendy. 'We can't have kids. So that put a bit of a spanner in the works.'

'Kids?'

'Yeah. I'm infertile now. Sperm count is a big fat zero.'

'Gosh, I'm sorry. I didn't think you wanted kids, anyway,' Wendy says.

'Oh, of course we did!' Sue says. 'We *love* kids. And I was... Sorry, Neil. I'll let you... whatever you decide.'

Neil nods and wipes his face with the flat of his hand. He clears his throat loudly. 'So, yeah... Sue was actually pregnant,' he says. 'She was pregnant when I got ill. And so we didn't – we kind of thought one was enough, one could be enough – and it wasn't 100 per cent sure I'd be... you know... infertile.'

'And I would probably have been too old to try again, anyway,' Sue says. 'I mean, it was a miracle I got pregnant then, in the first place. Well, we thought it was a miracle.'

'So yeah, we decided, well, if we can't have more, well, one's enough. So we didn't, you know, freeze any spunk.'

'But I lost it,' Sue says quietly, looking out into the garden. 'I lost it at four months. It was a boy. And we lost him. So...'

'We think it was the stress,' Neil says.

'Or my age,' Sue says.

'Well, they said it might be stress,' Neil says.

'And they also said that my age didn't help,' Sue insists.

'OK, yeah, so we don't know, not officially. But I think it was probably stress. All that business of me being ill.'

'And I think it was probably my age,' Sue says. 'But whatever it was, I was devastated.'

Wendy looks between her brother and his wife. She can see the pain in their eyes and can barely breathe because she's suddenly aware of how much of it there is. How did she fail to see this before? She feels like she's about to have a panic attack. Her pain. Her mother's pain. Their pain. It's all just too much. She could really do with a drink.

'Have you got...?' she starts to ask, but she sees Sue begin to anticipate the rest of her question, and realises that it will just add to their troubles – to everyone's troubles, including her own. So she stops herself in time. 'Do you think I could make more tea?' she asks.

'Of course,' Sue says, jumping up. 'Of course. Let me just put the kettle on.'

* * *

Wendy, Harry and John

John: Hello. No, no, please, stay seated! I'm sorry I'm so late. I had a bit of an emergency. Still, we're all here now, right?

Harry: No worries, eh, Wens?

Wendy: ... <checks watch>

J: So a couple of quick questions first. <uncaps expensive-looking fountain pen> I see here that you're married.

W: Yes, we are.

J: Since 1990, is that right?

W: Yes.

J: And you have two children, Fiona and Todd?

W: Yes.

H: We did already answer all of these questions. Your secretary gave me a questionnaire to fill in.

J: Yes. That's what I'm looking at now.

H: Indeed.

J: I'm just checking this is all correct.

H: Well, it is. I'm the one who filled it in.

J: Of course. And you're a teacher?

H: Yes.

J: And it says here you're a nurse?

W: Yes!

J: Great. So what can I do for you today?

H: Um... do you want to, Wens? Or...?

W: I can... If you want?

H: Sure. Go ahead.

W: So, our relationship has been... I'm not sure how to describe it really.

H: Going through a rocky patch? That's what people say, isn't it?

J: Yes. That is often what people say. And how rocky would you say it is?

W: Well, we have, kind of talked about whether, you know...

H: ... whether our future's still together.

W: Or not. But we think it is, I think. Don't we?

H: Yeah, I think so.

J: I see.

W: It all started during the lockdowns, really. I'd say that was when it all went a bit... wouldn't you?

H: Yes, pretty much. I mean, things weren't fa-a-abulous before that. But Covid definitely didn't help.

J: Well, a lot of people reconsidered what they wanted during Covid. Both professionally and personally.

W: Yes. I quit my job afterwards, too.

J: And I left my wife of thirty years...

W: *Really?* <glances at Harry> OK. Anyway...

J: So what job did you leave?

W: I was nursing.

J: Ah yes, of course. You're a nurse. It says that here, on the questionnaire.

H: Yes. It does. <sighs>

W: And my job, that was a part of... what went on with us... in a way.

J: The nursing? How so?

W: Well, it was the risk of bringing it home, really. I mean, Covid was everywhere. So I started staying elsewhere.

J: You mean you left the family home?

W: Yes.

J: And you stayed where?

W: Oh, just in a friend's Airbnb.

J: Is this a friend-friend, or a friend-friend?

W: Oh, no. Not really, just a friend who happened to have a place.

J: I see. And how long did you stay there, would you say?

H: It was on and off, really, wasn't it?

W: Yes. With, you know, the ups and downs of the pandemic. The infection rates and what-have-you... But overall, I was probably there, like, half the time, maybe? Over those two years?

H: I don't think it was half the time.

W: I think you'll find it was.

J: Well, I don't think we need to be exact here. But I get the picture. And why did you do that, do you think? Why did you leave the family home for such a significant amount of time?

W: Like I said, because of the risk of infection. I was working in a very high-risk environment, and everyone was scared. I was terrified of giving it to my kids.

J: You're referring to the risk of infection from Covid?

W: Yes.

J: And you truly believe that's the reason? Because for most people, well, Covid was little more than a cold.

W: ...

H: Um... <coughs>... Um, that's not really true. In fact—

W: Over two hundred thousand people died in the UK. Quite a few of them in front of me.

J: Yes. Of course. Your experience as a nurse will have been different, I suppose. I was merely pointing out that this wasn't the experience for most of us. Anyway, moving on.

W: Christ!

H: You OK to carry on, Wens?

W: Sure. Yeah. Whatever.

J: What I was trying to get at is whether you were happy to get away from the family home? Even a little bit. Please, there's no shame in admitting it.

W: Happy?

J: It's just a question.

W: No, I wasn't happy. I hated it.

J: OK. And you're perfectly sure about that?

W: Yes.

H: Um... Are you, Wens? Totally sure about that?

W: What? Yes, Harry! Of course.

H: It's just... I don't know...

W: What don't you know, Harry?

H: I just... sometimes I wondered. Sometimes I felt like you did enjoy getting away. So you could, you know... get hammered and watch Netflix without worrying about the kids. Without having me on your back.

J: Were you? On her back, as you say?

H: About the drinking?

W: I *was* drinking too much. It was my way of dealing with the stress.

J: Well, many people did find themselves drinking more during the pandemic. I certainly know I did.

H: Right. Um, OK.

J: I'm merely suggesting that wasn't entirely unusual.

W: Fine. Well, anyway, no I didn't enjoy it, Harry.

H: Hey, I'm not criticising, hon. I'm just saying that I don't think that's all it was.

W: And I'm telling you that you're wrong.

H: OK, fine. But you did also... she did also rent a place in France and bugger off there for six months. And that wasn't about Covid at all. Because it was over by then, wasn't it?

W: Yes, that was about getting my head together. You know that. And I was away less than three months. Not six.

H: *Was* it just about getting your head together, though?

W: You know it was. I needed to be on my own to think, that's all.

J: And how did it feel, being on your own, um... Wendy? Did you find that you liked it?

W: No. I've already said. I didn't.

J: Not even a little? Because most of us, after years in a long marriage, find some relief in being on our own.

W: No. I mean, OK, maybe a tiny bit. I was so tired, and stressed, and... So yes, sometimes it did feel easier being on my own. Not having to deal with other people...

H: You see. That's all I was saying.

J: And how about you, Harry?

H: Me?

J: Yes. Were you happier on your own as well?

W: I didn't say I wa—

J: Sorry, Wendy. I'm asking Harry a question right now. Harry?

H: OK, I... OK, but I wasn't on my own, was I? I had both kids with me.

J: I see. But what about Wendy. How did you feel about her absences?

H: Well, I missed her, of course.

W: Of course! <laughs>

H: But I was very stressed as well. And so were the kids. We all were. So if I'm being honest, having her take her stress elsewhere sometimes felt like a bit of a break.

W: Christ, Harry! Don't mince your words, eh?

J: No, this is good, Wendy. Harry's being honest.

W: Fine. Fine! Whatever.

H: Hey, don't get the hump with me. I'm only trying to answer the questions.

W: Hey, who's got the hump?

H: You have. I can tell.

W: Feel free to step in any time, John, before we end up hitting each other.

J: I'm just listening to you, observing the way you function. It's actually very interesting.

W: Great. Well, good for you. I'm so glad we're interesting for you.

J: So I'm hearing what's been pushing you apart. What, if anything, is still pulling you together?

W: If anything?

J: Yes. I mean, how, for example, is your sex life?

W: Oh... I'll let you field that one, Harry.

H: Um, it's pretty non-existent. I mean, it is non-existent. We tried, though, didn't we?

W: Yeah, we did.

H: But it didn't really work.

W: No, it was awful.

J: When you say it didn't work?

W: It felt embarrassing, really. Like we don't fit together.

J: I see. Those are quite profound words, don't you think?

H: Are they?

J: I think so. Don't you?

H: I think she's just saying we were all elbows and knees because it had been so long.

W: Exactly. That's exactly what I was saying.

J: Yes, but that's not what you said, is it, Wendy? Those aren't the words you used.

W: No. But it was the image I was trying to describe.

J: OK. So we've established that sex isn't pulling you together, right now. What else is?

W: If anything!

J: If anything.

H: Well, our... um... shared history, I suppose you could call it.

W: Yes. Yes! Twenty-odd years of marriage. That's not nothing.

J: Odd? Why do you say odd?

W: Oh, no... No, I didn't mean... I meant 'about'. Twenty-odd years. About twenty years.

J: OK. If you're sure that's what you meant. And is that a reason, do you think?

H: I'm sorry?

J: Just because you've been doing something for twenty-*odd* years. Would you say that's a reason to carry on doing it?

H: I ...

J: I'm merely asking the question.

W: Well, yes, it is.

J: If you've *enjoyed* doing it for the last twenty years, then I suppose one could argue that it is.

W: Enjoyed?

J: Yes. Enjoyed.

W: No one enjoys a twenty-year marriage.

J: They don't? I think it's very interesting that you think that.

H: Hang on, Wens...

W: No, what I mean is, no one enjoys all of it. It's not like one thing that you just enjoy.

H: Oh right.

W: It's a process. It's a shared experience, the good and the bad. It's trying to understand all... this... <waves her hand in a circle above her head>

J: All... this?

W: Yes! Life and death, and what's the point of any of it? And instead of trying to do that whole... thing... as a lonely little soul in a big scary universe, you team up with someone and try to do it together. That's what a marriage is.

H: Yeah. Exactly. That's good, Wens. I like that.

J: Well, thank you for enlightening me about life, the universe and everything, not to mention the purpose of marriage. And have you – made sense of it all, together – do you think?

W: Well no, obviously not.

H: I don't think Wendy means that's the aim. Because you can't really make sense of it, can you? I think she's talking more about the process.

J: Is that what you meant, Wendy?

W: Maybe. Yes. I think so. Look, I'm sorry, but what exactly is your role, here?

J: I'm sorry?

W: You, your role? What is it? Because I was under the – apparently mistaken – impression that you were here to help us fix our marriage.

J: Oh! <laughs> *That's* my role, is it?

W: Well, isn't it?

J: I don't know.

H: You don't know?

J: No, perhaps I see my role as enabling you to find your truth, whether that's staying together or admitting that you actually prefer to be apart.

H: Wow!

W: Yeah, wow.

H: Wens, shall we just? <nods towards the door>

J: You're free to go whenever you wish, of course.

W: Yeah. Come on. This is bollocks.

* * *

Harry and Wendy

'And I'll have a hot chocolate,' Wendy tells the waitress.

Harry nods out of the café window at a woman in a red coat, ringing the bell opposite. 'His next victim,' he says.

'Poor woman. We should warn her. He has to be the worst marriage counsellor ever, right?'

'Yeah, he was really shit, wasn't he?' Harry agrees.

'And the Covid stuff!'

'Awful. Should be barred. Unless...'

'Unless?'

'I just... I don't know...' Harry says. 'I mean, he was *so* bad...'

'And?'

'I can't help but wonder if he did it on purpose?'

'On purpose?'

'Yeah, you know... I mean, there's nothing like providing a common enemy to convince you to stick together, right?'

'Oh,' Wendy says. 'Yes, I see.' Then, 'D'you really think so?'

'Nah,' Harry says. 'No, I think he's probably just a bit useless.'

'Yes,' Wendy agrees. 'Me, too.'

The waitress arrives with their drinks. Once they have thanked her Wendy stirs her hot chocolate slowly, then asks, 'Who advised you he was good, anyway?'

Harry sips his Coke, then says, 'It was Steve Mason. You know, the PE teacher?'

'Oh, right. But didn't he...? I thought he got divorced.'

'Yeah, actually, he did,' Harry says. He bites his bottom lip and pulls a silly face.

'You idiot,' Wendy says.

'Yeah, probably not my best idea,' Harry says. 'Still, I liked what you said, about, you know, decoding the mystery, together.'

'Thanks,' Wendy says. 'Though he had no idea what I was talking about.'

'None,' Harry agrees solemnly.

'Actually, I'm not sure I know what I was talking about.'

'No,' Harry says. 'Me neither. It sounded cool, though. Quite poetic.'

'We are better off together, though, aren't we? You do think that, don't you?'

'Yeah,' Harry says, reaching across the table for her wrist. 'Yeah, I think we are. Definitely. Even if we don't seem to fit together anymore.'

'Hum,' Wendy says in a silly voice. 'Quite a profound statement, that one, don't you think?'

'Gosh, I just realised, we didn't pay,' Harry says. 'We didn't pay, did we?'

'Um, no. Well, I didn't, anyway.'

'Me neither.'

'Ha!' Wendy laughs. 'Well, serves him right.'

* * *

Wendy and Todd

Wendy: Hello, sweetheart.

Todd: Oh! Sorry, I thought it was Dad.

W: Yes, I bet. I'm on your father's phone. He lent it to me.

T: Right. Um, *why* are you on Dad's phone?

W: Maybe because you don't pick up when I use mine?

T: ...

W: I've left about ten voicemails, and I've called you maybe twenty times since I got back.

T: Look, I'm sorry, OK?

<Todd has always been quick off the mark with the world's most unconvincing apologies. He can even make an apology sound like an attack.>

W: For?

T: For not picking up. I just... I didn't know what to say.

W: About what, honey?

T: About, oh, come on, Mum. You know full well.

W: Something to do with the wedding, maybe?

T: Look, I'm sorry. I should have told you. I know.

W: I understand that was a difficult thing to say to me.

T: Cool. So, we're good, then?

W: But leaving it to your little sister was a bit weaselly, don't you think?

T: Yeah, I know. I asked Dad first. But he was just like, 'Do it yourself, lad.'

W: Interesting. Well, I don't blame him.

T: He says you've stopped drinking, though...

W: I have. And that's partly thanks to you.

T: Thanks to *me*?

W: Yes. Your ultimatum about the wedding helped me realise I have a problem. So thanks for that.

T: Oh. OK. Good.

W: I'd very much like to meet Amanda before the wedding, Todd, if that's at all possible.

T: Um, sure. OK. Maybe we'll come home for the spring break. And it wasn't me, you know.

W: What wasn't, honey?

T: It wasn't me who was worried about you at the wedding. Not to start with anyway.

W: I'm not sure I'm following you.

T: It was Sue and Neil. I mean, I don't want to get them into trouble or anything, but they were the ones who got Amanda all worked up.

W: Why? What did they say?

T: She was telling them all the plans. For the reception and stuff. And Sue said she didn't think it was wise. To have it in a pub.

W: Because of me?

T: Yeah. Kind of.

W: Oh, honey, I'm sorry.

T: And then Amanda got scared that there would be some awful sort of *Four Weddings and a Funeral* scene – that it would be the only thing anyone would remember. Especially what with you and Dad not talking and everything. Her folks are dead posh, too.

W: I'm not sure that—

T: I mean, they're a bit, you know... What people call 'stiff upper lip'. They wouldn't cope well. With a scene.

W: I think even posh people have domestics, honey, but I hear what you're saying.

T: Sorry, I didn't mean—

W: Todd, sweetheart, I get it. And I'm sorry I had you all worried. But everything's going to be fine. Because I'm not drinking anymore, at all.

T: You are happy for me, aren't you? About me getting married, I mean? Cos you haven't said it, you know.

W: God, of course I am, Todd! And you're right I should have said that first.

T: But are you really?

W: Look, I am. I just worry about you. I worry that it's too soon, that you're too young. All that stuff.

T: But we're in love, Mum...

W: Yes, I know. And I'm very, very happy about that. I just worry... It's a mother thing, I think. It's kind of non-negotiable, I'm afraid. It's what mums do. They worry.

T: Right, so are...

W: Yes?

T: Are we OK, Mum? Like really? Cos all this has been fu... Messing with my...

W: Todd?

T: I'm sorry, Mum, but it's been really eating me up. I felt so stuck in the middle. I've been feeling kind of pukey about it all. Cos if I tried to change the reception I'd have to explain why. And if I *didn't* change it then...

W: Please don't get upset, honey. Take a deep breath. Everything's fine. Everything's perfect. I'm sober as a judge, and I'm not upset at all.

T: Really?

W: Cross my heart, I'm thrilled to bits for you. And I love you. Because no matter what you do or what choices you make, I'm your mother. So that's non-negotiable, too.

FIFTEEN

THE WEDDING

The wedding takes place in St Michael's church in the bucolic village of Pirbright in Surrey, a couple of miles from Amanda's family home. St Michael's is a classic village church set in well-tended lawns dotted with ancient, often lopsided gravestones.

Forewarned by Todd that Amanda's parents are 'pushing the boat out', Wendy insisted that the whole family buy new clothes. Her first few months back home have been clunky, to say the least. She and Harry have organised as many team-building events as possible in an attempt at re-gluing the family together. They've done big family meals at home, day trips out and treats in posh restaurants – but the results have been mixed and unpredictable, sometimes lovely, others unexpectedly awful.

But the clothes shopping trip had been a success. They'd had fun together trying on different – sometimes silly – outfits, and as they step from the car and walk towards the church in the sunshine, Wendy feels proud, because as a family they have never looked better.

They pause at the gate while Wendy fixes Harry's new paisley tie and repositions her hat.

'Mine OK?' Todd asks, raising one hand to the knot of his own grey polka-dot tie.

'Yours is still perfect,' Wendy says, then to Fiona as she pushes her hair behind her ears (hair that Fiona immediately shakes back into place), 'And you look amazing, too, Fifi.'

'Can't believe you made me wear a dress,' Fiona, who's never been a fan of flowery dresses, says.

'Think yourself lucky I didn't insist on the floppy hat,' Wendy laughs.

'Hey, we can swap if you want,' Todd teases his sister. 'There's still time. Though that might give your game away.'

'You'd probably look *less* gay in a dress,' Fiona says, punching him in the arm.

'Stop it, you two,' Harry tells them. 'Be nice. Just for one day. Todd's getting married. You're not five anymore.'

'And when you're not punching each other, you both look absolutely stunning,' Wendy tells them.

Inside the cool church, they say hello to Amanda's parents, Prudence and Mike. Prue is wearing a Margaret Thatcher blue two-piece suit, and Mike, a severe black suit and tie that would be more suited to a funeral. He's in a wheelchair, which is unexpected and rather sad. His Parkinson's must have advanced faster than everyone had hoped.

'Such a beautiful day for it!' Prudence says.

'It is! We're so lucky,' Wendy replies.

They take their seats next to Sue and Neil then turn in their pews to acknowledge Todd's sporty friends – lads Wendy has never seen wear anything other than trackies. They have scrubbed up remarkably well.

She scans the church. Someone has installed three of the biggest flower displays she has ever seen, containing hundreds and hundreds of flower heads, the ensembles reaching six feet high. She can see peonies, roses and lisianthuses, scented stocks and irises plus a few exotics she can't name. 'The flowers are amazing,' she whispers in Todd's ear.

'Yeah, her mum's best friend's a florist,' Todd explains. 'Not my thing, though. They make me sneeze.'

'I hope you've taken—'

'... double dose of Zirtek,' he says. 'Hopefully I'll be OK.'

'You don't seem too stressed, anyway,' Wendy says. 'That's good.'

'Stressed...' Todd repeats flatly. 'Why would I be stressed?'

Wendy sits back in her seat, glances at Harry and pulls a face.

'I almost pooed myself before ours,' he says quietly.

'Well, that's because I'm so scary.'

'Not you,' Harry says. 'Your dad.'

'Oh yeah, Dad was terrifying,' Wendy laughs.

At that moment, the organ strikes up and they stand, twisting and craning to catch a glimpse of the bride. And now here she is, looking incredible in a simple off-white shot-silk dress and a veil with a daisy-adorned headband.

Everyone holds their breath for an instant as the bride leans down, kisses her father on the cheek, and then straightens and begins pushing his wheelchair down the aisle.

'How wonderful,' Wendy says, looking at the happiness on their faces, looking at the sunlight streaming through the high church windows, smelling the incense and losing herself in the deep bone-shaking swell of the 'Wedding March'. Harry reaches for her hand and she squeezes his back and turns just long enough to see that his eyes are watering too.

The service is short and sweet – barely religious, yet religious all the same, but also elegant, almost literary in a way – and then soon, too soon almost, they are outside in the sunshine, mingling, smoking, everyone chatting about how lovely it all is as they stroll towards the White Hart which, like the church, is almost absurdly English.

'I can't believe people still live like this,' Harry says, as they cross the road, 'It's like a flashback to 1965.'

Thanks to the good weather, the reception has been set up outside, two lines of tables side by side to host forty – beautifully set with white tablecloths and silverware. Miraculously, the floral displays have travelled undamaged from the church to the rear of the buffet, which is protected by two side-by-side gazebos.

The guests mill around, waiting to be told where to sit. The name cards are not yet in place.

Fiona immediately starts chatting to the best man's girlfriend, who it would appear she knows, and with Todd being in constant demand plus Sue and Neil having momentarily vanished, Wendy and Harry find themselves cast adrift, stranded in the middle of the proceedings.

'Look at us,' Harry says, sipping his Champagne. 'Johnny no mates. Just you and me.'

'Thank God you're here,' Wendy says, though even now, even after six months sober she secretly wishes he wasn't holding a glass of Champagne so close to her face. 'I can't bear these sort of things if I'm on my own.'

'I know,' Harry says. 'I know that about you. I can't count the number of times I've had to save you from standing on your own looking forlorn.'

'You'd actually be fine without me, wouldn't you?'

Harry shrugs and sips his drink. 'I'd just wander up to someone and start talking. I've never understood why that's so hard.'

'Who?' Wendy asks, looking around. 'Go on, who would you pick?'

'Er... that old girl in the massive purple hat, maybe?' Harry says. 'She looks crazy enough to be fun.'

Wendy studies the woman. Her lipstick looks like it's been printed slightly off-register and her eyeliner is almost fluorescent blue. She has about fifteen roses tucked into the band of a wide-brimmed purple hat. 'Great shoes,' Wendy says. 'Good on her for balancing in those at her age.'

'Ah, these Surrey girls live forever,' Harry says. 'Sexy shoes until the very end.'

'Maybe she's fifty,' Wendy jokes. 'Maybe all that Champagne makes them age really badly.'

'Christ,' Harry says, feigning fear and looking at his glass. 'I've had two. Am I looking older?'

'Nah, you're looking gorgeous,' Wendy says, checking him out. 'The sexiest man here, by far.'

* * *

Everything goes to plan and it really does feel like the whole thing has been exquisitely directed by Richard Curtis.

Wendy finds herself comfortably seated between Fiona and Sue, opposite her brother Neil, and Harry. The food is traditional and tasty if lacking in vegetarian options. But Wendy's never been averse, in a pinch, to a bit of fish, and lets herself enjoy the smoked salmon starter, plus the caramelised vegetables of the main course even though they taste suspiciously of duck. The sun continues to shine and the speeches are that perfect British mix of embarrassing anecdote, snide humour and repressed love. Everybody seems to be smiling, and Todd and Amanda look wonderfully happy. The bubble of chatter mixes perfectly with the clink of silverware meeting porcelain, and the jazzy music drifting from indoors.

Once the meal is over, the wedding cake is cut and the joint honeymoon kitty – to which they have all contributed – is revealed to be a staggering £4,000. Finally, people start to drift indoors where a DJ has set up his gear. About four, Todd and Amanda open the dance with a slow to Robbie Williams's

'Angels', joined by Todd's rowdy friends and Amanda's more restrained girlfriends as the tempo picks up.

After a brief embarrassing slow on the dancefloor with Harry, Wendy takes a seat at the far end of the pub next to the unplugged jukebox and waits for him to return from the bar.

'You're sure you're OK with me drinking?' he asks, when he finally returns with a pint and her ginger beer.

'Yes, it's fine,' Wendy says. Harry is already well on his way to drunkenness. 'I'm perfectly happy to drive home.'

'Lucky me,' Harry says. 'A dedicated designated driver. God, that's like a tongue twister.'

They chat, superficially, to various people, about the food, and the weather, and the music, about Todd and Amanda, Kent and Surrey. As afternoon drifts towards evening, the music gets louder and some of the older participants start to drift away. Just after six, someone manages to get the disco lights working, too.

Harry, bless him, does his best to stick by Wendy's side, but he can't help slipping into conversations with all and sundry – conversations which, as he drinks, become increasingly incomprehensible. It's the first time in years that Wendy has been surrounded by drunken people, and she marvels at how difficult it is to fit in without drinking, how difficult it is to even listen to – let alone enjoy – all the slurring rubbish that's being said.

Dancing, too, turns out to be impossible. Perhaps if there was a little less light in the room (the evening sun is now streaming in through one of the windows) then she'd feel a bit less self-conscious, but as it is, in broad daylight, on a sparsely populated dance floor with unfamiliar music, sober, she's left feeling like a clunky adolescent. The sensation of being all elbows and knees – of being the only sober person present – is unbearable.

Around six thirty, just as she's wondering how early she can reasonably convince Harry to leave and how early it's socially acceptable to do so, Prue's florist friend, Jennifer, crosses the dance floor holding two drinks, one of which she hands to Wendy before plonking herself down beside her. 'I thought you were looking a bit glum,' she says, leaning in conspiratorially. 'So I came over to cheer you up.'

'Thanks,' Wendy replies, examining and then sniffing the drink. For half a second, she forgets that she's not drinking – she really does forget that fact. And then for another few seconds she tells herself that befriending Jennifer is more important right now than the whole silly not-drinking thing. She raises the glass to her lips and the sweet liquid (it turns out to be vodka and tonic – oh my God, that taste!) has barely touched her lips when Jennifer says, 'Did you like the flowers? That was me, you know.'

'Oh, yes,' Wendy says, lowering the glass to reply, and as she does so thinking, *God! I nearly drank that.* 'Yes, they were amazing!'

'Thank you!' Jennifer says, raising her glass. 'Cheers.'

Wendy clinks glasses but then braces herself and – feeling like she's wrestling with her own arm – manages to place the glass on the table. 'I'm driving,' she says, meeting Jennifer's troubled expression with a forced smile. 'So...'

'Surely one won't do any harm, will it?' Jennifer says. 'Because, frankly, you look like you could do with a drink. Your shoulders are all hunched up. Trust me, I do reiki.'

Wendy bristles at this remark. 'Actually, it would,' she says, so quietly that Jennifer has to lean in to hear her over the thumping Britney Spears bassline. 'It would do harm. I'm on the wagon, so...'

'God, how dull!' Jennifer says. 'Poor you!'

Suddenly, Wendy finds herself on her feet, heading for the door. It's only once she steps into the garden that she understands why she has left, because it's then that she realises she is crying.

Aware that a few people are staring at her, she makes her way to the street, forcing a smile and muttering, 'All getting a bit emotional, that's all,' to the best man as she passes by.

As she strides away she dries her tears, and soon finds herself back at the church where some kind of service is taking place.

For a few minutes, she lingers outside, watching as people file into the church, and then when a stranger catches her eye and actually beckons at her, she continues on her way, past the graveyard, and then along a footpath beside a brook.

It is calm, green and lovely here, and the only sounds are birdsong and the burble of the water. *Nature*, she thinks. *It's so good for us, and we forget that fact so quickly.* She can feel her heart slowing down already.

After a few hundred yards she comes to a drystone wall, just low enough that she can clamber on top of it so that she can sit looking out at the brook. She pulls her cigarettes from her handbag for only the third time today.

She'd intended to stop completely – had thought that if she wasn't drinking then stopping smoking might be easier. But on her third, or perhaps it was the fourth visit, the therapist had suggested that stopping both alcohol and cigarettes at once might be over-ambitious. So though she has slowed down considerably, she's putting off stopping completely until next year. But, oh my God, that cigarette tastes good. Maybe she won't give up at all.

She thinks now about the drinking, specifically about the deliciousness of that tiny sip of vodka and tonic. Actually, it had been beyond delicious. She had sensed every cell of her body starting to vibrate in sheer anticipation. It's why she'd suddenly felt so scared.

She thinks about being told she's 'dull' for having stopped. That's going to be an ongoing challenge, she can see. There always seems to be someone to insist that drinking is normal and fun. And how to maintain sobriety without becoming a hermit? How to stop without refusing every invitation to every party, every dance, every night out...? Perhaps one day she'll get to the point where it doesn't feel so awkward. But she finds it hard to imagine.

She takes a deep drag on her cigarette, stubs it out early, and pulls her phone from her bag, just in case Harry is looking for her, but there's no news from him – he's way too busy having fun to notice her absence. But she has received a WhatsApp message from Manon.

These messages – with Manon making the effort to write in English, and Wendy doing her best to reply in French – have become regular occurrences, which was unexpected. They're sending each other multiple messages on most days of the week. She really does seem to have made a new friend there and that feels strange. It's so long since that has happened, after all.

How go the wedding? Manon has asked in her latest message. *Bless her*, Wendy thinks. *She remembered.*

Ca va, she replies, then even though she knows it's approximative, *Pas alcohol est tres difficile.*

You can do, Manon replies immediately. *You are strong woman.*

And just like that, she feels strong enough to make it through this. Sometimes a vote of confidence is all you need.

When she gets back the sun is setting behind a copse of trees. The music from the pub is pounding (she recognises the song: 'Rock Lobster') and only three people remain outside, a couple, snogging in the shadows, and Prudence, seated alone at the furthest pub table nursing a drink. All signs of the wedding meal have vanished.

Wendy takes a deep breath to prepare herself for another round of banal, socially acceptable conversation, and crosses the garden to join Prue. But as she reaches her table, Prue, whose back is turned, simply raises one hand and without even glancing to see who is there, says, 'Just give me another five minutes and I'll be in.'

Wendy freezes and starts to turn away. But something in Prue's voice – a hoarseness indicative of sadness – makes her hesitate. Instead, she touches the woman's shoulder and asks, 'Prue, are you OK?'

Prue shrugs her hand away and, again without looking, says, 'Yes, I'm fine.'

Wendy hesitates and then, decision made, rounds the table to sit opposite. 'Hey,' she says. 'What's going on? Oh, you've been feeling emotional, too?'

'Oh, well spotted,' Prue says, sounding more weary than anything else.

'Look, if you really want to be alone, then I'll leave you to it,' Wendy tells her. 'But if you want to bend someone's ear, I'm here. I just shed a few tears myself.'

At this news, Prue lifts her gaze from her drink to look Wendy in the eye for the first time. She sniffs and swipes at the corner of one eye. 'You did?' she asks.

Wendy nods. 'Yep.'

'Why? What do you have to cry about?'

Wendy laughs lightly at this. 'Oh, not much really. Especially compared with other people's worries, I suppose.'

'No, go on,' Prue insists, still sounding vaguely spiky, but perhaps softening. 'Maybe it'll make me feel better about my own mess.'

'OK, well, I... um... realised recently that I'm what people tend to call an alcoholic,' Wendy says. 'And I'm discovering that a wedding party without alcohol can be seriously hard work.'

'Oh, poor you,' Prue says, and Wendy's unsure if she's being genuine.

'It doesn't sound so bad when you, you know... just say it,' Wendy says. 'But I have been feeling sorry for myself, all the same. Even though this is a lovely do.'

'Yes,' Prue says. 'Still, the youngsters are having fun. That's the main thing.'

'You're right, they are. So what about you and your... what did you call it? Your mess? What's that all about?'

'Oh, it's just Mike...'

'The Parkinson's,' Wendy says. 'That can't be easy.'

'No,' Prue says. 'No, it's a horrible disease.'

'I had an uncle, as it happens,' Wendy says. 'So I do know a little about what goes on...'

'Yes, everyone does seem to know someone,' Prue says.

'I wasn't suggesting...' Wendy says. 'Obviously, when it's your husband, that's going to be far tougher.'

'I wasn't getting at you,' Prue says. 'I just sound like that sometimes. Forgive me. But yes, it really does seem to be frightfully common. And yet they still haven't given us a pill.'

'A cure, you mean?'

'Yes. I mean, he's on the L-dopa, obviously. But once that wears off... well, he just stops, really.'

'And where is he now?' Wendy asks, rather pointlessly looking around the empty pub garden.

'Oh, we had to sneak him out and send him home. He just, you know, froze. Please don't tell Amanda or Todd, though. He'd hate to think he spoiled their big day.'

'No, of course. I wouldn't. So that's all got to be quite tough on you.'

'Yes,' Prue says. '"Tough" doesn't really capture it.'

'Can I?' Wendy says, reaching for her bag. 'Do you mind if I smoke?'

'No, of course not,' Prue says. 'Not if I can have one.'

'Oh, I didn't know you smoked.'

'From time to time,' Prue answers, taking one from the proffered pack. 'Especially since I read about the whole Parkinson's thing.'

'The Parkinson's thing?'

'Yes. Apparently smokers get it less.'

'Really? Is that an actual thing?'

'Apparently so,' Prue says, speaking through smoke. 'Some people with Parkinson's even self-medicate with cigarettes and patches and what-have-you. Some find it helps a lot. I tried to convince Michael to try a patch. But his doctor said it was all rubbish even though he's got nothing else to offer. You know what they can be like.'

'Yes, I do. Anything that doesn't fit into their worldview...'

'Exactly. Even though there have been clinical trials in Europe and what-have-you. Anyway...'

'So how do you cope?' Wendy asks.

'Why? Does it look like I'm coping?'

'Yeah. It kind of does,' Wendy says, nodding gently.

'Well, good. That's definitely the impression I'm striving to impart.'

'But it doesn't feel like that? Like you're coping?'

Prue shrugs. 'I suppose I am, most of the time,' she says. She clears her throat and takes a hit from her cigarette before continuing, 'I feel so bloody angry all the time. That's the thing.'

* * *

They have escaped.

Todd and Amanda have been driven away, cans clattering, and though the party is continuing nevertheless, Wendy has convinced Harry and Fiona to leave.

Harry, in the front passenger seat, falls asleep almost immediately. It's not even ten o'clock.

So Wendy finds herself struggling to chat to Fiona in the

back seat, speaking loudly over the noise of the engine. 'Did you enjoy yourself?' she asks. 'You looked like you did.'

'Sure,' Fiona says, looking up from her phone. 'It was fine.'

Wendy, who saw her daughter dancing frenetically at various points during the evening, laughs. 'You youngsters are so stingy with your compliments. Would it strangle you to admit you had fun?'

'Fine,' Fiona says, feigning strangling herself. 'Yes, Mum. It was great.'

'I had fun, too,' Harry chips in, in a rare, sudden moment of wakefulness.

'Huh!' Wendy laughs. 'We noticed.'

They drive in silence until the M25 whereupon a loud snuffle and a snore from Harry prompts a fresh round of conversation.

'He really *did* have fun,' Fiona says just loud enough for Wendy to hear. 'I don't think I've ever seen him that drunk.'

'No,' Wendy agrees, checking the mirrors and indicating before moving into the middle lane.

'Is that a reaction to you stopping?'

'No, I don't think so. More to the fact that we haven't been to a party in years.'

'But you don't mind?'

'Your dad drinking? No, of course not!'

'It doesn't make it harder for you?'

'No. I mean... it is quite difficult being surrounded by drunk people when you're sober. So there's that... But not your father, specifically. I was glad to see him having fun.'

'He's a terrible dancer.'

'D'you think so? I've always liked the way he dances.'

Wendy glances across at Harry now. His eyes are closed, but he's smiling, and she can't tell if he's dreaming happy dreams or listening.

'You hardly danced at all.'

'I did, a bit,' Wendy protests.

'Like, once. Maybe twice.'

'OK, that might be true.'

'Too sober?'

'Yes, totally sober.'

'My friend Joe can't dance when he drives us places,' Fiona says. 'You know, when he's the designated driver? He says it's impossible.'

'Yes, it does feel hard. I'm not sure why.'

They drive on in silence for another half an hour, with only the thrum of the engine and noise of the wind and the road, the light from the orange street lamps sweeping through the cabin. As she drives, Wendy tries to get her brain around the idea that her baby boy is married. It seems unreal. It feels like only yesterday he was learning to walk.

Just as Wendy is guessing that Fiona has also fallen asleep and is considering switching on the radio for company, her daughter speaks.

'So in the spirit of not being stingy with compliments,' she says, 'you do know I'm impressed, right?'

'I'm sorry?' Wendy says.

'God, I knew you'd make me say it twice. I'm proud of you, Mum.'

'Proud of me? For what?'

'Because you've really changed, haven't you? You really got your act together.'

'Oh,' Wendy says, glancing back. 'Well, thank you! And I'm proud of you, too.'

'You know, we never thought you'd stop drinking. Todd and me, that is. We were going to place a bet, but we couldn't because we both wanted to bet you wouldn't stop.'

'Gosh!' Wendy says, pulling a face. 'OK.'

'It must be hard, though.'

'It's not easy, I'll admit.'

'So, what happened in France?' Fiona asks.

'What do you mean?'

'Well, you were completely different when you came back. You didn't have a fling, did you? I kind of wondered if that was it.'

Wendy shoots her daughter a look of consternation and then glances over at Harry, whose mouth has fallen open.

'God, I forgot Dad was even there,' Fiona says. 'Sorry.'

Wendy laughs genuinely at this. 'Don't be,' she says. 'And no, I didn't have a fling at all. I just... I don't know... I took the time to look at things, I suppose. And I made friends with that girl, Manon. She helped me a lot.'

'Really?' Fiona says. 'How so?'

'I don't know,' Wendy says thoughtfully. 'By being honest with me, I think. By connecting.'

'OK,' Fiona says. 'Fair enough.' Then, 'You were chatting to Amanda's mum for ages. You must have been out there for, like, an hour.'

'Oh, no, I went for a walk, actually. But we did chat a bit when I got back.'

'They're so stuck up,' Fiona says.

'Don't say that!' Wendy protests. 'I think she's nice. Prickly at first, but underneath I think she's all right. And she's going through hell right now.'

'Not your usual attitude to people like her,' Fiona says.

'People like her...' Wendy repeats softly. 'Well, perhaps I'm changing. Perhaps I'm trying to be a bit more understanding. Everyone has reasons why they're the way they are, you know. Nothing comes from a vacuum.'

'God, did you meet Ghandi out there in France?' Fiona asks. 'Or was it the Buddha himself?'

'Ha,' Wendy says. 'No, neither of those, unfortunately.'

She thinks, *No, the only person I met was myself. I just saw who I had become. And caught a glimpse of the person I could be instead.*

And even though the thought strikes her as one of the most profound thoughts she has ever had, she does not say it out loud. She knows it would sound like a cliché and that her daughter would only mock her for it. *One day*, she thinks. *Perhaps one day, when she's older, I'll explain.*

EPILOGUE

She turns off the ignition and sits listening to the ping-pinging of the cooling engine. *So here we are again*, she thinks. Through the windscreen the cabin is silhouetted against a reddening afternoon sky.

'You OK?' Harry asks, laying one hand on her knee.

'Yes, sorry...' she says, as if dragging herself from a trance. 'It's just so strange to be back!'

She releases her seatbelt and cracks the door. 'You know, it's warmer today than when I got here last time?'

'But you got here in autumn,' Harry replies, speaking over the top of the car.

'I know,' Wendy says. 'But the weather up here is nuts. Tomorrow might be sun or rain or snow. You never can tell.'

'God, I'd love it if we got snowed in,' Harry tells her, looking suddenly boyish.

'Believe me,' she says, 'it's overrated.'

She retrieves the keys from the lock box and leads Harry by one hand around to the front of the cabin.

'Wow,' he says, turning his back to the house to look out at the view. The sun is moving behind the hill and the sky is flaming in reds and purples.

'I knew you'd like it,' Wendy says, standing beside him. 'In fact, all the time I was here, I think that was the single thought I had the most often. Just how much you'd like it.'

'I'm guessing you alternated between that one and wanting a drink,' Harry says cheekily.

'Yes. That did come up quite a lot, too.'

Wendy turns back to the house and fiddles with the lock until the door opens. Inside there's a surprise: the cabin is warm.

'Hello, hello!' Wendy murmurs, crossing the room to crouch down in front of a new Japanese-style room heater which is belching paraffin-scented heat into the room.

'New?' Harry asks.

'Yeah, it was freezing when I got here last time. At least she listens to her renters' complaints.'

'It's still got the famous wood stove,' Harry says, walking around the space, peering at things. 'There's a note.' He swipes the envelope from the top of the unlit wood burner and places it between Wendy's outstretched fingers.

You are welcome to France again! the note inside reads. *I leave petrol fire for you. Please turn off immediately and put the fire to the wood pan for better smell.*

'She says it's a petrol fire?' Wendy says. 'That sounds dangerous.'

'I think she means paraffin,' Harry says. 'It smells like paraffin to me.'

Wendy laughs and hands him the note. 'Poor Madame Blanchard. I never did explain the difference between "welcome to France" and "you *are* welcome to France".'

'Maybe you should have given her English lessons,' Harry says, reading the note and pulling a face.

'You know, I never even met her. She could be one of those AI-computer things. Though she would probably speak better

English if that were the case... Anyway, I bet that's still better than your French.'

'Huh!' Harry says, feigning offence. *'Vous... serez – seriez ? – surpris, Madame !'*

'I think you can probably *tu-toi* me, though,' Wendy says, with a grin. 'Seeing as we do share a bed.'

'Merde !' Harry says. *'Bien sûr !'*

While Wendy lights the fire, Harry brings the shopping in from the car.

As they unpack and stack the items in cupboards, Wendy asks, 'So what do you think? You haven't said a word.'

'Oh, sorry, no, it's amazing!' Harry says. 'I'm a bit in awe, I think. My little Wens up here all on her own... I'm finding it hard to imagine.'

'I know,' Wendy agrees. 'I can hardly believe it myself. But what about the place? Is it how you imagined it?'

Harry pauses, a jar of jam in one hand, momentarily perplexed as he looks around. 'It's weird,' he says. 'Cos, I mean, you showed me photos, so it is, obviously, exactly like the photos. But it's also completely different.'

'How d'you mean?'

'Dunno,' Harry says, resuming his stacking. 'I don't think I ever imagined how the place would feel, I suppose. How it would smell, and sound... all that stuff... But, yeah, it's very cool indeed.'

'Fridge,' Wendy says, handing him a little pile of items containing a bottle of milk, a wedge of cheese and a block of butter.

Harry crouches down and opens the fridge. 'Ahh,' he says, pulling a bottle of prosecco from the door and waving it at her. 'I guess you didn't tell her about your new healthy ways, huh?'

'No,' Wendy says. 'She never knew about any of that. But that's fine. You can have it tomorrow with Christmas dinner.'

. . .

They heat their so-called 'luxury' ready meals in the microwave and once the fairly joyless event of eating these is over (because they don't taste very luxury at all) they move to the sofa to stare at the flames.

'So this is where it all happened, huh?' Harry asks, still constantly scanning the room.

'Yep,' Wendy says. 'This is it. And wait until you see the views tomorrow. I have a fabulous walk in store.'

'Tomorrow's going to be strange without the kids.'

'They wouldn't have been home anyway,' Wendy reminds him. Todd and Amanda are on their belated honeymoon in Bali while Fiona is at a friend's place in Brighton.

'Well, they promised to call, anyway,' Harry says. Then, 'Which reminds me. Must get on the old wifi for WhatsApp. I don't think I have much EU data in my plan. Does that work?'

'What, the wifi?' Wendy says, but by following Harry's gaze she deduces that he's referring to the Bluetooth speaker. 'Oh, yes. It's a bit fiddly to connect. But it actually sounds quite good.'

Once everything is connected and Harry's playlist is on, they snuggle on the sofa staring at the fire, Harry's arm heavy across her shoulders. 'My God, it's nice being here with you,' she says.

'And it's nice being here with you, too,' he replies. And then suddenly he's on his feet, holding out one hand. 'Dance with me,' he says.

Wendy laughs. 'I haven't been able to dance since I gave up the wicked booze.'

'I'm not asking you to do a bloody Charleston,' Harry says, yanking on her hand. 'Come on! Gimme a smooch.'

Faking reluctance, Wendy caves in, and she's relieved to find that their bodies do still fit together, at least enough to slow dance. When Billie Eilish ends and 'Something' by The Beatles begins, she jokingly comments, 'Why, I do believe thou art trying to seduce me, *Monsieur*! I've never heard this playlist before.'

'You know me,' Harry says. 'I'm like a Scout. Ready for anything.'

Wendy nestles her head against his shoulder and as they turn she studies the room to see what has changed since her last visit a year ago. Other than a couple of new cushions the place looks exactly the same and yet, it feels quite unfamiliar being here as a couple. It's like a different place entirely.

'Are *you* worried?' she asks, the thought having bubbled up from nowhere. 'About the sex thing?' It's probably the love song that has prompted the thought, she decides belatedly.

'Uh?' Harry says, also surprised by the sudden change of subject. 'Oh, no, not really. Why? Are you?'

'So you are a bit?' Wendy says.

'Er... no. Not really. I guess I'm still hopeful. Plus, if I'm being totally honest, I'd say I'm getting to an age where it isn't quite as important as before. Moments like this seem to mean more, if you know what I mean?'

'Yes,' Wendy says. 'Yes, I do.'

'Are you worried? Is it playing on your mind?'

'No, I... Never mind. It's silly, really,' Wendy says.

'No, it's not... go on.'

'I... Well, I suppose I worry that without being able to drink, it'll never sort itself out. A drink always seemed to make all that stuff so much easier. D'you know what I mean?'

'Yes,' Harry says, pulling her close. 'Yes, I thought that, too.'

'And I suppose I worry that you'll... have needs and...'

'And be tempted to look elsewhere?'

'Yes.'

'I don't think that's going to happen,' Harry says.

'But what if it does?'

Harry fails to reply for two full revolutions and Wendy, who can sense tears forming, starts to fear the worst. But then as she turns to face the front door again and George Harrison begins singing the final verse, Harry says, 'Well, if it does, then I'll let you know, OK?'

Wendy laughs genuinely at this. 'I'm not sure that would help things, to be honest.'

'Well, at least that way you won't be worrying all the time about something that doesn't exist. Right?'

This time it's Wendy who does not reply. When Harry eventually prompts her with a simple, 'Eh?' combined with a squeeze, she says, 'Can I have a think about it? Because between knowing and not knowing... I'm not sure. I'm really not sure what's best.'

* * *

She wakes up early the next morning to find that Harry is no longer beside her. She lies there enjoying the silence and the smell of woodsmoke, and for a moment the place feels like home again – it's as if she never left.

'Make me a cuppa, will you?' she calls out eventually, and when Harry does not reply, more loudly, 'Haz?' He's probably listening to one of his podcasts.

When he still doesn't reply, Wendy turns around in the bed and peers over the edge of the mezzanine. But Harry's not downstairs either.

Thinking, *He can't have gone for a walk already, surely? It's not even light*, she climbs from the bed and pulls on her dressing gown.

Downstairs the stove is roaring, proof, if proof were needed, that Harry isn't far, so she crosses to the window and peers out into the half-light to see him silhouetted against the brightening sky, wearing his overcoat, bobble hat and gloves, breath rising in steam-train puffs.

She cracks the door, letting in a rush of icy air, and calls out, 'You OK out there? Don't freeze!'

'Christ!' Harry says, turning sharply. 'You made me jump!' Then, 'Yeah, this is one of the most beautiful views I've ever seen. I'm waiting for the sun to come over that hill. It's almost there, look!'

In the distance a donkey brays, followed by the screech of a cock. 'It's cool, isn't it?' Wendy says before returning indoors. She always knew that he'd love it here, but she's still relieved he does.

They eat a leisurely breakfast of croissants and pains au chocolat, and then call the kids one after the other on Whats-App. It's mid-afternoon in Bali and their call finds Todd and Amanda on a beach.

'It's like, you know, all those photos of tropical paradises,' Todd tells them excitedly, before switching to the front-facing camera and performing a nauseatingly rapid 360 spin. 'Look!'

'Wow,' they say, in unison, even though the image is little more than a blur of sand and sky.

'I bet it doesn't feel like a proper Christmas, though,' Harry says.

'Oh, it does,' Todd says. 'It feels like the best bloody Christmas ever.'

The call to Fiona is more subdued. WhatsApp catches her in pyjamas in a scruffy lounge with a Lana Del Rey poster on the wall behind her. 'Everyone's still sleeping,' she whispers. 'Happy Christmas from Brighton. We're going to the pier in a bit.'

By the time they've made sandwiches, pulled on their trainers and left the cabin, it's eleven o'clock. As they start to walk, Wendy says, 'You know the main Christmas meal in France was last night? It's actually on Christmas Eve.'

'Yeah, I remember that from French lessons,' Harry says. 'There was a lot of stuff about Jean-Michel opening the oysters.'

'Your memory always astounds me,' Wendy says. 'I can't even remember the stuff I learned last time I was here.'

'I can still remember the word for oysters, too,' Harry says.

'Which is?'

'*Huîtres.*'

'Weeters?' Wendy says, trying to parrot him.

'No, it's he-wee-treus,' Harry says slowly. '*Huîtres.* With a silent "H" at the beginning.'

'Huh,' Wendy says. 'Unpronounceable. It's a good job I don't like them.'

They walk along the roadside in silence for a moment until Harry asks, 'Do you think she's OK?'

'Fiona?'

'Yeah.'

'Oh, I think so. Why? Don't you?'

'Dunno,' Harry says. 'Just a feeling. What was she like when she was here?'

'Fine, really. It was much nicer than I expected.'

'You weren't expecting it to be nice?'

'Oh, no, I wouldn't say that,' Wendy says. 'But I was a bit nervous. She'd been distant and spiky with me for a while. So it was quite a nice surprise. Until she told me about Todd's wedding, that is. That came as a bit of a shock.'

'So you don't find her distant?'

'Not really, why?'

'I just think there might be something she's not telling us. Like an elephant in the room that makes conversation about anything else a bit clunky,' Harry says.

Wendy laughs.

'What?'

'Oh, it's just that I know exactly what you're gagging to say.'

'You do?'

'I do,' Wendy says.

'Go on, then.'

'No, you first.'

'This friend of hers, in Brighton...' Harry says.

'You're thinking she might be more of a friend-friend,' Wendy says, smiling at the memory of the terrible marriage guidance counsellor.

'Yes!' Harry says. 'Exactly.'

'When did it first cross your mind?'

'I don't know,' he says. 'Maybe at Todd's wedding. You know, when he said—'

'... that swapping clothes might give her game away?' Wendy says, finishing his phrase for him.

'Yes. Exactly then!' Harry says. 'I mean, that could have just been banter. But...'

'You think Todd knows something we don't?'

'Well, it would appear that we kind of do know,' Harry says.

'I'd thought about it before, actually,' Wendy says. 'Ages ago. It's more like a slow dawning, really. But I did pick up on that, too – when he said that. I wasn't at all sure it was just a joke.'

'You think she might be seeing this Ada girl?'

'Maybe,' Wendy says. 'I haven't really thought about it a great deal, because I suppose it doesn't worry me much either way.'

'No,' Harry says. 'But it worries me if she thinks she can't tell us.'

'Yes, I know what you mean,' Wendy says. 'But she knows that I'm friends with Manon. And we've never said anything that would, you know... I mean, I'm sure she knows we're not rabid homophobes.'

'Yeah, I'm sure she knows we'd be cool.'

'But, you know, I think they're a lot more flexible about these things, these days. I remember Todd saying a couple of his friends were flexi.'

'You mean they do yoga?'

'No, I mean—'

'Joke, Wendy. Joke.'

'Right! So this is where we turn,' she says, pointing. 'The track up starts over there.'

'Gosh, sporty girl!' Harry says. 'Get you.'

'Yep,' Wendy says. 'Who knew?'

When they reach the final plateau, Harry bends over and rests his hands on his knees to catch his breath.

'You OK there, hon?' Wendy asks, doing her best not to sound out of breath herself. The walk up became vaguely competitive, probably because Harry is so used to being 'the fit one'.

'Yeah, it's just further than I thought,' he says. 'And bigger.'

'Bigger?'

'Yeah,' he says, straightening and looking up at the radar sphere towering above them. 'I imagined it as sort of small-car-sized, but it's massive.'

'And the view,' Wendy says, turning to face the coast. 'Look.'

'Yeah, amazing,' Harry says, '... reminds me of Greece.'

'Yes!' Wendy says. 'That island we were on with the mini mountain in the middle?'

'Exactly,' Harry says.

'You don't remember the name, either, then? That makes me feel a bit better about my failing memory.'

'I know it ended in "os",' Harry says. 'Paros or Kos or Ios or something.'

'That's the airport, over there,' Wendy says, leaning her head against Harry's shoulder and pointing to the runway where it juts out into the sea.

'And there?'

'That's Antibes.'

'Where you went walking with Fiona? She said it was amazing.'

'Yes. It's really nice.'

'If I'm good will you take me there, too?'

'Yes, if you're good, I might,' Wendy says. Then, 'This, over here, is my rock.' She moves, almost skips in fact, to 'her' rock, and then stands on top of it to take the panoramic photo. 'I took a photo of this view every time I came up here. I thought it would look cool if I got them all printed up on a single poster, but I never got around to it. Let me take one with you in it.'

'And then I'll take one with you,' Harry says. 'It's a shame there's nowhere to lean the camera. We could have—' He's interrupted by the arrival of other hikers.

So Harry asks the couple, in surprisingly passable French, if they mind taking the photo, and once that's done – once the image of Wendy and her husband side by side with the magnificent backdrop of blue sky and sea has been recorded to Wendy's specifications – the newcomers smile and wave and start to head back down.

Wendy leads Harry a little further up the ridge where they sit in a hollow to eat their sandwiches.

'... very low-maintenance Christmas dinner,' Harry says, speaking through crumbs. 'You're slipping.'

'Don't worry,' Wendy says. 'I've a surprise in store for tonight.'

'You have?' Harry asks.

'Uh-huh,' Wendy says mysteriously.

'Only, we did the shopping together,' Harry says. 'So maybe not so surprising. Unless you ordered pizzas?'

Wendy laughs at this. 'Almost,' she says.

'You booked a restaurant?'

'Nope,' Wendy says. 'Now stop before you spoil the surprise.'

* * *

The girls arrive at 7 p.m., and Harry is so surprised when Manon raps on the window that he jumps and spills his drink.

'Jaysus!' he says, as Wendy crosses to open the door. 'Now I get why you kept putting off the cooking!'

Manon is the first to step into the cabin, her arms laden with foil-covered trays, closely followed by Celine with a bottle of Champomy and a ribboned box from the bakery.

Once introductions have been made and the table set, once the pre-roasted veggies have been heated up and the salmon roulé sliced, they sit down to eat.

'So how is lovely Mittens?' Wendy asks. To Harry she says, 'He's—'

'... the cat you adopted, I know.' To the girls, he adds with a wink, 'She thinks I don't listen, but I do.'

'Mittens is fine,' Manon says. 'But now we call him Pattex. It's more French. It's because he is very... erh... sticky?'

'Sticky?' Wendy says. 'Oh, you mean, clingy?'

'Pattex never goes out,' Celine explains. 'Ever.'

'Really?'

The girls nod. 'We think he sees too much cold before. Now he sleep and sleep and sleep.'

'*Sur le radiateur,*' Celine adds.

'On the radiator,' Harry says.

'Yes, thanks, Harry,' Wendy says, laughing. 'I think I got that one.'

'I wasn't translating,' Harry says. 'Well, I was but not for... Oh, never mind.'

'And your brother?' Wendy asks, wincing at the realisation that this might not be the best question to have asked.

'Oh, he's OK,' Manon says brightly. 'So good... Oh, I don't remember how this one goes. *Pour le moment,* he's OK.'

'So far, so good?' Wendy volunteers.

'Yes!' Manon says. 'So far, so good.'

'And your father? He's OK too?'

'Yes, he's great. Now Bruno is OK, Papa is OK, too, you know?'

'Yes, I know exactly what you mean. We depend so much on our children for our own wellbeing, don't we, Haz?'

'I'm sorry, I don't understand,' Manon says.

'When our children are OK, we are OK,' Wendy paraphrases. She takes a sip of her fizzy apple juice while Harry tops up Celine's glass with prosecco.

'And you?' Manon asks, indicating Wendy's glass with a nod of her chin. 'I think you are so good so far, yes?'

'Yes,' Wendy says. 'Thanks to you.'

'*Moi ?*' Manon says, looking genuinely surprised.

'Yes, you really helped me, you know?'

'I don't do so much.'

'No, you did! By telling me to stop, for one,' Wendy says. 'And then telling me about your mother. You gave me quite a shake-up.'

'Oh!' Manon says, jumping up. 'You make me think!' She crosses to the sofa where she retrieves a photo from her coat pocket. 'Look,' she says, once she has returned to crouch down between Harry and Wendy. 'This is a photo of Maman. I want to show you.'

'Oh, crikey!' Harry exclaims.

'Gosh,' Wendy concurs.

'Yes, I know,' Manon says. '*C'est fou, n'est pas ?*'

The photo, of Manon's mother in her thirties, could totally be a photo of Wendy at the same age. In fact, had Wendy stumbled upon the photo out of context, she would have started trying to remember when it had been taken.

They stare at the photo in silence. Wendy shakes her head slowly and sighs. 'Can I take a picture of this?' she asks finally. 'Because our kids will never believe me.'

'Yes,' Manon says. 'Of course.'

Once dinner has been eaten and the chocolate log sliced and devoured, Celine says she's going to go outside for a smoke.

'Of course,' Wendy tells her. 'I think I'll join you.'

'But you are telling me you stop,' Manon says.

'Yes,' Wendy admits sheepishly. 'I know.'

'She almost has, really,' Harry says in his wife's defence.

'Yes, I'm down to three or four a day,' Wendy says. 'I'm doing it very slowly. But hell, it's Christmas Day, isn't it?'

Manon turns to Celine at this point and rattles off some rapid-fire French that neither Wendy nor Harry understand. But whatever she has said has instant effect, because Celine pulls a face as if she's been told off and settles back in her chair. 'She say I must ask if it's OK,' Celine says, looking disgruntled.

'Why? You want to smoke in here?' Harry asks. 'Sure, go for it. It's freezing out there.'

'No, not this,' Manon says. 'But Celine. She does not want to smoke cigarette.'

'She doesn't?' Wendy says uncomprehendingly.

'Oh, oh!' Harry says, as the penny drops. 'She wants to smoke a joint, right?'

Celine smiles shyly.

'Please,' Wendy says, gesturing towards the door. 'Be my guest. That's not a problem at all, is it, Haz?'

'Er, no!' Harry says, comically emphatic.

'You want?' Celine asks, pulling a pre-rolled spliff from her jacket pocket and pointing it at him.

'Absolutely, I want!' Harry says. 'It's been years.'

* * *

'Those two are lovely,' Harry says, once the girls have left. It's just after 11 p.m. and they are clearing the table, piling dirty dishes in the sink.

'I know,' Wendy says. 'They're great, aren't they?'

'D'you think that's why she befriended you? Because you look so much like her mum?'

'Not only,' Wendy says. 'But I suppose it might explain why my drinking upset her so much. It must have been so hard on those kids.'

'You know, for a minute I thought it was a joke,' Harry says, shooting her a slightly inappropriate grin. 'I thought it was photo of you and she was winding me up.'

'I know,' Wendy says, breaking into a smile herself, even though she's not sure why she finds it funny. 'Sorry... talking about that poor woman,' she says. 'Not quite sure why I'm grinning. It's clearly not funny at all.'

'No, but you looking so like her kind of is.'

'I suppose,' Wendy says.

'I can't stop smiling, either,' Harry says. 'I think it's the joint.'

'That was ages ago.'

'Well, whatever, it's nice to see you smile.'

'I think I am still a bit stoned,' Wendy says. 'You know, it made me feel like I was eighteen again? Do you remember those joints we smoked at Glastonbury with that hippy guy with all the piercings?'

'I do,' Harry says. 'I couldn't stand up for about an hour. We missed David Bowie because of that.'

Harry's playlist, which has been providing a pleasant soundtrack to the evening, moves on to 'Every Beat of My Heart'.

'Who's this?' Wendy asks, frowning. It's not like Harry to listen to soul music.

'Gladys Knight,' he says, putting down the coffee pot and holding out a hand. 'Dance with me.'

Wendy carries the final dirty plates from the table, adds them to the pile, then rubs her hands on her hips and steps between Harry's open arms. Their bodies seem to fit together more easily than yesterday. She wonders if this is another side effect of the joint.

'Since when do you listen to soul?' she asks.

'Since Spotify started suggesting it,' Harry says, sliding one arm round her back, and moving her into a playful tango hold.

'Clever Spotify,' Wendy says. 'I like.'

Because Harry breathes out heavily, she tips her head back to look up at him so that she can identify the nature of the sigh.

'I do love you, you know,' he says.

'Me, too. This has been one of the nicest Christmases ever, hasn't it?'

'Don't let the kids hear you say that,' Harry laughs.

'No, no, I won't.'

He kisses her then, and for the first time in ages – for the first time in years – she wants more. She opens her mouth to let him in.

'Allo, allo!' Harry says comically, once the kiss is over.

This makes Wendy crack up laughing for no reason she can identify. 'Allo, allo?' she repeats, in a silly French accent.

'Hey, you started it with your French kissing.' And then he wheels her in so tightly she can hardly breathe.

* * *

She wakes up the next morning to find herself spooned by Harry's body. She can feel his morning hard-on pressed against her buttocks and, feeling vaguely embarrassed, she edges gently away.

She pokes one arm out from the quilt to confirm what her

nose is telling her: that the cabin is once again freezing. 'Shit,' she mumbles.

'What?' Harry asks. He's apparently wide awake.

'Forgot to stack the wood stove. It's arctic out there.'

'Huh,' Harry says. 'I'm sure it warms up pretty quickly, doesn't it?'

'It does once *you* get up and relight it.'

'Sorry, don't know how,' Harry says, rolling onto his back. 'It's gonna have to be you, babe.'

'I'll give you instructions,' she offers, rolling over so that she's now cradling Harry. She tickles his waist in an attempt at forcing him from the bed.

'I still think, with all your experience...' Harry says, through laughter. 'OK, I'll get up and light the paraffin thing, if you want.'

'Ooh, no,' Wendy says. 'It stinks. Plus I don't think it's very healthy – breathing the fumes and what-have-you...'

Because it's ultimately easier to do it herself than to motivate Harry, she braces herself and gets up, returning five minutes later with mugs of tea.

'Here you go, lazy man,' she says.

'Oh, you love it,' Harry says, through a yawn. 'You love being my charwoman.'

'Huh?' Wendy says, sipping her tea. 'Charwoman? Now you've blown it!'

'Blown what?'

'There's a massive pile of washing up down there. Which is now entirely your job.'

'I don't mind washing up. As long as tonight is like last night.'

'Oh, sex for washing up, now, is it? I think that might actually be worse than being your charwoman.'

'You didn't seem to mind too much last night,' Harry says, nudging her.

'No...' Wendy admits, softening her voice to indicate she's no longer joking. 'No, last night was lovely. But can we manage it without a joint? That's the question.'

'Course we can,' Harry says.

'I hope so. Because it definitely helped me relax.'

'In that case, I have good news,' Harry says. 'Celine left me two more spliffs.'

'She did not!'

'Did, too.'

'Scoring drugs off the kids?' Wendy says. 'I'm not sure how I feel about that.'

'Well, don't get addicted,' Harry says. 'Cos there's no more where that came from.'

'I think I'll be OK. I've never craved a joint in my life. Cigarettes? Yes. Alcohol? Totally. But weed's never really done it for me. Generally just sends me to sleep.'

'Until last night.'

'Indeed. Maybe it's because she grows it. Maybe homegrown is different.'

Once they have drunk their tea, Wendy sticks a leg out before declaring it's still too cold. 'Let's snooze for a bit,' she says.

'What do you want to do today, anyway?'

'I don't know,' Wendy says. 'Lazy morning and then a picnic somewhere? Maybe Antibes, or Nice, or Cannes?'

'I take it you've visited them all?'

'Well, Nice with Jill, and Antibes with Fiona. But I've never been to Cannes.'

'Let's do that one, then,' Harry says. 'You know, I completely forgot she was here.'

'Jill?'

'Yeah. You don't seem to mention her much lately. I didn't dare ask.'

'No...' Wendy says thoughtfully.

'Did you fall out, or...?'

'Not as such. It was just the drink thing, really.'

'Yeah, Jill can certainly put it away.'

'I went to see her in... April maybe? I think it was April, anyway. I was toying with the idea of inviting them to Todd's wedding. I mean, I would have asked Todd first, obviously, but he really liked Jill when he was little, didn't he?'

'He was in love with Jill when he was about nine.'

'But they were both pretty far gone. And it was only eleven in the morning.'

'Ouch,' Harry says.

'I know. And she kept offering me drinks, too. She was really quite insistent. Even though I'd told her that I'd stopped... And I found that upsetting really... It seemed a bit disrespectful to put me in a position where I had to keep saying no.'

'She probably doesn't like the fact you've stopped.'

'No, that's exactly it. I think I'm like a mirror to the fact that she can't.'

'So you *have* fallen out?'

'Well, I phoned her a week later – I got her answerphone, repeatedly. So in the end I left a message saying that it had upset me – her trying to ply me with drink. And I said I was worried about their health. And she never phoned back. And that was April, as I say. So I think that friendship may have reached its expiry date.'

'I'm sorry,' Harry says, caressing her arm. 'It's hard losing a friend.'

'I suppose it's bound to happen at some point in a lifetime. But it does hurt. And I feel a bit guilty, I suppose. Because she's been good to me over the years.'

'She might come back, one day,' Harry says. 'She might think about what you said, and sober up.'

'I hope so,' Wendy says. 'Because otherwise, I worry that the next bit of news will be that she's in hospital. Or dead. Maybe I'll try again at some point, I don't know. It's a tough one.'

* * *

Because Wendy so wants Harry to see it, they end up back at Cap d'Antibes.

The sky is misty blue and it's far colder than when she came with Fiona, but it's beautiful all the same.

As they pass through the rusty gate and start their way along the coastal path, Wendy's phone, in her pocket, pings with a message.

'Kids?' Harry asks, from in front.

'No, just Prue saying happy Christmas,' Wendy calls back.

'You two are besties now, right?' he asks, moving to her side as the path widens. 'You lose one, you win one?'

'Huh,' Wendy says. 'No, it's not the same. It's not the same at all. I've known Jill for decades. But I do like Prue. I think she's OK. And she's going through so much.'

'Well, it's sweet, you being there for her.'

'I just try to listen, really. I don't think she has anyone else to talk to, and I don't know... somehow I feel like I get it.'

'Because of your uncle?'

'No, I was more thinking of Mum. Prue's angry. She's quite reasonably furious about the cards she's been dealt. And I know how that feels.'

'So you're a friendly ear,' Harry says. 'That's kind. As long as she doesn't bring you down.'

'No, it's more than that,' Wendy says, as they round the corner and climb a set of steps. 'It turns out, I'm quite a good listener.'

'God, it's lovely here,' Harry says.

'Yes,' Wendy agrees. 'I really like it. And look at that house over there. Imagine living there.'

In the distance, on an outcrop of red rocks, sits a mansion surrounded by crashing waves.

'The window cleaning on that place would be hell,' Harry says, then, 'And you are a good listener, I know.'

They walk on in silence for a while, with only the sound of the waves and the gulls. When finally Wendy decides that this is probably as good a time as any, she says, 'Actually, I've been thinking about something. And I wanted to get your input.'

'Sure,' Harry says. 'Go on.'

'I've been wondering about maybe retraining,' she tells him. 'As a counsellor. I mean, I've barely started looking into it, but...'

'Oh,' Harry says, surprised. 'OK.'

'I've still got some of Mum's money left. So I could work part time, and we'd still have enough to keep everything ticking over. And... I don't know – I mean, I'm not sure – but maybe this is what I want to do with it. I enjoyed seeing that therapist more than I thought I would. And I've enjoyed trying to help Prue deal with her feelings, too. I think Mum would have approved. But what do you think?'

'Sure,' Harry says. 'Why not?'

'But would you mind?'

'Er, no,' Harry says. 'How could I?'

'But do you think it's a good idea?'

'Well, I think you'd make a great counsellor if that's what you're asking.'

'Really?' Wendy asks, grabbing his arm, and pulling him to a stop. 'Because you must say. You must be honest if you think I'd be rubbish, or if you think we need that money for other stuff.'

'Hey,' he says, caressing her arm. 'If it makes you happy, I think it's a great idea.'

'Well, it would, I think,' Wendy says. 'And I don't think I could bear going back to full-time nursing. But there's you to think about. I want you to be happy, too.'

'You know what makes me happy?' Harry says. 'The fact that you're asking me. Because it means you're still thinking about us.'

'Oh, God, am I being presumptuous?' Wendy asks. 'Maybe you don't even think that we'll carry on—'

'Stop!' Harry says, grasping her forearms tightly. 'I do. I just wasn't... I mean, you never said... we've never said it out loud, since all that... happened. But I do. It's what I want.'

'Oh, thank God,' Wendy says, leaning into his embrace. 'We agree, then.'

'We do,' Harry says, giving her a peck. 'Isn't that great?'

They hug tightly for a moment and when Wendy pulls away she has to swipe tears from her eyes. 'Just the wind,' she jokes.

'Of course,' Harry says, blinking. 'Mine, too.'

'So!' Wendy says, turning resolutely back to the path.

'So,' Harry repeats, emulating her tone. 'When do we eat? Is there, like, a particular spot? Because I'm starving even though it's... Actually, it is almost two.'

'Yes! A bit further along here,' Wendy says, grabbing his hand and pulling him forwards. 'There's a little set of steps that lead down to the sea where I ate with Fiona. Come! Follow me. I'll show you the perfect spot.'

THE END

A LETTER FROM NICK

Dear reader,

Many thanks for choosing to read *Where Do We Go From Here?*. If you enjoyed it and want to keep up to date with future releases, please sign up at the link below. Your email address will never be shared and you can unsubscribe at any time.

www.bookouture.com/nick-alexander

The idea for *Where Do We Go From Here?* first came to me over a decade ago when I spent a horrific winter quite literally snowed under in a cabin in the Alps. The memory of that winter poked me in the ribs again during a Covid lockdown when I saw a Facebook meme depicting an isolated cabin with the tagline, 'You can spend a year here with no internet, no phones and no visitors – would you do it?'

Lots of friends had commented that they would simply *love* to spend a year in an isolated cabin, and I couldn't help but think, *They just have no idea!* And then I thought, *Hum, maybe this would make a good novel!*

If you think it did then I would be massively grateful if you could write a review. I'd love to hear what you think, and it makes such a difference helping new readers to discover one of my books for the first time.

However you choose to do it, and whatever you have to say,

I love hearing from my readers so please do get in touch through social media or my website.

Many thanks again.

Love and peace.

Nick Alexander

www.nick-alexander.com

 facebook.com/nickalexanderauthor

 instagram.com/authornickalexander

 bsky.app/profile/nick-alexander.bsky.social

ACKNOWLEDGEMENTS

Many thanks to my touchstone, Ro, for all her help and encouragement, and to Lolo for sharing all the ups and downs of this messy/challenging/brilliant thing we call life. Thanks to Laura, Jon, Becca and everyone else at Bookouture for all their hard work on this novel. It's been great fun working with you, and that's truly the most important thing of all.

PUBLISHING TEAM

Turning a manuscript into a book requires the efforts of many people. The publishing team at Bookouture would like to acknowledge everyone who contributed to this publication.

Audio
Alba Proko
Melissa Tran
Sinead O'Connor

Commercial
Lauren Morrissette
Hannah Richmond
Imogen Allport

Cover design
Ami Smithson

Data and analysis
Mark Alder
Mohamed Bussuri

Editorial
Laura Deacon
Imogen Allport

Printed in Great Britain
by Amazon

61537413R00211